Dreams of the Fisher Kings:

PART TWO ~ The Age of Afallon

Dreams of the Fisher Kings

PART TWO ~ The Age of Afallon

Robert Jacobs

MorningStar Press
2023

Dreams of the Fisher Kings: Part Two – The Age of Afallon

1. Historical Fiction 2. Folk Legend 3. Mythology 4. Mysticism

Copyright © 2023 by Robert Jacobs

First Printing: 2023

ISBN 978-0-9643840-4-0

MorningStar Press   PO Box 1287   Nevada City, CA 95959

MorningStarPress@yahoo.com

Dedication

To my amazing wife Letitia, whose continued encouragement, enthusiasm, unconditional love and support enhanced the experience of the writing of this book, as a joyous and fulfilling conversation in spirit.

Acknowledgements

Poetry, myth and dreams share the same language: a language of allegory and metaphor yielding archetypes and emotional currents, that speak to the soul of the attentive listener. I must acknowledge the articulate writers of this universal language, too numerous to list here, from ancient ages into modern times, who have birthed the Arthurian characters, from the ancient myths and legends for generations of writers to rediscover these rich treasures. Modern pioneers of psychology and comparative mythology Carl Jung and Joseph Campbell also deserve acknowledgement for their contributions and applied understanding, interpreting these eternal stories of the human psyche. My deepest gratitude goes to Caitlin and John Matthews, who have kindly advised my leap into this recent adventure in writing. John and Caitlin have opened doors and windows to the Celtic and Arthurian genre of literature throughout their decades of writing and mentoring, inspiring and encouraging my creative spirit to run and fly through those wise portals, prompting further exploration into expanding mythic realms. I also acknowledge the voluminous works of dedicted historians, archeologists and geneologists – namely, Peter C. Bartrum, John Morris, and John T. Koch – who have unearthed and compiled many of the intricate lost details that greatly served my imagination in the shaping of new impressions of the timeless characters from an obscure epoch of history and floklore.

Contents

ORCADES

CRUTTHNI
PICTS

HEBRIDES

MIATHI
PICTS   *Firth of Tay*

DALRIADA   WALL OF FORTH *Firth of Forth*

ALT   LOTHIAN
CLUD   YNYS
                         MEDCAUT
            BRYNEICH

GALLWYDDEL SOLWAY   WALL OF TYNE

            Solway Firth   RHEGED   BERNICIA

EIRENN   EBRAUC

            YNYS MANAU   DEIRA
                         ELMET
            YNYS MON   LINNUS

            Yr Wyddfa RHOS

LAIGIN   GWYNEDD POWYS

            CEREDIGION MEIRIONYDD   ANGLO–
                         ERCING   SAXON   ANGLIA
            DYFED BRYCHEINIOG   OCCUPIED
                                    TERRITORIES
            GLYWYSSING   *Thames*
                    Severn Estuary   YNYS THANET

            DUMNONIA   CEINT
                         SAXON SHORE   SAXONIA

CORNUBIA   Llyme Bay YNYS WEITH

                                        FRANCIA

MID SIXTH CENTURY   SOISSONS
BRITAIN
                                        Sequana

            ARMORICA   GALLIA

Chapter One ~ **The Odd Birds**

Opening to the infinite possibilities of immortal dream – I take flight! Held upon the air of imagination, reaching ascension, I embrace the expanse with arms extended in freedom and fascination, soaring on and on towards an inevitable landing, not unlike Icarus: ignoring the wise architect of these precarious wings. Yet, wondering if this atmosphere is fair or foul, wherein each day I arise from sleep, to find a place to alight or fall. Hatched here, cracked open from the cosmos, lies a plot, a dream, a new life born to be witnessed through a widening threshold. Awakened, I see from my own window, one small bird, a curious young merlin, flashing a richness of hue within his slate blue markings, alighted on the weather-worn window sill. He looked at this aging bard as if I would have some special gift for him: a nut, some seed, a crust of bread, perhaps a wheat grain. Seeing that I was without any kind of morsel for his hunger, he flew up within a tree, its branches expanding out into the western sky. Filling spaces of the upper reaches of this grand tree, the shadowy hawk's distant relations joined in a vociferous chorus of musical tones, cascading through the morning air, singing songs so glorious I could feel their heavenly intent without understanding a note. In startled response to the merlin's entry into the song filled foliage, a sudden wave of rushing motion, the minute thundering rhythm of wings released a flock of black patterned flight, vibrating out currents of collectively orchestrated air, glancing upon my ears for me to catch the sound of each fugitive feather.

I sit with a delicate quill; touched here, once and ever will be a feather, flown high above the hand it now rests upon; page after page sounding only echoes of soaring within a vastly different life. Ravens, kites, hawks, doves, and a merlin – they all have their ancestral arcs still traversing ancient skies, each eidetic finger leaving latent traces of avian paths. The bard attempts to fashion wings of words for the soul in flight from grave imaginings into lifted experience. We tend to see the eras that we live in as isolated from the distant past, even though old seeds are sown within our altered memory.

The forgotten past leaves a hallowed echo upon the soul; just as silence fell upon the land in the wake of a dark season of widespread plague. Pestilence was the encroaching war, unconquerable by vain flailing arms of suffering and archaic strategies. Flight then, seemed to be the only recourse against death. Birth and death of a world born in the mind is a gestating epoch that has untraceable parentage. Orphaned from its gods, the disowned idea appears to raise itself from an infancy vanished, yet streaming undisclosed truth below the obsessive tracks marking a trail into illusion. A mire of communal thought, fear and the bleak increase of fallen bodies left to be buried, shaped the shared nightmare of this time bound world – birthing an identity of flesh and blood merged with the lands of an evolving island realm. The staggering composite identities of the isles of Britannia are born and reborn: Prydain, Hibernia, Alban, Afallon, hyperborean isle of apples – bitten, cored, baked into fanciful pies and served from the faery realm, where mystery recalls faint cries of a lost language of birds and trees. Cutting truth with crude letters forms some semblance of these distant avenues of thought, often misconstrued, more ideally sung to be heard upon the heart. This is where the inspired speak the innate voices of the air – to listen and convey feathering song. From this earnest opening, we may hear our own true story.

I am a voice captured by quill to page, telling of that song that unfolded in history before me and continuing after me. Born into this life not knowing my parents, I had no assumed identity. Raised by druids and bards, my lineage was sketched as a trail left by clever otherworldly outlaws distinct from neighboring clans. When I was eleven years of age, Aneirin took me in, seeing some latent talent in my stringing of words together in verse. Earlier tutelage had been given to me from a bard known as Morfyn, mentored by Llywarch Hen. Morfyn was nearly a foster father, dying during my tenth year of this unusual mystical life. He and his elder sister, Claire, a priestess of Afallon, had cared for me from infancy. I became well acquainted with Taliesin, Myrddin Wyllt, Llywarch Hen and other bards of the day, through old Morfyn. This strange breed of soaring word wizards was what I understood to be my clan; just as many who know their parentage feel more akin to the odd birds they flock to away from their own parents' nest. For me, the choice had already been made. Verse, myth and dream were the first orders of understanding that I was introduced to, laying the foundation for my perception of the waking world and its history. All of my teachers revered that great Raven of Awen, Emrys Myrlyn, mentoring us from the Otherworld. His legacy allowed me to feel that elusive presence deep within the wooded groves, ascending above the heights of Yr Wyddfa, finding my own voice of the quill, conveying this meandering tale of druids, bards and mystics, in a time of wars and shifting boundaries.

History is like the forest floor: layers of fallen leaves cover the common ground, new sprouts rising up between the damp perpetually turning blankets of time. Blood, bones, and bodies of centuries past lay buried, feeding the roots of trees stretching up extended limbs into the sky, where winged life may take flight from these skeletal branches, breaching nature's silence with each new breeze. Much of what rests upon this ancient floor of fauna and flora is unknown: as words sung by those treading over it, hear profound resonances within a season of history; and yet carry their own interpretations. Thought molded as words conjured into human forms finds its clothing among the scattered leaves, hiding a nakedness that is uncovered to reveal our world soul. Identities enter the skins of this earth to animate our story again. It is a dark complex unfolding to expose a simple light. Myths merge with dream; and roles are played to form the rooted tree. The tree is language and drama planted within us – its universal speech given voice through diverse tongues that tell their tales, and battle over differing deliveries of the same primordial message. Leaf by leaf the bard picks up pieces to form his song, some notes familiar, others disputed for their oddity. He allows Awen to guide him where to begin to draw the patterned veil: revealing, concealing, creating, eliminating and sustaining that grand story washed upon the senses. It is a flood of thought, channeled word by word, line by line, to catch the eye, ear, mind and heart. We enter the stream and let it take us along where it will, from rooted earth to expansive skies.

Astrologers have long prophesized progression of the guide star in the north. The polar star has moved from Draco to Ursa, prompting these observers to foretell of that bear king leading a northern kingdom – in the way they foretold of a spiritual king born in Judea, announced by alignment of bright heavenly bodies. The earthly heritage of the ancient Prince of Peace and our northern bear king are debated, as many believe that lineage continues through the Fisher Kings. Whether they are descendants of a line of blood or a line of light, legendary identities of priest kings pose a challenge to histories favoring the surviving hierarchies. Expectation of the "Arthwyr" repeatedly enthralls storytellers of near and distant kingdoms, with generations of his namesakes arriving and departing. To the realist, Ambrosius or one of his warlords was the most likely candidate. Mythic leaders leave such enormous shadows to eclipse others that most mortal men tend to slip about them like a drunken sailor on a storm-ravaged ship. Bardic songs of heroes of legend take on mythic attributes, allowing these colorful histories to paint pictured icons, fulfilling roles for the spirit of countless listeners to reflect upon their own inner battles. Each icon blends with local lore through time, leaving us with the greatest visionaries, healers, and nurturers of our souls to traverse the fields of myth, fantasy and dream. We meet them within our dreams, as these images are still painted upon the innermost imaginal corridors of every human being.

It is within dream that Vivianne was first conceived, her father the Myrlyn courting her mother Nimue through their lucid realms of the psyche. These were the avenues that led to the discovery of lost treasures of the Cymri, nothing being hidden from the deepest depths of the otherworldly mind. Visionary images of his Lady of the Lake were first held by Myrlyn about his beloved Nimue, their daughter Vivianne inheriting that mantle when she became High Priestess of the Afallon Ysgol. Wed to the role of preeminent leader and guide to the sisters of Afallon, while also wed to the Pen Bard of Rheged Taliesin, Vivianne balanced her personal and spiritual life between earthly bonds and mystic inspiration. She and Taliesin shared that lineage of light from her grandmother, the Fisher Kings, and distant dynasties.

Defining where and when it all began is as difficult as defining the birth of wisdom, that daughter sprung from the godhead, named Athena or Sophia by the Greeks, and Shekinah by the Hebrews. She, in her feminine aspect, is protector and nurturing presence to all children, and therefore every soul. Also called Aine by the ancient Cymri and Scotti, she embraces the infinite source of light and expanse. Her mystically descendant daughters are the Anns, the Marys, the Maré and the Meira of the Magi – wise sisters and masters of their own merit. Through the legacy of these divine daughters, the first fruits of wisdom were carried forward to the protective isle of Mannan Mac Llyr – Ynys Manau – priestesses of Afallon tracing their lineage of light from the Sicambrian and Sarmatian Queens of the Caucasian Steppes. Their lineage paralleled the biblical prophets, the wise men of distant mountain retreats, or stark desert solitude, and the descendant holy messengers fulfilling the legacy of a threefold Hermes – source, spirit and offspring of a divinely emanated word. These were the manifested cosmic seed and egg serving as progenitor and womb for the world soul. Mothers of earth and sky birthed philosophy with their innate love and wisdom; often voiced and projected into the waking world by their sons, while a nurturing remembrance of the loving source of life originated before the spoken word from the mother's essence and constant presence.

The greatest among us remind us of the truth of who we are, often because their mothers, fathers or wise mentors never let them forget that truth. Within the descending shadows of time, it is the curse of humanity that we may lapse in our awareness, falling asleep to our shared integrity by forgetting the truth of our identity. It is an abduction of sorts: perpetuated by mind and emotion as each soul assimilates into a world gone mad. Fate and destiny seem to turn on one seemingly random event. A babe born into the fluid stream of time is cast upon its current, retrieved as an innocent water-ling, to become a new Moses, a Perseus, a Jason, or just another child open to listen for the flow of their calling.

The Foundling

Vivianne knew her calling; because her parents were two of the wisest souls among the sixth century Cymri. Vivianne's way of living in this outer world was led by her inner awakened vision. Although she could often see events before they transpired, she could not readily affect their course. Even with the powerful innate heritage of her matriarchal ancestry, shifting the tide of history seemed beyond the gifts of the Priestess of Afallon, in a world ravaged by the tempers of men. During the quietest hours of the night, Vivianne entered into her visions of mindful sleep. She found herself searching hurriedly within a fog draped forest, following the haunting sounds of a babe's crying voice through the dark pillars of towering trees. Soon she caught sight of a young woman of nobility, carrying an infant swaddled in her royal blue cloak, the lady's eyes opened wide with surprise by Vivianne's sudden appearance. The piercingly harsh sound of an arrow hitting the noble woman's back sent a blood-stirring look of shock across her face, as she fell forward, reaching out towards Vivianne with the babe in her arms, as if to pass this fragile young life into her safe keeping. Without a word spoken, the woman collapsed, the last light of life exiting her plaintive eyes, the infant child landing gently on the forest floor between the fatally stricken woman and Vivianne. Startled awake from this nightmare of tragedy, Vivianne sat up in bed, recalling the vivid details of the dream vision, knowing this imagery was not detached from the waking world, but foretold of events about to occur. Vivianne also knew this forest in the dream was far to the northeast, near the coastal lands of the Votadini. A sudden surge of urgency compelled the priestess to immediately rise from bed.

Vivianne was quite certain that a mother and her child's lives were in grave danger.

"Sister," Vivianne said to her chambermaid, "quickly alert Galehaut; have his men wake him. We must prepare for travel and leave at once."

"Where are you going Sister Vivianne?"

"To Gododdin and the forests of Bryneich – make haste sister!"

Galehaut and two men at arms were soon waiting outside the residence hall of the Afallon Ysgol. Vivianne came out to greet them.

"What is the urgency my lady?" Galehaut questioned.

"I am directed by an intense vision to proceed east to the forests of Bryneich. A child and his mother are in grave danger. This child is of great consequence. His life and destiny are just beyond my reach. We may save him, if we move swiftly," Vivianne explained.

"In what part of Bryneich will we find this child?" Galehaut inquired, having complete confidence that her vision was as accurate as any dispatch from a seneschal or winged courier.

"Near Gefrin," she responded.

"Very well, we can arrange for extra mounts in Caer Lliwelydd; and I assume Taliesin will join us there," said Galehaut.

"Quite possibly, and we should retain a wet nurse there as well."

"Yes my lady, whatever you shall require."

Galehaut and his men escorted Vivianne to the shore where they gained passage on the timely departure of a ship that morning for Rheged. Despite billows of morning fog, the voyage from Ynys Manau to the Solway Firth brought them to Caer Lliwelydd well before mid day. Vivianne's cousin Urien, son of her Uncle Cynfarch, was the reigning King of Rheged, continuing the legacy of Coel Hen and the Gwyr y Gogledd. Taliesin and the King were surprised by Vivianne's unannounced arrival into the great hall with Galehaut.

"Vivianne!" . . . Taliesin exclaimed, rising to greet her with a kiss and a warm embrace. "I wasn't expecting to see you until tomorrow at the Ysgol. What prompts this sudden visit to Caer Lliwelydd?"

"Cousin," Vivianne said, turning with a curtsy to King Urien, "and my dear," she continued, glancing toward Taliesin. "I must act upon an urgent vision. I have seen a child of great destiny in serious danger to his own life and his mother's life. I am guided to intervene in hope of saving at least the child."

"Where are this mother and child?" King Urien inquired.

"Bryneich Sire, in the forests near Gefrin, I will know the exact place when I arrive there – I am certain," Vivianne affirmed.

"Bryneich . . ! These are uncertain times in Bryneich, since Ida's increasing dominance toward the north. I caution you, cousin: Gododdin, Alt Clud, Ebrauc and Elmet have all been on edge in recent weeks. You may have whatever you need for your journey and protection, to assist Galehaut with a small detachment of warriors," Urien offered.

"We thank you Sire," Taliesin replied. "I will join them. Vivianne, shall we prepare straight away? It would seem there is no time for delay."

"I believe we must act swiftly," Vivianne answered. "As you well know, these things become clearer as we delve into them. However, I have never had a vision of such urgency before. We must collect our company and leave at once."

"Very well my dear – our adventure begins!" Taliesin announced with a loving smile and a wink to his prescient wife.

They traveled on the Roman road east, below the Wall of Tyne, until they reached the Dere Ystryd, heading north. Turning northeast beneath the foothills, they crossed Afon Aln, following the road east of Afon Til, where Vivianne began to recall further visions from her dream encounter.

"The forest is near, and so is the time of danger," she said softly to Taliesin and Galehaut as they signaled to the men to keep silent while easing forward.

After moving into the wooded groves, Vivianne stopped, dismounting from her horse. She walked between the trees with Galehaut, Taliesin and a few warriors following thirty or more paces behind her. Vivianne motioned for them to stop as she proceeded to the crest of a hill within the woodland. There she recalled the cry of the babe from her dream. Beyond her range of sight, an aging nobleman and his young wife were being pursued by a small troop of Bryneich warriors. The nobleman fell to his knees, his eyes rolling back into his head as he collapsed. The woman with babe in arms knelt down, her delicate fingers gently closing the eyes of her husband as she wept. His body showed no movement, or any hint of breath from the stillness of his lips, touched by her trembling hand in a final farewell to his departing soul. Hearing the warriors approaching, she scurried toward a ravine, below the crest where Vivianne could see her. A wave of recognition swept over the Priestess of Afallon, bridging ancestry stretching back to eastern lands of the continent. She knew this babe held within the woman's arms and his father was of Vivianne's own ancient lineage. A thickening forest fog rolled over the hillcrest as Vivianne and the mother with child finally met in the flesh, the young woman's noble life cut short by that sudden single arrow. This time Vivianne scooped up the babe, disappearing into the mist and over the hill. The pursuers were soon to run past the slain noblewoman, cresting the rise to face Galehaut standing fast, as Vivianne, Taliesin and a few others rode away to the southwest.

"Good day lads, out on a hunt?" Galehaut addressed the murderous company of warriors.

"Why, yes – what brings the Cymri of Rheged out to Bryneich?" Their leader questioned, recognizing the clan tartans of Galehaut and Urien's men.

"Well, much like you lads, we just follow the whims of our nobles through the lands of their ancestors, and try not to spill any more blood than is needed for their protection," Galehaut intimated a peaceful withdrawal.

"You're right there – it gets us all back to a pint and a maid before nightfall. Where are you lads headed?" The Bryneich warrior responded.

"Due west – lest our lord and lady change their whims, delaying us from a pint and a maid," Galehaut answered, inspiring chuckles from the posturing men of Bryneich. "We'll be on our way. Good morrow then."

"Good morrow!" The Bryneich leader responded, leading his men east, back into the woodland.

Vivianne cradled the infant child in her arms, now a league and a half away from the deadly scene of his parents' passing. She turned to Taliesin saying, "I fear we have not served his parents well, by leaving their bodies to be claimed by their assassins."

"We have saved the child, and that serves the legacy of his parents. Regrettably, we could not do more without some loss of our men, or loss of our lives with them. Hopefully this noble family has someone to see to their fallen bodies. If this was treachery or an act of war, then we will hear of it; and further Cymric forces may be engaged in battle with Bryneich or their invaders. There is much that is not revealed here. We are blessed with the care of this child. His life has been spared through your vision and action upon that vision," Taliesin reassured her.

"My visions revealed to me that this child is of our ancient lineage, blessed in that his identity is born of that stream of light. While sadly I mourn any loss of blood, and the fact that his parents will not see the fine man he becomes," said Vivianne, as she softly brushed the brow of the babe she sheltered within her protective arms.

Vivianne knew this innocent infant was a tiny part of a much larger pattern of dynastic conflict: not only within the Cymri, but within the royal families of the continental kingdoms. Members of her own lineage through her great grandmother Ywrhica, the Merovingians and the Sicambrian Franks carried the heritage of the Fisher Kings. These priest kings were the descendants of an ancient priestly line from Palestine. True heirs embodied bloodlines of noble ancestors and the sacred lineage of light. It doesn't take the discerning eye of a bard or druid to see that wisdom and purity of spirit are not inherited qualities of the blood. And yet, the idea of a sacrosanct birth plays into the unfolding drama of the divine right of kings – each eldest male heir claiming God given ascendancy to the throne of a Christian kingdom. Since the age of Constantine the Great and his conversion to Christianity nearly two and a half centuries past, kingdoms aligned with the Roman Catholic Church have been on the rise. Decades ago, around the time of Baddon, Francia too, under Clovis, became a Christian kingdom. Clovis, grandson of Merovech, cemented the undisputed supremacy of Merovingian ascendancy to the thrones of the northern continental kingdoms as champions of the Roman Catholic Church. For generations there have been dynastic marriages between the royal lines of continental kings and the lineages of Cymric, Scotti, Angle and Saxon kings of the isles. With the rise of Christian kingdoms or a few Saesneg kings converting to Christianity, the claims of divine right over pagan precedent fed greater conflict in these contentious times. Fewer and fewer of the Fisher Kings or Sicambrian Queens who were of that purity of wisdom and light sought to rule feudal earthly kingdoms. While those less enlightened cousins who could claim that lineage for their worldly gains were likely to use pedigree to justify tyranny.

The trickling of bad blood across the channel was not a new occurrence, nor was the hypocrisy of its adopted holy source. The Romans, who had conquered and reshaped so much of these lands with the roads carrying travelers for centuries, were ruled by Caesars claiming their own godhood, as identities inflated by the enormous accomplishments of the Roman Empire. Hadrian's Wall stands here before us, spanning the width of our isle, reminding Cymri, Scotti, Picts and Britons of the encroaching power of continental kingdoms. For more than two centuries the Roman Church and its hierarchies have been the heirs of Roman foreign dominance, seeking more than control of the lands of these rolling hills, stubborn crags, and majestic waters, grappling hearts and minds for the immortal souls of all of us who walk these lands – lands holding standing stones erected long before the births of Roman emperors, Roman bishops or the High Priests of Palestine.

Vivianne, Taliesin, Galehaut and their company journeyed west along the ancient wall, most of its mile castles abandoned and crumbling, the line defined by the Roman builders becoming more vague with each passing decade. Their travel of less than three days seemed timeless to Vivianne, with the newborn holding her attention, his bright blue eyes taking in the expansive world. They all felt the sea air off the Solway as they neared Caer Lliwelydd. Upon their entry into the great hall, Urien greeted Galehaut, Taliesin and his cousin Vivianne, relieved to see them safely returned from Bryneich.

"I see the infant rescue was a success!" King Urien announced, as several noble ladies hovered around Vivianne and the babe.

"Yes Sire." Taliesin responded. "Sadly, we couldn't save his parents, undoubtedly avoiding a greater conflict by arriving and departing precisely when we did."

"My dear cousin's vision clearly brought about this fortunate timing. Were there any swords drawn?" Urien pursued his inquiry.

"None by either side," Galehaut answered. "The Bryneich patrol was a small band of toughs. They seemed to be after the parents, the father likely ambushed and killed first, with the mother taking a fatal arrow in the back. Once the deadly errand was done, they were more intent on a pint of ale and a saucy wench than any of their own blood spilled by us. I don't believe they even knew of the babe. Whoever sent them must have wanted to end that family line before this infant heir was born. The errant thugs didn't follow through."

"Were they all Bryneich men, or perhaps Angles or even Franks?" Urien followed up.

"They appeared to be from Bryneich; but only one of them spoke." Galehaut responded. "Do you suspect a greater treachery here Sire?"

"Possibly," Urien continued. "With Ida's movement on the coast, and waves of dynastic chaos among the Franks, I suspect this noble heir and his parents were exiles seeking refuge in Bryneich, and then fleeing west, tragically too late."

"Why would the Franks be sending assassins to Bryneich?" Vivianne entered the conversation. "Isn't their Salic Law enough of an iron hand to strangle succession?"

"Chlothar and sons, Clovis' heirs, are multiplying with avid polygamy. I suppose they fear they'll run out of land for each of them to hold a kingdom," Urien retorted.

"Ha, ha, yes of course, you have your father's wit, cousin," Vivianne responded, laughingly. "It is clear that Salic Law instituted by Clovis ended matriarchal succession for the Franks; and his alliance with the patriarchal Catholic Church further wounds the Fisher Kings through their ancestry of Sicambrian Queens – but have they now sent male heirs of distant cousins fleeing for some western happy isle to dance with the faeries in exile?"

"Ha, ha – you have your father's wit too my dear! I would not put it past them to send assassins; as we should be cautious of our own cousins, with the diminishment of kingdoms enabling every pompous male heir the chance to be king of a hill. At least we retain the Cymric Cylch, unsteady as it seems lately. But I fear Bryneich may be the infestation of a new plague of little kings, easily exploited by the cloven hooves of greater foreign powers and influence," Urien concluded.

Vivianne and Taliesin stayed on in Caer Lliwelydd a few more days, traveling back to Ynys Manau with clear skies at the morning tide. Recollections of her fleeting visions, hinting the shared lineage Vivianne had with this infant lad, flashed through her mind as she held the babe on the voyage to his new home. These glimpses arose as if generations of ancestors stood-by witnessing their descendants, held in a loving bond manifested over time during their earthly lives, but formed eternally beyond the veil of transient physical images within the unfettered realm of the Otherworld. From that timeless domain each child's soul leaps into the nurturing center of a mother's love, beginning a great adventure of rediscovered identity. There were other children embarked on that great rediscovery at the Ysgol: some born to young widows of war who had entered the life of a priestess of Afallon, or orphans rescued by the wise sisters, and even children of the local families who were granted rare opportunities for an occasional child to be educated by the sisters of Afallon or learned tutors.

Taliesin and Vivianne had named the foundling babe Llenlleawg, meaning "parting of the veil", because he came into their world from another one across the sea, foretold by dream vision, guided from the mystic Otherworld. He was a peaceful babe, adjusted to his surrogate parents and a school of adoring adolescent elder sisters of Afallon. Even as a toddler, little Llen was uniquely handsome. His big blue eyes and endearing smile caught the heart of every female who gazed at him, drawing them in when he let out a laugh or chirped an indiscernible word from his dimpled cheeks. Winning them over in an instant, he began to realize his powers of subtle influence early on: if not consciously, then certainly by the sheer evidence of favor and attention afforded to him by each minor capture of a feminine eye.

Vivianne tried to instruct the novice lasses by this budding display of how some, perhaps most, men of the world who did not overtly attempt to take them by force or by right, would surely seek to woo them with clever charm. Here was a near infant already exploiting his power over them. This would serve, in Vivianne's view, as a safe example for them to observe the rising of masculine allure, before he matured and potentially all hope of their rational detachment would be swept away. Taliesin and other male mentors would have to step in and guide the lad in his responsibility to respect these bourgeoning wise women of the first fruits of spirit. These lasses held power too, of course: along with their innate feminine nature attracting the unaware male libido, each novice sister of Afallon was learning to move the subtle energies that flow between us and around us. Their responsibility was to the higher levels of this movement of unseen power, for healing, for positive influence, for joy and for love. It was not magic or spells cast upon the unsuspecting that they had learned, but rather to be the intangible wafting current moving the veil between realities.

The senses can be deceived and deluded by altered states of mind or emotion, enticed by attraction – a vision capturing the eye, arousing desire and imagination. Beneath this lies an alchemical current: some movement of that dust of matter and dream composing our veritable forms in the waking world. One can be led to believe a lie, when moved by hidden impulses. Priestesses of Afallon could not combat the brute force of men, in most cases; but they could disarm them through trance, through herbal potions, or by leading them to believe something not rightly recognized. Even with the disparity of physical force between the sexes, strength of intent, deeper understanding, and a bond with the forces of nature seem more acutely attained by these sisters of spirit – posing the most feared threat to the patriarchs of temporal and ecclesiastical powers.

Potentially shared power and ascendency with a matriarchy was an avenue of influence that kings and pontiffs actively conspired to blockade. The Roman Catholic Church furthered the imprint of patriarchy by becoming the dominant religion across the continent. Islands of Britannia were spiritually divided, not strictly by kingdoms, but divided within individual clans and regions. Allies of the Cymric Cylch attempted to bridge these differences, but passions ran high when injustices or outright attacks of violence occurred. Ever since Clovis and the Franks secured their pact with the Roman Catholic Church, other dynastic lines became increasingly targeted by his heirs. Ancient lines of nobility had been migrating into continental and island kingdoms for centuries. Certain dynasties, however, gained greater influence by suppressing the matriarchal lines. If this could not be achieved by Church decree, then the slaying of sisters, brothers, cousins or even infants carried forward the dark scenarios found in strains of every race, religion and culture. Human sacrifice continued, not as an act of appeasement to the gods, but as the bloody arm of political expedience. The alleged heresies of the so-called "pagan nature religions" and their "blasphemous" priestesses were justifications for violent cleansing by the Christian kingdoms.

The death of young Llenlleawg's parents exposed the cloaked removal of dynastic heirs and matriarchal lines to Vivianne and her cousin King Urien. Llen's surviving cousins on the continent were in constant danger, seeking refuge within Frankish kingdoms; while turmoil between the heirs of Clovis left fewer and fewer safe harbors. Clovis, grandson of Merovech, had married Clotild, granddaughter of Nascien, joining the lineage of the Merovingian Fisher Kings with the Sicambrian lineage during the late fifth century. Nascien and Merovech were cousins, grandsons of Faramond and Princess Argotta – Fisher King and Sicambrian heiress of the late fourth century. These were sacred lineages intent on merging throughout the centuries to maintain that divine strain of their birthright. Clovis and Clotild were in fact cousins, he the son of Childeric son of Merovech, she the daughter of Chilperic son of Nascien. The lineages of the brothers of Chilperic, Zambor and Galains were the lineages in greatest jeopardy from the heirs of Clovis and Clotild. Clovis had left the Kingdom of Francia divided between his four sons upon his death in the second decade of the sixth century. Childebert ruled from Paris, Chlodomer in Orleans, Theuderic in Rheims, and Chlothar in Soissons. Chlothar's kingdom absorbed the kingdoms of the Burgundians – including Narbonne and encompassing the alpine haven for the heirs of Zambor and Galains, where the Archdruid Lamech, son of Nascien, had been born. Galains was the ancestor of Llen and his continental cousins. These were the true heirs of that divine strain of lineage – Priest Kings of the sacred ancient heritage. The so-called "Catholic" or universal authority sent to flight any souls deemed heretical by their prejudicial hierarchy. Chlothar and his brothers were quick to capitalize on this bias, not out of religious devotion, but out of their thirst for power and dominance.

Quest of the Hart

These were the turbulent kingdoms that little Llen had been born into; but the only world and home he knew was that of Ynys Manau and the Afallon Ysgol. He was nurtured and protected there. Vivianne saw to his every need from the first day that she saw him and carried him to safety. She provided a wet nurse, Meiddryn, a lass seeking to become part of the Afallon Ysgol, yet not of noble birth and without means of entry into that life. Llen became her blessing of good fortune, ushering the eventual placement of her and her own son Bercnaf at Afallon. Naturally, the lads were immediate mates, both being fatherless and nursed by the same woman. As they grew, Llen received early education from a tutor, Cenfigen, the orphan foundling always wishing to include Bercnaf in his opportunities. Nonetheless, there was greater attention and privilege given to Llen. Both lads developed affection for the many hounds raised for hunting game, kenneled upon the extensive grounds surrounding the ysgol. Bercnaf particularly took interest in the care and training of hounds, while he was less inclined to schooling. Llen's active mind, however, thirsted for knowledge of the outside world beyond their island refuge. The two lads became especially fond of a couple of the hunting hounds: one trained as a lymer and the other a naturally swift greyhound. Lymers could be of varied breeding, possessing a keen nose for the scent of game. They were called lymers because of the leash or lyam that their handlers held them by when tracking prey. Llen and Bercnaf's favorite had sharp and alert attention, with a pleasant disposition. He was often sought as the lead lymer, so they named him Tywyswr, meaning leader or guide. The greyhounds or grechion are the faster and leaner members of the chase, making up in speed what they lacked in stamina, usually held back until the clear scent and trace of the game had been found, culminating the hunt by rapidly catching up to the prey. The lads' favorite greyhound had a regal look to him, his stance proud and extended – so they called him Tywysog, which means Prince. It wasn't until a lad reached the age of seven that he would take part in his first hunt, or "quest of the hart", the "hart" being a mature buck of at least five years. Llen had learned to shoot a small bow with a blunt shot when he was five, gaining the use of a somewhat larger bow at seven. Galehaut himself, master of most all weaponry and a leader of battle, taught young Llen the archer's skill, taken as he was by the lad's charm and quick ability to learn.

"You have an agile mind, lad," Galehaut would tell him, "and a sharp eye. As you grow in stature, you will most certainly be a fine archer."

"Thank you, sire. I aim to never miss the mark in all I can learn," Llen replied.

"Good lad, you will find that the ease of your every breath will calm your hand and extended arm to draw the bow, releasing a shot clear and true. You become the center of the movement. If you are true; the shot is true. This will guide you in all you seek to learn," Galehaut explained.

The lad learned well, joining in on several quests of game before he was allowed to take the shot. Older lads and experienced huntsmen held that privilege most of the time. Galehaut was there to teach young Llen the importance of respecting the prey.

"These beasts are both part of the land and part of spirit, just as every man and woman is part of this waking world. The blood of the hart, the stag, or any game we take, feed our blood, joining us with them in spirit and flesh. Our ancestors lived from their ancestors. We are bonded to them in reverence from the Otherworld into this world. The sacred beast leads us into the quest of spirit. It is up to us to honor their role in our lives, and honor their death, when their shared blood is surrendered to us," explained Galehaut.

"Are you saying that they come to us willingly?" Llen questioned.

"Not entirely, no," Galehaut continued. "They are one with the land, as we are one with the land; and we both are one with spirit. We play a role and fight for our survival. They fight for their survival too. A careless huntsman can be killed by the horns of a stag. I have seen it. There are elements that commune between man and the gods. We share in that sacred communion with the stag – the hart of the quest. We respect them as that otherworldly element, and as a power sustaining our lives; just as you will learn in battle to respect your enemies. They can be ruthless and dangerous; but they have souls as well. We are joined in this land, in this world; while men seek to control and dominate the land of other men. The stag has his domain also. He prepares us for battle; and he feeds our body and soul."

Young Llen began to learn that all men were not as honoring of the elements of spirit, the beasts of the forest or of other men. He had seen

Galehaut reprimand older lads in the hunting parties, chiding them for their behavior and attitudes. Llen's tutor, Cenfigen, had a manner and attitude that Llen did not trust. At first he thought it was just his way of discipline, keeping the lads in line, like Galehaut on the hunt. But something else was lurking within the character of this tutor. Cenfigen was not an appealing man in either appearance or demeanor. He was stern with his young charges, sometimes brutal; while he was pitifully sheepish around the novices and priestesses of Afallon. Llen could see how they nearly cringed at his awkward approaches to them. True to their training, they were kind and polite; but even young Llen readily perceived how differently they behaved towards Cenfigen, compared to him. This was also obvious to the tutor, clearly instilling a sense of resentment for the blue-eyed little charmer Llenlleawg. He didn't blatantly abuse the lad. It would have been too overt, drawing attention to his growing envy. Cenfigen would, however, find cause to chastise Bercnaf, Llen's closest mate. Bercnaf was a bit of a rascal, even as a lad. Short in stature, he was bounding with energy: one of those lads that wouldn't settle down until he had run out the day. Then he would nap like his beloved hounds – only to wake at the next bark. Cenfigen had the bark and bite; even whipping the lad, if he could catch him. So Bercnaf's schooling soon became rather sparse, spending his time with the hounds or with Llen after school.

By the time the lads neared ten years of age, they both had been part of numerous hunting trips across Ynys Manau. One late spring, Galehaut received an invitation from his clansmen in Gallwyddel to join a hunting quest in his old homeland with parties from Alt Clud and Rheged. It was a rare meeting of related northern clans to hunt for game in camaraderie and competition. Galehaut was glad to accept the invitation, and believed it would be a fine opportunity for young Llen to see more of their northern realms, presenting the idea to Vivianne and Taliesin, just as they were finishing a meeting with the tutor, Cenfigen.

"Our lads have been invited to a quest for game in Gallwyddel, a challenge of rival parties," Galehaut informed them. "I would like to take young Llen with us. He is of the age that I believe the experience would serve him well."

"He is growing up so fast," Vivianne reflected. "We were just discussing his education – I would not wish to shorten his spring schooling."

At this point, Cenfigen, who hadn't left the meeting hall yet, interjected – "If I may suggest, my lady, I would be willing to join this adventure, acting as an additional guardian and tutor for any younger lads that might be traveling to Gallwyddel."

"Ah, yes, that presents further opportunity for the lad's education in new territory," Galehaut promoted the idea, although he had some misgivings about this tutor.

"I am eager to join the hunting quest and the journey as well!" added Cenfigen, as Vivianne looked to Taliesin with reluctance and concern.

"The lad is growing up. We cannot shield him from everything. At some point he must venture out into the world beyond Afallon," Taliesin reasoned.

"I have been a hand in his destiny thus far. And even though I hesitate, I must not hold him so dear that I limit all I believe he can be," Vivianne discerned. "You must promise me, here, his two most active mentors, that you both will ensure his safety."

"Yes my lady," said Galehaut.

"Most assuredly," added Cenfigen.

"Alright then, we'll tell the lad," Vivianne said, as Taliesin nodded.

"Thank you my lady, we will take good care of the lad," Galehaut said with a bow, he and Cenfigen leaving the hall together.

"Have you actually been hunting in recent years?" Galehaut questioned the tutor.

"No, not in recent years, but I am greatly looking forward to doing so again!" Cenfigen answered.

"I'll be watching you, schoolmaster. I bring you along for the lady's concern, not by my choice," Galehaut cautioned him.

"You are master of the quest, and I follow your command, sire," Cenfigen bowed in deference with an uneasy smile. "Good day. I will now retire and begin to prepare for the journey."

Vivianne and Taliesin met with young Llen that same day, to talk to him about his new adventure, Vivianne saying: "Galehaut has been invited to bring a hunting party to his homeland in Gallwyddel for a challenge quest with his clansmen from Alt Clud and Rheged. He asked if you could join them." The lad's face lit-up. Vivianne continued, smiling lovingly at the lad and Taliesin – "and we said yes, you may go along."

"Thank you, Mother, Father," young Llen responded with joy, hugging them both, brimming with excitement.

"You must heed every directive from Galehaut and your tutor," Taliesin instructed the lad.

"Cenfigen is going on the hunting quest too?" Llen questioned.

"Yes, your schooling will continue while you are away," Vivianne clarified.

"Can Bercnaf go along as well? He is such a great keeper of the hounds. I know he would be of value to the hunt," Llen eagerly asked.

"That is for Galehaut to decide. We will speak to him and the lad's mother. They have the final word," Taliesin told him.

"Yes, I know. I will respect their decision. Surely they will say yes," Llen responded.

"Surely they will; now let us help you prepare for your grand adventure," Vivianne said, holding him close once more, her eyes beginning to tear.

Bercnaf was allowed to go with Llen and the others to Gallwyddel. He was a valued hound-lad, recognized by many of Galehaut's men for his natural way with all breed and manner of hound. It was clear he would soon be a top trainer and handler. The party gathered the best mounts and hounds for the grand quest across the Solway in the north. Galehaut was heir to lands there; but through shifting alliances and dynastic marriages between the clans, the lands had been acquiesced to Afallach, descendent of the ancient King Afallach of Ynys Manau. So Galehaut became the active guardian and battle lord of Ynys Manau, while the island's descendant heir became king of Galehaut's own homeland of Gallwyddel. Most clans from Gallwyddel trace their lineage to Eirenn, the Cymric word for the Scotti of Eirenn being Gwyddel.

It was quite an expedition, just short of a battle or a well planned siege of a fortified town. Llen and Bercnaf were thrilled to be included in the fortnight adventure. At their destination in the forests of Alt Clud, near Gallwyddel, the camp was a rousing sight, cousins of Galehaut crashing their leather scaled hauberks together like rutting bucks, or sparring brown bears. Roaring laughter and tales told around campfires kept the hunters up into the night, consuming enough ale or wine to relax into sleep without dulling their minds too much for the next day's hunt.

All of the horsemen and handlers had the mounts and hounds fit for a great quest early in the morning. This event would involve several days of hunting, with a tally of each party's game over the course of the week, changing the direction of pursuit for each party each day, culminating with a fantastic shared feast of the spoils – with no true victor beyond the boasting. The first day ended without a clear leader, each party yielding few deer and small game. On the second day, a sudden storm cut short any prospect of a hunt, leaving the men huddled in tents, professing bragging rights for what was yet to come, with Llen and Bercnaf subjected to hours of tutoring from Cenfigen. Early on the morning of the third day, the sky was clear and the air crisp; but all were awakened by a currier from Alt Clud urging Galehaut and other clan leaders to meet with the northern Cylch concerning a rising threat within Bryneich, to their eastern borders. Galehaut and several other Wledig decided to ride east straight away. At first he felt that he better take young Llen with him; but the lad wanted to stay at camp.

"Sire, please let me stay, now that the rains have stopped, and the quest can begin fresh," Llen pleaded.

"I swore to protect you lad. How can I do that if you're not by my side?"

"I have not been by your side every moment thus far. Your liegemen, huntsmen, and my tutor have been my added guardians these several days," Llen debated him.

"The lad's right sire," Cenfigen interjected. "I'm here; the hounds and huntsmen are here; all the lad's newfound brothers surround him."

"You must guard this lad from harm with your lives, as your own blood – hear me!" Galehaut said sternly, looking around at his men. "I will return as soon as I can. The Lady of Afallon would not have this; so give no cause for her to find harm or danger to this lad. Or I will truss, gut and carve away the hide of any man responsible, until his last breath, when he will remember only his grievous error."

Galehaut, several clan leaders and their liegemen headed northeast to meet with King Tudwal and Prince Rhydderch of Alt Clud at a northern hillfort; while Llen and Bercnaf eagerly awaited a day of the hunt. The hunting party from Ynys Manau was reluctant to take the lads with them, harkening to Galehaut's threatening words.

"It might be best if you lads stick to the camp," Rheu, the lead huntsman suggested. "I don't care to be coddling barely weaned babes, while I'm on a quest for game."

"You old bugger, we were weaned as young as hounds; and I run with these lymers and grechion like the kin of their litters," Bercnaf barked at the huntsman.

"Huh, ha, that you are, you little cur," the huntsman snapped back. "It is Llen that we'll be skinned for, not you. So stay with him; and let your ysgol llygoden take the risk of his skin."

"Leave us with Tywyswr and Tywysog then, you cheese arrow buggers; so we can give curée to our favorite hounds when the prize hart walks right into camp!" Bercnaf shouted back.

"You're a pit-hound yourself, rascal bastard. Keep your favorites. It'll rest 'em for another day," Rheu the huntsman said, as he brushed his hand across Bercnaf's disheveled head of hair.

After the last of the hunting parties left camp, Cenfigen brought two fine horses over to the lads. As they looked-up with surprise the tutor said: "Well lads, shall we set-out with a party of three men and two hounds?" rousing them to their feet.

"Aren't you afraid of Galehaut's wrath?" Llen asked.

"I resent these lording huntsmen and their masters. They brought us here for the hunt. So let us begin our own quest," Cenfigen declared.

The lads hurriedly grabbed their arms and gear, Llen and the tutor each mounting their horses; while Bercnaf held the lyam for the hounds, running along beside Llen and his palfrey. It was a swift young steed, set aside for a lad or lady – just right for an experienced young horseman like Llen. Cenfigen seemed ill-suited for his mount. The mare was as impartial to him as any woman that the toad-like tutor ever touched with his feeble palm. Bercnaf and Tywyswr soon took the lead, the lymer catching scent in the one direction no other party had taken. The terrain became rough, edging down toward a stream. At some point Llen, Bercnaf and the hounds left the awkward loping tutor behind; he, attempting to prod his mare aggressively along, soon tumbling down an embankment, twisting his ankle. Llen and Bercnaf kept their focus on the chase, following trace of a fine buck along the stream, until it crossed over to the south; where Llen saw the proud beast flash through the morning light between the trees on the other side.

Llen took after his prey across the water, leaving Bercnaf and the hounds to find a shallow fording spot. Soon Llen sighted the grand hart standing in a distant glade, its ribs rising with a deliberate rhythm, now upwind, unable to gather the scent of Llen and his palfrey. The lad dismounted, securing his horse, pulling his bow overhead from around his shoulder, and setting an arrow from the quiver between his fingers on the bowstring. His breath was calm and steady, as he stood still and silent in the shade of a tall oak. Llen concentrated on what Galehaut had taught him – the mark, or point of focus, where the breath, calmness of thought, feeling, and intent join with the life-force of the hart and the aim of the archer. The lad took a breath, slowly, holding his eye two hands below the spine, left of center behind the shoulder, the axis of this regal body, to be intersected with a defining shaft, marking that point between mortal and eternal life. The hart and he were at the center of everything – all existence. He was innocent of the life he was about to take; because he was not separate from the hart in that instant. The body of the stable sacred beast would lose its life; but Llen would greet that shining stag of spirit within his own center. They became one with the land, the blood of the hart one with his – inseparable from the earth, the breath, the blood, and ignited light of life itself – one spark muted, to be caught as one spark waking. This was the gift of the hart: the sacred life shared and honored in that infinite marked moment of recognition and union with all life and death – a point of sacred ground. The hart was guardian to an open portal; as the arrow hit its mark, and as animal life passed, a chill swept through Llen; and he knew he was forever bonded with this sacred being.

Llen slowly approached the fallen buck, with his palfrey in tow. He looked down upon the beautiful beast, the arrow feathers pointing up to the late morning sun bursting through the cathedral pillars of trees. This was his first kill of a hart, a hart he revered as both an adversary and an elemental spirit, guiding him on, leading him into the life of a warrior. It wasn't long before Bercnaf and the hounds caught up to Llen. Tywysog ran up first, sniffing at the dead buck.

"Clean kill mate! You're a huntsman now!" Bercnaf cheered him, with a slap on the back. "He's a beaut!"

"I felt him, mate," Llen said with solemn reverence.

"He's got a fine coat and eight points," said Bercnaf, running his hand across the deer's body, "Feels good."

"No, I mean I felt him join me; when I took the shot." Llen clarified, with an earnest expression in his eyes.

"Join you . . . you mean the spirit of the buck?" asked Bercnaf, a bit staggered by Llen's somberness.

"Yes. It was at first a chill, a shudder of something touching my soul. He was a proud beast. I felt an instant of fear, not mine, but his; and then his raised rack reaching to the Otherworld, my spine arching with his. As he collapsed and fell to the side, I felt that bold hart enter my heart. He is with me still, now."

"You sound like a druid, mate," Bercnaf responded.

"This is our nemeton," said Llen, looking up to the sun pouring through the treetops, his arms spread wide. "This hart is our sacrament, the forest floor our altar. His blood marks the turning point in our lives."

Llen knelt down, touching the blood of the hart, looking at him with loving reverence, as if a great warrior and ally had leapt into the Otherworld, a hero of battle. He took his bloody fingers and traced a line of blood on Bercnaf and his own face from their foreheads down the bridge of their noses. The two lads lifted the buck onto the back of the palfrey, trussed him up; and Llen cut a small portion of flesh from the deer for each hound.

"Here's your curée, pups," Bercnaf said as he gave the wagging lymer and the greyhound their rewards.

The lads tasted the blood too, nodding to each other, and embracing forearms in a Roman handshake.

"We're brothers of this blood, wherever we go from here," Llen declared.

"You're master huntsman and archdruid to me, mate. That was a grand kill; and you're starting to talk like Galehaut or your Ta, the Penbard."

"Ha ha, I'm no bard, but this buck here shook my soul to wake – and you're on the journey to wake with me. Let's journey on mate!"

"Let's journey on!"

The lads headed south, past the stand of trees beyond the stream, Llen believing there was a road ahead. And there was one, as he predicted.

"See there, guided vision, I'm tellin' ya mate – you're a druid now!" Bercnaf jested with Llen.

"Stop it, or I'll turn you into a toad!" Llen fired back.

"You did turn us to the road!"

"Huh ha ha ha" – they both laughed.

"Good rhyme, maybe you're the bard," bantered Llen.

They walked nor-eastward on the old Roman road, in the direction of their hunting camp. Within less than a few ystaden they came upon a young noble walking his nearly lame horse, both the lad and his mount beaten and haggard. Clearly startled, the noble lad turned back to see them, frightened a bit at first glance; but quickly realizing they were just two lads and two dogs, with a palfrey and fresh deer kill. He waited until they reached him.

"Hello lads, nice buck, took him yourselves?"

"Yes, Llen here did," answered Bercnaf.

"Fine shot, Llen is it?"

"Yes. Are you in danger lad?" Llen surmised by the stranger's nervous manner.

"Yes, well, my family was ambushed by rouges from Bryneich. I narrowly escape. We were exiled from the continent. I'm trying to reach the fort of Tudwal in Alt Clud, but got turned around eluding capture. Now my mount is hardly able, and I'm fearful for my life," the young noble explained.

"Why do you seek Tudwal's fort?" Llen asked.

"My family had . . ." the youth began to break into tears, "my family had evidence of treachery between Bryneich and dynastic heirs of Francia. Tudwal and the northern Cylch must be informed at once."

"Our master Galehaut of Gallwyddel and Ynys Manau rode to meet with Tudwal and other clan chiefs this very day!" Llen added with astonishment. "You must take my palfrey and head nor-east to join them. Here, let us move this buck to your mount."

"You're godsends lads," the young noble said with relief, helping to hurriedly untie the buck and lift it over to his weakened horse.

Bercnaf assisted, perplexed, questioning Llen off to the side: "Are you sure you want to give up this palfrey for that bag of bones?"

Llen nodded yes.

"Thank you lads, I'll tell Galehaut of your kindness," the noble lad said, quickly mounting his palfrey and riding swiftly off up the road, giving a wave of his arm back to them as he rounded the curve of the road ahead; while Bercnaf, looked at the troubled horse that they had received in the exchange, wondering how their abusive tutor Cenfigen was making his way.

"What do ya think happened to Cenfigen?" Bercnaf asked as they slowly walked on.

"That mare probably killed him and ate him," Llen jested, causing them both to double-over with laughter; while the hounds looked-on, puzzled and wagging their tails until the lads settled down, able to walk again.

As it grew late in the afternoon, the lads came upon another stranger: an old gent, resting beside the road with a fine greyhound, a bow, and a full quiver.

"Hello! Had a long day of hunting?" Llen greeted him.

"Yes, my good lad, long day without a bird or rabbit to show for it," the old man responded.

"Ah, another day a better hunt," Bercnaf chimed-in.

"Well, true, but it is the night of my granddaughter's wedding feast; while I, the host, have no meat for the table. My son, her father, fell in battle nigh three year ago. I wished so much to make this a grand event. Now I must return empty handed."

Llen looked at Bercnaf, looked at their fine buck, and looked at Bercnaf again. Bercnaf shook his head no, frowning, his shoulders dropped.

"Here sir," Llen said, raising his hand toward their slain deer, Bercnaf turning away, shaking his head and stepping back a few steps. "Take this fine fresh kill for your granddaughter's wedding feast. It will honor us both and the life of the deer to serve such an occasion."

"Why, lad, are you sure? He's a fine animal," said the old man, standing-up to examine the deer more closely.

"His first kill," Bercnaf noted, pointing at Llen with a slight bow.

"First kill? I thought you lads were returning this buck for an elder huntsman," said the stranger.

In the meantime, the two greyhounds were getting acquainted, fascinated by each other, wagging tails, sniffing about, nuzzling their heads together. So much so, it drew the attention of the old man and the lads.

"Look at these two; they could be brothers from the same litter," Llen commented. "What's his name?"

"Tywysog," the old man answered.

"No, that's our hound's name," Llen responded with surprise.

"Ha ha," laughed the old man. "Two princes, met on a road between kingdoms, ha ha. They very well could be brothers. He was sired in Gallwyddel. Where was yours sired?"

"Gallwyddel," Bercnaf answered. "Our master, Galehaut, brought him from Gallwyddel as a pup."

"Well, I'll be – say, these hounds should not be separated again. Let me give you the hound, in return for this fine buck," the old man proposed.

"Done!" Llen agreed, his arm extended for a shake, sealing the bargain.

"Very well then, it turned out to be a good hunt after all," the old man gratefully acknowledged.

They untied the deer and the old man slung it up on his shoulders, much to the lads' amazement, his surprise success giving him added vigor.

"Are you alright with that?" Bercnaf asked, seeing the old man's posture bending under the added weight.

"Oh sure, I've not far to go. It's such a grand victory today for my dear young lass." With that, he trudged off to the southwest, singing an ancient song in the dialect of the Gwyddel.

Llen and Bercnaf slowly made their way back to camp, nearing sundown, blood-marked from their kill, with no deer, a pitiful horse, and a new hound. Cenfigen approached them straight away, hobbling with a makeshift wooden crutch.

"What is this raggedy old mount? Where is that fine palfrey? Where have you lads been all this day? I called to you when my mare took a fall. Didn't you hear me?"

"No sire, we were fast on the trace of a fine hart buck," Llen responded.

"Llen's first kill, clean . . ."

Cenfigen cut Bercnaf off, his temper rising – "Hart buck! Where? I see no game, no kill, just your painted faces."

"We gave the deer to an old man we met on the road," Llen tried to explain.

"He gave us this fine hound," Bercnaf added.

"An old man you say? And did he turn your fine palfrey into this feeble mount, barely standing here?"

"No, there was another younger man. We gave him the palfrey to ride to meet Tudwal and Galehaut," Llen answered.

Cenfigen railed back at them with sarcasm – "Oh now the cast of characters in this tale gets long enough to include a king and your master; were there any faeries trading hounds and horses as well?"

Bercnaf volleyed a flippant return – "No faeries, or ysgol llygoden either!"

Cenfigen raised his hand to slap the lad; so Llen stepped in front of his mate, saying, "This new hound is worth two palfreys. It's not our fault you couldn't keep up with two lads and two hounds on a mare that wouldn't have you mount her."

This enraged the tutor so; he struck Llen twice across the face with his open hand. The lad hardly blinked, scowling at the rattled little man. Responding to the tutor's blows, the hounds began barking and lunging forward, Bercnaf holding them back with the lyam; until the tutor struck one of the hounds with the side of his rough hewn crutch, drawing blood from the hound's flank. Llen quickly pulled his bow from off his shoulder, blocked away Cenfigen's crutch, causing the angered tutor to lose his footing and fall, the lad striking the man repeatedly about the head, breaking his bow, leaving Cenfigen bleeding from his balding pate. By this time, three huntsmen had run over to put an end to this pitched battle of tempers, separating the lads, the hounds, and the tutor.

Rheu, the lead huntsman stepped-in asking – "What in the bloody hell is all of this fray about?"

"These little bastards were about to feed me to their hounds!" Cenfigen's shrill voice shouted with agitation.

"Not much of a meal then," Rheu responded. "I was about to mount a search for you lads."

"He struck Llen first!" Bercnaf piped-in.

"It was when he struck the hound with his crutch that riled me," Llen added. "I took his discipline for my words, but not his abuse of the hunting hounds."

The huntsman examined the hound, seeing the fresh wound he sneered at the tutor, asking Llen – "What did you say to this ysgol llygoden that brought him to blows?"

"I said it wasn't our fault he couldn't keep pace with two lads and two hounds on a mare that wouldn't have him mount her," Llen answered, dipping his head to hide a smirk, inspiring the three huntsmen and a gathering circle to laughter.

"That's a randy statement for a lad nigh ten years – but funny lad, very funny," Rheu acknowledged. "So where's the palfrey, and where's your meat from the blood of the kill?" He questioned further, lifting the lad's chin to look at his proud battle paint.

"We traded the palfrey to a young noble desperately riding towards Tudwal's fort, with urgent news from Bryneich," Llen answered as the huntsmen looked to each other with raised eyebrows. "The meat was given to serve as a feast for an old man on his granddaughter's wedding night."

"You've been busy lads. Did he leave anything out, barking Bercnaf?"

"Llen's first kill was a fine hart buck, clean center shot, one of the best I've seen. And the old man gave up this great grech; could be the brother of Tywysog – bearing the exact same name!" Bercnaf added.

"Huh ha – two hounds named Prince, not quite an omen from the gods, but they do look like twins – aside from the fresh scar," the huntsman said as he turned away from the hounds and lifted Cenfigen to his feet, the tutor wincing from the weight on his turned ankle.

"When Galehaut returns we'll straighten this trouble out. Until then, no hunting, no bickering and no ill-tempered tutoring," Rheu said with finality.

There was plenty of game from the day's quest, each party finding deer, rabbit and fowl. A great meal was shared around the campfires, the young lads falling fast asleep after their long day's adventure. Cenfigen was understandably restless, with pain in his ankle and concern over Galehaut's potential retribution for the tutor's deplorable guardianship. Rheu took the lads with him on a short hunt the next day, feeling assured that the novice huntsmen could handle themselves. He enjoyed pointing out to the lads traces of game along the paths in the wood.

"Here, see, the hounds caught the fumes a ways back," Rheu said, picking up dry deer droppings. "These are yesterday's, early; but look here, see the fewt. There was an old stag and a hind. The blunter print and the wider heel is the old fellow, the sharper slot is the hind. See her gate?"

"How do you tell the print of the hind from that of a young buck?" Llen asked.

"Well lad, see here the gait of the hind is more varied, the hind foot up to meet the fore foot. When she is with fawn, her hind feet splay-out wider than the fore. But here, she's prancin' afore the old stag – struttin' her stuff, huh huh."

Late that afternoon, Galehaut and the other clan leaders returned from Tudwal's fort. Llen eagerly greeted Galehaut, running up to him as soon as he dismounted his horse. The young man riding the traded palfrey gave the lad a wave of his hand.

"I've returned your horse," he said to Llen.

"Yes, I see, thank you."

"That was a kind gesture, lad." Galehaut told his young charge. "This heir of Francia brought startling news of events in his homeland. I hear that you landed an eight point hart. Only wish I could have been there for your first kill. How is it that two lads and two hounds were out alone, no guide or guardian about?"

"Well sire," Llen began, "Cenfigen took us out on a quest, even though Rheu had told us to stay at camp. By the time Bercnaf and the two hounds caught trace of the hart, Cenfigen had fallen behind."

"We didn't know he'd really taken a fall and buggered his ankle," Bercnaf added.

"We never saw him again all day until we got back to camp," said Llen.

"You never looked for him, or wondered what became of him?" Galehaut questioned.

"We had crossed a stream to follow the hart, and I was well sure the Roman road laid a short way ahead, thinking it a better route with our game trussed-up and all," Llen explained.

"The tutor was a poor rider, we thought his mare must have taken a temper or somethin' – he is a full-grown man, I believe. We lads had to look to ourselves, and our game of the day," Bercnaf defended their actions.

"And then on the road, as you know, we met this noble lad in distress headed to meet King Tudwal. I knew he needed the palfrey more than us. I was sure it wasn't many leagues around the bend until we'd come up to the Basses Bridge and back to camp," Llen elaborated.

"Oh you did, now?" said Galehaut, with a smile.

"To Cenfigen's credit, sire, he had been tutoring me in the lay of the land as we traveled from Solway, with maps and cipherin' of leagues and ystaden to chart the journey," Llen added .

"I see. So you brought your fine kill back to camp, just the two of you lads?"

"Well, no, not exactly," Llen continued. We met a sweet old man who had been hunting all day with no meat for his table on the wedding feast night of his granddaughter. So we gave him the hart; for his need seemed greater than our glory."

"That was a very noble thing to do lad," said Galehaut.

"And the old man gave-up his fine grech in return, named Tywysog – could be our Tywysog's brother hound, sired in Gallwyddel," Bercnaf was quick to add.

24

"You lads have had quite a quest," Galehaut remarked. "Although I'm not too pleased with the way it all started out. I must have some words with Cenfigen. He is still lurking about, isn't he?"

"He's here somewhere. But I don't suppose he's too eager to be skinned alive sire," Llen answered.

Lead huntsman Rheu soon informed Galehaut of the skirmish between Cenfigen and the lads, prompting Galehaut's response: "With the lads unharmed, I had hoped to wash over this lapse in their care. Knowing Cenfigen struck the lad and the hound, I will need to take action, and tell Lady Vivianne and Taliesin of the tutor's ill-temper. I have suspected that he had beaten Bercnaf before, but that hound-lad is too tough to cry out."

"The ysgol llygoden is a man, though not much of one. He has no call to strike that favored Llen like a slave. And to draw blood from a hunting hound, I would have beaten the tutor myself, if Llen hadn't already broke a good bow on the chatty little creep," Rheu admitted. "Both lads are impressive: Bercnaf a bit rough, like his hounds – but he'll be a lead handler on the hunts before long."

The hunting parties had another day of questing game, ending with a fine feast and plenty to carry back to their neighboring kingdoms. Galehaut considered binding the tutor, realizing he couldn't hobble far on his bad ankle; he gave him freedom of the camp. After a round of playful taunts, the huntsmen from the northern lands went their separate ways, returning to home and hearth. Galehaut, Llen, Bercnaf, the Frankish noble lad and the men of Ynys Manau set sail from Solway to Afallon.

The Gift of the Hounds

During the night before Llen's bold hunt, in the early hours prior to the courier's arrival at the hunting camp, Vivianne was stirred by a profound visionary dream at the ysgol in Afallon. She was running through the misty forests of Armorica with the immortal goddess Diana. Behind them wafted the panting canine breathing of seven hundred regal greyhounds, the rhythmic pounding of synchronous paws creating a pattern of sound to match the meter of Vivianne's beating heart. Each hound wore a jeweled and gilded collar, denoting their lineage to a sacred pedigree from ancient times. Ahead of Vivianne and Diana galloped an enormous white stag, brilliant with radiant light emanating from ten points of his antlered crown. The stag led them into a great dining hall in the kingdom of Soissons in Francia; the doors springing wide open as the grand hart stag reached the threshold.

Inside, seventy of the grey shimmering hounds ran figure-eight tracks around, under, and between the pillars and tables of the great hall, as nobles and commoners reveled with drunken laughter. A king wearing the Crown of Francia stood-up at the head of the table, bleeding from his eyes and ears, holding a broken sword out before him. He shouted, "The princes must die!" as the greyhounds rounded and rounded the hall, two in the lead shifting shape from hounds to lads and back to hounds over and over again, the Frankish king now holding in his arms the body of his own dead son; while the lads who shifted shape to hounds ran from the hall behind Diana and Vivianne. The grand hart stag trotted-up to the table of the king, raked-up the royal scepter in his horned rack, the scepter streaming with blood from its golden orb, spiraling 'round its shaft, a line of blood trailing a trace behind the luminous stag all the way from the king's table, following the proud beast's turning to a galloping leap through the large arched celestial window at the hall's end, creating a shattering of multicolored glass and an effusion of intense light, completely permeating all vision. Within this near-blinding light, Vivianne saw the goddess Diana and the image of Mary Magdalene merge, embracing her with saturating radiance and abounding love, continuing even after she awoke.

Days later when Galehaut and the hunting party returned, Vivianne was certain her dream vision would be illuminated further by their report. She and Taliesin discussed the dream in depth. This was their frequent discourse in the early morning hours, when the potent images were fresh in memory.

"How would you interpret the significance of the Magdalene? Clearly, Diana is innate to priestesses of the natural world, and Mary is a significant matriarch in your ancestral legacy of wisdom," Taliesin put forth.

"Yes, most definitely, Mary Magdalene is a significant Maré, revered particularly in Francia." Vivianne responded. "She was the protector of princes of the Fisher Kings. We owe a great debt of gratitude to her for our own legacy of both priest kings and priestesses of the sacred mystery schools. Afallon itself is a tribute to her legacy – a tributary of truth – Magdalene and the Maré embody the heart of awareness. My vision was rich with blood and light, displaying dualism catalyzed explosively as primal forces: this energy intensely coursing through me. The Magdalene constantly stands as witness to the transcendence of dualism: the light and the blood, the patriarchal powers and the matriarchal essence are clearly at odds in this vision. Light prevails, and the goddess of the hunt guides me to the rescue of two lads who are somehow both hounds and princes."

"Having shared many a pint of ale or casks of wine with princes, they readily shape-shift to hounds, to the peril of innocent maidens or whatever prey their appetites fancy," Taliesin described the metaphor.

"No doubt, but here I perceive both literal and figurative allusions waiting to be discovered." Vivianne continued. "The celestial window is shattered to expose a greater light."

"Yes, by that ten point stag as the transcendent four-footed or fourfold force: where the earthly quest and the celestial heart are together as inner and outer radiance expanded," Taliesin perceived.

When the hunting party returned from Gallwyddel, Llen was first to rush to Vivianne and Taliesin, immediately telling them of his first kill and the new hound named Tywysog.

"So now there are two greyhound princes. That is quite fascinating. How will you tell these twins apart?" Vivianne asked Llen.

"One is marked on his flank; but that should heal-up." Llen answered.

"What happened to him? And where did you get this new greyhound?" Taliesin asked the lad.

"I gave the hart buck to a discouraged old man who had no meat for his granddaughter's wedding feast; so he gave us the hound."

"That was very kind; and a wise trade," said Taliesin. "How did the mark on the hound's flank occur?"

Galehaut stepped forward saying, "My Lady, Sire – the hound was struck by Cenfigen."

"Cenfigen?" Vivianne questioned.

"A courier came to our camp on the third morning with urgent news from Tudwal. Several Wledig and I went to Tudwal's fort in western Alt Clud at his request. I left the lad in the care of my huntsmen and the tutor; but Cenfigen took it upon himself to take the lads on a quest. Well, Cenfigen faltered; thrown from his horse with a turned ankle, and left on his own; while the young lads proceeded to have a successful hunt. Beyond that, Llen showed kindness and generosity to two strangers: the old man, as you heard, and a lad with a failing mount, urgently on route to inform Tudwal of treachery from Bryneich. Llen traded his fine palfrey to this lad," Galehaut pointed to the young Frankish noble, "for the failing mount. By the time the two lads returned to camp, Cenfigen was so incensed, he struck Llen with open hand, and scarred the hound with a rough wooden crutch."

The tutor sheepishly bowed his head, as Vivianne and Taliesin glanced at him with scorn.

"I have suspected Cenfigen of whipping Bercnaf; but the bold little fellow takes it like a man – no doubt to keep his post as hound-lad and to be near his mate Llen. This quest of theirs was impressive for any huntsman, let alone two lads and two hounds. Cenfigen, it is clear, is ill-tempered and ill-suited for his post. Rheu or I would have beat him for his violence against the lad or the hound; but Llen himself stood-up to defend his mate and the hound, whipping down this miserable guardian with a bow 'til it broke. I'm proud of the lads. I advise Cenfigen be dismissed. If he were one of my men, his punishment would be far more severe," Galehaut reported, giving the tutor a look that could skin a fresh kill.

"Well, quite a report. I am proud of the lads, intrigued by what the noble from Francia has to share, and disgusted with you, Cenfigen," Vivianne declared. "I entrusted the care of children to you. Your actions offend me, and are an affront to the Afallon Ysgol. My temptation is to hand you over to the huntsmen to receive their stern justice; but I would treat you better than you would treat a hound. Leave this island at once, or I will send these men to hunt you down. You will not find placement in Rheged as a tutor either, if I have any influence with the nobility ruled by King Urien, my cousin."

Cenfigen bowed and departed, never to be seen again.

"Now, shall we meet our guest from Francia and hear his accounts of the treachery on the continent and in Bryneich?" Vivianne directed.

"Thank you, my Lady," the young Frankish noble said, bowing to her and Taliesin. "I am Llamorhad, descendent of Nascien and Zambor, from the lands of the Burgundians. More than half of my life, my family has been in hiding or exile from the increased aggression of the heirs of Clovis towards our lineage. We had news of the heirs of Galains, our cousins, believed to be dead, two lads aged ten and eleven are held captive after years of hiding. Chlothar of Soissons holds them; and spies loyal to our lineage told us of his plans to kill these lads after the feast of the Magdalene." Vivianne's hand clutched Taliesin's arm as the noble lad shared these details. "My family," Llamorhad continued, "escaped to Bryneich seeking refuge, where we heard of this treachery. There are Frankish conspirators, rouge mercenaries, aligned with factions in Bryneich, who are plotting rebellion against the northern Cymric Cylch, to gain lands by allying with the Angle heirs of Ida. This was the urgent news for Tudwal and the Gwyr y Gogledd. I fear for the lives of my cousins, the young princes Llewyrch and Baeddan – especially now . . ." the lad hesitated, choked-up with sorrow – "now that my own family has been slain or taken captive."

"Thank you Llamorhad for your courage in delivering this urgent news." Vivianne responded. "I have had disturbing visions concerning what I now know to be the dangerous threat against your cousins. We are all descendents of the Fisher Kings and the Sicambrian Queens. You honor our lineage. We embrace you as a kinsman and welcome you here to Afallon to stay with us as long as you desire. I ask you to join Taliesin, Galehaut and me in council that we may discuss a plan of action to rescue these young princes."

"Thank you my Lady, I am grateful to serve in any way I can. I am young, and more of a man of letters than of battle, aside from my own family's fight for survival," Llamorhad said, bowing again.

Vivianne, Taliesin, Galehaut, the lad Llamorhad along with a young huntsman and another priestess of Afallon met together in a closed chamber to discuss the plight of the two princes.

"Thank you all," Vivianne began. "I have invited the young priestess Diana to join us, as well as Myr Heliwr, one of Galehaut's liegemen. They both have lived in Armorica and Francia, well spoken in local dialects. Diana was a clear choice to lead the rescue of these young lads, because she has the strength and courage of her namesake, goddess of the hunt. My recent visions showed me two princes shape-shifting to greyhounds, with hounds, chaos and mayhem in Soissons, the goddess Diana merging images with the Magdalene in celestial light."

"We are all awestruck by your lucid augury, my Lady," said Galehaut, breaking the moment of silently stunned reaction. "What do you recommend for this rescue in Soissons?"

"I believe we must appeal to King Chlothar's vanity, offering him gifts: a pack of greyhounds and three barrels of triple-strong ale. The ale will be laced with potions that incite distorted visions of the mind – elixirs from the enigmatic druids."

"And perhaps I could compose a bawdy drinking song to be sung by our well spoken rescuers, inducing the muddled images of the treacherous captor's delusions," Taliesin suggested.

"Brilliant my dear," Vivianne went on. "We'll dress the royal lads in grey leggings and tunics, donning hounds masks at the time of peak intoxication of the hosts, the lads exiting on all fours amidst the hounds. King Chlothar would hardly suspect a tavern maid and a young huntsman to abduct two princes from a well guarded fortress."

"It's a bold plan," Galehaut commented. "The key will be in the power of your elixir, and the disheveled drunkenness of Chlothar's entire retinue. I know Myr appears to be a lad of slight build to all; but he will lay open any man of any size before they realize his threat. I suggest the princely lads be carted from the fortress in empty barrels; and that we enlist a troop of Armorican warriors waiting in the nearby countryside to escort them back to friendly territory and safe passage across the sea."

"Wise advice, my friend," Taliesin agreed. "Let us prepare for this grand mission to save these royal heirs, keeping the details of our plans in close confidence among ourselves."

The plan was well provisioned: a ship setting off from Ynys Manau long before the mid-summer feast of the Magdalene, complete with empty barrels and the elixir for the beguiling ale, as well as seven well-trained greyhounds. Diana and Myr made a great pair of daring rescuers: both skilled in their individual talents and deeply dedicated to the cause, working together to cover every detail, drawing on their Armorican contacts and diverse language skills. They soon found a tight band of warriors to assist their entry and retreat from Soissons. A skilled Frisian brewmaster in Armorica prepared the barrels of ale, adding a small cask of triple-strength brew without the besotting elixir and a few empty tankards to the cargo, to adequately whetten the assistance of guards and gatekeepers along the way. The ale was a northern style, accented with spices that helped mask the elixir intended to disable their foes. Priming each gate with a pint allowed Diana and Myr surprisingly easy access to the center of the Soissons fortress. The greyhounds were a sensation too: every guard with a passion for the hunt admiring the look and temperament of the seven grechion. Chlothar was no exception. After a thorough vetting by his liegemen, the Cymric rescuers finally gained access to the King.

"What fine hounds!" Chlothar exclaimed, as the seven grechion stood poised awaiting command. "I hear they are a gift from Armorica?"

"Yes Sire," Myr Heliwr answered, "a gift of goodwill from Tewdr Mawr the King of Armorica."

"King Tewdr Mawr, well this is a fine gesture," Chlothar acknowledged.

"We have also brought several barrels of triple-strength ale for your celebration feast tonight. Would you care for a taste, Sire?" Diana added.

"Ah, tonight, certainly – but I'll wait until then. I hope that you can join us for the celebration before your return," said the king, smiling at Diana.

"Thank you Sire, we would love to," she coyly responded.

Before evening, Diana was able to find the two princes, playing on their own in a small courtyard, somewhat secluded, lightly guarded by a dosing old warrior who was easily distracted by a pint, giving the young priestess a chance to speak to the lads alone. She quickly set them aware of the evening plans, assuming they would be allowed to attend the feast on the eve of their rumored demise. The lads had been fairly well treated these few months of captivity, aside from being taunted by Chlothar's youngest illegitimate son, Chlod. This eve would mark the celebration of Chlod's entry into manhood. As Diana suspected, Chlothar showed a modicum of generosity with the gift of a last meal before the final sunrise of the captive lads' short lives.

Once the festivities began, the ale was presented to the king. Chlothar proceeded with caution, allowing his tasting servant to absorb the effects of a pint or so, the other nobility and their attendants readily following the taster's safe indulgence well before the king took his first swallow.

"My, this is a fine ale. Brewed in Armorica?" asked the king.

"Yes, by a Frisian brewmaster, Sire," Diana informed him.

"Ah yes, the spice, quite a taste – excellent – everyone must drink!" The king shouted, raising a gold cup above his head. "Tonight we recognize Chlod as a prince, as he now enters manhood. Here is the sword of his ancestors," holding the sword of Frankish kings high in the air, "beside the crown and scepter of Francia," laying the sword on the table where the scepter was displayed, resting on an ornate silver stand, the crown on a velvet pillow.

"Drink everyone!" The king shouted again, "drink by the gracious gift of Tewdr Mawr, who no-doubt seeks an ally against my warring brothers."

Drinking and merriment ensued with great abandon long before the feast of a grand stag, wild boar and pheasant was to be served. As soon as the entire hall of revelers was sufficiently pissed and near delirium, Myr led the crowd in a rousing song taught to him by Taliesin, just before the voyage.

"Raise a draught from the hunting horn, of good strong ale at table. No throats are dry, and all the while, the maids are all the wetter. Double the maids, and double-strong ale, still while the lads are able; But thrice-breasted maids, and triple-strong ale, is thrice as good or better.

Drink, drink, drink it all down, until the maids are triple. Drink, drink, drink it all down, until the lads see double. Drink, drink, drink it all down, until we've had rounds and rounds. Drink, drink, drink it all down, until the lads are greyhounds. Drink, drink, drink it all down, until we sire no trouble."

Myr roused them again and again to sing, as the pounding of tables rattled the hall, chorus after chorus; until finally King Chlothar stood, wobbling, pointing at young Llewyrch and Baeddan – "Drink lads, drink! Give them cups!"

As soon as a full cup was placed before Llew, he flung it into the face of the king, drenching Chlothar's eyes with ale, and cutting his head with the edge of the cup. Most of the hall was so engaged in song and drunken laughter, that few saw the altercation. Diana and Myr were fully aware, having only lightly imbibed of the ale without elixir. Chlod, defending his father, lunged at Llew with a dagger, Llew swiftly grabbing the king's sword off the table, swinging it fast and wide to cut through the throat of Chlothar's son. Baeddan rose, seizing the golden scepter, clubbing the Frankish prince;

while the seven hounds suddenly released by Myr, ran wild through the hall. Chlothar rushed to his son's side, the lad collapsing in the king's arms, Llew and Baeddan swinging their weapons wildly in retreat. Chaos consumed the hall as some cowered in defense, others struggled to attempt an attack of the lads, while many or most were still lost in drunken reverie and increasing delirium. Diana had Llew and Baeddan rapidly don masks, drop their weapons and scramble towards an exit on all fours. Chlothar, deliriously sighting the departing hounds, appearing as nine hounds and then nine lads, and then hounds again – fumbled for the fallen sword, reaching it, managing an overhead strike toward Diana. She, following behind the hounds and lads, turning as she exited an archway, barely escaped as Chlothar's strike hit the stone arch, shattering the blade, the broken edge slicing the right side of her lovely face from the brow to the cheekbone. Myr, a step behind, struck the king, allowing him to slump aside the base of the archway as Diana, the lads and Myr escaped the hall, sending the hounds another way back in, around to a second entrance. Outside, the rescuers promptly dropped the lads into two empty barrels on the cart, covering Diana's face with her hooded cloak and a veil serving as a bandage, then trotting the carthorse toward the gate. Myr greeted the guards with fresh pints as Diana leaned beside him into his shoulder.

"Quite the drunken row in there lads, this one's done, she's out," Myr said, gesturing a turn of his head towards Diana. "She can't hold a drink, off to sleep. Here are a couple pints for you lads. Good morrow!"

"Right kind, lad, how about leaving a barrel behind?" plied the portly guardsman.

"Sorry lads, empties headed for refilling – maybe next time," Myr answered, tapping a hollow sound on the barrel tops concealing Llew and Baeddan.

"Ah, just our luck, good morrow then," said the guard, waving then on.

Reaching the nearby wooded grove away from the local township and farms, Myr picked-up the pace until they reached the meeting place of their Armorican warrior escorts. They treated Diana's wound by a stream, Myr stitching the cut closed as best he could, applying a poultice of herbs that Diana pulled from the water's edge.

"You'll likely have a nasty scar, lass; but praise your namesake, your lovely eyes were untouched by the blade," Myr told her.

"A kind and loving field surgeon you are lad," she said as she leaned-in to kiss him on the cheek.

Arriving at the Frankish coast north of the Seine by dawn, they gained safe passage to Ynys Manau, rounding the point of Dumnonia and beyond to the Sea of Eirenn. The two rescued princes were eager to discover a new land of safe harbors. They recognized Llamorhad straight away. He was overjoyed to see his young cousins alive and well.

"Llewyrch here looks a lot like young Llen; don't you think so, my Lady?" Llamorhad said to Vivianne.

"Yes, a handsome lad, both of you lads are striking young men," responded Vivianne, warmly embracing them. "I am sure you lads will get on famously with Llen. Oh, here he is now – Llen!" Llenlleawg ran up to greet the royal Frankish brothers.

"Llen, this is Llewyrch and Baeddan, they're going to be living here for a while with us," Llamorhad introduced his cousins.

"Llew et Baedd," young Llew said in his native dialect, holding out his hand to shake Llen's.

"Can I show them our hunting hounds?" Llen said excitedly, looking to Vivianne.

"Of course you can," Vivianne answered, the three lads running-off as Llen waved them on towards the kennel.

"Well, that was quick," Llamorhad commented.

"Lads and hounds, it's a universal language," said Vivianne.

The lads became fast friends, accepting Bercnaf to round-out the foursome. It was an idyllic island for them to grow up on, with little threat from outsiders. Afallon was held sacred by most neighboring kingdoms. Even daughters of the Scotti of Eirenn entered as novices on rare occasion, the Roman Church being so dominant in Eirenn since the time of Saint Patrick. Any Scotti noble choosing the old ways of the ancient priestesses for their daughters' education would find Afallon a welcome refuge.

Vivianne was sad to see Diana scarred by the rescue struggle in Soissons; but clearly noticed the affection between Myr and the young priestess. Myr began training with Taliesin, in addition to maintaining his post with Galehaut. The priestess Diana had stirred Myr's interest in the mystic arts. Taliesin had been training the younger lads in the ways of understanding the elemental energies of the infinite sky, the sea and streams, the land and its inner fire, and the power of their dream journeys. He noticed the changes in Llen since his first kill in Alt Clud that led to meeting Llamorhad and the rescue of the foreign princes. Eventually Llen came to Vivianne and Taliesin to tell them of his recurring dreams and visions.

"Since the moment of slaying that great buck, I have seen him," Llen confided.

"Where have you seen him, lad, in the day, in your dreams, within your mind?" Taliesin questioned.

"All three: I see him through the distant wooded groves. I see him in the mist by a stream. I saw him in a dream last night."

"Tell us about your dream," said Vivianne.

"There was a man of great wisdom and power, dressed in a black robe. His hair was black as a raven, with one white feather of a streak above his forehead. He led me deep into the wood, where light beams shot through the towering trunks of giant trees, the trees so tall that they reached to the Otherworld. I could feel their roots reaching far beneath me, and their limbs embracing me. The man in black began to move in the way that you Taliesin have taught me, with the power of the mountains and streams. From this, I knew the man was Myrlyn, your father, Lady Vivianne. After we had moved together in this way of the mountains and the streams, the Myrlyn turned, walking into the light, his cloak spread like great wings; and in a flash, he turned into a raven, flying high up into the tree tops. Then, upon the earth, between the trees I saw a lynx darting from place to place within the light rays shining through the wooded grove. I ran after the lynx faster and faster until I had climbed a hill. Atop the hill stood the hart buck, his rack of eight points turning to ten and the heart beneath his strong breast aglow with light. That light pierced me like an arrow. It was not painful, but sharp, and then opening, opening in me a well of light. Then I knew the hart buck and me were one being, not beast or lad or man, but something else. And then I woke up."

"This is a grand vision lad," said Taliesin. "Vivianne, what do you see here? It seems so rich and clear to me."

"You are a bright lad, young Llenlleawg. The quest you had this spring was your initiation into the life of a warrior; but it was also an initiation into the great heritage of our ancestors. Master Myrlyn was there in your dream to acknowledge this, just as the hart buck has been with you ever since your day of the quest. Your old tutor is no more, and your new teachers have appeared: Myrlyn and others in your dreams, Galehaut, Llamorhad, Taliesin, me and others in your waking life. You showed the quality of your character of kindness, of justice, of honesty, of honor, of respect, of how you embody love in this life, when you behaved as you did on your quest. Myrlyn is the Raven of Awen, an inspiration to us all. I am his daughter. I had thought when I was a lass that the lynx was him; but I am the lynx, in my connection to him and all spirit, here, in dreams and in the Otherworld. You have bonded in spirit with the hart buck. He is your connecting link to elemental spirit and the ancestors in a powerful ten-pointed form of light-radiance and the infinite spark of Awen. In my dream vision the ten-point stag broke through the celestial glass, the veil between the world of blood and the lines of blood into the realm of light; where our ancestors, the sacred quest goddesses and our ancient mothers embrace us. This dream of yours, dear Llenlleawg, is a parting of the veil between worlds. It shows to you the hart as a form of guidance upon your path of love and light, your quest of the hart that unfolds into your future. Your destiny, dear lad, is the path of the conscious heart."

Chapter Two ~ The Wells of Sovereignty

The heart is the deepest well of every soul. We draw from it for our vitality, our pulse of blood, our inspiration and our compassion. Each birth of an innocent heart awakens to an expanding life. This lad, Llen, Llenlleawg – he might as well have dropped from the sky, landing on Ynys Manau in the Sea of Eirenn, to come into the lives of Vivianne, Taliesin and Galehaut. Is he truly of royal blood? From what divine well does this fount of blood spring? Where did any of us derive life essence? We enter without a trace of our return to our source: with only our senses, our perceptions, and our awareness of the world around us. I am an orphaned bard, a crafter of tales, attempting to find some understanding of it all, within this illusory stage; where most beings are merely struggling to survive. If not for his rescue, the babe Llen would most likely have been killed or raised in ignorance of his calling, his unfolding quest and his part in divine sovereignty. We all seem to be on a quest for our source of Awen: the inspiration welling-up within us; be it passion, or purpose, or our living breath – longing to live free of pain and healed from suffering. Afallon seemed to be a refuge and sanctuary for many young souls who, at least for a time, eluded the darker trials of life.

This island of Manau had its birth from the sea: the sea surrounding it, and the sea of serenity that it imbues. Ancients came here, erecting stones and cairn to merge sacred earth with human blood and the light of the stars. These were marks made by mankind reaching beyond their time into ours, sustaining those connective roots feeding the sovereignty of all souls. In this joining, we all partake of the first fruits of being alive. A tree of humanity sprang from one seed, foresting this earthen realm with diverse wooded groves. Afallon is one such place of the conscious heart. Nature and its elements encompass this physical life, making earth our womb of origin. She is in effect the authority of material life. The Otherworld simultaneously engulfs her, seeding her with an elemental spirit that inhabits all life-forms. This world and the Otherworld are inseparable, yet not readily perceived by all wandering souls planted here. So herein lays the quest: finding roots that are never truly lost. Our sisters of Afallon manifest the loving care of a sovereign goddess within a waking world, ransacked by patriarchal powers, violent patriarchs claiming the sovereignty of their vain glorious gods of vengeance.

My foster mother Claire and her brother Morfyn mentored me in the history of this sacred isle of apples. It is a story of two Afallons: one of a remote island kingdom within waking life, and one of an encompassing realm of spirit, seeding mythic dream. Ancient history is confounded by legends expressed in the language and forms of myth. Not that these stories are untrue; but rather, they shape truth with creative voices. We hear myth and dreams differently than the scribed annals dictated to clerics. One form records elapsed time, another conveys the shifting phantasm of our collective thoughts, passions, and the traumatic dramas of awakening souls.

Any druid or priestess of depth is a healer, mending and nurturing troubled lives. Afallon's island haven emerged from the womb of earth to heal the outward body of humanity. Ynys Manau was not a scrap of sod torn from the land, hurled by Manannan Mac Lir or any other mythic immortal god into the temporal sea; but it is that patch of a wounded earth within fluid waking life that the marked son of this sea of humankind draws from his worldly flesh and imagined form to rejoin with the healing of his cosmic birth. We have returned to the same dramas, portrayed in varied mortal forms, to learn from the ancestral voices still speaking wisdom to us. Afallon is a place of listening. Our quest begins by being aware enough to hear, to feel the movement through the silent passages within the lucid dream we are living.

Ancestors of myth founded this place of vague history. They have been called the Tuatha de Danann or children of Dôn, tribes of the gods revealing opening portals for the Sidhe to meld with us in our spectrum of time, or pryd in the Cymric tongue. Prydain is this waking realm of time, of matter, of the seasons of life and death. Myth and dream bridge our world with the Otherworld. Afallon itself forms such a bridge; Manannan Mac Lir being the mythic builder of that bridge, leading the Tuatha de Danann through the Otherworld within the conscious heart; where they guide us as the Sidhe, as the shining ones. Their cylch is reflected in the heavens as the crown of stars or silver wheel, formed as daughters of the sky. Priest Kings and Priestesses of Afallon descend from this mythic heritage, fusing light-streams with bloodlines, blurring realities within the storyteller's craft. Dôn weds Beli Mawr, Manannan weds Aine endowing their descendants with the gifts of prophesy, necromancy, and the arts of cryptic language – gwyddoniaith – all held in the crane bag handed down to the druids of the isles. Cranes gather at the shores, near streams and wells, as sentries to liminal gates of the Otherworld. Afallon's trees bear the everlasting apples, fed by sacred wells and streams. The tree, the fruit, the waters – they are all one fluidity of life, fulfillment, and active foundation. Within us is the fruit of all we have ever been, and the seed of all we will ever be. The waters and the wells of being are what each voice of song is here to care for with loving resonance. Priestesses of Afallon drink from that cup of the sacred wells, holding it out to us all for the imbibing of spirit's essence. Across the isles these divine founts exist, attended by the fair maidens of Afallon, dear sisters of the first fruits devoting themselves to usher-in the flow of sovereignty from the deepest wells of our joined mystic aquifer.

Afallon and Ynys Manau have been protected by surrounding kingdoms since the days of Roman occupation, when the sacred druid sites were attacked, the nemetons burnt down, and the surviving druids escaped from Ynys Mon. There has been an understanding among the Cymri and the Scotti of all neighboring lands to maintain a peaceful accord with Afallon. It is a holy place, where both native and later Christian priests have lived their monastic lives without fear of harm from a warring world. Kings of Gwynedd, Rheged, Dalriada, Eirenn and Gallwyddel have honored this peaceful accord. The Picts, the Miathi, and the Cruithni of the far north respect Afallon and the ancient ways of the Attacotti, the race of the foretime who have merged with the Sidhe, still shining through their descendants of spirit within the waking world. From the Ring of Brogar in the Orcade Isles to the brochs, maen and cairn of the Alt Clud, the legacy of the Attacotti lives on within druids, priestesses and even dynastic heirs. Waters of sacred wells, the streams, the depths of lakes and pools, cascading falls and the sea – all speak the mythic language of that flow of eternal voices. We are born of these waters, nurturing the roots of the tree of life. Mythic heroes are portrayed with births from the eternal waters, sources existing beyond conceived time: Perseus, Moses, Manannan Mac Lir, even Dyfrig, Dewidd of the sea cave, their legacies of the Dyfrwyr, and the Myrlyn's charges conveying the powers of the mountains and streams. Each generation tells of the birthing or discovery of these babes as gifts from the sacred waters received and nurtured by a rescuing goddess, priestess or maternal presence. Like Aphrodite rising from the sea, nymphs of the streams, or priestesses of the waters are the receiving arms of the fluidity of love, embracing the heroic soul.

The Hawk of May

In the north, beyond the lands of the Cymri, the Miathi and the Cruithni are the Orcades, named by the Greek explorer and navigator Pytheas, he, the son of an oracular priestess, a Pythia from nearly nine centuries ago. The Orcades are arrayed in the northern sea as if giant scattered runes had been cast from the realm of the gods to settle there; reflecting the cauldron of the cosmos, that large-bellied pot beyond life and death, named the Orcus by ancients, as the transient expanse holding answers to vast mysteries traversing worlds. These spiraling islands at the edge of the charted earth were hallowed places, farthest sacred points to the north rounded by ancestral dolman builders, settling there to create the Ring of Brogar, consisting of sixty immense stones of brittle rock in a giant ring reaching up to carve a mortal connection into immortal skies. Power exudes from this grand stone oculus of the ancestors. Maes Howe Cairn of the ancient enigmatic Attacotti lies across the watery channel from Brogar's renowned ring of monoliths.

It is in the Orcades that Loth, brother of Urien of Rheged – son of Cynfarch ap Meirchion ap Gwrast Lledlwm – cast his seed into the womb of the primal goddess. He, the most recent conqueror of these distant islands was drawn by forces of dynamic magnetism to the young priestess Morcades, descendant of the Attacotti and mystic heiress to the oracular lineage of the Pythia of Delphi. Theirs was a union of passion, not conquest: even though illicit for the newly crowned King of Manau Gododdin already wed to his Cymric queen. Morcades' passion was drawn from her visions of a child of destiny to be born to her. She knew his worldly father would sire him and then depart. Her son would never be bound to the kingdom of Lothian, but would instead be an ardent champion for otherworldly queens.

Terrestrial queens carried the inheritance of many northern kingdoms, with matriarchal conveyance of land being the continued tradition of the

Picts. The annals often exclude or speak little of the wives of warlords, warriors and kings; yet these women of ancient times were nearly inseparable from the lands of their mothers and the goddesses of all form. It is these feminine entities that carry and bring all worldly life to form, while holding in their hearts the essence of reality that is the pulse of life and love. Battles rage-on between warriors birthed upon the land by mothers that cradle the land as they did their sons. It is truly to the land that these grown sons are wed. The patriarchal powers seek to possess and control the land, and therefore capture the power of the princesses, queens and priestesses of the earth. These warriors and kings plant a seed, at most, held in the womb of the goddess, to be born a defender of their sacred mother or become her assailant. Each child is left to choose a path following their own inner guidance or the powers perceived in the outer world. Kingdoms could quickly enter into conflict, following the death of an heir, the siring of an heir, or the wedding of an heiress. Many family feuds, battles and recurring wars were incited or held in balance by the fact that heiresses often held the land, while the male heirs led the armies.

Morcades was heiress of the Orcades, a priestess bonded with divine feminine powers of nature, and a woman of rare beauty. She didn't look like the other young women of the isles: her hair as dark as night, with her fine features holding the allure of an exotic distant queen. At first glance she appeared lithe and fragile, but moved with an otherworldly strength and agility that was startlingly unexpected. When just a lass, not a year past her first blood moon, her father King Wyre was murdered while protecting the lass and his wife. Morcades and her mother Cundri escaped, remaining in hiding until foreign invaders were repelled. Cundri was descended from the mystic Attacotti, wielding much influence and prophetic power within the northern regions of the Orcades. Rival tribes and their duplicitous druids envying her gifts, seeking to silence her and her progeny, eventually killed Cundri. Morcades had grown into womanhood by then, well trained and developed in her own gifts of the mystic arts, remaining more reclusive as an adult priestess than her tragically departed parents had been.

By this time, the Orcades were dominated by Loth: Cymric ruler of Manau Gododdin, the land south of the Firth of Forth renamed the Kingdom of Lothian. As brother of Urien of Rheged, Loth respected the sacred authority of the Priestesses of Afallon and the arcane heritage of the Attacotti. During one of his many journeys by sea to the Orcades, Loth and a pair of his liegemen arrived at the Ring of Brogar early on the morning of Gwyl Awst. There he first caught sight of the enchanting Morcades, cloaked in a dark hooded robe from her head to foot. She turned suddenly, exposing her face to him for an instant, her piercing emerald eyes seemingly peering into his soul. Then she quickly vanished between the massive stones, Loth unable to discover where she had gone, as the island mist soon engulfed the scene.

"Sire!" His liegemen called out.

"Here I am!" Loth answered.

"We thought you sunk into the bog, Sire."

"No," the king responded, emerging from the fog, "just the passion of my heart, captured by some ghostly goddess."

"What say you, Sire?" His liegemen asked, finally seeing him.

"Did you see her?"

"See who Sire?"

"Clearly not . . . a young woman of intense beauty in a hooded cloak locked eyes with me, for an instant that bridged worlds."

"No Sire, she must have departed our world before we caught-up to you."

"No matter, this is indeed a mystical place. I shall return here again before we depart for Lothian."

"Yes Sire, as you wish."

Loth did return every morning for several days, hoping to see the mysterious maiden again. On the fourth morning, Loth arrived without his liegemen, walking around the Ring of Brogar, longing for an encounter with the intriguing young woman on his final day in the Orcades. Rounding a tall slab of the ancient maen, he nearly stumbled into the lass, standing there before him as if arisen from the ether.

"My pardon lady – I did not see anyone else here."

"There is no one else, just you and I."

Stunned by her intense gaze, he replied, "Ah, yes . . . I am Loth, ruler of Gododdin, and these isles."

"Of course Sire . . . I am Morcades, born of the spirit and essence of these lands."

"Yes . . . I, I, I am drawn to you as if the pull of winds and tides are within your eyes, lady."

"Here, in the Orcades at the great Ring of Brogar is the center of all that exists, in this instant. You cannot help but know this, whether you understand it or not," she said with a voice that melded with the atmosphere surrounding them, dropping her hood as a waft of air lifted a lock of hair onto her lips. As she brushed the hair away with her delicate hand, Loth could feel her touch upon his astonished face; even though he stood at least a pace away from her extended fingers.

"Yes, I don't understand. And yet nothing matters but seeing you here before me," Loth responded, entranced.

"I knew you would be here," she said with a quiet certainty.

"You must know I have been here every day since I first saw you, on Gwyl Awst," Loth admitted.

"I have known for months, the very day and hour that you would sire my child, here, at this great ring," Morcades candidly divulged, shocking King Loth with her command over him.

"I am flush with passion, following your every word. Are you flesh or spirit?" Loth responded, dumbfounded, his mouth agape.

Morcades stepped towards him, first placing her fingers to his lips, then kissing his mouth. As he pulled her closer she said, "I am both flesh and spirit, both waking life and dream. I am yours, and you are mine, in this instant Sire."

Against a monolith of ancient ages, sliding down within its moist shadow, they released their passion, she, mounting him upon the ground of his conquest, her legs astride the king until the rumbling boom of thunder from dark gathering voluptuous clouds announced the peak of their intensity, both drenched in a robust downpour from above. And as quick as she had come, she was gone, leaving him saturated by the sudden storm. Loth stood-up again, perplexed, fumbling with his muddied and twisted leggings and tunic, looking about in disbelief, finding no sign of the mysterious seductress, aside from her scent and sensation still upon him, slowly dissolving within his sensual apprehension amidst the pouring island rain.

Loth searched for Morcades the next morning, before departure to Gododdin, sending his men to ask of her at the nearby fishing villages and farms. She could not be found. Many knew of her. And some had known her mother. The only solace Loth was given was from one old fisherman who said, "She will be seen when she wants to be seen, and no sooner." Loth returned south to his queen and kingdom of Gododdin, somewhat assured he hadn't dreamed the entire episode.

Morcades was told by the old fisherman about the king's search. She knew the stoic old man well. He had protected her privacy for many years; as she continued to live in mysterious solitude, only appearing when there was need for a healer, a mid-wife, or to impart a prophetic message to the people. By Beltaine of the next year, Morcades delivered a child, her own child, alone at the edge of the roaring sea. As the bold babe entered the world, crying out, taking his first breath, a golden hawk circled the air, voicing an echoing cry of creation. Morcades washed her infant son, anointing him with myrrh, saying to him tenderly: you are born of divine love and vision, your name, clearly given here today as Gwalchmai – the Hawk of May.

Morcades raised the lad in the wild lands of the Orcades with the help of that old hunter and fisherman named Gawain Gwinau, also a descendant of the darker race of ancients. The young lad was of fairer coloring, reddish-auburn of hair, with a countenance akin to the highland Cruithni or northern Cymri. Gawain was like a father to the lad, teaching him to survive off the land, to track both beast and man, and to wield the weapons of a hunter and warrior. This wise mentor had fought alongside the lad's grandfather against countless invaders, later becoming a devoted protector of young Morcades. He loved her as a little sister or daughter, but also revered her as his priestess of the unseen world. Between these two parents, the lad received initiation into both worlds, knowing the pulse of nature and spirit as one realm. Gawain and the lad spent month upon month, year after year hunting and fishing the lands of their ancestors, sacred maen and cairn reminding them of the islands' long venerable heritage.

The Orcades were a coveted northern door for the seafaring people of greater Britannia. Roman ships rarely ventured this far during their centuries of occupation. Scotti raiders made their way around the Hebrides from the west, and northern Saesneg from the east. Cruithni, Miathi, and

Votadini of Gododdin sporadically invaded and claimed the distant islands as their own over the centuries. By the age of the Cymric kingdoms of Alt Clud, Lothian, and the Scotti kingdom of Dalriada, each of them sought to dominate the Cruithni and the Miathi of Pict Gwlad by holding that northern sea door of the Orcades. Heirs of Maelgwyn Gwynedd clutched the Pictish purse of their maternal heritage when Bruide ap Maelgwyn ruled the Cruithni neighbors of the Orcades, becoming a repeated adversary of Rhydderch and the Alt Clud.

After the passing of Gabran, king of Dalriada, Bruide festered a dynastic feud by invading the Orcades, aggressively jabbing at the patience of his recent brother-in-law Aedan mac Gabran and Aedan's peaceful co-existence with Cymric Alt Clud and Lothian. Lothian claims extended back to Gwawl, daughter of Coel Hen, maternal ancestor of Loth's wife Anna Morgause. But Gwawl was also the great aunt of Maelgwyn; adding to Bruide's Pictish maternal ancestry, citing enough lineage for his dual matriarchal claim. This wouldn't hold water with Prince Aedan of Dalriada, married to Domelch ferch Maelgwyn, Bruide's sister. All Bruide needed as grounds for invasion was a druid's recitation of his lineage and a sharpened blade. Bruide's invasion of the Orcades began as small raids, pressuring strategic islands to accept his dominance, banding with their Cruithni neighbors, rather than Cymric Lothian. The raiders were actively taking farmers and fishermen as slaves, blaming Lothian for these abductions. One such raid confronted Gawain and Morcades' young son, when the lad was nigh twelve years of age. Old Gawain quickly defended him.

"Run lad, they're slavers or worse!" Gawain ordered, prompting Gwalchmai to bolt from their hunting perch, while releasing a few swift arrows at the raiders. Soon they overtook his mentor, ending the old man's life then and there. The lad – tall for his age, agile with a short sword – gave a good chase and held his own until finally cornered, a quick blow to the back of his head blindsiding him. At that instant, Morcades felt a sudden jolt at the base of her skull, knowing her son was in peril, and Gawain was dead. The lad awoke hours later, bound hand and foot with other captives miles from his homeland. They were taken into unfamiliar terrain, through many hills and valleys to the southwest. Morcades had been reaching deep within her inner sight to find her son. Tragically she could only recover the body of old Gawain, floating lifeless in the marshes of the Orcades. She cried and held him close; calling to the hawks of the air to protect her dear son, knowing somehow that he still lived.

In the slave camp, the anxious lad was fed some pottage and then put to work harvesting timber for a fortress, to be built near a confluence of streams deep in the interior of the Pict Gwlad. He knew he must break free the first chance he saw – perhaps tonight, he thought. Tired as he could ever remember being, the lad fell fast asleep shortly after nightfall. He dreamed of his mother, weeping, holding the body of his mentor Gawain. Then Gawain rose-up, his wounds exposed, emanating beams of light, Morcades touching them, as if to heal them, but instead guiding the light up into the sky, rising through the darkness to illuminate a hawk soaring overhead.

Hearing the faint cry of the hawk, the lad awoke. The camp was quiet, all souls sound asleep. This was his chance. Even though he was bound, he realized that he wasn't secured to anyone or anything else. Silently he moved himself across the forest floor, careful not to crack a twig or branch, managing to make his way to the nearby stream, entering the moving water. It was quite cold; but the lad was charged with an invigorating need for survival. Soon he could hear the rushing turbulence of water becoming louder and louder ahead, knowing he must reach shore or be caught in rapids or a plummeting falls. All this time his hands and feet were still tied, hampering his every move. Seeing a branch held fast by roots near the water's edge, he was able to catch his bound wrists around the dangling limb. Slowly he walked his hands along the branch, reaching the shore. In the moonlight above the stream bank, he clearly saw some sharp edged stones, sharp enough to cut him free. Diligently he worked at grinding away against the ropes, first his hands, then his feet.

Before dawn the lad was swiftly following the stream on foot, dipping in and out where he could do so with ease to cover his scent. By mid-morning he reached an open meadow, staying close to the tree line, continuing in the cover of shadows. He had little notion of where he was or where he was headed. He believed the stream would lead him to the sea; but which sea? He could tell by the sun, he was moving generally east, and away from his captors. But was this the right direction? Around mid-day he saw a hawk soaring high above the stream, then diving down, winging its way above the surface of the water, talons stretching forward to snatch a salmon from the stream. Inspired by his airborne namesake, Gwalchmai soon fashioned a spear from a branch and waded into the shallow current. After a few failed attempts, he was able to spear a good sized fish. Slicing it open with a sharp rock fragment, the lad bit into the raw flesh of the fish – best meal he had in days. The mentoring hawk had circled back around, seemingly guiding the lad to the south, away from the stream. A sense of clarity rushed over the lad, knowing within his heart and mind that old Gawain or his mother had somehow sent this guide to him. He had to follow it. Living on berries, grasses, and remnants of the salmon and other fish he was able to spear, the lad wandered-on for days and days, hearing the call of the hawk as his beacon of direction. He crossed stream after stream, valley after valley, rounded lochs and crags, ever following the guide hawk and his high-pitched call. The lad was led away from villages and farms, remaining in the wild lands, never risking capture by the Pictish slavers. Somehow the hawk knew, he reasoned. It was as much his faith in his mentor's spirit soaring over him, and his mother's love still embracing him, that kept him open to follow a greater vision. The hawk, he knew, was the outer sign of that inner direction.

Asleep in a glade one morning, Gwalchmai was stirred awake by the prodding end of a quarterstaff, and a stern voice saying: "Wake-up lad!"

Startled, the lad rose abruptly, clutching his rough wooden fishing spear, taking a defensive stance.

"Easy, cub warrior, we mean no harm!" A young noble perched atop a towering stone at the edge of the glade shouted down, as his liegemen on the ground below gestured with open palms near the lad, indicating a peaceful lack of threat.

"Do you live near here lad?" The noble asked.

"No Sire."

"Are you lost?"

"No Sire."

"Do you know where you are?"

"No, Sire, but I'm not lost."

"That's confident!" said the noble, as his liegemen laughed. "What is your name lad?"

The lad hesitated, and then said: "I am Gawain, Sire."

"Gawain, that's a fine name. Are you Cymric?"

"No, Sire. I hail from the Orcades."

"The Orcades, you're a long way from home lad. How did you get here?"

". . . by cart, by capture, by stream, and by sheer wits and vision, Sire."

"Well, that's a damn good answer lad," said the noble, as the liegemen laughed again. "I can see you're a resourceful young warrior. How old are you lad?"

"Nigh twelve, Sire."

"Twelve? You're a strapping lad for twelve. You must eat well!" The noble jested as the liegemen laughed.

"Yes, Sire, until recently," young Gawain responded, engendering more laughter.

"Well Gawain, just to inform you, you are many leagues from home, likely abducted some days ago by Pictish slavers, mercenaries of Bruide of the Cruithni. I am Aedan of Dalriada, soon to give Bruide a good whipping for misbehavior. And, we can likely get you back home to the Orcades. Does that sound like a good plan, master Gawain?"

"Yes, Sire . . . a good plan!"

"First off, would you like some breakfast?"

"Yes, Sire . . . a very good plan!"

Aedan and his liegemen laughed heartily, and then fed the lad, who devoured every morsel placed before him. Contented by his first cooked meal in many days, the lad readily joined Aedan and his liegemen on their return home to the fortress of Dun Airigh in the south.

Gawain asking Aedan: "How did you know I'd been taken by slavers?"

"I can see the marks on your wrists, and of course you own mention of 'cart and capture'. Bruide of the Picts has used these tactics when he has attacked neighboring kingdoms, working lads like you to near death," Aedan answered.

"I saw an old man drop from toil, and then beaten senseless, on my only day of work on their fort. Then I knew I had to flee at my first chance, while I still had strength," Gawain confirmed.

"Where was this fort being built?"

"To the northeast, or is it northwest, between the fork of two streams, many a day's walk through the highland valleys from here – as best I can tell," Gawain attempted to recall.

"You're lucky to have made it this far, lad. We'll head south from here, taking some time in Crionan to equip ourselves at Dun Airigh, later making the journey by sea, from the Firth of Loairn around the western isles and north to the Orcades. Your parents must be frightfully worried about you. Are they alive and well lad?"

"My mother is, most assuredly. I never knew my real father, but was raised by a wise and kind man who bore my name, Gawain. He was killed by the slavers, the day of my capture. Old Gawain was the only father I knew. He taught me how to survive on my own, in the wild. I have thought of him often, as I made my way here."

"You've done a fine job at survival in the wild, lad. I'm sure old Gawain would be proud. I pledge to return you safely to your mother, when the time is right."

Aedan, young Gawain, and the small patrol of Dalriadan warriors soon reached Loch Eil, boarding their concealed currach, following Loch Linnhe through the lands of their ancestors toward their own homeport. Young Gawain asked Aedan as they drifted past the shores of the great northern lochs of the Scotti: "Are these your lands Sire?"

"These are the lands settled by my great grandfather Fergus Mor and his brothers Loairn and Aengus. Conall, my elder cousin rules Dalriada. These lands around us here are of the Cenel Loairn, my other cousins."

"Are your clans of the Scotti of Eirenn then Sire?" Gawain asked.

"Yes, that's right."

"Is it true that your ancestors brought the Stone of Destiny here; and that future High Kings will be crowned in these lands?" Young Gawain expressed his curiosity.

"That's correct lad. You seem well taught in prophesies and legends of kings. How do you know these things?" Aedan questioned.

"My mother taught me of the history of the many kingdoms, and of prophesies she knew. She is a seer; and has told me that I should prepare myself to be a leader of warriors and a counselor to kings."

"Well, I believe you are off to a fine start lad. Fate has set you here in my care for now. I can see that your life holds great promise. You are a strong and bright lad."

"Thank you, Sire."

"You're nigh eight years older than my eldest son. But there are others at Dun Airigh closer to your age. And, I'm sure all the lads will be interested in meeting you and hearing of your adventures in the north."

Fortress of the Kings

The journey down the firth was nearly as far as the lad had traveled on foot, but took only a fraction of the time to arrive at Dun Airigh. Aedan's hilltop fortress was built crowning a massive rock formation rising above the winding river and surrounding marshlands, as an archaic highly defensible site, reestablished by Fergus Mor. Aba Airigh – meaning river of the king in the ancient tongue of the Scotti – flowed around the gigantic rocky edifice.

Aedan and company moored their currach near the base of the rock, where sentries guarded the entry to the steep path that wound its way around the great crag to the broad rising summit. Four outer walls surround the keep at the highest rise of the terrain, near a cliff edge. As they drew closer to the keep, through the passageway hewn out of the existing rock, young Gawain placed his boot within the footprint carved into the natural stone floor.

"Not quite big enough to fill those shoes," said Aedan, pulling the lad away; then placing his own foot into the royal divot, "See lad, it may be my footprint someday, or my sons."

"Is this the Stone of Destiny?" Young Gawain asked.

"No lad, but this is the stone upon which the kings of Dalriada are crowned. Perhaps my son Eochaid – with the same name as Eochaid, husband of Tamar, the princess of Judah who brought the Stone of Destiny to Eirenn – perhaps he will stand here to be crowned one day."

"Would he be the next heir after you?"

"No, he's barely weaned. His brother Artúr would follow me, unless one of our cousins gained the honor first. Conall, son of my Uncle Comgall was crowned here, as was my father Gabran when I was only the size of wee Artúr. Kings rarely see their own sons crowned, with the father's death usually marking the son's ascension."

"Don't you believe that our fathers watch from the Otherworld, looking after their sons and daughters? I will be listening for old Gawain, believing he still guides me on," young Gawain reflected.

"You're right lad, and very wise for your years. Thank you for reminding me of the presence of our ancestors," Aedan acknowledged.

Nearing the keep, Aedan's wife Domelch emerged to greet him with two year old Eochaid and four year old Artúr in tow. Aedan knelt down to hug the young lads, and then rose to passionately embrace Domelch. Gawain introduced himself to the wee lads, steering his eyes away from Aedan and Domelch's display of affection.

"Now you must be Artúr and Eochaid. I am Gawain."

"This is our fort," said Artúr. "Where do you live?"

"I live in the Orcades . . . islands in the north."

"Oh. Is it far?"

"Yes, quite far."

"Bringing home stray pups?" Domelch quietly asked Aedan.

"The lad's journeyed for days, escaped from slavers." Aedan responded with a hushed voice, leaning into his wife's ear. "Gawain, this is my wife, Princess Domelch," Prince Aedan introduced the lad.

"Hello Gawain," Domelch responded, extending her hand.

Gawain's eyes were sharply drawn to the swirling designs of tattoos covering the length of the princess's arms, as he touched her hand, bowed slightly and said, "It's a pleasure to meet you my lady. Are you a princess of the Cruithni?"

"Yes, I am the daughter of Princess Dwysedd, and granddaughter of Girom, great king of the Cruithni of Pict Gwlad. Are you a warrior prince from distant lands master Gawain?"

"No, my lady – but my mother is a great seer of the Orcades. And although I don't know my father, my mother tells me that he is, or was, the King of Gododdin."

"Then you really may be a prince." Turning to her husband she said, "Aedan did you know this lad may be one of Loth's bastard sons?"

"Well, you are quite sharp, and courageous," Aedan answered, looking directly at the lad. "You carry within you a great warrior's blood, lad. I saw that straight-off."

"How ever did you find your way to Dalriada, Gawain?" Domelch asked.

"I didn't know I was going to Dalriada. I followed a stream at first; then I followed a hawk."

"How long did you follow this hawk?" Domelch questioned further.

"I followed him for days and days."

"You followed the same hawk for days and days, watching it in the sky?"

"Well, sometimes I just heard his call," the lad explained.

"Are you a seer too, like your mother?"

"No, not so much . . . I'm more of a listener, following sign in the wild."

"That's a great skill to work on, lad." Aedan encouraged him.

Young Gawain went on, "You almost feel the way to go: as if a pull or touch of something moves you on."

"I'd say you're more of a seer than you know lad," Domelch observed.

Entering the keep, Domelch made room for Gawain with her young sons, treating him as one of her own. Leaving the lads alone together, she and Aedan found some time to themselves. Not wasting an instant, they quickly disrobed to lie with each other on a warm bear skin placed before the fire. Aedan was strong and muscular, scars crossing the rippled sinews of his arms. Her arms and legs, tattooed like sleeves and leggings, wrapped around him as if writhing serpents drew the Dalriadan prince rhythmically into her nakedness. After their passion subsided, they rested peacefully in the stillness of their long awaited and satisfying embrace.

"Were the slavers that abducted the lad from my clan in the north?" Domelch asked him as she rested her head upon his chest.

"I don't know for certain; but your brother has been employing mercenaries, leading the Orcadians and Miathi to believe the Lothians were the slavers." Aedan expressed his suspicions.

"Is there war brewing with Lothian?"

"Bruide seems intent on expanding his power, like your father. He knows his chances are better with the Miathi and Orcadians on his side. The Cymri of Alt Clud and Rheged won't sit idly while he moves on Gododdin. And if he could persuade Rhun or Gwallwen's warriors of Gallwyddel to move against Urien and Rhydderch, then there would be war – a war we never want to see. I couldn't stand beside Bruide in this. We have too many ties to Alt Clud, Rheged and Afallon to let your brother bring your clans against us."

"Would he seek to take Dalriada?"

"You, your mother, and your grandmothers are the true heirs of the north. If he forgets that, then he engages war with the sovereign goddess."

Domelch was the daughter of Maelgwyn Hir, Pendragon of the Cunedda clan and King of Gwynedd who died of the yellow plague, as so many souls did in the mid-sixth century. Domelch's northern tattooed brother Bruide was quick to capitalize on their mother's lineage when he became King of the Cruithni of Pict Gwlad. Bruide and Domelch's half-brother Rhun Hir was eldest heir to Maelgwyn's kingdom of Gwynedd, and also son of Gwallwen of Gallwyddel. Sixth century Britannia, from the shores of Dumnonia to the furthest reaches of the Orcades was rife with arising disputes within clans and kingdoms, sibling rivalries and backbiting cousinage, gnawing away at dynastic lines drawn-out in the bad blood of deceit, infidelity and spurious claims of sovereignty.

Challenges arose to Rhun's succession in Gwynedd over his legitimacy as a bastard son of Gwallwen and Maelgwyn. Roman and Christian ideology weighed-in against his natural blood relation; although battlefield supremacy usually defined the ripeness of scattered fruit from a family tree. The contentious spouse of Maelgwyn's daughter Eurgain – from Maelgwyn's Christian marriage to Nesta, Princess of Penllanw – Elidyr Mwynfawr of the Dyfnwal Hen lineage staged an assault on Gwynedd, suffering defeat and death at his landing point on the shores of the Menai Strait. Elidyr's second cousin, Rhydderch Hael of Alt Clud sailed in force to Gwynedd to avenge him, striking a blow against the sons of Maelgwyn by burning down Caer Afron, and then returning north. The military action against Rhun, however, inspired the King of Gwynedd to display a show of immense strength remembered for generations. Rhun amassed an army of thousands, marching them through southern Rheged past Caer Lliwelydd, beyond the Solway, across his mother's Gallwyddel and into the Pict Gwlad of his half-brother Bruide. Bruide was the ever festering Pictish thorn in the northern side of Rhydderch's kingdom. Rhun met no resistance, inciting no conflict with Alt Clud, but delivering a clear message to the northern kingdoms that the sons of Maelgwyn were not to be challenged.

Heirs of Vision

The seers of the lands and islands of greater Britannia were spinning with visions of these impending clashes. They could only warn the kings and warlords of the recurring signs. Whether this prescience was heeded or sparked aggression lay beyond their reach, but hopefully not their influence. Morcades saw these things to come, as many of her visionary sisters had, though often time and place, even the exact nature of the trouble was unclear. The wise sisters lacked the animosity or desires for revenge of the warlords, making their pleas seem less urgent. Morcades could see some form of reckoning was to be set in motion. Hoping to avert imminent trends of darkness from rising, Morcades journeyed by sea to the western islands, to find her son, and to confer with her wise sisters of Afallon.

Aedan's plans to reprimand his brother-in-law were postponed, cautioned by Domelch and King Conall of Dalriada. Gawain was beginning to feel like an uncle or at least an elder brother to young Artúr and Eochaid.

The hawk of his inner guidance was not leading him anywhere else, for the time being. But much to his surprise, a boat arrived at the entry dock to Dun Airigh, as he once again heard the call of the hawk. Morcades had seen in visions the distinctive sight of Dun Airigh, rising above the lands of the ancient Creones. The seer knew of all the ancient peoples of these northern lands, as she continued to commune with spirits of the ancestors. Her mother and grandmother had taught her well, from their legacy of adepts accessing that visionary gift. Visions of her dear son, joyfully at play with the son's of Aedan led her to the great fortress of the western isles. Sentries announced the young priestess' arrival to Aedan and Domelch, both of them coming out to greet her with young Gawain. As soon as he caught sight of his mother he ran to her. She opened her dark hooded cape, embracing him as he melted adoringly into her arms.

"Mother, I believed it was you arriving, when I heard the hawk call above the cliffs this morning."

"I came as soon as my visions led me to you. I knew that you were safe here; but I needed you to know that I was safe too. I love you my dear Gwalchmai."

"I love you too, Mother. I believed you were safe; and now you are here at last. I have been so sad about Gawain, feeling him with me, all along my journey here to Dun Airigh," the lad confided as she held him close.

"Welcome, Morcades," said Prince Aedan.

"We have heard so much about you from young Gawain," added Domelch.

"Yes, my dear Gawain," Morcades responded, with a quick wink of approval to her son, while brushing her hand through his hair, "named after his wise mentor, our protector for so many years. Thank you both for keeping my lad safe from harm."

"Of course, we've loved having him here. Come, join us, tell us of your voyage and all about the Orcades," said Domelch, leading them into the keep.

Soon the young sons of Aedan appeared, excited to meet the mysterious and beautiful visitor.

"Artúr, Eochaid, this is Gawain's mother – Morcades," Aedan told his young lads.

"Are you a princess too, like our Mum?" Artúr spoke right-up.

"No," Morcades answered, laughing. "I am a priestess of the Orcades."

"Is that like a priestess of Afallon?" Artúr questioned.

"Yes, dear, that's enough questions for our guest," Domelch cautioned the wee lad.

"It's alright," Morcades said, kneeling down, reaching her hands out to both lads, Eochaid a bit resistant at first, but then both of them took her hand, unknowingly giving the priestess a quick visionary sense of their innocent souls. "You are both blessed princes of Dalriada."

Domelch smiled warmly, feeling as if her family had just received a divine gift. The princess quickly made arrangements for Morcades and Gawain to have their own room together. The keep was a round stone structure, similar to the brochs dotting these northern lands, with a wood beam and thatched roof covering the main hall and adjacent rooms. Other smaller round dwellings lay around the keep, within the inner walls of the fortress, smoke from their individual home fires wafting between them, rising into the salty coastal air. Quickly settling into one of these thatched roof homes, the priestess of the Orcades and her brave son were secure once again.

"I am so proud of your courage my dear Gwalchmai: how you made it all this way by yourself," Morcades lovingly said to him, gently touching his handsome youthful face.

"I wasn't sure where I was being led, just following the hawk, who remains my guide – even today."

"You have learned well, my dear. The hawk is most certainly your guide. You are connected with this soaring spirit being to the Otherworld. That clear tone of his call and those wings of vision guide you through this uncertain world. You honor Gawain Gwinau by taking his name, while you now more fully understand your spirit name: Gwalchmai."

"Yes, I do Mother. When Prince Aedan asked me my name, Gawain was the first thing I could say. I don't know why for sure."

"It was your first step into manhood, my son. Gawain led you there, and then departed. You honor him and begin to assert yourself in the world, in a new place and identity. He will always be with you in spirit, as I will. Now you have begun your own journey. New mentors will arrive and depart; and you will mentor others. This is the way of things: the things of spirit and destiny."

"I can see that Mother, now that I have touched my own future, off alone, but not alone, even by myself."

"Yes, you remembered, you are never alone. The hawk, old Gawain, the ancestors, the Sidhe – they are here with us. It is so wise of you, my dear Gwalchmai," Morcades assured him, holding him close.

Morcades and Gawain joined Aedan, Domelch, their children and other warriors and their families for a grand feast in the main hall of Dun Airigh. Everyone seemed intrigued by the visiting seer from the Orcades. Both Aedan and Domelch were curious and had been pondering throughout the evening what visions Morcades might have concerning the destiny of their own sons. Finally when the feasting and celebration had settled down, and the children put to bed, Aedan asked the seer what she saw.

"Have you had any visions of the destiny of our lads Artúr and Eochaid? Your Gawain has already told me that he will be the leader of warriors and the counselor of kings."

"Ha, ha, ha – well it is true. He will. It is often the burden of the seer to see too much or too far. I knew of my son's birth, the man who would sire him, and the greatness that resides within the lad, as you must have recognized too," answered Morcades.

"Yes, I saw a strength and presence in the lad straight away; which I know well, having to weigh the mettle of men who might stand by my side in battle," Aedan acknowledged.

"Thank you. I'm glad you see that in him. As for your sons, they will fill you with pride. Each one will be a great warrior and leader. One will be king, and other sons will follow them. You yourself will lead the north, and survive all of your enemies, except that adversary all mortals fall to – time. Beyond that, I can really say no more of your sons. Much unfolds that can alter the course of their lives. As choices are made, destinies change. In the Otherworld, time does not exist. My visions glimpse into both time and the timeless, from a point that is present here and now, and yet eternal. This may not seem sound to you, lacking common reason. I only tell you these things to explain the different nature of a seer's vision; and why I may leave many questions unanswered. Know that your confidence in your sons will be well deserved. And, your confidence in my son Gawain will have its rewards for you as well."

"What do you mean by that? Have you seen more of your son's destiny?" Aedan pursued questioning her.

"Ever since his abduction, I knew he would be safe, even though I did know the details of his capture. I also knew he would meet a new foster father or mentor. I believe that man is you, Prince Aedan. I have not spoken to my son of this, only to say the he would have other mentors after old Gawain. I will be taking my son with me to Ynys Manau for the season, joining my sisters of Afallon. But upon our return, I would ask of you if you would consider mentoring or fostering Gawain. Your confidence in my son confirms my visions."

"I believe I know the answer, but thank you for giving me the time to consider this, and discuss it with Domelch," Aedan graciously replied.

Morcades and her son stayed with Prince Aedan and family a few days before taking passage by ship through the coastal lands of Dalriada, around Gallwyddel and across the sea of Eirenn to Ynys Manau. Galehaut had been alerted by Vivianne that a visiting priestess would be arriving soon. Upon first sighting of the ship, he met Morcades and son at the shore, escorting them to the Afallon Ysgol. Vivianne, old enough to be a grandmother to Morcades, greeted her warmly.

"Oh my dear, you have grown into such a beauty, and I see a powerful light of spirit around you and your son."

"My mother spoke so very reverently of you my lady, and of your wise and extraordinary parents. This is my son Gwalchmai, also called Gawain, honoring his childhood mentor of that name," Morcades addressed the High Priestess of Afallon.

"It is a pleasure to meet you, my dear lad. I have heard the call of the hawk, guiding you into your coming of age. Your mother has taught you well, I am sure, in feeling the touch of this subtle guidance that surrounds us," said Vivianne, surprising young Gawain with her immediate insightful awareness of his inner nature.

"It is an honor to meet you Lady Vivianne. I have never felt such a strong power of spirit in anyone other than my mother until now, with you my lady. Thank you for allowing us this visit. I feel the wisdom of this place is already beginning to shape my destiny," young Gawain responded.

"You are most certainly welcome, bright lad. I am heartened by your awareness of spirit and openness. This is rare in one so young, but not entirely surprising, considering your heritage. I was very fond of your grandmother, Cundri, who was a gifted priestess here at Afallon many years ago. You and your mother clearly carry on her heritage. I asked Galehaut to introduce you to some of the lads of your age, now, if you like."

Looking to his mother first and then seeing her approval, Gawain answered, "Yes, of course my lady."

Galehaut led young Gawain out to meet Llen and the other lads, who were working with Bercnaf and the hounds at the kennel.

"Hey lads, this is Gawain, visiting from the Orcades. Be good hosts now, and show him around a bit – alright?" Galehaut directed.

"Hey Gawain, I'm Llen, this is Bercnaf our hound master, and these two butt-ugly fellows are my very distant cousins from across the big eastern pond – Llew and Baedd. Oh, and these four-legged members of the crew are Tywyswr the lymer, and the grechion twins Tywysog I and Tywysog II."

"Hello, one and all – how do you tell Tywysog I from Tywysog II?" Gawain replied, while looking-over the near identical hounds.

"We don't always know, but they don't seem to know either." Bercnaf chimed-in. "Sometimes it's just because one goes number one and the other goes number two."

All the lads laughed, and then Gawain asked, "Have you got them trained to go number one or number two on command?"

"No, he's good, but not that good," Llen answered.

"I'll work on it – number one," Bercnaf responded to Llen.

"By the way," Llew spoke-up, "He only calls my brother and me butt-ugly because he looks so much like us and can't get over himself."

"Sounds like a lot of number two going on around here," Gawain added.

The lads all laughed again, with Llen saying – "You're alright, Gawain of the Orcades. You'll get-on here with this bunch of misfits just fine."

Within the Ysgol, Vivianne and Morcades had time to talk about some shared concerns that they both had been having in recent years.

"I felt it of utmost importance that I speak with you about certain increasing visions I have had. I am concerned for our sisters and the sovereignty of these lands," Morcades got straight to the point.

"Yes, I have had these disturbing visions too," Vivianne responded. "There have been so many challenges to matriarchy with each passing decade; and yet the power hungry patriarchs will use matriarchal claims to serve their own ends."

"Yes, I see this too, even in the north," agreed Morcades. "My darker visions display more violence upon our sisters and sisters of the Church as well. I fear an increasing disregard for the sanctity and sanctuary of the sisters of all paths."

"I understand, sister," Vivianne related, "Within my visions too, there appears a rising surge of this violent assault and abuse of physical power over sisters of spirit, royal heiresses, and women of every station. I have tried, and I am sure you have as well with your son, to instill a deep respect for the divine feminine within the charges here at Afallon, hopefully raising a generation of protectors, champions of the sacred goddess. But I too fear a rising darkness encroaching upon us all."

"What can be done to alter this ominous course of events that we both perceive?" Morcades beseeched answers.

"We must endeavor to see it differently, reshaping our visions – if possible. We must cultivate that essence of love and respect, so that more hearts and minds are nurtured by the atmosphere emanating from wells of divine resource within us all."

"Yes Lady Vivianne, I see that is what we must nurture within ourselves – but can we, we rare and few sisters purify a poisoned well, a well that time after time is defiled?"

"We must reach beyond ourselves, enlivening an inseparable dynamic of reality. We must do so by realizing that any brutal external forces are only the rough husk of humanity, no matter how cruel or unkind. The pure core is the prevailing reality, the essence of truth. These visions should only encourage us to redouble our efforts to break this outer shell, to repel the dark husk of human behavior and let that aberration dissolve into the pure power of greater love."

"Thank you, Lady Vivianne. We must work together from this fluid stream of awareness to join as sisters."

"Yes, dear Morcades, and within that stream concurrent with the Otherworld, where there are no perceived limits or looming weightiness, we can enlist those unseen powers and ascended entities to shift all beings above the specter of mounting external tides."

"Thank you for reaffirming that truth within me, Lady Vivianne. I will continue to work for this call of our reserve deep within us to shift these deceptive dark tides. We must shift between worlds, realizing there is truly only one world within us. Love prevails."

"Yes my dear. Love prevails."

The two priestesses embraced each other. Then, sitting quietly until dusk, they resumed the work they had pledged to do: rising within the eternal stream, raising the resonant atmosphere of influence, healing worlds within worlds.

Well before sundown, Galehaut returned to see how the lads were getting-on, accompanied by two older lads – Llamorhad, and Owain Prince of Rheged – nearly five years older than Llen, Gawain and the others.

"Well, what is happening here with all of you scruffy pups?" Galehaut teased the five young lads around the kennel.

Llen answered back, "Just waiting for Tywysog number three, sire!" rousing laughter from the others by referring to the Prince of Rheged.

"I guess we know who's cleaning the kennel tonight," Owain fired back at Llen.

Galehaut followed-up, looking straight at Llen, "If you're going to sling it, you're going to shovel it! But now, why don't we show Gawain here about the power of the mountains and streams. Llen, you can give Gawain some pointers."

Gawain, a bit puzzled by the directive, followed Galehaut and the lads over to a level clearing where they all formed a circle, facing each other.

"Here, stand with your legs like this," Llen said to Gawain, showing him the proper distance between his feet. "Bend a bit here, with your hands this way – then just do what everyone else does."

"Alright lads, you are the sky and earth. You are the mountains and streams," Galehaut said, as they all began to move in unison, their arms rising up as if brandishing sword and shield, their bodies turning as if to dodge axe or spear.

"Your arms extend the length of javelins. Feel the power of the streams, rushing through, out into the cosmos. Your legs are rooted into the earth, like a mighty tree, the power of mountains building your strength," Galehaut described to them.

"Hold your hands like this," Llen corrected Gawain, "as if you hold the boss of a shield.'

Galehaut led the lads in several different movements. Then he had them stand still, allowing the power of the mountains and streams to rush through them.

"These are the practices of Master Myrlyn, Vivianne's father," Llen told Gawain in a hushed voice.

Gawain could feel the power already. He had enough awareness form his mother's teaching and even old Gawain's mentoring to step right into the deeper sense of what was being taught there. He already knew the touch of spirit, and the elemental nature of the wild: it was in his blood and bone. Galehaut could see this straight away.

"You're a natural, Gawain," the master quietly said to the lad as he walked around the circle, checking the posture of the others.

"Alright, stand aside – Owain and Llamorhad take up sword and shield," Galehaut commanded, "Defense!" He shouted, coming at them with his sword swinging in short serpentine motions, each tall lad blocking his blows with shield, unable to strike before Galehaut was on them again, all the while teaching them.

"The stream is in the strike. The wind is in the movement. The roots are in the stance. The fire is in the blade. The elements are in balance. The battle is won before it begins, at one with power of mountains and streams."

With those last words he had scattered the two shields of Owain and Llamorhad to the side and sent each of their swords flying from their hands.

"Soon these lads," Galehaut said, pointing his sword at Owain and Llamorhad, "won't allow me to do that so easily. One day all of you lads," he said pointing his sword at the others, "will be able to do the same, becoming masters of the mountains and streams in your own right."

Gawain continued to train with the lads for several days; while Morcades and Vivianne joined together with the priestesses of Afallon to work at healing and transforming the subversive seeds of germinating turmoil that seemed to be spreading across the land. It became clear to Morcades that Gawain felt truly at home at the Ysgol, well supported by his new youthful comrades and elder mentors; Galehaut, Llamorhad and Owain each taking lead of the lads from time to time. Witnessing Gawain's adept progress, Morcades decided to delay her return to Dalriada and the Orcades.

Taliesin soon became an influence on Gawain as well. He had been tutoring Prince Owain at Urien's citadel of Caer Lliwelydd for a number of years by then. Owain was raised as heir to the kingdom of Rheged. Vivianne received frequent visions of the lad long before he was born on the Winter Solstice, nearly five years before her timely vision of the babe Llenlleawg. She had said to her cousin Urien, "Between Samhain and Imbolc, an heir will be born to you from your wife Orwen, of this great stock of the Raven Kindred." The babe Owain was born at the darkest hour of night, on the shortest day of the year. His mother Orwen – daughter of Ceredig ap Cunedda – found a raven's feather on the window sill of her bedchamber on the morning of the prince's birth. She handed the raven's feather to Vivianne the next day, asking if this feather was an omen of great portent.

Vivianne smiled, turning the feather in the morning light, saying to her: "This is a gift from my father Myrlyn, letting us know that he watches over this child, welcoming him into our clan."

"Will my son be a druid, a warrior, a bard, or a king – and will he be a happy child?" Orwen eagerly questioned the priestess.

"He is a blessed child, right now. He may become any or all of these identities in his rich life. Master Myrlyn invites your son to mature without limitation. He, and no doubt my mother Nimue will be there to guide Owain from the Otherworld, as wise emissaries of his awakening vision." Vivianne explained. "Your son descends from the great lineages of the Cymri: that of Cunedda through you; but also the Attacotti, the Fisher Kings, Dyfnwal Hen, and the Brychan clan from Urien's mother Nyfain. That is the clan of my father Myrlyn. And now, you have me, Taliesin and the wise counselors of your king and husband to guide this Prince of Rheged in his new life."

As the babe's dark hair began to grow upon his tiny crown, it was clear he had been kissed by his ancestors, as a pale feather-shaped patch appeared above his brow. Owain quickly grew to be a sharp young lad, nimble with his hands and balanced on his feet quite early. Even as his speech developed, the wee lad would mimic the sounds of various creatures, birds in particular, providing great amusement for his parents. Urien was certain that his son would become a keen hunter. The child loved to see how close he could get to birds in the gardens of Caer Lliwelydd, stalking them like a cat.

The feather that was discovered after Owain's birth was placed above his crib, and later over his childhood bed, at Vivianne's suggestion. This was an open invitation from the Sidhe and ascended masters from the Otherworld to inspire the lad's dreams. Young Owain often dreamt of hunting with his father, or hunting alone, guided by the creatures of the forest – a wildcat, a raven, or a raven sometimes following a wolf. He dreamt of flying with the ravens, changing form between a raven and a running lad, following a buck, boar or bear through dense wooded groves, where the trees took on the animated life of breathing creatures. His skills with bow, sword and spear improved with each passing year, hunting with his father, his cousins and the men of Rheged. Urien taught Owain the ways of war, of military strategy and siege craft, becoming battle savvy in those tenuous times. Taliesin and Urien often played the strategic game of gwyddbwyll with the prince, training his mind to anticipate the moves of his opponent, seeing the shifting turns of pieces on the game board, their strengths, their vulnerabilities, and the way each player's actions betray his intentions.

Although Owain trained with Taliesin in Rheged, the prince's visits to Ynys Manau became more frequent; especially as he began to train the younger lads in the powers of the mountains and streams. Both Vivianne and Taliesin encouraged young Owain to delve into his dream visions. The raven and the lynx were regular visitors to the lad's nocturnal world, becoming a presence in his life, as the guised mentors of his lineage. One dream stood-out among many, occurring shortly after the arrival of Morcades and Gawain to the Ysgol. Vivianne and Taliesin were together there at Ynys Manau to hear Owain tell them about his visionary encounter.

They both listened intently as Owain began: "I seemed to awake from sleep, sitting-up in bed, yet knowing that I was still within a dream. As I viewed what took shape in the room, I could hear a voice within my mind describe to me the nature of what I was seeing. Two ravens appear – one is thought and one is memory: memory of the past and thought about the future. A white raven lights between them, illuminated by the sun, disappearing in the light of a blinding flash. In that instantaneous burst of brilliant light, the dark ravens vanish too. A cacophony of caws and the clamor of wings pound upon my listening ears, the sound of a hundred thousand ravens, crows and magpies echoing on throughout time. Then – silence . . . and a dove appears. The whiteness of the dove expands as its wings extend, becoming a pure white raven hovering, its feathered strength rhythmically pulsing against the stillness of the air, beating with a cadence of my heart, my breath, of life itself. The voice within my mind speaks to me with this innate metre of my own pulse, saying: 'The blood of countless ravens rushes through you, speaking to you, calling to you. The fount of your discovery awaits you.' Then the white raven rises up into the dark void of the ceiling above, until it vanishes. My attention abruptly shifts to the vision of another raven flying within the bed chamber, floating still, as if gliding upon a mysterious wave of lofty air above me. With a dip of a wing, he drifts to the left side of my darkened bed chamber and then back to center, room windows allowing moonlight to illuminate the scene rushing past the edges of my sight – the walls seemingly in motion. All the while, the great raven and my alert sense of self are completely still; even as the raven touches down to the floor, shifting into the hooded semblance of a young druid. With the lowering of his hooded cowl, his raven-black hair settles to his shoulders, revealing to my attention a stark patch of white strands rising from his hairline. I know then, he is the Myrlyn, my great uncle who I have never met in the flesh. As he stands before me, the whiteness of his one tuft of light hair spreads across his crown, through his long locks and into his growing beard, framing a wise and radiant face, shifting from youth to old man, to bird-like being, to white raven, to blinding beam of light – and back to Myrlyn's image once again. Then he says to me, 'your name is Owain ap

Urien. Others named Owain within the Cymri have come before, and many will follow. Owain Ddantgwyn, also son of a Pendragon, became my charge. Owain Finddu, the black lips, came generations before him. They slew fierce giants. You, Owain, will also confront giants, within and without. These ogres obscure the light with their shadows, restricting the flow of truth with their dominating clutches. They claw and grab for power, a power they cannot grasp, a power that consumes them and devours them. You must find the power that flows from truth, from love, the power that flows through you freely, for you to preserve this flow, to nurture this flow, to sustain this infinite flow of the fount of love. You are my charge beyond time. You are of my sacred kindred. You are a guardian of the fount.'

Chapter Three ~ The Calling of Exiles

$\mathcal{T}$he fount of our source is a precious thing. We touch it with our own depth, our depth of love and our depth of awareness. Most men of this waking world are grossly unaware, battling, striving, killing, wounding – only to more deeply wound themselves and humankind as a whole. There are those brave souls, however, who rise above the fray, reaching to fulfill a greater vision. It is their calling to lead us all to a higher place. Mentoring these courageous souls is a grave responsibility, because they will face adversity and often fail. And yet, what they expose, what they keep alive, what they rescue with that extended reach of devotion – is the truth that cannot be overshadowed. The light of truth must prevail. It is not a truth held by one man or one god or certainly not a wrathful god's rambling prophets. It is a truth that lives within all illusory forms, beneath the armored facades of battle that divide and fortify tender hearts against the love they fear to embrace.

Saints, druids, bards, seers, mentors, mothers, and fathers – they stand at the edge of the wells of truth, at the fount of love, seeking to sustain their own essence, reflected within the eyes of those souls in their care. It is the same in every age and every region on this diverse earthen stage of waking life. In sleep, dream or through our highest aspirations, we are opened to the Otherworld, where the thin veil of our illusions mirror back to us what we are asked to perceive, understand, and respond to from our most sacred source. This is where we all may realize we are here to uphold an enduring legacy of beneficent kings, insightful bards, and wise saints. It is not a legacy of royal blood, but one of preeminent light.

All true paths of the soul are infused with divine light. It is the structures of men, built-up by patterns of belief that often obstruct that resolute inherent light, leaving confused pilgrims to make their way through the shadowy labyrinth of these convoluted human patterns. Mysterious guides present themselves along the way, imparting their visions and foresight, mentoring as best they can earnest travelers treading recurrent paths. Llen, Gawain, Owain and many others to follow had the generations before them to mark signposts at each turn, each turn toward the light or into perplexing shadows. Taliesin mentored bards. Vivianne mentored priestesses. Galehaut mentored the heirs of kings. Saints of the Church mentored priests, novitiates, and the laity of their faith. Across the isles visionaries shed their awakening light upon exiles from both unknown and familiar family homes – each soul searching for a home of destiny, to finally root their prosperity within that light never truly forgotten.

The Dove of Exile

Ever since the legendary Stone of Destiny was brought forth to the ancient isle of Eirenn, the legacy of light, of leadership and of visionary dream was carried into all of these northern isles. Fergus Mor and his brothers, the patriarchs of Dalriada brought that stone of Princess Tamar and Eochaid – said to be the Hebrew patriarch Jacob's sacred pillow – across the Sea of Eirenn to the new lands of the Scotti. At the dawn of the sixth century a pivotal visionary was born on the isle of Eirenn, who would follow that defining path of the Stone of Destiny, guiding descendant kings of its legacy. Earca – the daughter of Loairn, brother of Fergus Mor and king of the northern isles of Dalriada – was wed to another royal heir named Fergus from their ancestral isle of Eirenn. These two heirs were the grandparents of a gifted lad born to Eithne of Laigin, and Fedhlim, Chieftain of the Clan O'Donnell of the Ui Neill. They named the lad Crimthann, anticipating him to be clever as a fox. He later became known as Colum, for the peace of his spirit, gentle as a dove, surrounding him. As son of a chieftain, the lad was trained in the skills and methods of war. And yet, he longed to inspire others with his voice of song, becoming a student of the bard Gemman of Laigin. The lad showed promise, continuing to compose verse; although he found his heart being drawn to the priesthood of the Church. His parents were somewhat divided on this shift in direction. Crimthann's mother had encouraged his bardic talents, also recognizing his prophetic gift and highly intuitive nature, she having introduced the lad to the famed Gemman of her own homeland. Crimthann's father saw his son as a leader of men of battle, capable of inspiring their devotion to the Clan O'Donnell. The lad's entry into the monastic seminary of Clonard, under Father Finnian – also originally from Laigin, a student of Dewidd of Dyfed and Catwg of Llancarfan – marked the decisive turning point in his future.

After the young tonsured priest was ordained at the Abbey of Clonard on the River Boyne, he went on to found an abbey in Daire Calgaich of his father's tribal lands. This was the land of the Ui Neill, descendants of Niall Noigiallach, great patriarch of northern Eirenn. As in other kingdoms across the isles of greater Britannia, dynastic rivalries spilled the red blood of cousins, brothers and countrymen upon the emerald isle. In those early years, conflict fed off the division between the ways of the druids and the increasing dominance of the Church, ever since the time of Saint Patrick. The Clan O'Donnell and their cousins of the northern Ui Neill still held more to the old ways. The High King Diarmait mac Cerbaill of the southern Ui Neill touted his Christian faith, at least outwardly. When the north struck a blow against the high king to return leadership to the north, Crimthann, now known as Colum or Columba was torn between his faith and his clan.

Diarmait had also intervened in a dispute between Colum and his old teacher Finnian over a sacred Biblical text that Colum laboriously copied without permission to use for the teaching of his northern kindred. Finnian claimed any copy of the text belonged to him. King Diarmait ruled in Finnian's favor, equating the phrases: "As a calf is to a cow, so is the copy to the book". Colum rejected the decision as an irrational and untenable intrusion of the king upon the dissemination and free expression of the Word of God to the people. Culmination of this brawl over the book and fight for the crown of Eirenn occurred at the Battle of Cuil Dremhni. Finnian prayed for the armies of Diarmait, while Colum prayed for the victory of his northern kinsmen, suffering the spiritual wounding of his embattled people and a physical scar that he carried for the rest of his life. Colum's kinsmen of the northern Ui Neill prevailed.

The defeated former High King and Father Finnian pressed the Church for the excommunication of Colum, claiming the rouge priest supported the pagan druid overthrow of their Christian kingdom. Colum confided to his confessor Lasrain of his own conflicted actions in the face of the hypocritical attempt by Finnian and the defeated king to thwart his conveyance of Holy Scripture. Lasrain petitioned the Church for Colum's acquittal, bargaining for a voluntary exile from Eirenn, while maintaining Colum's ordained status as a priest of the Church. Colum was compelled to "depart on pilgrimage" for the isles of Dalriada, hastily sailing into the Firth of Loairn, and lands of his great grandfather. While passing by the southwestern isles held by the sons of Gabran, Colum could feel the reverberating resonance of spirit speak to him of his new sphere of influence, there on one and many of those secluded islands. Colum first sought out Prince Baetin of Cenel Loairn, his kinsman at Dun Ollaigh. Soon after arriving there, his closest island cousins directed him south to meet with Conall mac Comgall King of Dalriada to be granted an island suitable for the home of his new monastic abbey.

The meeting with the King of Dalriada took place at Dun Airigh, where Conall was the guest of his cousin Aedan mac Gabran. Morcades and her son Gawain were also there, having returned to Dun Airigh that same summer after spending over four-hundred days on Ynys Manau at the Afallon Ysgol. Colum arrived at Dun Airigh with a dozen monks who had made the journey from Eirenn with him, including Colum's uncle Ernan and Lasrain mac Feradaig. The procession of Colum and a dozen monks with their tonsured heads and plain dark robes trudging up the long path to Dun Airigh was a strange sight: queues of boisterous bards, flamboyant seers, and tattooed Pictish druids being the more common occurrence at Aedan's court. As the monks entered the gate to the fortress walls, they were greeted by Aedan's brother Prince Eoganan and a few of his liegemen, Eoganan espousing the Christian faith, eager to meet the renowned priest Colum Cille.

"Welcome Father, I am Eoganan. I will present you to King Conall and Prince Aedan straight away. I hope your journey was peaceful Father."

"Thank you, Eoganan; it was calm and divinely inviting, a refreshing contrast to our brusque departure from Eirenn. Bless you my dear son for your concern," Colum said as he blessed him with the sign of the cross.

"Thank you Father, as you may know there are many here who do not hold to our faith. It is a great honor and blessing to have you and your brothers among us," replied Eoganan with a gentle bow.

"I bring the Lord's blessing to all of His children. This universal acceptance is precisely what led me here to these islands and my kindred of Loairn mac Erc. In truth, we are all brothers of divine kindred," said Colum.

As they walked on towards the keep, Colum noticed a lone sparrow fly swiftly around the upper level of the main tower to suddenly disappear, followed by the sound of a thud. "Just a moment," Colum said, lightly touching Eoganan's arm, then walking briskly through the grounds below the keep, departing from his brothers and the Dalriadans, they, curiously watching his sudden urgency. Rounding the keep, Colum saw Morcades and young Gawain, both kneeling down to observe the fallen sparrow on the fortress floor. Morcades gently scooped-up the bird in the palm of her hand, holding it close to her face, whispering something to the fragile motionless being. Rising slowly, extending her arm, holding the tiny creature up to the sky, the bird miraculously lifted-off in flight, fluttering out of sight.

"Good day, my Lady, lad," Colum addressed them, drawing their attention.

"Good day, Father," Morcades responded.

"I see that you are a healer, blessing all of the Lord's gentle creatures."

"It is the bird's nature to soar, and be unobstructed by man's walls and windows."

"Well isn't that the plain truth of it. Forgive me I am Colum, just recently arrived from Eirenn."

"I am Morcades of the Orcades, and this is my son Gawain."

"It is a pleasure to meet you both. I was drawn to the sudden movement of that tiny bird, and heard the disturbing thud of its impact."

"Yes, we did too, coming around from the other side. The poor thing must have struck the upper window."

"What type of prayer were you whispering to the little bird that seemed to inspire its flight?"

"I wouldn't call it a prayer, Father. I was simply and clearly present, affirming the life that is, the life that exists and moves through all creatures, stating that fact to the tiny feathered being, silently resting in my open hand," Morcades said to the priest, looking directly into his eyes, as if to join with him in that same healing moment.

"That is beautiful. The Holy Spirit surely moves through you, my Lady. Although I am a man of God, and of the Christian faith, I see divine love where it exists. I know divine love has no bounds."

"Yes, Father, boundless love is the healer, not me, or any other person or belief."

"I hope that we have a chance to speak again, while I am here; to get to know you and your fine lad. Now I must return to my hosts, good day."

"Good day, Father," Morcades replied with a bowing nod.

Colum returned to the entourage of Eoganan, the monks and the liegemen, waiting patiently on the pathway to the keep.

"All is well! Shall we proceed?" Colum announced; then, turning to Lasrain, said, "I just met the most extraordinary young woman and her son."

Lasrain nodded his head and smiled with his eyebrows raised in a somewhat stunned response. The party entered the keep led by Eoganan and Colum. Prince Aedan and his cousin were conversing intensely, seated in two large hewn timber chairs on a raised terraced platform at the far end of the main hall. Their conversation was interrupted by Eoganan's announcement of Colum's arrival.

"King Conall, Prince Aedan, may I introduce Colum Cille of Eirenn, Father of the Catholic Church, descendant of the Ui Neill and of Loairn mac Erc."

"Greetings, Colum Cille – is this your given name or a Christian title?" King Conall questioned the priest.

"Blessings upon you, King Conall and Prince Aedan," Colum responded.

"We thank you for your blessing, cousin," said Prince Aedan, acknowledging their kinship.

With a short bow to Aedan, the priest continued, "in answer to your question, Sire: I was given the name Crimthann at birth, and acquired the agnomen Colum Cille through my devotion in solitude to the Lord God of my faith."

"And where is your 'cell' now, my holy cousin? You are far from the home of your birth." Kink Conall pursued his questioning.

"Yes, Sire . . . I am seeking some property among the many islands of Dalriada to form an abbey and monastery, serving the Lord and his expanding flock of Christian kindred souls of these lands," Colum explained.

"And what do you offer in exchange for this property, if granted? Has Rome or Byzantium or the Christian kings of Eirenn sent you here with coffers loaded full of the immense wealth of the Church?" Conall challenged the priest.

"No, Sire. I am only a humble servant of the Lord," said Colum.

"It is my purpose to serve the souls of humanity, and ease their burden through the love of Lord Jesus Christ. These are the treasures that I bring, by following Christ's example of charity, and sharing His message of love and salvation. I will assist in the guidance and healing of your people to serve this kingdom and the divine kingdom of God, by building an island sanctuary, to give refuge to struggling souls, turning their hearts, as a hub to a wheel of renewal and hope."

"Aedan, Eoganan, do you believe it is wise to invest in this holy man's illusive treasures? Is it of any benefit to our kingdom and the intangible souls of our people?" King Conall reluctantly opened the dialog.

"I certainly believe," Eoganan responded, "that this great soul, our distant cousin Colum should be given a place within our kingdom. Divine grace will shine upon us for our welcoming of him to serve our people."

"As I understand it," Aedan added, "he comes to us after being shunned by the clergy of Eirenn for his gracious embrace of all beliefs and traditions: druids, Picts, northern Saesneg, and seers of all supernatural vision. He is a gifted seer himself, whose foresight and knowledge of other tribal peoples could benefit his own Dalriadan cousins; if we support him and his monks in their efforts of kindness. He has founded abbeys and schools in Eirenn. Such schools of higher learning and their teachers in our lands will allow our heirs to become more learned, wise and powerful leaders in this changing world of kingdoms in conflict. I say we grant this holy cousin of ours a place to build his community of God."

King Conall paused for a moment, just staring at Colum, without expression or intensity. Then he said, "If we were to grant this holy cousin of ours some island to build upon, where would it be? Do you have a place in mind holy man?"

"My first response would be a smaller island to the west, in the Firth of Loairn. I am drawn to one island in particular, off the coast of Mull." Colum shared his thoughts.

"That sounds like Iona, which is already a sacred burial place of our shared ancestry," Eoganan added with enthusiasm.

"Iona is a bit far afield for transport of provisions, labor and timber for a settlement," Conall debated.

"Perhaps Hinba could serve as a site for a short time, until Iona is developed," Eoganan suggested.

Then Aedan committed himself, "Colum and his brothers could reside here at Dun Airigh until we resolve the issues of transport and building timbers. The sacred isle of Iona seems fitting. I would be willing to work with Cenel Loairn to provide these holy brothers with what they need for Iona's abbey."

"I am certain we can make this happen," Eoganan agreed, with a sense of excitement.

"Alright then, cousins, I will leave it to you to assist these friars in their island abbey endeavor," King Conall concluded.

Colum bowed to the king saying, "You are most generous, Sire. I will make every effort to enhance this kingdom with the help of my devoted brothers."

Eoganan immediately embraced Colum Cille and several of the monks before they departed the main hall. King Conall continued the conversation with Aedan, while Eoganan led the monks to their lodging.

"My concern, cousin, is that in granting this holy man a foothold in our lands, we risk more kingdoms becoming an arm of the Church."

"I share your concerns," Aedan agreed, "but this Christian faith is already here. My brother's giddy embrace of these monks bears that out. Having an abbot of our own clansmen, who is here by exile, or forced pilgrimage by overbearing Church authority, at least gives us a clergyman as an ally. Politics and religion are bathed in blood on the isle of Eirenn and here, with our Pictish and Cymric neighbors drawing long knives as we speak. Colum is an exile of Finnian's hypocrisy and Diarmait's duplicity, he the so-called Christian, crowned by the ritual blood rites of the 'Feis Temro'. I believe our cousin Colum, or Crimthann is both sincere and clever, willing to serve kings of his own clan that he can rely on."

"I trust your balance cousin," King Conall responded. "With a Christian brother and a Pictish wife, you may have a better grasp of whether this holy cousin of ours will be more of a dove or a fox. Keep me informed of his abbey's progress."

That afternoon, Conall departed for his own fortress to the east, holding the borderline between Dalriada and Alt Clud. Eoganan and Colum were already planning a sailing expedition to Hinba and Iona, surveying sights for the potential abbey. Later in the day, Colum took a stroll around the upper fortress grounds, enjoying the distant view from the highest parapets. He saw a great hawk gliding above the terraced citadel, casting a shadow on the fortress floor below. There was young Gawain, watching the bird in flight, his hand shading the sun from his fixed gaze, as he turned side to side following his avian guide. He noticed the friar waving to him from the parapets. Colum came down from the high defensive wall to speak to the lad.

"Good day, Gawain."

"Good day, Father."

"Are you an aspiring falconer?"

"Well, no, I haven't really tried that; but I am amazed by the high flying hawk. My birth name is Gwalchmai. I have taken the name Gawain to honor my mentor, who was murdered by slavers more than a year ago. This hawk seems to have been with me ever since. He is my guide. He led me here the first time, last year."

"How do you know it is the same hawk, laddie?"

"I followed him through the wild, from north Pict Gwlad to Loch Eil. He showed me where the salmon leap. He kept me from harm and recapture. How do I know he's not the same hawk?"

"Ha, ha, yes, it is rather convincing," Colum acknowledged with an amused chuckle.

"So you traveled from Pict Gwlad, all the way to Loch Eil?"

"Yes Father, I was captured by Pictish slavers, but escaped, following a stream and then the hawk."

"When was this lad?"

"It was over a year ago."

"How did you come to Dun Airigh?"

"Aedan and his men came upon me in the wild and brought me here by boat through the Firth of Loairn to their fort"

"And your mother, she came for you?"

"Yes, but we have been on Ynys Manau until a fortnight ago."

"Will you return to the Orcades?"

"I don't know. I would stay on Ynys Manau if I could."

"Ah, you must have mates there now?"

"Yes, Llen and Bercnaf, Llew and Baedd, they're all just about my age."

"You mentioned your mentor, Gawain. What of your father lad?"

"I never really knew my father. Mother said he is King Loth of Lothian."

"You are of royal blood then lad."

"Yes, I suppose. What of it? Can a king soar like a hawk? That hawk and old Gawain have been better guides to me than any king."

"Yes lad, I can see that," Colum said, looking at young Gawain with compassion and subtle admiration. "Guidance will find you, as you seek it. It has been a pleasure talking with you, Gwalchmai. Keep listening for that higher guidance. We will talk again soon. Good day, lad."

"Good day, Father."

It was a rare opportunity for Prince Aedan to have Colum Cille a prescient seer of the Church and Morcades an arcane priestess of the Orcades there at Dun Airigh at the same time. Domelch had said to Aedan on that first day of Colum's arrival, "If we could just bring a Pictish druid, a priestess of Afallon and a northern seer casting runes and bones before them all – then we would have a real mystic circus to marvel."

"I can see you dancing around them, clothed in nothing but your richly painted flesh," Aedan played along with her fantasy.

"Your vision inspires a more private performance," she said, kissing him passionately and pulling him off to their bed chamber.

Father Colum and Morcades were destined to have their own entirely Platonic encounter within the confines of Dun Airigh. They found each other walking the grounds of the fortress at the same time one morning. It is hard to imagine these two diverse seers would meet out of sheer coincidence, unforeseen by their prescient awareness. It was surely intentional.

"It is a fine morning, Lady Morcades. Would you care to join me on my early contemplative stroll?" Colum invited her.

"Thank you, Father – What is the nature of your contemplation today?"

"Well, I find my thoughts occupied with the future abbey planned for a nearby island, the school there, the souls that I my touch in the years ahead."

"In what way would you touch them Father? Is it to turn them to the Christian beliefs and rituals?"

"I am compelled to open any heart that I encounter to the love of our Lord Jesus Christ."

This response prompted Morcades to challenge him further. "You have witnessed my love for my son, and the love of healing shared with that tiny gentle creature, momentarily stunned from flight. Need I, my son or anyone else open their heart to a prophet who lived five centuries ago? Is not that boundless love here now, open to any heart, by any name?"

"There is only one true Son of God who came to save us. It is His message of love and salvation that I bring."

"What of all the sons of gods of the ancient world scriptures? What of all their wise mothers and daughters? Who will save us from the patriarchs of the Roman Church who claim allegiance to one patriarchal deity and his son? Why is this divine son's mother girdled by a perpetual virginity? Was she not a woman? Was her son not a man? Is it not our greatest hope that all men and all women can realize the innocence of divine love in their embrace of every soul?"

"Ah, I hear the Pelagian idealism of our purported innocence. We are born into sin in this world, and are perpetually tempted. The Virgin Mother has been kept to her purity, as has her son, the Savior."

"Your Church then implies that this life is inherently impure, and that nature has fallen from grace. All creation in nature is divine. My son's conception and his birth were just as divine as any soul's. The purity of my soul or his was not altered by birth into this world. The impurity of human life is in what people inflict upon each other: instilling fear, anger, and dominance. A Church that dominates belief and suppresses the divinity and innocence of any soul has lost its way from loving grace. It requires a maternal love more than a paternal fear."

"I am speaking of the temptation of divine life upon this earth. I have no fear of my Father in Heaven."

"Then why fear the mothers of the earth? A goddess, a queen, a priestess, or a natural mother may inspire us as much as any bishop, priest, god, or son of a god. We raise our own divine children with love."

"There is only one Son of God who rose from the dead," Colum refuted her argument.

"If I am not mistaken Father, you are a seer as well as a priest. Certainly you have seen visions of departed souls as I have. Certainly you have had visions of angels or prophets or ancestors of the Otherworld as I have. Have they not risen from the dead to continue to commune with the living? Are we but a few of a vanishing breed of gifted seers, soon to be forgotten, crucified or burned alive, only appearing as the seventh son of the seventh son, or rebellious consorts of a demon? Certainly you see that Yehoshua the Nazarite was demonstrating that the dead are not dead; while most of the living are not even fully alive. Upon death every living thing becomes one with the unseen; and in that, more fully connected to everything that ever was or ever will be. We draw the unseen to us through our love. The love of the Master and the love of his disciples drew them together, in life and after life. The Nazarite is not greater by way of a unique paternal lineage to some distant divine king, but greater through his greater love."

"You are a fascinating woman, Morcades. I can hear the challenges that I will face as I encounter diverse beliefs. It is not as simple as the 'old ways' opposing the Church. I hear that. I see that. And, I find a clarity and passion within you that cannot be denied. Even as I disagree with your ideas, I respect you, and the essence of that boundless love that you have demonstrated. Your son has the gift of a thoughtful mother, as strong as she is loving. If you would allow me, I would be happy to assist your son with his education, as a tutor, while we are all here at Dun Airigh."

"As long as you realize, he is not a soul that needs saving. He would benefit from your knowledge, and it would serve him to understand Christian viewpoints. However, you must recognize that he already knows a great deal of his spiritual reality: knowing it cannot be compressed into one holy book and its beliefs, no matter how diligently it was copied. My son has been raised to think for himself; but even more so to understand beyond thought. I thank you for hearing me out. You may find that you will learn much from my son, to further your own education."

"I look forward to the opportunity, my Lady. And I also look forward to the challenge of our spirited friendship. My faith tells me that there is always more at work here than we realize," said Colum.

Gawain was tutored by Colum Cille for those months that they both resided at Dun Airigh. The lad also benefited from the mentoring of Aedan and his men, many of them seasoned warriors, rugged huntsmen and crusty seafarers – all manner and facet of individual eccentric types. Gawain did his best to pass along his acquired gifts by tutoring young Artúr with some early training in the power of the mountains and streams, continuing to enliven this skill within himself, since his time on Ynys Manau. As much as Gawain valued those potent months at Dun Airigh, he longed for the Afallon Ysgol and his new mates. Those lads were his wayward brothers, all of them in effect exiled from their homes and families, yet united in a current of shared destiny.

Gwyr y Gogledd

The lads of Ynys Manau traveled a parallel life path with the sons of Prince Aedan and the sons of other clans, clans of the northern Cymri – the Gwyr y Gogledd – most of them descendants of Coel Hen, patriarch of the north. It would seem all bards have sung of Old King Coel, who held the rank of Dux Britanniarum, commander of the Roman forces of northern Britannia at the end of Roman occupation, more than a century and a half in the distant past. Born of Romano-British heritage, he was as much a Cymric king as a Roman commander. Coel's daughter Gwawl wed Cunedda Wledig, king of the Votadini tribal clan of Gododdin and founder of the dynastic kingdoms of Gwynedd. Coel Hen's descendants controlled the northern Cymric lands for generations. His wife and queen Ystradwal was the granddaughter of Cynan Meiriadoc, the first Cymric king of Armorica. Patriarch of the other dominant Cymric lineage of the north was Dyfnwal Hen. His ancestor Ceredig Wledig held Alt Clud and the Wall of Forth around the time when Coel Hen's forces held the Wall of Tyne. Ceredig ruled from Dun Barton at the mouth of the Firth of Clyde, his ruling heritage going back a dozen generations to ancestral kings of the Picts.

In the days of Conall and Aedan of Dalriada, Rhydderch, descendant of Dyfnwal Hen ruled Alt Clud. Called Rhydderch Hael, the generous, known to be magnanimous to his allies and comrades, he often became a ruthless warlord and a fierce defender of his kingdom and the Cymric Cylch. His capricious queen Gwendydd ferch Madog – a fifth generation descendant of Coel Hen and twin sister to an enigmatic bard mentored by Taliesin, Myrddin ap Madog ap Morydd of Penllanw — Myrddin and his twin sister were born of the same generation as Rhydderch Hael, from a lesser branch of the Coel Hen lineage, residing in the mountainous backbone region of Cymric lands. Madog ap Morydd had been eager to align his twin heirs with the powerful northern dynasties. Myrddin displayed an early talent for verse and oracular vision, enabling him to be accepted as a charge of Taliesin at the court of Rheged. Both Urien and Taliesin were elder distant cousins of Myrddin and Gwendydd from the Coel Hen lineage.

Brother and sister found favor with the court of Rheged: Myrddin by his wit and imagination, Gwendydd by her charm and striking blonde beauty. It wasn't long before competition arose for the affections of Gwendydd by the princes of the north, first among them Rhydderch ap Tudwal of Alt Clud, and a close second by Gwenddoleu ap Ceido of Solway. Myrddin himself was quite enamored with his own twin, as an enchanting feminine reflection of himself, haunting his childhood and adolescent desires. The Prince of Solway, Gwenddoleu was by far the most aggressive suitor, always vying for dominance over his rivals of greater standing. Solway's boggy marsh at the sea edge and inlet of the firth, framing the mouth of the River Eden and the ruinous Roman wall, was a lesser kingdom waning in its importance ever since the withdrawal of the Romans. Gwenddoleu's detractors had been calling him "Tywysog ag Mawnog" prince of the peat bog, riling his volatile pugnacious temperament. Rhydderch took no pleasure in taunting Gwenddoleu as others did. Instead, he intently impressed Gwendydd with his breeding and character, believing his romantic chances with her far outmatched her combative cousin from Solway. Rhydderch's blind confidence underestimated the attraction between Gwendydd and Gwenddoleu; while Myrddin saw the fascination straight away, steering the strategic choice of their father to broker a match with the heir of Alt Clud. Myrddin never trusted Gwenddoleu, fearing he would use his sister, eventually casting her aside for a princess with a larger dowry. No man was right for Gwendydd in Myrddin's view. He saw himself as her eternal mate, bonded in the womb. It was his sacred duty and obsession to guide his sister, to keep her close and untouched by any other. Their father Madog's ambition to link his lineage to the Alt Clud through wedding his daughter to the highly esteemed Prince Rhydderch was finally achieved, and envied by many dynasties.

Neighboring ruler, the widowed queen Gwallwen of Gallwyddel would have relished the chance to wed her daughter Modron to Rhydderch. Tensions between Dalriada, Alt Clud and Gallwyddel made that match increasingly unlikely, Gallwyddel being already a subkingdom to Alt Clud and Rheged. Princess Modron inherited her mother's shrewd power to entice and manipulate kings and heirs of kings. Gwendydd had been her rival for their attention, but now Modron saw her prime years of allure passing by too quickly, pressing her to set her sights on King Urien of Rheged. Few but the most prescient knew the true parentage of Modron, rumored to have been sired by her grandfather Afallach, others describing her as "daughter of the underworld king". It is true that Modron lured Urien to a hauntingly remote bridge crossing between Rheged and Gallwyddel known as "Rhyd y Gyfartha" – Ford of the Barking – no doubt the wild and restless hounds of devilish desire howling their private rendezvous into popular legend. Modron's daughter from this passionate clandestine union, Morfudd, would marry the brother of Rhydderch, Morcant Mwynfawr. These afflictions of illicit courtly liaisons did not escape the wide vision of Vivianne and other wise cousins of the ruling dynasties. Morfudd's birth, occurring on the same day and hour as her half-brother Owain's birth, signified the arrival of cosmological twins, marking a parallel and yet divergent dynastic bloodline. Conflicts within dynasties could arise as quickly from a spark in a bedchamber as a bridgehead, inevitably leading to the battlefield. An ominous sense of these wafts of impending turmoil troubled the visionary awareness of the Lady of the Lake and Morcades of the Orcades; their conscious work inspired to move the elemental powers toward peace.

Gawain and his mother returned to Ynys Manau after a season at Dun Airigh. The lads were glad to see Gawain rejoin them, forming a band of foster brothers of Afallon, rapidly growing into manhood. These bourgeoning lads were primed for life, while residing next door to a blossoming field of beauties: the young novitiates of Afallon, nearing their time to be wed to a mystic druid, a princely heir or to declare a celibate life of spirit. Needless to say the simmering stew of fertile expectation for the young lads and ladies of Afallon was frothing to the rim of containment. The anticipating imagination of fond glances between both frisky genders was observed, noted, and discussed by their elder mentors, hoping that their cautionary reminders instilling chastity and restraint would be sufficient to suppress the virile and fragrantly ripe rising powers of nature. Inevitably a covert conspiracy arose, involving five lads and five novitiates slipping from their respective beds one enticingly full moon to enter a secluded warm water spring in the wild. Bubbling and fluid as the secretive encounter was, no fragile maidenhood was breeched, even as amorous fondling behavior clouded the scintillating waters, furthering their sensual edification without any sudden engendering of unsanctified future progeny. After playfully exposing their curiosities, the elated and mischievous adventurers were discovered upon their giddy return by Priestess Dianna and Myr the huntsman, who had been sent on an errand to investigate the disappearance of certain novices, their empty beds having been revealed in the awakening visions of Vivianne and Morcades. Ten teenage late night fugitives were apprehended by Dianna and Myr as they gleefully cavorted along a moonlit path through the wood.

"Desire is a wild thing, hopefully tamed and not allowed to ravage our innocence prematurely," Dianna said to the astonished escapees, as she appeared suddenly from the leafy shadows with Myr by her side.

"No maiden was violated this night!" Llen immediately declared.

"Glad to hear that mate," Myr the huntsman responded.

"It is true. We took care," one earnestly concerned novitiate pleadingly confirmed.

"The sisters will certainly verify that after your return. I will escort the ladies, and Myr will escort the lads. I am sure Lady Vivianne will have plenty to say in the morning," Dianna asserted, leading them back to the Ysgol, she and Myr successfully keeping their amusement over the entire escapade well concealed.

Each group of would-be satyrs and wood nymphs were soundly lectured on the dangers of their unrestrained passions, the lads by Galehaut and Taliesin and the young ladies by Vivianne and Dianna. It was clearly time for the lads to advance in their training abroad, specifically military and scholarly attainment, youthful temptations and curiosities having been quelled for the moment. Llen, Llew and Baedd spent a few seasons in Eirenn at Durrow, gaining further education; while Gawain's mentoring shifted between Ynys Manau, Dun Airigh and the new Abbey on Iona. Father Colum was one of Gawain's surrogate fathers and wise counselors, imparting his outsider's view of the bristling Cymric, Pict and Scotti factions. Colum Cille had founded the school in Durrow before his voluntary exile to Dalriada. The schools of Eirenn were renowned centers of learning for dynastic heirs, many with a mixed Scotti and Cymric heritage, both secular and Christian.

It was during these seasons abroad that the lads became fascinated with the triennial competition of arms at Loch Garman, bustling seaport of Laigin, twenty leagues across the Sea of Eirenn from Dyfed. The Aenach Garman was a festival and contest of strength, endurance and skill. Young men from Scotti and Cymric kingdoms came to prove themselves and vie for the honored title of champion of arms. Generally, lads younger than eighteen years were not yet tempered by many seasons of battle; so they rarely ever competed for the ultimate victory of the games. It would be a few years before Llen and the lads of Ynys Manau would test themselves against the best of the isles. They continued to train with Galehaut, Taliesin and Owain ap Urien. It was clear that Llen and Gawain stood out among the lads, soon equaling or besting Llamorhad and Owain.

Peredyr of Ebrauc

Owain and Llamorhad regularly traveled to Elmet and Ebrauc, eastern Cymric kingdoms near the Dere Ystryd, lands of Owain's cousins and his widowed aunt Erfiddyl. They were descendants of the Merovingian Fisher Kings and the Maré through great grandmother Ywrhica Meira. Cousin Gawain joined his comrades on this eastward journey, he also a nephew of Urien and Erfiddyl by way of his distant father King Loth of Lothian. Erfiddyl was former Queen of Ebrauc to King Eliffer Gosgorddfawr "of the Great Following", renowned for their spearmen and javelin ranks, a tradition dating back to the time of Bedwyr or earlier. Eliffer and five of his sons perished on battlefields well before the coming of age of triplets born to Erfiddyl, two sons and a daughter. The former queen swore to raise her last three children away from the world of battle, by resettling into a modest home within the sheltering woodlands of western Ebrauc, north of Elmet. This was near the long recovering wastelands, devastated during Roman occupation as a scorched fire-line against the northern tribes. Erfiddyl brought up her triplets Gwrgi, Ceindrych and Peredyr within the forested arms of nature, away from that encroaching edge of conflict. All three of her surviving children were blessed with a deep connection to the spiritual world. Gwrgi was drawn to the philosophical realms of contemplation and the interpretation of dreams. Ceindrych, she had the gift of vision, seeing and feeling events yet to come, communing with the Sidhe and her departed ancestors in the Otherworld. Peredyr was a curious lad, intrigued by the woodland creatures and the dynamic elements of nature, determined to discover the hidden mysteries of life.

Peredyr spent hours and hours in the wood, hunting game for his family. Sometimes his brother Gwrgi or sister Ceindrych joined him; but he was quite content to venture out on his own. The sights, scents and sounds of the forest filled his senses, his aware vision heightened, peering through the towering layers of trees housing countless creatures. He had no fear of life in the wild. He knew this world. It was the world of men and women, of kings and queens, of war and religious belief that he knew so very little about. These things did not concern him. He hardly knew he ever had a father or five other older brothers. His mother, his closest siblings, and the woodlands were his life. A keen hunter, Peredyr could hurl a dart or javelin with a sling over a hundred paces to his its mark, taking down fowl, deer, rabbit, or squirrel – whatever he set his acutely focused eyes upon. His sister told him many times – unbeknownst to their mother – that he would travel far, becoming a great warrior of the Cymri. He knew her gifted vision was sure and true; but did not wish to bring sorrow upon his dear mother, for her loss had already been so profound. Peredyr kept to his private woodland world. Although, each time his cousin Owain came to visit, young Peredyr could feel the temptation to go out and seek his destiny.

When Ceindrych had one of her potent visions, all three children and their mother knew. It was as if the lass's hair had stood on end, creating wings that reached to the sky into the Otherworld. That is why they called her Penasgell, meaning winged head. Not that her hair actually rose up: but they all three clearly felt lifted by the current of her vision rushing through the family. Ceindrych was the oldest, Gwrgi next, and Peredyr the youngest – only by a few minutes between them. Gwrgi acted as the balancing temperament, with Ceindrych Penasgell in her visionary raptures and Peredyr on his exhilarating hunts. Early one morning, Ceindrych woke them all.

"Later this afternoon, our cousin Owain and Llamorhad of Burgundy will be arriving . . . with Gwa . . . with Gawain of the distant isles – also our cousin."

That afternoon, Peredyr watched for them from a high perch atop the trees, eager to catch the first glimpse of their cousins' arrival in the distance. A glimmer of light reflected off one of their helmets as they crested a hill far to the west.

"I see the light of angels rising over the horizon!" He shouted down to Ceindrych; and then scurried down the giant elm to hurriedly greet his older cousins on the road.

"They are angels: your guardian angels, bringing your destiny," she called back to him.

"Come on, let's meet them halfway!" Peredyr directed with enthusiasm.

"Go ahead, I'll catch up. And, try not to hold them too highly. Remember, they're only men. In truth, we are our own angels," Ceindrych Penasgell advised him.

"Yes, my wise sister," answered Peredyr as he gave her a glancing kiss on the cheek, dashing out of the wood towards the road, the lad waving madly to the three warriors as they drew closer.

"Is that a distress call or a greeting?" Gawain asked the others.

"Looks like Peredyr, a bit taller now," said Llamorhad.

"Yes, and that must be cousin Ceindrych sauntering behind him," Owain added."

Peredyr shouted out as he approached them, "Greetings, Owain and Llamorhad!"

"Hello lad," Owain responded, nearing Peredyr, "You have certainly grown up since we last saw you. It seems years, although I guess it hasn't been so very long. You look strong, lad. This is Gawain, our cousin, son of Uncle Loth."

"I am pleased to meet you, cousin. What manner of hauberk are you wearing? I know so little about the warrior's armor. Where did yours come from?" Peredyr asked, noticing Gawain's unusual armor.

"I am from the Orcades. My old mentor and my grandfather wore this form of breastplate," Gawain answered.

"The armored attire of your mentor and namesake, son of Morcades – I am Ceindrych, another of your cousins."

"And quite prescient, I am stunned," Gawain immediately responded, taken by that current of power he knew all too well from his mother and Lady Vivianne, recalling their wise words: "Spirit recognizes spirit."

"Yes Gawain, now you see why our wise cousin is also called Penasgell," Owain added, as the two newly acquainted cousins seemed to be absorbed in a melding of kindred spirits.

Then Llamorhad asked, "And the other member of the trio – Where's Gwrgi?"

"Where do you think? He's back at home delving into a musty old scroll, too involved in deciphering ancient language scratching to join us here at the road." Peredyr explained his brother's whereabouts.

"Ah, the scholar – I see by the darts and sling, you must be the huntsman of this trio," Gawain observed.

"Yes, he's definitely the huntsman." Ceindrych answered.

"Come, join us cousins, for a fine feast of game from my hunt," Peredyr invited them all.

They soon approached the round thatched home nestled into a clearing deep within the wooded grove. Erfiddyl was standing in the threshold as the visitors arrived.

"Hello Auntie," Owain greeted her, stepping down from his horse, giving her a warm embrace.

"Welcome, welcome, my wayward nephews," she said with a smile, giving Owain and Llamorhad each a peck on the cheek.

"This is Gawain, Loth's son from the Orcades," Owain introduced him.

"Oh dear, another handsome lad in the family," Erfiddyl said, giving Gawain a consuming hug, "so pleased to have you here Gawain. Your mother is Orcadian? That's what Penasgell told us, our own little seer."

"Yes, Morcades, daughter of Cundri," Gawain answered.

"Oh yes, I met your grandparents, years ago, seems another life, another world," Erfiddyl responded gazing-off, a tear coming to her eye. "I'm sure you lads are hungry. We've been roasting venison for your arrival."

"You knew we were arriving today?" Llamorhad asked.

"Oh lad, with Penasgell, we knew you were arriving long before you did!" Erfiddyl answered, arousing a round of laughter.

After a wonderful meal, songs and tales of recent adventures around the fire – Gawain telling about his young journey escaping from the slavers through the highlands, Gwrgi reciting countless lines from heroic poems – they settled-in to sleep for the night. The lads bedded under the stars, the ladies by the hearth. Peredyr awoke early, roused by a vivid dream. Ceindrych Penasgell knew, of course. After breakfast she prodded him.

"Well, are you going to share your dream with us?" The sharing of dreams were their frequently recurring conversations.

"A lad has no chance to keep anything from a sister who is a seer, does he?" Peredyr declared.

"No. Not this sister."

"Alright then, gather round. The first thing I remember is that I entered a clearing in the wood. There was a great tent, bigger than our house, like a grand church or nemeton. I felt compelled to bow before I entered. Inside was a beautiful maiden, dressed in a wisp of a gown, seated on a golden chair. She welcomed me in. There was a huge feast presented on a long table at the far side of the pavilion. I said to her, 'I am Peredyr of Ebrauc. Whose pavilion is this?'

'It belongs to Balchder O' Rhywun,' she said.

'Are you his Lady?' I asked her.

'Yes, I am Awydd, come have your fill,' she said, directing me to the table, rising from her chair to briefly expose her bare legs.

"I went ahead and sat at the table, feasting on every kind of meat, fowl, cakes and food I could possibly imagine. There were two full flagons of wine, which I only drank of to clear my pallet. The entire time, she just watched me as if my appetite excited her. I offered to give the maiden payment in return for the meal; yet I had nothing of value except a gilded torque of father's. I began to remove it from my neck, and she stopped me saying: 'No, no, it is too much. But I will accept a kiss.'"

Peredyr paused to see if his mother was listening, glancing away, seeing she was out of ear-shot, he continued.

"So I started kissing this beautiful maiden, praising her beauty, her generosity – she responding, wanton and passionate, I, I, became aroused."

"Here we go!" Gwrgi said, looking away to watch for their mother.

"But I was embarrassed by it, having never been with a lass, in that way. There I was, big as life, armed with no skill, as it were. So I stumbled back, trying to cover myself with my cloak, the maiden laughing at my, my armed but unready stance. So I said, 'Excuse me, I must be on my way. Your husband may return, and I don't know what I'd do.'

"She kept laughing, saying, 'My husband will return, and you don't know what to do!'

"She kept laughing as I left the tent and went to retrieve my horse. As I untied the reigns, I saw a jewel on the ground, picked it up, and turned to ask the maiden if it was hers. But the grand pavilion had vanished. The maiden and all of her trappings were gone. I stood there, staggered for a moment. Then I got back on my horse and rode on.

"After a while I came upon a strange man and a woman, very short in stature, standing at a crossroads. Their arms and legs were small, and odd looking, their heads of normal size, but large for their short bodies. I thought they might be elves or faeries of some sort. I greeted them; but they would not or could not speak. As I looked closer, I saw that each of them had a countenance that looked like our family: an aunt or uncle, or our parents, but much older. The woman offered me a piece of bread, torn from a loaf as long as she was tall; as the man cut a slice of cheese from a round as large as he was wide, pulled from a satchel slung on his back. I thanked them. They nodded and smiled, then waved, beginning to walk away. I stopped them, and tried to give them the jewel that I had found. They refused it, shaking their heads no, touching their hands to their hearts, with expressions of gratitude, bowing to me, and then traveling on, still waving back to me as they disappeared into the distance.

"I journeyed on, down a different road, soon to realize that I must have circled around; because I came upon the same old couple again, baffled by seeing them ahead of me. The man had been slain, lamented by the woman, weeping and wailing over his lifeless body. 'Who did this?' I asked'

"The woman looked up at me with anger, shouting through her tears: 'Balchder! Balchder! Balchder is the killer!' She fell over the body of her husband, crying oh so very painfully, taking what was her last breath, dying right there with him, out of her deep sorrow. Then I awoke."

"Clearly Balchder is pride," Gwrgi began interpreting the dream, "the old man's pride is your pride, our pride, our father's pride: the old couple appearing like dwarfs and resembling our family, as our diminishment, our loss, a sense of dwarfed identity through the pain of tragedy. Also, as the specter of the maiden's husband, and her laughing at you, wounding male pride – Balchder was the killer – for what: the jewel that would not be received?"

"They will not take our treasure," Penasgell continued the interpretation, "even if we wish to give it away. So what is its value? Why do we desire it? The maiden is desire, enticing yet fleeting. The big tent, our pavilion of perception, shades us from the light; until we journey-on, sometimes coming full circle, discovering what we carry in our satchel, or what has been handed down to us: the length and breadth of what we carry."

"Well, I am amazed and inspired by finding such aware young cousins," Gawain expressed with awe. "I feel quite at home with this kind of discourse. It jars me to reflect upon my own life, and how things may unfold in the coming days. I could linger here for weeks, but our journey takes us north to Lothian. There I will meet my father, your uncle King Loth for the first time. I have had many wise guides and fatherly mentors in my life thus far, while Loth may be a large part of that unopened satchel I have been carrying."

"If I may speak freely, cousin," Penasgell began again, as Gawain nodded. "Loth would have sought you out. But it was not your destiny as a lad, as your mother knew, allowing many other important mentors to become part of your life. I have seen that your meeting of him will be positive, in most respects. However, be wary of his wife Anna Morgause and her clan. They carry both light and shadow. Duplicity and manipulation are only some of the dark traits carried in their inherited satchels."

"Thank you for that caution, and the encouragement, my wise cousin," Gawain responded. "It will serve us well to be aware of what anyone may carry into each new encounter."

Their cousins from the west stayed-on with Erfiddyl and her three bright young teens another day. Owain led the lads in an initiatory session of the powers of the mountains and the streams, Peredyr taking to it quite rapidly, Gwrgi questioning the details of this inherent flow, Ceindrych Penasgell simply becoming enlivened by the presence of this elemental current that she knew so very well. On the third day, Owain, Gawain and Llamorhad prepared to depart at first light. As her cousins were preparing their horses, Ceindrych touched Gawain's shoulder, gesturing with her head toward Llamorhad, saying quietly: "Stay close to your friend. He carries a heavy weight in his heart."

Gawain, glancing toward Llamorhad, and then back to her, saying, "Thank you, Penasgell," taking her hand and kissing it.

"I look forward to our next meeting," she said smiling.

Peredyr was doing what he could to suppress his eagerness to travel with his elder cousins. Ceindrych hesitantly spoke with her mother just after the three visiting young warriors rode away.

"Mother, I know your deepest sorrows and fears. You have always known of my gift. And you have three loving children who have been by your side. You know, as I believe all mothers do, your children have their own destinies to follow. It is clear to me that Peredyr is hearing his call, his call to begin his journey."

"You are such wise children," Erfiddyl replied, "but still so young."

"I know mother. We do not completely choose our time. It just arrives. Then we must choose. Let the lad make his choice."

"Peredyr!" Erfiddyl called him.

"Yes Mother, what is it?"

"I know you enjoyed this visit with your older cousins, more than any visit before."

"Yes, Mother, they are fine young men."

"Yes they are. Are you compelled to join them?"

Peredyr paused, struck by his mother's openness, asking — "Now, today . . . or one day?"

"Now, today," she answered.

"Yes, I would, but for you and our family . . ."

"Ah, yes, but then . . . I believe you must join them, for you and our family."

"Really, truly, are you certain Mother?"

"What is certain in this life? My love for you is certain. Your destiny draws you. Where it leads is uncertain. But you must answer its call and follow your inspiration. Awen must not be denied."

"Thank you Mother. I will be careful, and learn from Owain and Gawain all that I can. I will return soon, and tell you of all my adventures."

"First, there are some things I must ask of you."

"Yes, Mother, but I must prepare and catch up to them on the road north."

"Yes, I know. Please follow these things; promise me that you will."

"Yes, Mother."

"If you do not meet your cousins on the road well before nightfall, promise me that you will return home."

"I will try my best, Mother," Peredyr answered as he began to rummage through an old wooden chest of long discarded parts of leather plated armor, belts, grieves, caps and visors, the outgrown belongings of his long lost brothers.

"Many of these things that I ask of you, you know well – but I remind you now, just the same."

"Yes, Mother," Peredyr said, and then leaning out the window, "Gwrgi, Gwrgi, could you find that saddle for the dappled-grey?"

"On your journey," his mother continued, "whenever you see a church, a nemeton, a cairn, or a burial site, be sure to bow in reverence. When offered food or drink, accept it with gratitude; and if none is offered, take only what you need, while leaving something of value in exchange. If you ever hear a scream or cry of distress, go near it, and defend any woman, child, or elderly person. If you find a jewel, or gold or silver that appears to have no owner, take it to give to someone in need; and you shall be praised for it."

Peredyr stopped what he was doing for a moment, caught in reflection upon his dream of finding the jewel – "Yes, Mother."

"If you encounter a beautiful woman, praise her, be kind to her, even if she rejects you. It will make you a more noble man by your respect of her."

Peredyr's eyes widened, and a smile flashed across his face, surprised again by the similarity to his dream – "Yes, Mother."

"If you encounter great nobility, or people of great learning, do not be too glib, asking too many questions, or getting too talkative about yourself. Try to listen and learn. And lastly, never forget who you are: born a divine child into the peace of nature. Seek to see that in others."

"Yes Mother, I see that in you, in Ceindrych, in Gwrgi, and my cousins. I must go, but will return soon, as best I can," Peredyr said, gathering-up his quiver, his javelins and darts, and his satchel stuffed with hurriedly chosen odds and ends. "I love you Mother."

"I love you too, my dear son."

Peredyr hugged and kissed his mother, his sister, and gave his brother a firm hug and a slap on the shoulder, Gwrgi responding with a harder slap – "Easy lad!" Peredyr said. "Check those traps by the stream, should be supper waiting. Remember what I showed you on the hunts. Maybe take a stroll between scrolls."

"And you watch out for trolls . . . and enticing dream maidens, little brother," Gwrgi teased him.

"Little? Maybe a little late, like today, that's all," Peredyr said as he cinched the saddle to his horse.

"I'll be watching out for you from afar. Listen to your guides. The Sidhe will be with you," Ceindrych Penasgell assured him.

"Thank you, my guardian angel," he said, mounting the old dappled-grey mare, riding out into the woodland, to the northern road beyond and to the adventures of his expanding world.

Liminal Bounds of Lothian

Peredyr tried to keep a good pace with his aging horse; but she wasn't capable of being pushed too hard. He could see the tracks of three horses headed north toward Lothian for quite some time, although, distinctive marks got muddied well before the River Tees after intersecting a number of crossroads. As dusk approached he remembered his mother's request to turn back before dark. He was committed and sure that he'd come upon his cousins' camp soon, urgently deciding to act upon his sister's advice.

"Alright then, brothers and sisters, masters and ancestors of the Sidhe, guide me on! If I am to find my cousins, help me to see a clear path. If I am to return home, then let me know now . . . or soon . . . perhaps very soon – thank you," his eyes surveying the periphery of his vision, hoping an apparition of guidance might arise. In that moment he was able to see the soaring flight of a peregrine falcon, aware that his sister's name, Ceindrych was similar to the Scotti name for the peregrine, ceinthireach; as Gwrgi had told him numerous times before.

Answering to this grand bird's call above the unfamiliar landscape, he said: "I hear you. I'm listening. Speak to me, okay? I'm just used to asking my winged-head sister about these things."

As the glow of the sun painted the western sky in brilliant tones of gold and vermillion, the lad faintly heard what sounded like a more mature version of his sister Penasgell's voice saying: "Two more leagues, turn down the deer path, east, round the a tall crag before the wood."

Peredyr smiled, saying, "Wow, sister of mercy – I love you." To his glee and amazement, after two leagues he saw the tall crag before the wood, following a deer path, east, into the darkened forest. Gradually his eyes adjusted to the darkness, feeling quite at home in the wild, only wavering with the thought: "Is this Bryneich? I hope it's not Bryneich." He could hear the sound of the peregrine, calling through the evening air outside the wooded grove. "She'll find some dinner out there" then he heard the hawk. "Yes, Gwalchmai, I must be getting closer." Soon he could smell a campfire, and then saw the glow of light ahead in the distance. Before he reached the clearing, Owain appeared from the shadows with a drawn sword and a firm grasp of the dappled-grey's bridle.

"Peredyr, what are you doing here? How did you find your way to our camp? Is Penasgell with you?"

"In spirit, I'm sure; in the flesh, it's just me."

"Is all well at home?"

"Oh, yes cousin, fine, fine. I just knew I had to follow you lads, to follow my destiny."

"Welcome to the Gwyr y Gogledd." Owain said, leading the lad into the camp, announcing his arrival to Gawain and Llamorhad.

"Look what brigand I found out here, fast on our trail."

"Peredyr!" both Gawain and Llamorhad happily welcomed the sudden arrival of the adventurous lad.

"He's joining us to travel up to Lothian," Owain added.

Gawain attended to Peredyr's horse, jesting, "This mare of yours is looking a touch sickly, lad. Did you have to carry her part way?"

"Almost, she's a good old gal. I caught up to you old-timers with her help. I guess she's closer to **your** age," Peredyr razed his elder cousins.

"Oh, is that how it is? Well, at least you're weaned. I don't think she'll be nursing you all the way to the Firth of Forth," Gawain shot back.

"Alright, enough of the pissing contests for now, these rabbits are roasted and ready," Llamorhad chimed-in.

They all shared a meal, settling-in to sleep by the fire, telling tales of Cymric warriors of the past, expanding Peredyr's knowledge of his heritage of kings.

"Do you know much about your father lad?" Gawain asked young Peredyr.

"Only what little my mother has told me: his bravery, his pride in his sons, and his leadership in building a great following, many now sadly perished. And, my sister has told me of her visions of our father and brothers, appearing to her from the Otherworld."

"Your sister and my mother sound very much alike – true seers. With the blessing of her guidance and some fine mentors, I have not felt the absence of my father. Has it just been the four of you there at the forest cottage all these years?" Gawain inquired further.

"My mother has tried to shelter us from the outer world, the world of battle and conflict. She lost so many in her life to war. My brother and sister and I have been mentors to each other, each one with their own strengths. But I know so little of the kingdom once ruled by my father Eliffer, or his ancestors. I have no idea how one would rule such a land and its people. Do you know how your father, how our uncle Loth became a king?" Peredyr asked.

"Yes I do. It is rather complicated. In the north," Gawain explained, "as in the Pict Gwlad, they often follow the old ways: where the land is their fertility, the womb of life, belonging to the sovereignty of the goddess, and thus handed down through the grandmothers and mothers to their daughters, who marry princes and kings to defend and preserve those lands. Many conflicts can arise from disputes over the claims of lineage and sovereignty. My mother could not claim sovereignty over her land, a land conquered by foreign kings. But, she could give birth to an heir, sired by a king who ruled over her ancestral land; even though that king had a wife and queen of his own in a distant kingdom. I am that heir of the Orcades. And if I had a sister, she might regain the land by her matriarchal sovereignty. My farther, your uncle, is the King of Lothian, the land known as Manau Gododdin. Nearly two centuries ago Ceretig Wledig held the Alt Clud and the Manau of the Votadini, called Gododdin, while Annun Dynod held the Isle of Manau. These were the early marks to the north made by the clans of the Cymri. Ceretig's daughter, Ingenach was heir to the sovereignty of the land. She married the son of Brychan, patriarch of the southern Cymri. Their granddaughter Lluan married Gabran of Dalriada. Their son was one of my mentors, Prince Aedan. The sovereignty would pass to a daughter of

Brychan and Ingenach: either Nyfain who married Cynfarch of Rheged or Gwawr who married his brother Elidyr. Nyfain and Cynfarch are our grandparents, the parents of Urien, Loth, and your mother Erfiddyl. Your mother waived the right to sovereignty over Manau Gododdin when she married your father Eliffer, Prince of Ebrauc. When Brychan and Ingenach of Manau Gododdin died, an alliance of the Cymri was formed between Alt Clud and Rheged over Manau Gododdin and Gallwyddel, since the passing of Afallach, making Gallwyddel a subkingdom to Rheged and Alt Clud. Manau Gododdin was to be ruled by Loth, the matriarchal line existing through his mother, our grandmother Nyfain and great Aunt Gwawr, passed on through Loth's wife, Anna Morgause of Gallwyddel, my stepmother and your aunt."

"What of Aedan's line in Dalriada is there any claim through his mother Lluan?" Llamorhad asked.

"No. Neither Gabran nor Aedan have had daughters, and Lluan was a granddaughter of Ingenach and Brychan. Gabran's Dalriada went to his brother Comgall and then to his son and heir Conall, through their Scotti patriarchal succession. Aedan's wife, however, is a Pictish princess of the north, true sovereign heiress of the Pict Gwlad ruled by her troublesome brother Bruide mac Maelgwyn," Gawain explained. "Does that answer your question, cousin Peredyr . . . Peredyr?"

"I think he went to sleep somewhere around the middle of the alliance of Gallwyddel, Rheged, Alt Clud and Gododdin," Owain observed. "What we all best watch for in the months and years to come is the remaining contention between Alt Clud and the heirs of Ceretig, but even more so between Bryneich and their heirs of Coel Hen, eager to gain Gododdin and control the Firth of Forth. But try not to battle-on between dynasties through the night. Our young cousin leads the way now, hopefully in peaceful dreams. Sleep well lads. We've got some leagues to cover tomorrow."

"Good night," said Gawain.

"Sleep well," said Llamorhad.

Early the next morning, the lads headed north, following the Dere Ystryd where it was safe, diverting west to other roads or across open country when they neared enemy territories.

"Are we in Bryneich? I know Bryneich is not a good place." Peredyr asked, with a look of foreboding on his young face.

"No, we're not in Bryneich," Owain answered.

"I thought I was in Bryneich yesterday, was I?" Peredyr asked again.

"No. Unlikely, lad, not unless you went too far north and doubled back to find us," said Owain.

"Oh, no, no, I don't believe I could have done that," Peredyr said, looking a bit puzzled.

"Bryneich isn't half as bad as Bernicia. That's why we're going west. We won't get to Bryneich 'til the morrow," said Gawain.

"What's so bad about Bernicia? I thought Bryneich was worse?" Peredyr kept asking.

"Did anyone ever tell you not to ask so many questions?" Owain continued, a bit agitated, "Bernicia or Bryneich for you lad, would be a matter of preference: do you want to be gutted by an Angle bastard or a bastard from Bryneich, not that it would make any difference – when you're dead."

"Bryneich has been unstable for more than two decades, with some factions allied with Angles or Franks from the continent," Llamorhad added.

"Where's the continent from here?" asked Peredyr.

"East, across a big treacherous pond," Owain answered.

"So we'll stay west." Peredyr stated.

"Yes, we'll stay west, hopefully far enough west of the Angles," Owain repeated.

"Where did you dig up that rare mix of plated leather, laddie?" Gawain asked their curious young companion. "It looks like one shoulder, and front to back come from different gear, pilfered off foreign armies."

"I have an old wooden chest at home full of remnants from my older brothers, gear they trained in, or grew out of, some parts lost, others damaged. So I pieced together what would fit and hold up. I don't even know who wore what. My mother wouldn't speak of it. She almost burned the lot, 'til I begged her to let me keep it," said Peredyr.

"It will do for now lad. We'll get you some better gear once you grow out of this. We all had training gear at one time." Owain related to the lad.

Owain wore a dark, nearly black, leather plated hauberk, with round metal disks attached to the plates across the front. Llamorhad's gear was similar, only lighter in color, dark brown tones, with square metal plates over the leather. They both had helmets of the late Roman style, round with hinged side guards to protect the jaw, and a nose guard covering past the bridge. Gawain's hauberk had much smaller plates. His helmet was a weathered bronze, round with a crested ridge, and no side guards. All three wore leggings in the tartan of Rheged, a dark plaid, cinched into short boots. Each of them carried a round shield with a boss in the center. Owain's was dark with a faint image of a raven's head in profile. Gawain's was olive green, with dark spiraling finely crafted lines marking three pentagrams inside pentagons inside of each other, the smallest pentagram star on the center of the boss. Peredyr on his dappled-grey mare with odds and ends of armor appeared as an ill-made copy of the other three, riding boldly on their strong warhorses. It would take two and a half days to get to Lothian, if weather was mild, and no extra detours or sudden altercations with marauders occurred.

On the second day, after the four of them turned to the east to get back to the Dere Ystryd below the wall of Tyne, a band of a dozen men of Bryneich came dashing towards them at full gallop, emerging from a wooded grove just past a rise in terrain. Owain, Gawain and Llamorhad quickly formed together, Owain in the lead, the others alongside him, and Peredyr holding back behind.

"Stay there lad. If you can get-off any javelins or darts, fire away. **This** hunt is for your life. If it goes bad for us, head west and follow the wall to

Caer Lliwelydd," Owain shouted back as he led the other three, swords drawn into a charge at the attackers.

Peredyr dismounted, telling the old dappled-grey mare: "stay put, old gal, it's just another hunt." Then the lad looked up to the sky as he drew a javelin from his quiver saying, "Great guides above and beyond, guide this javelin or guide us home."

Peredyr felt suddenly more alive than he had ever been, his stance and movement poised and directed to reach an arm of rescue to his new brothers facing poor odds against hardened warriors. He released the first javelin, taking one distant warrior down, clean off his horse, Owain turning a glance back with a smile and a nod, sending a clear message – keep firing. And Peredyr did, the second javelin wounding another attacker, leaving him as easy prey for a Cymric sword. By now his cousins were too close-in for a shot; as a warrior in a red leather hauberk bolted past them and another marauder with battle axe also racing towards the lad. He quickly fired and hit the axe-wielder, as the red warrior kept coming. Down to his last javelin, without a breath of an instant to spare, Peredyr let loose his final throw, acutely seeing the intense anger in the warrior's eyes, his battle-cry rattling the steady lad only after the javelin left his hand. The warrior, leaning forward, tight to the reigns of his mount was struck straight through his eye, the javelin driving into the back of his skull, out the scruff of his neck and into the neck of the horse, forcing the steed to buckle at the front legs, plowing into the earth just a pace or two before the astonished lad, standing ready, with a dart in one hand and a butcher's knife in the other. Horse and rider were dead. His cousins had battled or run-off the remaining eight attackers, each lad exhausted, exhilarated and blood spattered. Owain, Gawain and Llamorhad rode back, amazed and grateful to see the young lad standing dumbfounded over the fallen warrior and his horse. The dappled-grey had retreated to the hills, out of sight during the final fray. Peredyr had yet to notice.

"Oh my lad, that was the finest javelin wielding I have ever seen. You carried your weight and more today," Owain honored him.

"Those throws were fierce lad, fierce!" Gawain added.

"I say we strip this Bryneich bastard of his gear, and reward young Peredyr with a fine red leather hauberk," said Llamorhad, looking over the lad's final kill of the day.

Peredyr looked at the warrior he had just killed, pinned to his dead horse, blood draining onto the ground at the lad's feet. Then he turned suddenly, bending over to throw-up his breakfast. "First time I've seen a dead man up-close," the lad said, wiping his chin.

"It's all right lad," said Llamorhad. "There's a lot to stomach here, your first day out."

While Llamorhad and Peredyr pulled off the bloodied gear from their dead adversary, Owain and Gawain rounded-up the horses from the other fallen marauders. It wasn't until later that they discovered the old dappled-grey, run-off in fright, stumbled in a ditch, leg broken and her heart finally given-way. They buried the mare, but left the marauders for wolves, ravens, and crows, their ravenous calls sounding as Owain led the lads north toward Lothian. Peredyr rode one of the retrieved horses from the Bryneich attackers – a sturdy young bay mare with a black mane and a white blaze on her brow. At the first stream they crossed, the lads stripped-off their clothes to bathe, rinsing blood from their arms and faces, and chilling their frenzied nerves from the day's sudden ambush.

Llamorhad noticed Peredyr's surprised glance at Gawain's naked form, saying quietly to the lad, "We tell him it's his Monster of the Loch."

Peredyr snickered, "I never saw a man so large."

"He's not likely human, part giant, or Orcadian sea beast," whispered Llamorhad.

Peredyr washed his new hauberk in the stream, scrubbing-off the blood of the fallen marauder, cleansing the battle gear that had become his own. He hung it from his saddle to dry for now, as they rode on. The fit of the armor was a bit large for the lad. He was yet to gain his full height and fill-out in the shoulders. Everyday his elder cousins trained with him, using shield and sword. Peredyr found the axe too heavy, taking more to small arms: the javelin, darts and sling that he could already use quite well. He thought of his father and brothers that he never knew, as he practiced the skills of combat – the bloody reality of the beast of battle made vividly clear on that day of his first encounter near the border of Bryneich.

Late afternoon on the third day, the lads reached Arthsedd, site of the towering fortress of Lothian. It was the same hilltop citadel overlooking the Firth of Forth ruled by Brychan II a century before. Greater stone reinforcement and structures had been added over the decades, making the stronghold even more impregnable, giving the distant profile of the crouching bear a stony crown. Sentries at the base and all along the well guarded incline up to the summit recognized Owain, Prince of Rheged, nephew of King Loth. He and Llamorhad had been there several times, most often with his father, King Urien. Like Dun Barton to the west and Caer Lliwelydd to the south, Arthsedd was a strategic prize, coveted along with its matriarchal lineage spanning generations, giving this northern fortress the agnomen "Caer Morwynion" – Castle of the Maidens – its queens soon surrendering their maidenhood with the dower of their sovereignty. Owain and his cousins were announced at the main hall of the keep. Queen Anna Morgause and her sons greeted the travelers, the oldest slightly older than Gawain, the others one and a half and three years younger.

"Hello Owain, Llamorhad, it is so good to see you both. You lads look well. Who are these other fine lads?" Queen Anna inquired.

"These are my cousins, Gawain and young Peredyr of Ebrauc," Owain answered.

"Welcome to you all. Come meet my sons, your other cousins: Agrefain, Gweheris, and Gweirydd. Gweirydd and Peredyr look about the same age. How is your mother, Erfiddyl, she is well?" The queen inquired.

"Yes, my Lady," Peredyr answered.

"And Gawain?" . . . She questioned.

"I'm from the Orcades," Gawain answered.

Just then, King Loth entered the great hall, bellowing: "Hello lads, it looks like we have a young troop gathered for a hunt! Owain, Llamorhad – you're looking strong, lads," giving them each a firm forearm hand grasp and a pat on the shoulder.

Then he turned to Gawain as Owain said, "This is Gawain, my cousin from the Orcades."

Loth giving him a Roman handshake as well, sensing a familiarity, "Ah the Orcades, fabulous land, the Ring of Brogar is quite stunning."

"Yes indeed, Sire," Gawain answered.

"And, Peredyr, Erfiddyl's lad," Owain added.

"Oh my dear nephew," Loth immediately embraced the lad, and then held him apart at arm's length to get a good look at him. "You're a fine lad. How is your mother? It has been so very long since I've seen my dear sister, she's well?"

"Oh yes Sire, as are my sister Ceindrych and my brother Gwrgi," Peredyr replied.

"What a surprise – we must have a feast; and you can tell us of all your adventures lads. Seneschal! Come, let's find you lads lodging, while the hall is prepared," Loth directed with festive joy in his voice.

All this time, Anna Morgause had noticed the manner and movement of Gawain, how he carried himself like her husband the king. This sent her mind racing: "his repeated journeys to the Orcades, his fascination with that conquered land. And how, something in his expression when he met Gawain, Gawain a cousin of Owain – but how? What is his lineage? Who are his parents? He could just have traits resembling Urien, as does Loth. And, do I really want to know the truth, if it means Loth was untrue to me from the beginning? The lad is Agrefain's age!"

Before the feast, Queen Morgause was busy overseeing the preparation of the meal; and Loth was showing the lads around the fortress, allowing the cousins some time to get acquainted. By dusk, the king, his liegemen and their ladies had joined the queen in the great hall for the evening. Loth presented the visiting lads to the court as his nephews, sons of Urien and Erfiddyl. Llamorhad, of course, was no relation, but considered a foster son of Vivianne and Taliesin of Ynys Manau. Last mentioned was "Gawain of the Orcades." A grand feast was served, all the while Anna Morgause watching Gawain laughing with her sons across the room, unable to shake-off her troubled curiosity about him. Llamorhad found himself unusually attracted to the queen that evening, observing her frequent glances at Gawain. He wondered if it had been the season of Beltaine, which masked ladies, liegemen and nobles would slink away together for an uninhibited night of amorous escape. Music and boisterous conversation filled the hall, interrupted periodically by orations of verse from bard Aneirin ap Dynod of Penllanw, one of the many bards mentored by Taliesin. As the evening carried-on, Loth stepped-out to walk along the parapets and take the air. Gawain, noticing his exit, followed after him for their first chance to speak alone.

"May I join you Sire?" Gawain asked.

"Certainly lad, the view from here is commanding, Loth replied.

"Yes, the moonlit waters draw me back to the north."

"Ah, the Orcades – I know what you mean. Now, how are you a cousin to Owain? What other clan are you from lad?"

"The Attacotti, Sire, my mother is Morcades. She tells me that you knew her briefly."

Loth stopped and turned, facing Gawain directly. "Briefly? Are you **my** son lad?"

"Yes, that is what my mother told me?"

Loth put he hands on Gawain's shoulders, looking him straight in the eyes, "You are lad, you are, I can see my younger self in your face! Another son, how miraculous, and your mother, how is she? She was like a fleeting dream to me."

"She has that way about her. She is well, living in Afallon these days," Gawain answered.

"Gawain, is that a family name?"

"Not exactly: I took my mentor's name. He was like one of the family, the only family I knew besides Mother. Old Gawain was killed by the Picts when I was eleven. Gwalchmai is my given name."

"The hawk of May, is that your month of birth?"

"Yes, the first day."

"Ah, yes, it all adds up."

Queen Anna Morgause suddenly exited an upper chamber to see the two men talking. "There you are!" she called-out, coming closer. "I wondered where you two were off and about," then she saw the looks on their faces, revealing her suspicions. "Is it true? It must be." She blurted-out.

"Is what true dear?" Loth asked, feigning ignorance.

"Is Gawain just a cousin? Or is he your son?"

Loth put his arm around the lad's shoulders, looking at him with pride, "Yes, I believe he is my son."

Morgause stood in shock, the confirmation of her fears gripping her in a cascade of emotion, a tear falling down her cheek.

"I think I'll return to the hall now," Gawain said, bowing to each of them, and then walking away.

"My dear, it was a long time ago." King Loth fumbled an excuse.

"I know exactly how long ago it was. I was carrying Agrefain; and you were on a conquest in the Orcades."

"It was nothing."

"Nothing? Nothing? A full-grown man is something. Another son is something. Did you ever feel something for me? Did you? Do you?"

"Yes, of course I do," said Loth, he reaching to her, she pulling away.

"I know there were others. But now I see that there were always others. You were never really wed to me. Why did I ever believe there was more?"

"Because you wanted to believe, and there is more: maybe not what you think it should be. I am what I am. Men are what we are. I know few nobles without a mistress or two. You are my grandniece, after all. We wed, and you were fully aware of this, we wed as part of an alliance of sovereignty."

"Oh, that is so conveniently barren of feeling. I am the mother of your sons – except one, that I know of. We, the queens of this land, give you birth upon the earth. And you, you kings of conquest, just ride over it all on your brutal mounts." With that, she stormed back into the keep, leaving Loth to ponder these new revelations of his fatherhood.

Gawain and others noticed the queen's fiery attitude as she returned to the hall, rapidly forcing down a tall cup of wine, as if to submerge and drown her anger. It seemed to only fuel it. By the time Loth entered the gathering again, Morgause was well-primed. Nearly stumbling, she drew a sword, swinging it wildly in an arcing motion towards her husband. Loth stepped back, his arms spread wide, gesturing for people to step away.

"Stop, my dear!" shouted Loth."

"Dear? Dear? What is dear to you?" The enraged queen replied, walking closer to Loth, the sword held firmly with both hands at waist height.

"What are you doing?"

"Has everyone met my husband's son Gawain?" She shouted, spinning around full-circle, pointing the sword at Gawain, and then at Loth again.

"What now? You've made your announcement. What do you want from me? . . . My head? . . . My balls? . . . You cannot erase the past with a sword. Many have tried and failed." Loth taunted her, the hall quiet and motionless.

Morgause began to weep, her arms dropping the sword point to the floor, its metallic sound breaking the silence. Gawain and Llamorhad came forward to each side of the queen. She, reacting suddenly, raised the sword as Gawain leaned forward, the tip of the blade grazing his neck as he jerked back. A gasp from the crowd voiced the shock on their faces, Gawain quickly touching his hand to the scratch from the blade, while Llamorhad embraced the queen from behind, removing the sword from her hand, she, collapsing into his arms. Llamorhad kneeled down, holding the queen, her face blank, lost in an emotional stupor. Looking up at Gawain, Llamorhad could see that he was fine. Agrefain and some ladies of the court soon took Morgause from Llamorhad's arms, carrying her to her bedchamber.

"Drama!" bellowed King Loth across the hall, "And now, music! Continue the music! Enjoy the night everyone!"

As the musicians started-up again, and the clucking of the crowd began reviewing the gossip of the king's exploits, Loth approached Gawain.

"Are you alright lad?"

"Yes, father, it's just a scratch."

"Father, I like the sound of that from you, son."

"Was she capable of taking your head?"

"Not likely, it's hard as a stone. Although, she could have done some damage, drawing my blood, or our blood. You've been officially announced, my son. Not exactly how I might have staged it."

"Spontaneity, Father, that's how I came into your life. Luckily, I didn't exit that way, tonight of all nights."

"It was lucky for us all, lad, lucky for us all."

The festivities continued unabated for hours, until only a few drunkards remained, asleep where they sat, slumped over a table, or out-cold on the floor. Gawain fell deep asleep in the bedchamber he shared with Owain, Llamorhad and Peredyr. The evening fed his vivid dreams, conjuring images as profound as any he had ever known.

Gawain found himself within a great hall, much like the one he had been in all evening at Arthsedd. He was attending the most marvelous feast, full of music and merriment, until the enormous doors of the hall sprang open, streaming light shining into the darkened evening of candlelight and fire pit glow, in a blinding flash of rays around a giant silhouetted figure. A warrior entered on horseback, his fantastic horse rearing-up with sounds of a whinny that echoed the call of a hundred cries of hawks. The warrior was more fierce that his horse, leaping off the dark steed onto the floor of the hall, his feet instantly becoming rooted to the stone flooring, tendrils of roots sprouting from his toes like wriggling worms, finding entry into the earth between the individual stones. Already gigantic in stature, the warrior grew in height, his beard and hair creating shoots of vines and foliage, fanning-out to form a spectacular tree. Each branch conjured the semblance of varieties of birds and beasts, appearing for a moment and then vanishing from sight. As the warrior leaned forward, his face appeared as every mentor Gawain had known within his life thus far, settling into the countenance of his birth father, King Loth. Queen Morgause appeared from the crowd wielding a sword, she disturbingly turning different hues of color across her face and arms while standing before the transforming warrior king. The grand woodland king displayed over his shifting visage all the variations of hues of green: from the darkest tones of the deep forest, to the vivid emerald grasses, to the most brilliant chartreuse bursting buds of spring.

The reactive queen swung her gleaming sword wildly as the mutating warrior king bellowed back to her – "Take my head and my balls if you can; and I will grow more back again!" The suddenly emotionally deflated queen fell to her knees weeping, the king calling out to the hall – "Who among you all will stand-up for the queen?"

Gawain stepped forward; and the king handed him a double-axe, by holding it out from his bark-encrusted limb of an arm, swinging the weapon to and fro, with the axe-head slicing through the air in the downward motion of a pendulum. Gawain reached out and took the axe by the highest point of the handle he could grasp and control, as the gigantic green warrior king said, "Take my head with this axe; and if I live, I will return to take yours after the turning of four seasons. I will meet you at a nemeton, deep in the woodlands, in the most hallowed place of the trees."

Miraculously, the green warrior became diminished to the size of a very tall man, extending his neck forward, the hair on his head blowing back as if a sudden gust of wind moved a leafy willow branch. Gawain swung the axe high, bringing it down upon the strange warrior's massive neck, cleanly severing his head from his body. The truncated neck rapidly began sprouting vines, first red, then yellow, then green – seemingly searching for the fallen head lying on the floor, its crazed eyes scanning from side to side to find the detached body. The twitching body, minded by extended vines, discovered its own head again, picking-up the disoriented capstone of identity, placing it firmly onto its vacant neck, as Gawain and the court stared in awestruck silence.

Then the dark viridian reconstituted warrior mounted his fiendish horse again, roaring at Gawain – "Four seasons, and your head is mine!" Turning his horse, laughing so ferociously loud as to shake the walls of the hall, he rode out of the open doors of the keep, leaving the room in a stunned silence; once again illuminated only by the fire pit and candlelight, dimming slowly into quiet darkness.

Suddenly, Gawain found himself in a darkened bedchamber, lying upon a bed, perceiving a brightening of light around him. A woman had entered the room carrying a candle, the flickering light dancing across her naked body. She climbed upon his bed, straddling his loins, arousing herself above him. When she tilted her head back, her hair falling away to expose her face, Gawain saw that it was Queen Anna Morgause, his father's wife. Gawain realizes he cannot do this. She answers his thoughts, saying, "Then accept a kiss." Leaning forward, she kisses him on the lips three times, and then vanishes through an opening door that floods the room with light. Gawain arises from bed, stepping through the door out into the morning light, brightly shining on a rich green meadow spreading out before him. Leaves of the trees rapidly begin changing to autumn colors, swiftly becoming covered with snow, the snow quickly melting, with the sprouting leaves of spring opening and extending instantaneously. As the temperature warms, Gawain moves into the light. He walks across the verdant fields, flowers blossoming among the green blades of grass, opening their petals as he wanders through them, brushing against the bare flesh of his thighs. He stands there, completely naked, viewing an expanse of towering trees forming a grand nemeton at the end of the meadow. Walking on, he enters the nemeton, looking up through an oculus of treetops to observe the clouds traversing a resplendent blue sky, the etheric light catching diaphanous edges of the billowing vaporous entities, creating intense spectral hues of color. From the corner of his eye he sees the ominous green warrior appear from the shadows, wielding his double-headed axe. Approaching Gawain he says: "Four seasons have past, four seasons begin," swinging the axe as Gawain steps back, his neck exposed, the razor sharp axe-head just shaving the skin of Gawain's naked throat before he swallows and sighs in relief. Then Gawain awoke, touching his neck to feel the scratch from the sword wielded by Morgause at the feast.

Sitting up, Gawain sees that Llamorhad is not in the room. So he gets up, quietly putting on his boots and tunic, carefully opening and closing the door, off to find a chamber pot or an open window to relieve his bladder. Llamorhad had awakened earlier, disturbed from a dream stirred by the clash with the marauders from Bryneich, remembering his narrow escape as a youth when his entire family was killed by the mercenaries hired by his Frankish cousins. He thought a walk in the night air would clear his head. After Gawain released a good strong golden stream out a window above a steep cliff edge of Arthsedd, he too decided to take a stroll. Nearing a corner he heard the passionate moaning of two lovers, clearly reaching the climax of their encounter. Gawain proceeded, stepping gingerly to peek around the corner, seeing Llamorhad, his leggings around his ankles, bare buttocks thrusting rhythmically into his lover, her gown hiked-up around her waist, legs in the air, with hands grasping the corners of the parapet. As her long auburn hair flipped to the side during her passionate response, Gawain could clearly see it was Queen Anna Morgause.

Gawain quickly ducked back behind the corner with this eye-opening revelation, taking a deep breath as he leaned against the wall; then he slowly tip-toed back to the bedchamber. Llamorhad slipped into his own bed before dawn, Gawain silently aware of his return. The next morning they all awoke to Owain's ringing stream upon the chamber pot from his resounding relief. The others soon did follow, Llamorhad noticing that Gawain hadn't added to the communal pot.

"Shall I dump this or are you contributing," Llamorhad asked him after the others left the room.

"Go ahead, I stepped-out earlier." Gawain responded.

"Oh, up in the night?" asked Llamorhad, wondering if Gawain had noticed his absence.

"Yes and . . . you know that the penalty for violating the sovereignty of the queen – even if by her consent – is a public beheading," Gawain said, slapping him on the back.

Llamorhad, slightly rattled, almost spilling the chamber pot replied: "Good to know mate; best to keep those things quiet."

"Mum's the word," Gawain replied with a cautionary stare.

The day that followed was a lively adventure of hunting, six cousins – Owain, Gawain, Peredyr, Agrefain, Gweheris, and Gweirydd – with Llamorhad, King Loth and a number of his liegemen. They spent hours in the forests south of Arthsedd, yielding much game for the table, returning by dusk laughing boisterously as if the events of the night before had never occurred. Another feast was set before them, yet all retired earlier this time, the lads intending to depart the next morning. Queen Anna Morgause did not attend the second feast, keeping to her bedchamber. The following morning the lads were exiting their room, on the way down to breakfast, when the sons of Loth confronted them.

"Hold-up lads! We have news that we must act upon," Agrefain shouted, stopping their cousins and Llamorhad.

"What, trouble from Bryneich?" Owain questioned.

"No, Prince Owain – trouble here!" Gweheris answered.

"What's this?" asked Gawain.

"Llamorhad has violated the Queen and he must forfeit his life!" Gweirydd shouted, drawing his sword. "His head will be taken!"

Owain and Gawain drew their blades, stepping back in response. "What is your proof, Princes of Lothian?" Owain questioned, with his sword held firmly before him.

"Our mother has admitted this violation and her attending ladies have confirmed it."

"Admitted? Then this intercourse was by consent?" Owain responded.

"It makes no difference. It is the law. Llamorhad must pay with his head!" Gweirydd yelled, shaking his sword in the air.

"We cannot stand by while you slay our brother-in-arms," Owain answered.

Llamorhad stepped forward, looking to Gawain's concerned face, and then confessing, "It is true. I met with Queen Morgause on the night before last. She gave herself to me willingly and passionately. Whatever regrets she may have now – I have none."

"There it is! He must die!" Agrefain declared.

"We **all** leave this fortress today, or your blood will be shed here and now," Owain challenged them.

Then Llamorhad leapt up onto the parapet, facing them all saying: "I cannot allow the blood of cousins to be shed today, over me. I am the only one who is not of your blood. I am the one here who was reckless in his passion. I end it all now." With that he turned and jumped from the parapet, plummeting down the steep cliff onto the rocks below.

Catching just a fleeting glimpse of his leap, the queen ran out, reaching her arms to the empty air, wailing – "No, no, no!" Agrefain quickly grabbed her, fearful she would follow Llamorhad. She collapsed there, weeping, her son lifting her up and taking her back indoors. All swords were sheathed again. They buried their friend in a meadow near the wood where they had their last joyous hunt together. The son's of Lothian still insisted on Llamorhad's beheading, while allowing his brothers-in-arms to bury his noble head with his body. Soon after, they departed to the south again, traveling to Peredyr's forest home in Ebrauc.

Both Ends of the Wall

It was a mournful journey, each lad shaken in their own way. They stayed well west of Bryneich and Bernicia, approaching the forested lands of Peredyr's family after a somber and uneventful three days of riding. Penasgell was at the edge of the wood to see them arrive.

"I see Llamorhad is not with you, and your saddened faces confirm what I believed to be his passing. I am sorry for your loss of a true brother of spirit. While you were away, dear brother," she said, touching Peredyr's hand as he reached down from his horse, "our mother passed in the night as well. She went peacefully, in her sleep."

The lad slumped off of his horse into his sister's arms, both of them crying, deeply immersed in grief. Their cousins looked at each other, shaking their heads in disbelief. Peredyr walked along with his sister to their home, their cousins following behind with the horses. Gwrgi greeted his siblings with a tearful embrace. The three of them huddled together consoling each other for quite a while, before entering the cottage where their mother was lying on her bed. They were so very young when she had lost her other five sons and her husband, King Eliffer. It seems that the triplets had been born into sorrow, their mother shielding them from that grief as well as she could. Now they had a greater sense of her hidden suffering, standing over her silent face, her still, cold, mortal form, with eyes closed and devoid of that loving glimmer they knew so well.

Soon Gwrgi and Penasgell learned the whole story about Llamorhad's death. Their prescient sister had confided her fears, seeing the weight that their Burgundian friend carried in his heart, and knowing of his tenuous fate.

"Nothing is for certain," she said to them on that sorrowful day. "And yet, these shadows follow certain people. Many emerge, survive, and prosper with great courage and compassion for the sorrows of others. Others may struggle with the temptation to take that leap between worlds, suddenly diving into the lost hearts of their loved ones, releasing the pain within their own to join them. Llamorhad's courage was invoked to spare the lives of others, to stop the bloodshed of cousins against cousins."

"It was his leap of grace," Gwrgi added: "As if his self-sacrifice was his purpose from the moment that he was born and took his name."

"I knew he had been with the queen, my stepmother," Gawain confessed. "I warned him of his folly, and the penalty if found out. He must have had a deliberate flirtation with death, defying danger for forbidden passion. Maybe that act made him feel more alive while on the brink of death, ecstasy, and somehow a spark of creation."

"It is our mothers that are so intensely present for that spark of our creation," said Penasgell. "Our dear mother brought us into this life, and now has made her exit. She came to me in the night, her spirit body raised out of her physical form. She told me how much she loved us all; and was confident that we were able to be on our own. She said, 'I go to embrace your father and brothers, once again. Watch over Peredyr and Gwrgi, as I know they will watch over you.' Then she faded from my vision."

They buried Erfiddyl there, near the cottage. Gwrgi decided to carve a headstone for her. The lads helped him move a slab over to the grave site.

"It has some warm tones of color in the veining. Mother would like it," he said, wiping away a tear.

"It will be wonderful," said Penasgell. "I am grateful for the years we have had here; but I feel drawn to the opening future of my life. I am sure I will return here. Yet now, I feel called to Afallon, to meet and know my sisters of spirit. I believe Peredyr is ready to continue his adventures toward his destiny; quite soon I'd say."

Yes, I am sister," Peredyr responded.

"How do you feel about your future here or beyond here, Gwrgi, after you complete Mother's headstone?" She asked her brother.

"I think I will stay on and keep the place up, for a time at least. My place is here for now. I will be fine alone. I want both of you to follow your calling and your unfolding destiny. Quiet contemplation is my way, as you know," Gwrgi replied.

Peredyr, Penasgell and their cousins stayed on another day, before traveling northwest and along the Wall of Tyne toward Rheged. Peredyr reminded Gwrgi where the best hunting and fishing spots were, prior to their departure.

"I know, I know," Gwrgi answered. "I remember very many things, dear brother; even if I wasn't the hunter in the family."

"Well you'll need to be the hunter now, so remember to eat," his sister said. "Don't spend all of your days lost in thought – alright?"

"Yes, I'll keep that in mind," he said with a smirk.

She embraced him with a consuming hug and kissed him on the cheek. Peredyr shook his hand, pulling him close for a full embrace, both lads tearing-up. Then the four rode off, leaving Gwrgi behind, hearing the tap of hammer and chisel slowly diminish as they passed through the wooded grove surrounding the cottage. They headed due west after nearing the Wall of Tyne, its serpentine ridge undulating over the green rolling hills. Many of the fortifications had been raided for the Roman cut stones, the dismantled structures hauntingly appearing through the brume as empty ghosted dwellings of another time. Some of the forts were maintained and manned by warriors of the Kingdom of Solway, King Gwenddoleu exerting his importance where he could. He happened to be at one of the milecastles when Prince Owain and his cousins were traveling west on their way to Caer Lliwelydd. A patrol of sentries approached them as they neared the wall.

Penasgell cautioned Owain: "This king is of a dark nature. I do not believe he or his men will harm us without cause; but he may toy with us to flex his power."

"Thank you cousin," said Owain. "Keep your wits lads. Don't provoke any conflict."

"Greetings, men of Rheged," the leader of the sentries said, recognizing the tartans of Owain and Gawain, "My lady," he added, bowing his head slightly. "Our King Gwenddoleu would like to have a word with you nobles. He waves from the tower."

They could see Gwenddoleu raising his arm in welcome from the stone fort. Obliging, Owain and his party followed the sentries to the wall.

"Owain! I did not recognize you from a distance. Will you join me for some refreshment, before you journey on?" Gwenddoleu shouted from the top of the wall.

"Certainly Sire, a brief repast before we journey home to Caer Lliwelydd," Owain hollered back.

"Marvelous!" The king replied.

So they rode up to the ancient Roman garrison and dismounted. Sentries saw to their horses as Gwenddoleu greeted them.

"Owain, you're looking good lad."

"And you as well, Sire."

"Tell me, who joins us in your party?"

"Yes, my cousins, Ceindrych and Peredyr of Ebrauc and Gawain of the Orcades."

"Ah, children of Eliffer Gosgorddfawr – we are cousins! Your father was my uncle, brother of my father Ceido. You are the rightful heirs of Ebrauc, now ruled by Gwallog of Elmet and his heirs. These family trees are so entangled across the land. Now, what is your lineage, Gawain, is it?"

"Yes Sire," Gawain replied, stepping up, "I am the son of King Loth."

"Ah, well, an entourage of princes and a princess," Gwenddoleu said, taking Ceindrych Penasgell's hand to kiss it, she, relinquishing to his gesture, while a flash of vision rose within her mind of this depraved king watching over captives who he had been tortured, serving them barely alive to vicious predatory birds; the skin on Penasgell's delicate hand crawling with repulsive sensation rising up her arm when the king's lips touched the knuckles of her fingers, still feigning her smile and curtsying, demonstrating her breeding while concealing her clear reading of his character.

The king had a table prepared in the open air, now that the morning fog had lifted on that fine sunny afternoon. Wine, bread, cheese and some smoked meats were served. Gwenddoleu spoke with one of his servants to the side in a couched manner. The man nodded, departing quickly, returning later with a small table and two chairs.

"What is the nature of your travel, Prince Owain, if I may ask?" Gwenddoleu inquired.

"I was visiting my Aunt Erfiddyl, my Uncle Loth, and my cousins in Ebrauc and Lothian," said Owain.

"And are they all well?"

"Sadly, Sire, Erfiddyl passed away, and I return home with her son and daughter to join us for a time in Rheged."

"Ah, I am sorry to hear of your loss," said the king, rising to touch Penasgell again on the shoulder, she doing her best to accept his condolence.

"Thank you, Sire. We look forward to our time with family at Caer Lliwelydd."

"Yes, of course, my dear – you must visit our court in Solway too," said Gwenddoleu, stroking her shoulder.

Peredyr abruptly stood up, his action causing the king to immediately withdraw his hand from Penasgell, the lad saying: "It has been a tiring journey for my sister, and an emotional time for us all. We really should continue on to Rheged soon."

"Yes, the lad's right," said Owain. "Thank you for your hospitality, Sire. My father Urien will hear of your kindness."

"Yes, of course, you must be on your way. But, first, if you could just indulge me with a brief game of Gwyddbwyll," the king responded, his servant bringing out the board and pieces for the game, setting them upon the small table with the two chairs.

"Perhaps another time, Sire," said Owain.

"Really, I insist, a short game, I have so few worthy opponents. We are noble neighbors, after all," the king pressed him, as an increasing number of armed sentries appeared nearby.

Owain glanced toward Penasgell, who gave him a short quick nod, and then he said, "Alright, just a short game then."

"Good lad, good lad, thank you," said the king as he hurriedly arranged the pieces.

"It's a beautiful set," Owain complimented him on his game board.

"Thank you. I had it specially crafted by a gifted eastern artisan. It's my pride and joy!"

The perfectly square game board was patterned in squares of gold and ivory: eight by eight squares outlined in silver. Each game piece was finely sculpted of gold for one side and ivory for the other.

"Shall we draw for sides?" asked the king before they sat down.

"Your choice," Owain acquiesced.

"Very well," said the king, sitting down in front of the gold pieces. "I have heard your father taught you this game. He is a very fine player."

"Yes, Sire," Owain said, surveying the board.

From then on, their playing was relatively silent, the weight of a piece being positioned or captured the only sound made by either man. Peredyr, Gawain, and Penasgell watched intently, as each player's focused concentration seemed to move the pieces of their own accord, each action having a hypnotic effect upon their audience. Penasgell perceived the complex game within her mind's eye from a broader visionary field, seeing each piece as a living, thriving being: as pawns moved about, sentries around the fort moved in tandem with the game. She saw kings and queens of neighboring kingdoms inhabit the identities of the pieces as they were directed across the board. When pieces were captured, the gifted young seer watched their warriors and liegemen respond in dismay, engaging in efforts of rescue, battling on horse with sword and lance. Bishops conferred, advising the security or advancing of kings. Time became distorted, as all attention, movements of the sky, or temper of the air felt bound to the game and the two intensified players. Many pieces had fallen, removed to the side. A fierce balance of power held Owain and Gwenddoleu rigidly in their chairs. Suddenly, as the number of sentries upon the wall behind the king greatly increased; a distant call of ravens rose within the air, drawing clouds to hover over the Roman wall, creating an enveloping shadow. Then the ravens came. Hundreds and hundreds of loud cawing ravens filled the air, rising as a wall of wings and sound behind Owain.

The Prince of Rheged looked up at Gwenddoleu staring directly into his eyes and said, "I believe we have a draw."

"I believe we do," the king responded.

"Another time then?" asked Owain

"Another time," said the king.

The sky was clear, free of clouds, without a bird in sight. The sentries were once again sparsely placed. The servants cleared the tables. All things seemed to be as any afternoon in that pastoral setting, with no one suggesting it had ever been otherwise.

As the cousins departed the fortified wall, Penasgell smiled at Owain, handing to him a single black raven's feather, and saying: "Good game, Prince of the Raven Kindred."

"Thank you for playing along. By that I mean your restraint, as that lecherous bastard was almost drooling over you. The lads and I were near inciting war to protect you," Owain reflected.

"Thank you. I am grateful, for both your concern and your wise restraint. His advances were utterly repugnant, oozing up from his dark disgusting soul. I saw into him. It took all of my forbearance to keep from cringing and jolting away in disgust. This king is a dark stain upon the Cymri."

Her description of the shadowy king left them all silent, as they rode on to Caer Lliwelydd. Finally reaching that grand stronghold below the Solway Firth, the citadel felt safe and secure. Owain and his cousins were greeted with immediate attention to their horses and an announcement of these noble heirs at the main hall. King Urien and Queen Orwen were quick to welcome the new visitors, embracing them warmly.

"Where's Llamorhad?" Urien asked, immediately noticing his absence and the saddened pause in Owain's response. "Oh no, what has happened, is he gone?"

Owain explained the tragedy; and then relayed the sad news of his aunt, the king's sister. Urien responded with mournful silence, sitting down in his regal chair, dropping into reflective memories: poignant moments of their childhood, her wedding to Eliffer, their pride for their many sons. Quickly he turned to Peredyr and Penasgell.

"I am saddened by this news of your dear mother. You must know that you are received here as our own children now," said Urien, while grasping the hand of his wife and queen, she nodding, looking upon their niece and nephew with compassionate eyes.

"Where is Gwrgi? Is he well?" Urien inquired further.

"Yes Sire," Peredyr spoke up. "He chose to remain at home, hold down the fort, as it were, carving a lovely headstone for Mother."

"He is a bright and learned lad," Penasgell added, "I am sure he will engage you in a spirited discussion of history and philosophy one day, Sire. For now, his solitude is his refuge."

"Very well, we all must mourn in our own way. He sounds like an insightful young man. I look forward to meeting him."

After the guests had some time to relax from their journey, they joined their aunt, uncle and cousins to dine. Both Owain and Gawain were eager to boast of Peredyr's handling of a javelin during their encounter with the marauders from Bryneich.

"That disgruntled little kingdom has become a thorn in the side of the Cymri," Urien commented.

"What is their gripe?" Gawain asked.

"Three things, as I see it," Urien explained. "Firstly, they are a branch of our Coel Hen lineage from Garbinion that has only retained a smaller portion of the north. They are without matriarchal estate: so their sovereignty is held by brawling with and dominating their cousins. Second, the Angles are at their back doorstep, inciting them to jab at these continental neighbors or bed them, neither seemingly satisfying. Third, yet not fully proven, even after all these years, there seems to be a covert alliance with some faction of the Franks, sons of Clovis actively backstabbing each other while trying to eliminate distant cousins as they seek refuge here, in our lands. Our dear Llamorhad was a shattered survivor of these malicious conspiracies, and one of his last battles was against those Bryneich villains, who still are likely attempt to bring in Frankish support against the

Angles – those serpentine keeled sons of Ida that continually threaten all the Cymri."

"How long have these Angles and other Saesneg been invading our lands?" Peredyr asked.

"Well over a century and a half, laddie." Urien continued. "Vortigern, in the south, opened the sea door to the Jutes and Angles. Bryneich may think they can win at Vortigern's dangerous game."

"He certainly lost than one, up in flames, having a Saesneg wife didn't stop his in-laws from backstabbing the Britons." Owain added.

"Yes, Gwrgi told me of the 'Night of the Long Knives' and Ambrosius and Einion Yrth, and other Pendragons before you, Sire," Peredyr eagerly said to the king.

"And there was my Uncle Emrys, the 'Myrlyn', have you heard of him: who as a wee lad faced Vortigern, redeemed his faulty tower, saving his own young life from a bloody death?" Urien quizzed the lad.

"Yes Sire, the 'Myrlyn' was then our great uncle as well, not by blood, but by marriage to great Aunt Nimue," answered Peredyr.

"Very good lad," said the king, "yet he was a distant relation by blood through his Brychan mother, Ebradil. Your grandmother Nyfain was a Brychan."

"Sire, what of the Arthwyr, as prophesies foretell? Will there be such a king from the north to lead the Cymri, against Angles, Saxons, and all the Saesneg?" Peredyr probed the old prophesy.

"Ah, the 'Arthwyr' – perhaps Ambrosius was the Arthwyr, perhaps my cousin Arthwys from Elmet, perhaps Owain Ddantgwyn, perhaps Einion Yrth, perhaps my son Owain will be? Perhaps the 'Arthwyr' is in each of us who fights to save the Cymri from all invaders, especially those that lurk within us, pitting cousin against cousin. It was the Myrlyn that said this is where every battle is won or lost, within the soul of each of us."

"I believe it was in young Myrlyn's dream, Sire," Penasgell described, "the dream of the two dragons; I had heard of this from the heirs of Elmet. In Emrys Myrlyn's dream were a red dragon and a white dragon, battling for the soul of the Cymri, a battle between the blood and the light, a battle within each of us."

"Yes, yes," Urien said, stroking his chin. "I have spoken with Taliesin of this dream vision. In the end, the dragons merge as one."

"Ah, I see," continued Penasgell. "The light and the blood are one essence, manifested in our lives, our human forms, our departed ancestors, and our unborn heirs – with us now, in the Otherworld."

"My uncle, the 'Myrlyn', the 'Raven of Awen', was a fascinating figure. We are happy to have you here with us, Ceindrych Penasgell. Afallon calls to you, I am sure. Your wisdom and insight at such a young age displays that so clearly," King Urien recognized.

"Thank you, Sire. You are most gracious in receiving us here so warmly. It does indeed seem to be the time for me to step away from the history with my brothers to the destiny with my sisters," said Penasgell, bowing to the king and queen.

Ceindrych Penasgell did travel on to the Afallon Ysgol with Gawain and Peredyr, finally meeting her mother's cousin Vivianne and Gawain's mother Morcades. Penasgell was instantly accepted by her two new mentors, assuming the loving roles of a wise mother figure and grandmother to her. They were the gifted feminine seers of their time, brought together as timeless sisters of Afallon.

Gawain was glad to return to his mates on Ynys Manau; but burdened with relaying the sad news of Llamorhad's death. Llen seemed to take it the hardest. Llew and Baedd had witnessed so much loss in their Frankish homeland that Llamorhad's sudden passing was taken as yet another blow upon the emotionally battered bodies they had been born into. Until reaching the idyllic life on Ynys Manau, these lads were severed from their families of origin. Their new bonds of brotherhood had been forged with wise surrogate parents, shaping them with the skill of brilliant smiths of metallurgy into the gold of wisdom, the silver of knowledge, the bronze of valor, and the steel of strength. They would be emerging from this forge once again, soon, to compete at the Aenach Garman that summer season. Owain had been seeing to the guardians of the wells throughout the kingdoms of Rheged and Gallwyddel. Each well was protected by a single warrior, where one of the maidens of Afallon served the sacred waters to travelers and visitors on pilgrimage to the holy wells and fountains for healing and spiritual inspiration. Owain's appointment as defender of the wells was a great honor bestowed upon the Prince of Rheged by the priestesses of Afallon. This season Owain planned to compete with his brothers-in-arms at the Aenach Garman. Kingdoms throughout the isles would be attending, maintaining a truce from all strife and division that plagued their relations. An air of confidence existed among the kingdoms, each believing their own young men would honor the kings and queens of the Cymri with heroic abilities displayed at the grand games. It was a unique respite from the often troubled world.

Garman and the Gates of Eden

Aenach Garman was a sacred occasion for the Scotti, the Cymri and even the Picts, many of the dynasties of those northern lands intermarried with heirs of southern kingdoms. The festival was held every three years at the coastal hub of Laigin, Scotti kingdom and ancestral home to the Brychan clan and other Cymric nobles. Kings of Laigin had hosted this grand event for centuries, drawing the best warriors from across the lands. Skills of battle and athletic ability were the most anticipated events, allowing rival kingdoms to challenge each under a truce of peace. Bards and storytellers would fill the night air with their lyrical songs and fantastic tales of adventure, wowing the crowded campfires after each day's strenuous activities had subsided with the setting sun. The fortnight of events began with a sacred honoring of the dead who had lost their lives in past seasons of battle, or to disease, or to the inevitable passing of time. This was followed by a great celebration of new beginnings, with mass marriages, betrothals, or "hand-fasting" – where couples would become engaged for an informal period of time to test the temper of their love to one another. In between events and ceremonies, artisans and craftspeople displayed their creations, for sale, barter, and judged competitions. Smiths, jewelers, weavers, armorers, woodcarvers, and imaginative folk of every stripe convened. Three ships from Afallon and Rheged alone carried the lads, Taliesin and several bards, horses, weaponry, crafts and goods of varied kinds, barrels of wine and casks of ale, with fresh meat and fowl for the feasting.

Prior to this grand event, there had been tensions among the northern neighboring kingdoms. Dalriada had arising disputes with Alt Clud over borderlands near Gallwyddel. The King of Solway, Gwenddoleu was eager to stir this conflict, finding an ally in Aedan of Dalriada, if war broke out against Alt Clud. Aedan was not too keen on any commitment to Gwenddoleu. Between Aedan and his cousin Conall they found that they could play both sides to their advantage through shrewd diplomacy: Aedan duplicitously proffering an alliance with Solway and Conall with Alt Clud.

After Rhydderch's marriage to Gwendydd, Gwenddoleu was still determined to have the Queen of Alt Clud to his bed, and take the kingdom as his royal bedding if he could. It became the ardent task of Myrddin, Gwendydd's protective twin, to pull the King of Solway off of his obsession with the capture of his sister's coital fig leaf. Myrddin had become favored by the king, not for his verse, but precisely for the purpose of furthering the king's insatiable vice. The fact that he could not openly have Gwendydd, made her even more desirable to him. Much to Myrddin's consternation, his sister was strangely drawn to Gwenddoleu, even though she married Rhydderch – albeit arranged by her parents, not by her desires – impulsively open to the advances of Gwenddoleu. Myrddin found himself unwittingly in the position of a procurer rather than protector of his twin sister's fidelity. She repeatedly engaged in passionate liaisons with the King of Solway, on the pretense of visits and support of her bardic twin. Myrddin was completely distraught by his loss of his sister to two different men, feeling violated upon his own body, seeing her as his intimate prenatal mate for life. Conjuring his most earnest and resolute powers of imaginative coercion, Myrddin devised a scheme to appeal to Gwenddoleu's basest appetites and lust for power. After sufficient time elapsed between his sister's liaisons with the libidinous king, and as rising frustration had been mounting within Gwenddoleu, Myrddin planted the seeds of his manipulative ploy.

"Sire, I am continually stunned by the lack of respect and recognition that you have received from the Cymric Cylch. You and your ancestors have been the foundation of this Wall of Tyne, ever since its erection by the Roman Emperor Hadrian centuries ago. Your stature is clearly evidenced by the complete loyalty and respect held by your warriors and liegemen. Few kings can claim such devout fealty. I can think of no other king that has had a history like yours, except possibly the legendary and renowned Niall Noigiallach of Eirenn," Myrddin set the snare for the king's conceit.

"Of course, I know of the great King Niall Noigiallach; but I do not recall the details of his early life," Gwenddoleu responded.

"I am happy to tell you of his legend and history, which I'm sure you will recall, Sire," Myrddin continued. "Niall was the son of the great king Eochaid Mugmedon. Niall's brothers were the sons of Eochaid's queen Mongfind; but Niall was the son of the king's captive Cymric slave, Cairenn. So then, Niall had no claim to the throne as a bastard son of the king's slave. He was raised with the other lads, but was not given the same respect, always needing to prove he was worthy. After reaching maturity, Niall and his half-brothers were on a long hunt, becoming lost after a rigorous chase through the deep forests of northern Eirenn. Wandering through the maze of wood and bracken, they became grievously hungered and thirsting. Finally they came upon a secluded fountain and well, guarded by a hideous horse-faced hag and her vicious beasts, forbidding their relief, unless one of the lads were to give the monstrous hag a kiss. Niall's half-brothers were revolted by the request, refusing to go near her and her odious stench. But Niall was not only un-dissuaded; he kissed the hag incessantly and made passionate love to her, while the others looked-on in disgust at his robust mounting of the hag. At the peak of this heroic performance, the hag transformed into a beautiful goddess – the goddess of the sovereignty of all the lands of Eirenn. Niall and his half-brothers drank of the fountain and were given a feast. Their path of return was presented before them, and Niall was declared High King, by right of the sovereignty of the goddess, conferring that right to rule upon Niall and his progeny throughout time. This was the first 'Feis Temro'."

"Ah, yes, the ritual mounting of a mare by the new king, ceremonial bathing in her blood, and the feast of her flesh as the sovereignty of the land – 'the Feast of Tara' – do they still do that in Eirenn?" Gwenddoleu questioned.

"I think **not**, Sire," Myrddin answered. "Here is where the enactment of the myth has disregarded the essence of Niall's power and sovereignty. This old legend refers to his union with a Maré, not a mare, not a hag, not a monster, but a priestess of the well, a goddess on earth. What I propose, Sire, is that you wed a maiden of the well, a priestess, a Maré, bathed in the blood of her virginity, breaking the veil of her chastity, and remaining loyal to her as your goddess of sovereignty. You could seize claim to sovereignty of all the northern lands you desire, for you and your progeny, ordained and anointed by your union and devotion to the virgin goddess who surrenders all to you. Perhaps you could even be, if I dare suggest, the Arthwyr."

"Perhaps, perhaps . . . I believe you have defined this clearly, Master Myrddin, what it is to be finally recognized, to be the embodiment of sovereignty, the unquestioned and unrivaled power." The king responded, dazed, in stunned awe of his own self-aggrandizement. "I must find this perfect virgin goddess and devote my attention to her."

"You are truly a wise king to see this Sire. I am at your service, at any time you require further advisement," said Myrddin, bowing repeatedly as he exited the king's presence.

Myrddin was elated, nearly bounding out of his skin to believe he had finally convinced Gwenddoleu to leave his sister Gwendydd alone. It appeared to be a complete success. The king had rebuffed Gwendydd's attempts to covertly meet him on numerous occasions prior to Myrddin's departure for the Aenach Garman that season. Myrddin joined his mentor Taliesin, with two other bards, Aneirin ap Dynod and Llywarch ap Elidyr, another cousin of Urien, to expound their verse at the festival in Laigin. Many warriors of the Cymri, as well as spectators of noble birth from their kingdoms made the voyage across the Sea of Eirenn. Most every king felt secure enough with the pact of truce during these few weeks to leave the defense of their lands to subordinate troops, while many of their most elite warriors competed at the Aenach Garman.

The festival opened with the traditional rituals. Prayer and chanting, honoring the dead, soon shifting to a celebration of the living. Kings, druids, and priests of Laigin presided over the ceremonies and events, with the chosen princess of the festival later to be awarding the prize garland crowns to the victors of each endeavor. This season the selected princess chosen for her beauty, charm, and noble breeding was Gwenhwyfar of Laigin – crowned the bestowing maiden of Aenach Garman. Llenlleawg found himself transfixed by her every gesture, expression and breath, glancing her way any opportune moment he could.

"Are you drunk or something mate?" Bercnaf questioned the lunacy of his friend's gaze toward the princess. "You best sober-up if you want to be up for this trial of your life."

"Oh, I'm up. Awen and the Sidhe are charging my veins and sinews with the power of mountains, streams, and eternal passion," Llen answered with the joy of a smitten romantic.

"Shite! Don't tell me, the princess maiden of the entire festival – could you set your sights a little higher?" Bercnaf realized as he saw Llen's attention spellbound to the princess. "No, don't think so, no, the moon, that's it – shoot the moon, mate."

"The moon, the stars, the heavens, from there and there alone comes my victory!" Llen announced boldly, slapping Bercnaf on the shoulder as he dashed off for his first event.

Llen took charge of his opening contest masterfully, riding his horse with precision, wielding weaponry with speed and agility through a maze of obstacles. Gawain excelled in both falconry and hand to hand fighting. Peredyr, a bit younger than most contestants, amazed the crowds and judges with his distance, skill, and accuracy of javelin throwing. Owain did quite well with sword and shield, a highly competitive field, especially against multiple attackers, his heightened sense of hearing and side vision allowing him to catch and anticipate his opponent's every movement. All of the lads trained by Galehaut and Taliesin seemed to have an extra edge, beyond normal response and perception, baffling many of their older and more experienced adversaries. After the action filled days of competing, they had time to confer about this sense of mastery with their brothers of Afallon.

"Is it just me, or are you lads feeling a second wind rising up against these veteran legends of Eirenn and elsewhere?" Owain directly posed the question.

"I know what you mean, lad. I always engage with confidence, but those first few throws of my match with a fierce Pictish brute, surprised me as much as him," Gawain confirmed.

"It's the mountains and the streams, lads," Llen said with complete certainty. "I don't believe any of them know it. The Raven Kindred of your Uncle Myrlyn has instilled in us that flow of power. Galehaut and Taliesin taught us well. The Raven of Awen assists our every move."

"It must be true," Llew added. "Baedd and I did far better than we ever thought we would at each trial."

"Not to say the competition was weak, far from that; I said to Llew today – I don't know where it came from, but I bested one of these ogre-like monster-men, shocking the shite out of him, leaving me feel like some kind of a David defeating Goliath!" Baedd said, rousing a round of laughter.

"It is oddly laughable. But we have been at this for years, lads," Llen said, moving his arms in one of the practiced training motions. "Feel it? It is there within us. It is just as Galehaut and Taliesin told us: keep at it, and there is no stopping the Cymri."

The Cymric bards also did exceptionally well, dazzling crowds and critics, shifting from their native tongue to dialects of the Scotti and Picts from time to time. Aneirin soon received the agnomen "Gwodryd" – of the flowing verse. It was on the final day of competition that Llen and the other lads showed their true prowess. Llen bested every archer from every kingdom in events of riding and standing archery. As a leader in several events, he was set against a few other leaders in single combat, using various weapons of choice. Most competitors were near battle-weary by this final day, having run a long and arduous foot race, a chilling swim in Garman Bay, and a dangerous climb of the cliffs on the day before. The Cymric lads of Afallon, again, led the pack that day.

When Llen faced his final foes of Aenach Garman, no man was by any account fresh and fully rested. Each match was declared at first blood. No man was expected to face death during this contest of skill in a time of truce. Llen managed to make the first cut with sword in his two opening matches. His final opponent was of the Ui Niall, distant cousin of Colum Cille, possibly the finest swordsman of Eirenn. Llen mustered all he could of the fluidity of streams, and the strength of mountains to meet his adversary with every strike, parry, and movement. In a close clash of blades, nearly catching the skin of Llen's arm to draw first blood, Llen broke free, quickly striking the rattled descendant of Niall Noigiallach with the pommel of his sword, staggering the swordsman of Eirenn, breaking the skin of his brow to bleed down his cheek. The man dropped like a felled tree, face down, motionless. Llen just stood there at first; but then sensing something terribly wrong, sheathed his sword, kneeling beside the man, rolling him over on his back. The man of Eirenn lay there still as stone without a breath. Llen laid his hands upon the man's head and chest, as members of his clan dashed forward to either assist or attack Llenlleawg. As they neared, Llen raised one hand, gesturing for all to stand back. And then, he entered a place within his own heart, a place of the source of strength, of love, and of healing he had come to know quite well from his life at Afallon. He leaned down as if to kiss this fallen warrior, but yet only to allow the center of his own soul to merge with the man of Eirenn. Momentarily, the man's eyes opened, Llen pulling his adversary to his breast, helping him to stand and greet the cheering crowd. Cymri, Scotti, Picts and men of distant kingdoms rushed in to lift Llen above the throngs, carrying him in triumph to the steps of risers where the kings and the maiden princess Gwenhwyfar were waiting.

The King of Laigin rose proclaiming: "It is clear we have our champion of arms today – young Llenlleawg of Afallon."

With that, Gwenhwyfar crowned Llen with a gilded wreath, kissing him upon the lips, looking at him as if she was in the presence of a god. This moment of intimate contact through her eyes to his soul, seemingly silencing all outer sound, sight, senses or motion around them fused a profound connection that was his deepest reward of the day. Then and there, he knew she was the mirroring of his heart and spirit in eternity, revealed as his mate for this life and beyond.

Much celebration followed this fortnight of competitive adventure, culminating on the eve of Lughnasadh, or Gwyl Awst. Peredyr was awarded master of the javelin, from then on called "freich dur" or steel arm. Gawain received the awards for both hand to hand battle and falconry. Finally the Cymri of Afallon were recognized as the champion team. And young Llen as the champion of arms of Aenach Garman was to be called by kings, warriors and bards of many kingdoms – Llenlleawg Gwyddel – man of Eirenn.

Aside from his great victory, Llen and Gwenhwyfar were so powerfully drawn to each other that day, making every effort to meet somehow later in the evening. She suggested a secluded waterfall, upstream, well beyond the mouth of the river descending into Garman Bay. Each of them took care not to be seen riding out separately from the late night celebrations. Arriving at the site chosen for their secret rendezvous, they were compelled into each other's arms like the force of the falls. Disregarding all caution, immersed in the showering vapors, they were soon stripped naked and unguarded, savoring the flesh of their senses exposed to the enveloping moisture. And yet, he refrained from compromising her maidenhood, as he so easily could have, and as they both so greatly desired. Their pleasure and passion was nonetheless fulfilled as if they had revealed what lay beneath the veil of a new bride to her bridegroom. Later that night, in utmost secrecy, they held their own private handfast ceremony, pledging what their souls had already determined at the Aenach Garman. Returning to their separate beds before dawn, they did not know when they would have such time as this together again. Llen would return to Afallon that day, and she to her family estates, as a princess soon likely to be publically betrothed to a prince or king.

The short voyage to Cymric lands was joyous to his brothers-in-arms, but to Llen it was a triumphant wrenching of his heart – as victor of battling arms, yet longing for Gwenhwyfar's tender touch. This was but a foreshadowing of sorrow. Arrival at Ynys Manau was met with grave news. The foreboding signs that the prescient women of Afallon had been seeing had become manifest in the kingdoms of Rheged and Gallwyddel.

While most of the Cymric kings and warriors attentions had been upon the games of Aenach Garman, Gwenddoleu, King of Solway chose to enact his destiny in a grasp for lust and power. Inspired by Myrddin's elaborate ploy to have the king take a Maré, a maiden of the wells to wife, he took her and others by violent assault, many at night, snuffing-out their innocence like the fragile candles of light they were. At numerous sacred wells near and north of the River Eden, Gwenddoleu and his loyal troop of warriors sought-out his prize Maré, seeking the one most exceptional beauty to stimulate his desire and fulfill his hunger for dominance. With each fountain and well grossly under defended against attack, this depraved king and his predatory pack of vermin, made their way across the land, raping maidens of the holy wells, murdering their protectors, and robbing the sites of sacred artifacts. Until the savage Gwenddoleu found his chosen bride, he allowed his men to repeatedly rape the maidens that they encountered on their grotesque rampage over purity and sanctity. Most of these young innocents were killed or became hostage whores in the wake of being violated. Others cowered in the forests, some, tragically taking their own lives in a last futile attempt of escape from the horror of capture. Trampled like the rows of corn they rode through on this errand of evil, the dark king captured and raped his chosen slave bride, taking her to his lair, extending her torment at his leisure.

The Cymric kingdoms, their kings, their queens, their liegemen, and their sworn warriors were enraged. Civil war against the kingdom of Solway was imminent. Even the land, the earth, the trees of the forests, the crops of the fields, the bloodied grasses of the meadows seemed to grieve from this horrendous assault upon the true sanctity of life. There had been grievous conflicts among the Cymri in its darkest moments of history: from Vortigern and Sawyl Penuchel to Cwm Llan – but this struck at the pure nature of existence. The island world of Britannia, oft-time called Prydain was hit by a severing crack in time, jarring the eternal. Sadly, dark events like these continue to occur in this tenuous world of time and matter, as they did in ancient ages of fallen kingdoms. Prydain is a persistent yet crumbling realm, attempting to survive and rebuild itself from its own rubble. It is limited by contracted entities insisting that this incremental reality is their own identity, conquering and abusive of others forced into servitude. All the while, the Otherworld fluidly supports and surrounds these islands of identity that we cling to and claim to be defined by. The land does not stop at the shore, it simply goes deeper. Trees find rooted footings, even as the earth and its children are raped. The innocents bear children; and we continue. We create, protect, conjure, and assail trees of the first fruits, trees of family, trees of kingdoms, trees of belief. From these grand and terrible trees, from vile acts against our own nature, from roots and shadows of these trees thriving to grow and change with each turning season, and now I, submerged within the tiny cup of mind that I believe myself to be; this bard has become aware as blood, as light, and as love – I was conceived by this shocking event. And from here, I am born into life.

Chapter Four ~ Battle of the Trees

$\mathcal{A}$ violent knock on the unhinged door of humanity has hit us all as squarely as that first slap of our bare buttocks at birth. Like a sharp rap on the head, rooted conflict begins within the serpentine core of the mind: its vibration in the bones arming the backlash of hardened heads to strike-out against brothers – drawing blood. Just cause soon becomes irrevocable, dividing states enflamed by searing cuts of deep wounding. These embattled states are not of plotted lands, but of kindled thought and riled fervor, roots of tormented souls, striking upon the earthen beds of fallen bodies, burrowed into their own separate knotted skulls. A seed was planted, hundreds of generations before, sprouting now to birth a recurring beast – the serpentine parasite of humanity – clawing its way over each branch to strip bare the bark, breaking the boughs. Any fallen seed could rise into a greater tree – the true oak – flourishing for centuries, though scarred by each brutal season. From this most mighty tree we can gather limbs and leaves to build with, cushioning the blows, generating language that can heal, not harm. Every family of trees has its role, its best suited purpose; and our loss of one mars the life of all. A leaf becomes a letter; letters become language; language becomes our creed; and we become our words. The words linger, mimicking and mocking an appearance, a dream, a vision. It is the role of the druid and bard to shift the shape of words to carry more than they appear to hold, allowing the listener to hear more than is spoken, becoming a knower of the oak, becoming once again seed and branch of the immutable tree of truth. We eat of fruit or poison; we burn or build; we shelter with love or crucify – our heartwood split for the fire.

The Master Pen Bard Taliesin answered his calling to decry the violence against innocence. His haunting call to watch and bare witness speaks to us all, for our embattled soul of one family tree, destine to be reborn again and again until all of our roots reach the opening sky, joyfully bridging worlds; whereas each entry into war repeats humanity's insane venture into the bowels of the beast. Violence begets violence as a mind warped field of battle is formed by trees and shrubs, who, animated with madness violate natural law, uprooting themselves from their common shared earth, while blinding clear sight of the sky.

Battle of the Trees	**Kat Godeu**
I have been absorbed in the fire.	Bum yspwg yn tan.
I have been wood in the thicket.	Bum gwyd yngwartan.
Nothing have I not been since	Nyt mi wyt ny gan
in this small chanting	keint yr yn bychan
chanting the battle of treetops	keint ygkat godeu bric
racking time-bound rulers.	rac prydein wledic.

Fleeting hundred candled daughters
intruding corruptors
– a thousand aggrandized fleeting –
upon nine hundred head of corn of age
which battle for endurance
under base of tongue.

Gweint veirch canholic
llyghessoed meuedic
gweint mil mawrein
arnaw yd oed canpen
a chat er dygnawt
dan von y tanawt.

It is another battle
in the skull-scruff,
black toad forks
upon nine hundred claws
the pied-crested snake
a hundred animated
   impregnated deceptions
torment in the flesh
becoming fortified, benumbed,
watching seedlings debauched
wanderers wailed
captives chastised
unraveling the britons
who best wrathful
appearances upon heaven
upon accusations of grace.

A chat arall yssyd
yn y wegilyd
llyffan du gaflaw
cant ewin arnaw
neidyr vreith gribawe
cant eneit trwy bechawt
aboenir yny chnawt
bum ykaer, uefenhit
yt gryssynt wellt gawyd
kenynt gerdoryon
kryssynt katuaon
datwyrein y vrythron
a oreu gwytyion
gwelwyssit ar neifon
ar grist o achwysson.

When they find deliverance,
some part of the abundance,
that which answers to faith
through language and elements
conjured liberated trees
from silence in the hosts
and hindered masses
prepare to handover battle
when enchanted trees
the hopeful trees
divergent trees
out of fourfold spark
increase around heiresses
truncated in sadness.

Hyt pan y gwarettei
y ren rwy digonsei
as attebwys dofyd
trwy ieith ac eluwyd
rithwch reidawc wyd
gantaw yn llutd
a rwystraw peblic
kat arllaw annefic
pan swynhwyt godeu
y gobeith an godeu
dygottorynt godeu
o pendrydant taneu
kwydynt am aereu
trychwn trymdieu.

Disarmed garden maidens
issued around remorse
first lineage, first maidens
invest sleepless lives
not sewn in hymns
blood upon men's thighs
increasing three injustices
that bitter pause

Dyar gardei bun
tardei am atgun
blaen llin, blaen bun
budyant buch anhun
nyn gwnei emellun
gwaet gwyr hyt an clun
mwyhaf teir aryfgrt
a cheweris ymbyt

as if a druid	ac vn a deryw
out of flooded sense	o ystyr dilyw
which is the Christ crucified	a Christ croccaw
that brother's day of reckoning at hand.	a dyd brawt rac llaw.
First lineage is Alder	Gwern blaen llin
that feeble summons	a want gysseuin
Willows that laugh	Helyc a cherdin
soon in the evening world	buant hwyr yr vydin
Plumwood is scarce	Eirinwyd yspin
from the molestation of women	anwhant o dynin
correcting riff-raff	keri kywrenhin
mutinous objectifying	gwrthrychyat gwrthrin
quite quick-wood	fuonwyd eithyt
against host sinew	erbyn llu o gewryt
sewn passion	auanwyd gwneithyt
best not asserted	ny goreu emwyt
the encompassed life	yr amgelwch bywt
Rosewood and Woodbine	Ryswyd a Gwyduwyt
as ivy of the mind	ac eido yr y bryt
like quick-grass to the dirt.	mor eithin yr gryt.
Cherries were sought	Siryan seuyssit
Birch of the high mind	Bedw yr y vawr vryt
was late arrayed	bu hwyr gwiscysseit
not of the cowardice	nyt yr y lyfryrder
but of the grandiose	namyn yr y vawred
Laburnam idealized mind	Auron delis bryt
that interpreted loud foreign land	allmyr uch allfryt
Fir and Pine is the portal	Ffenitwyd ygkynted
seat of conflict	kadeir gygwrysed
Ash most exalted	omi goreu Ardyrched
ranked before sovereign	rac bron teyrned
Elm of the masses	Llwyf yr y varanhed
not side-stepping footpath	nyt oscoes troetued
for gifts and ankles	er laddie a pherued
and unto the very end.	ac eithaf a diwed.
Hazel trees judge	Collwyd bernyssit
airing our inscription	eiryf dy aryfgryt
hedge of blessed life	gwyros gwyn y vyt
bull battle-fierce state	tarw trinteryn byt
sea edge and inlet	morawc a moryt
Beech trees prospering	Ffawyd ffynyessit
Holly sprouting	Kelyn glessyssit
becoming valorous	bu ef y gwrhyt

Whitethorns beckon	Yspydat amnat
infecting outward grasp	heint ech y aghat
fitting oppression	gwiwyd gorthorat
oppressing the gate	gorthoryssit ygat
plundering ferns	rhedyn anreithat
broom-rape rack and rant	banadyl rac bragat
in that trenched wound.	yn rychua briwat.
Quick-grass never became stuck	Eithin ny bu vat
by those rabble	yt hynny gwerinat
Heather beckons benefit	Gruc buddy amnat
those rabble bedeviled	dy werin swynat
as far as men are prosecuted	hyd gwyr erlynyat
Oaks quickening	Derw buanawr
god-reckoning tremors out of heaven	racdaw crynei nef allawr
innate brave porters	glelyn glew drussiawr
name in earth-breath	y enw ym peullawr
Cudgelwood tares	Clafuswyd kygres
comrades remain	kymraw arodes
forsaken, rejected	gwrthodi, gwrthodes
others from piercing	ereill o tylles
best pear-sweet tyranny	per goreu gormes
in a plummeting wide field.	ym plymlwyt maes.
Most sublime word	Goruthaw kywd
and sweat veiled tree	aches veilon wyd
Chestnut of shame	Kastan kewilyd
mutinous marsh-wood	gwrthryat fenwyd
layers of bitter stones	handit du muchyd
layers of bent mountains	handit crwm mynyd
layers of hazel-wood lands	handit kyl coetdyd
layers of great myriad wedge.	handit kyn myr mawr.
Watch for when the hour	Er pan gigleu yr awr
within bower of Birch tops	an deilas blaen Bedw
within developed resolution	an dathrith datedw
within entangled Oak tops	an maglas blaen Derw
out of besieged benefit of the Oak.	o warchen maelderw.

The Cymric Cylch would confront the dark army of Gwenddoleu, in the field of battle since called Arfderydd; where the arms and weapons of the Oak would begin to reclaim sovereignty for the wounded hearts of Eden's valley, as Cherubim with flaming sword, to keep the way of the tree of life. "Arfderydd" was the call to arms of the ancient druids, when nemetons of oaks had been severed by invading armies. This time the invasive venomous strain within their own clans must be held to account. The brutal stage was set. All effort in the past to avoid civil war had been futile. It seems the peace could only be held for a time, when dark ambitions like those of Gwenddoleu were lurking. His finagling attempts to broker alliances were pointless, now that he had assaulted and defiled what was held most sacred to everyone, aside from his accomplices in the rape of these precious innocents. Those who had considered an alliance with the dark king before, abandoned that grotesque illusion after his egregious rampage. Strangely, Gwenddoleu still believed he would be revered as high king. Somehow his delusion of complete power was fed by this savage assault. His immediate followers and fellow perpetrators were also thriving on this abhorrent fleeting victory, unconscious of the blighted legacy that would scar the land and the Cymric people.

Myrddin and Gwendydd were of the few within Gwenddoleu's inner circle who realized the impact. Gwendydd, already dismayed by the King of Solway's rejection of her, was suddenly and thoroughly repulsed by him, stricken as if by illness, her own body feeling a debilitating and revolting reaction to her past intimacy with the depraved king. Her twin Myrddin seemingly lost all touch with reality, knowing it was by his own persuasive manipulation of the deranged king that led the aspiring despot to launch his vile campaign. Myrddin disappeared, retreating into the woodlands of the north, mentally afflicted by the inevitable carnage that would unfold between his kinsmen – imagining the violent cleaving strikes upon each one from his own words – haunted by visions of the raped and battered, the butchered, and the dead.

Rheged and Alt Clud rallied for battle, Gallwyddel allying with them, joined by Ebrauc and Lothian. Penllanw was divided, with many of Gwenddoleu's villainous accomplices being kin of those clans. Rhun Hir of Gwynedd had feigned alliance with Solway, mainly by reason of his tensions with Rhydderch and Alt Clud. Aedan and Conall of Dalriada were in a similar position, leading Gwenddoleu to believe he was not alone. This, again, was his delusion. Gwynedd and Dalriada would no more support Solway now, than they would join the Saesneg. They too felt the assault upon divine sovereignty and that heritage of the goddess bestowed upon them from their Celtic mothers, grandmothers, and matriarchal ancestors through this ungodly attack of sisters, daughters and blessed mothers of the Cymri. Gwenddoleu believed he could ride straight into Caer Lliwelydd and take control of Rheged, imagining Alt Clud and Lothian would follow his grand instatement as High King of the Cymri. His self aggrandizement and Myrddin's self descent into madness were equal yet opposite breaks with reality, insidiously infecting Gwendydd with a flooding visceral pall upon her, as that fickle and forbidden object of desire for those two madmen and her cuckold king of Alt Clud.

The battle lands had been marred for centuries, and would be again and again, in that region where the ancient wall met the Solway Firth and its marshes. Somehow it held an eerily strange beauty – an area demarcating disparate worlds, a land of creatures surviving at the edges of kingdoms. Overhead, the disquieting, whirring drone of snipe tails etched against the dead silence before battle, as dragon flies and reptiles gathered, awaiting the return of the giant heath butterflies, released from their cocoon crypts,

ushering fleeting mites of souls, only to be met by the carnivorous sundew –
seeded in the wretched mire, their sticky leaf pads clutching, arresting,
trapping and smothering tiny wings. Any attempt at flight was to be cut
short, devoured by the persistent and recurring beast, ever lying in wait
within forms of death, beneath the deceptive surface forms of life. Between
the rivers Esk and Lyne, between river and bog, into that hollow and marsh,
bloodied, beheaded or drowned, soddened and smothered by the peat lands,
the army of Gwenddoleu fell. Peat domes of the Solway mosses had formed
dead, stagnant pools, building for millennia, leaving wet hollows, now filled
with the dismembered dead. Heads and limbs, castrated parts and grotesque
fragments of the dark army were placed on pikes for carrion of scavenger
beasts. No prisoners were taken. No trials were held. No burials were
performed, only swift and dishonorable deaths, for the untamed natural
world and its vermin to reclaim their own.

Many of the kinsmen of Myrddin and Gwendydd were killed or had
retreated before the final fray. Even their families, descendants of Arthwys
ap Mor who opposed Gwenddoleu, deeply carried the scars of this battle,
holding to their mountainous lands, no longer a vibrant arm of the Cymric
Cylch. Rhun Hir ap Maelgwyn saw enough of this devastating assault and
conflict to realize division within the Cymri would not serve his kingdom of
Gwynedd. Urien of Rheged and Rhydderch of Alt Clud emerged even
stronger from the quelled break of the northern peace: now holding the
Solway as their own, no longer contending with the erratic Gwenddoleu.
Aedan and Conall of Dalriada also mended fences with Rhydderch, Aedan's
son Artúr coming of age to witness the carnage of Arfderydd at his first
battle. Most of the lingering conflicts in the north were instigated by Aedan's
brother-in-law Bruide of Pict Gwlad, waged against Lothian and Alt Clud,
Bruide's southern neighbors. The lads of Afallon – Llen, Gawain, Baedd,
Llew, Owain, and also Peredyr – all now had become seasoned warriors.
Arfderydd was that seminal event shattering any sense of worldly innocence
they may have retained, stepping into a new era of the Cymric Cylch and its
descendants.

I was born into that era. My mother had been a priestess of the
fountains. Her life ended giving life to me. I am a true son of Afallon, born
into the arcane mystic life, never knowing my worldly birth father, likely
killed at Arfderydd. I did not know of this tainted legacy until I was told later
as a young lad. All I had known of my origin before that time was the
priestess Claire and her brother, the bard Morfyn who cared for me from
birth. They were the parents that I knew. My roots of love had been formed
with this elderly pair of wise souls who acted as fostering grandparents to
me. When they told me how I came to be born, it seemed foreign, unreal,
sounding like a shrouded tale from some distant land of long ago. I grew to
understand that the atrocities of Gwenddoleu and the carnage of Arfderydd
were the wounding of the Cymric kingdoms, a wasted promise marked upon
the land for generations. The maidens of the wells were attendants to our
source waters, our fountains of life. They served pilgrims and travelers the
sacred waters from golden cups. These vessels were taken, abused and

discarded. I am one of the children of this tragedy. From that day on, the priestesses of Afallon sought to heal this wound upon the human spirit, heal the land, and heal the generations born into an uncertain future. This monumental task was not new; and yet the recent shocking event made it more immediate. The lads of Afallon saw this as their quest: to search for the restoration of divine accord. Humanity had fallen from grace – again. A new hope needed to be born to enliven the discovery of our sacred link to the source of divine grace. Whether this was to be found through acts of faith and devotion or the revival of sacred symbols, souls hungered for release from their suffering. Perhaps the return of the sacred vessels, those vessels serving humanity for countless ages, may provide clues to heal this great wound and bridge the divide in the human psyche. Quests for the grail hallows rose from this spiritual longing. Mystic vessels of diverse cultures became conflated with biblical legend, reaching back to Yusef Ram Theo, called Joseph of Arimathea, Yehoshua ben Yusef, known as Jesus the Christ, and even to Jacob ben Isaac and his youngest sons Joseph and Benjamin. Terrible atrocities of rape and murderous revenge were recurring bloody scenarios of the archaic biblical sagas, resurfacing and infecting human behavior as if a deadly plague of madness lies dormant within angry souls. My own birth and Myrddin's madness were two legacies of the violent moral and ethical disaster resurfaced. I would at long last reflect upon it; while Myrddin would at first unravel from it.

Myrddin Wyllt

He ran into the woodlands to find a place where no human life would infringe upon his shattered psyche. There was no one to speak to, nor anyone to listen to, except the wild creatures of the forest realm, allowing him to abruptly shift into becoming one of them. As thoughts invaded his rattled mind, he responded with the screeching caw of the crow, the guttural squeal of the boar, or the soulful howl of the wolf – repelling the discordant voices from within his emotionally addled mind. He lived on wild grasses, roots and berries, grubs and snakes, acorns and mushrooms, his clothing becoming tattered, crusty with dirt and stench. Bearded and graying, he began to merge with the shadows, his filthy, matted, overgrown head of hair cluttered with leaves and twigs, forming the appearance of an abandoned bird's nest out of his bushy crown. Gradually one voice emerged from his invasive thought streams, speaking from an image dominating his nightmares, an entity who attempted to take command of the chaos.

"Caw! Caw! Caw!" Myrddin screeched at this shadowy intruder of his dreams. The towering presence just stood there, ignoring Myrddin's mad ranting and crowing, the crazed dreamer leaping and crouching with the panicked gyrations of a franticly trapped forest fowl. After the disturbed bard settled down, the entity finally spoke.

"Have you had enough? Sounding-off as a creature will not awaken you; neither will it clear the putrid carrion from your mind. To do so, where you are now, you can only become as I am."

"And who are you?" The disheveled bard asked, with indignation.

"I am Lailoken."

"Well, Lai lo ken, o' ken, o' shite, I care not who or what you are!"

"But you do care. That is why you have lost yourself," Lailoken responded, giving Myrddin pause.

"It does not matter. Nothing matters. It is all shite. I am shite."

"Then what or who am I?"

"You are more shite!"

"No, I am just here," Lailoken resolutely stated.

"Where . . . where is this – here, now?"

"This is within you."

"Within me, what the bloody shite does that mean?"

"It means, I am you, if you recognize me as who you are," Lailoken cryptically answered.

"Shite! This is all shite! I am shouting at you, you, you vague image – La La Lailoken. I am not you!"

"Who you think you are is an idea. Weeks ago you thought you were a bard from Penllanw. Today you think you are a bird, or a boar or shite. Why not become the wisest voice within yourself?" Lailoken explained.

"And you, you claim to be that wise voice? If I call myself Lailoken, will I then become wise, and all becomes straight away right and tidy again?" Myrddin questioned again, in an increasingly sarcastic tone.

"Nothing significant will change by changing your name; but much will change by not reducing yourself to shite. All that I ask of you is to listen, listen deeply. Do not wallow in your disgrace, your guilt and your fear. Loss, sorrow, and death have impacted you. Now you can find a way to live again. You can find a wiser voice. If it helps you to become Lailoken, as an identity, then do so. But that is not who you are. You do not need to be another identity. Only by living and being life itself, will you live again."

Startled by a fallen branch from a nearby tree, Myrddin awoke from his dream encounter with Lailoken, into his newly demented waking reality.

"Who is there? Which one of you woodland giants drops debris on me? Rubbish! Rubbish! Rubbish thrown at shite – meaningless! Explain yourselves, dark stoic arboreal phantoms! Alders, what do you throw-off to become the smithy's charcoal? No one heard your feeble summons of foresight near the marshes and moors, near the fountains and wells. Speak! Speak now, sullen trunks of silence. Or you there, Beech bark, mark-down words for Alban's mountain book, give us the wisdom of Jupiter or Zeus, confirm our proven past knowledge of hindsight, where we become wise from repeated ignorance. . . . Hah! Just as I thought – silent! Are you all dead wood? Encroaching ivy will get you too: ivy of the mind, like golden chains of Laburnum poisoning this dense wood of nightmares, stock for howling pipes and chilling drones. Shake it free if you can. Vines of thought choke this life! They spring upon me, like weeds of poplar, shoots of doubt, fear, and remorse – the entrance of my own hell. And who stands there: Lailoken, my inner Laocoon? Is he a guide? Or is he the grisly reaper of time: old age come too fast, Chronos raping the first fruits of Gaia, castrating the eternal, concealed in a hewn timber wooden horse. Trees, bloody trees speak to me! Sound your timbre! Don't just stand there in silence! Battle with word of wood! Creak! Moan! Right this miasma of Myrddin!"

He stood there, silent, looking straight up, seeing the treetops begin to sway, first this way then that – the illuminating sky peering through with flashes of light and color enlivening the dark shadowed foliage. Then the seemingly languid limbs began to groan a compliant response.

"Ah, ah, I hear the Rowan Ash, axe handle of this world tree. Can I recover, and find roots again? What? What do I hear? Do you sway me to cairn and circle . . . but how? And who am I to be . . . Myrddin or Lailoken?

The wind rose through the trees, creating a distorted language of the wood, releasing creaks, squeals and warped howls from diverse branches and straining narrow trunks. Myrddin construed their sounds as direct missives on the moving air to his confused reasoning.

"What? Bull eh? Bard bull eh? Bard bull eh shev? Shev neh? Is this who I am now – Bard Buile Suibhne? What else do you say, arboreal guides? Is this my way? Or is it wind – breaking wind – hah – wind through my ears, or out my arse?"

Just then a branch of hazel fell at his feet, formed in a most perfect 'y' bouncing before him as if it was alive.

"Whoa, now, there it is: a divining rod at my feet."

Myrddin promptly picked it up, feeling the hazel branch pulling him forward, his mind hearing verse to be voiced.

"And here I grasp divining rod, from out of time of mind and sod, a Herculean cudgel spoke, to crown a king of wood and oak, the ancients flung these branches hurled, wielding axis arms of worlds."

Myrddin fell to his knees, in supplication to the tree guardians who seemed to answer his angered prayer. He knew he was not healed; and yet there was some avenue of recovery opening to him, perhaps even more profound than he had ever known before. The entire forest was now his nemeton, each tree standing as elder brother and sister druids, subjects of the true oak, high king of the wood, all grounded in Gaia, that ancient matriarch of a distant foretime, living here and now within his roots. He held the divining branch of hazel in his hands, allowing it to pull him to and fro, grasping for direction out of his mental muddle. The woodland sounds seemed louder now, his ears and eyes attuned to every alteration of timberland and thicket. Creatures stirred around him, he was certain, moving as if parts of his own gestures led their actions. His daily diet off the forest floor had fed his hallucinating visions, heightening his imagined sense of an ever expanding natural world. It had become his reconstituted and shed sylvan skin, serpentine and transformed each day into another manifestation of self awareness. No longer able to be the person he had been, he became the elemental environs of his rapidly shifting perception. Leaves were a literature of light. The earth was the heat and dampness of his flesh. The air was the taste upon his tongue. Every stone was his firm stance, stabilized across the terrain. Each tree was his skeletal frame, holding him erect into the infinite sky above. At one within the forest – he now was the forest. The world he had known before had vanished from his troubled memory.

Myrddin's sister, Queen Gwendydd had no idea what had happened to her twin brother. She ordered the battlefield searched for his remains, fearing he had been killed with their kinsmen at Arfderydd. Rumors soon surfaced that Myrddin was seen heading into the woodland regions many weeks before. Gwendydd pleaded for Rhydderch to send a troop of his army to scour the wilderness to find her brother, tracking down any hint of his last appearance. Finally a patrol came upon the man of the wild, perched high in a tree. If not for a huntsman's sharp eye following a hawk through the tree tops, Myrddin may never have been seen. It was a tiresome task to retrieve the madman from the lofty limbs without harm; but they managed. Roped and lowered to the forest floor, Myrddin resisted like a cornered badger, clawing at his captors, until a knock on the head left him docile enough to be secured for the journey to Dun Barton.

The grossly disheveled bard was bound within a cage built of saplings, mounted on a cart. As he was brought into the inner yard of the fortress, curious onlookers gathered around the cart to see what strange sorry wretch was held within the cage. Myrddin cowered, covering his ears to avoid the chatter of the crowd. Four men at arms slid two long shafts through the top of the cage to lift it off the cart, carrying the secured madman into the main hall of the keep. King Rhydderch approached the cage immediately after their entry.

"My God – could it be, Myrddin?" said the king, walking around the cage, and peering-in to discern any resemblance of his missing brother-in-law.

"Myrddin?" the king inquired again, leaning toward the poor huddled soul, suddenly stepping back as Myrddin lunged at the wooden bars of the cage.

"Bard Buile Suibhne!" Myrddin shouted, his eyes opening wildly, the whites bulging from the shadowy pitch-toned color of his filthy cheeks and brow. A guardsman abruptly rapped on the bars with a long staff, sending Myrddin to recede back into a corner. Soon Queen Gwendydd entered the hall, first believing a caged creature had been brought in from a hunt.

"What strange beast have you discovered now, Rhydderch?" the queen questioned from across the hall.

"Come closer dear; but prepare for a shock," Rhydderch responded.

Gwendydd approached with some hesitance, squinting to focus-in on the odd cowering being, the guard standing-by with staff in hand. As she drew closer, she was suddenly stunned – "Oh my . . . Myrddin . . . is that you?" The captive remained silent, his eyes darting side to side, his chin tucked into his chest. "Oh dear, oh dear Myrddin, what has become of you? Oh dear God – please, free him! He must be bathed, and shaved – and those rags burnt. Oh my dear brother," Gwendydd reacted.

"Best take-care my lady: he's not right in the head – near gouged-out a man's eye when we caught him. We'll clean him up alright; but give us some time to see him regain his senses," the lead guard said to the queen.

"It must be some form of battle madness, dear. Let these men try to bring him around before we get too close. Our dear Myrddin does not know what he is doing," Rhydderch tried to explain, comforting his wife, putting his arms around her, pulling her close as she wept.

Myrddin had become quite strong and agile from his primative roaming of the forest, climbing into the trees and living as a wild beast. It took several men to restrain him with ropes, stretched-out on a rack to wash and groom the woodland vagrant. After a few days he became much calmer, although restrained with chains, preventing any sudden attacks. Myrddin spent hours just standing, staring out of his cell window at the beckoning treetops, visible in the distance. He was well cared for, without the abuse most prisoners received. He ate what was put before him. But, he did not speak. Gwendydd would visit him; and he would not even look at her. He just stared out of the window, emotionless and silent.

"I know you can hear me. Why won't you answer me? I love you. All of our lives we have never been so distant. Please, dear brother, tell me what has happened to you," she pleaded to no avail, leaving him, rushing out of his cell in tears and frustration.

The guards gradually began to allow Myrddin to walk around the enclosed garrison courtyard. He looked up to the expansive sky above the walls, oddly smiling as if something appeared there, seen only by him, as he lumbered along, dragging his chains. Finally, Myrddin was brought before the king and queen, his chains removed as he stood in front of them in the main hall. Again, he stood silent, gazing up to the nearest window.

"Myrddin, will you speak? Will you give us some idea of your current state of mind? Will you not even speak to your own sister?" King Rhydderch challenged him.

Gwendydd stepped toward her twin, standing right in front of him, silently, looking deeply into his face with an empathetic intensity, as he continued to look away, up and out of the window above. Men at arms stepped closer, preparing to protect the queen as she reached out to touch her brother's face. When her fingers gently touched his cheek, he turned his attention to her, seeing a tiny autumn leaf caught within the blonde locks of her hair. Myrddin slowly lifted his hand forward, quickly plucking the leaf from her hair, examining it intently – as if reading countless scrolls of information within the minute textured patterns of the leaf. Then, with a look of revelatory shock on his face, he looked directly into his sister's startled eyes and finally spoke to her.

"Woman, you have been deceived; and have deceived your king. The leaves contain the life of trees: the trees that live for years and years, the trees that shade our graves and fears, the trees that stood through histories of kingdoms come, kingdoms gone, and kingdoms yet to be. And in this tiny leaf I hold, I see the histories unfold. I see the futures born in past. I see the wars – the battles cast, the lies, the bloody thirst – the last to fall just as the first. I see the terror men have known. I see the seed each thought has sown. I see the Cymri stricken down. I see the built and broken crown. The future is calamity, in waves of waning sanity. An entity is puffed in spring, to fall in autumn, a dead thing: a face, a leaf, a scroll, a lie, a place, belief, a blinded eye. It is one thing, shattered here. It is one life, one love, one fear, one blood, one breath, one truth, one death. What dear sister you concealed, I read within this leaf, revealed, your carnal lust stole away, in bed with dead King Solway."

The king and his retinue were shocked. Rhydderch looked to his wife, who reacted with scorn and sorrow over her brother's convoluted ramblings.

"He is insane! This is the ranting of a madman. I am both repulsed by this deluded lie, and saddened by my brother's strange dementia: claiming to see these revelations in a leaf – a leaf! We could ask him anything, and he would likely answer with lunacy. I could repeat the same question and he would surely give a different answer each time. Oh, how have you lived like this my sad brother? How will you die, my dear demented Myrddin?"

Myrddin stared deeply into the leaf held there within his hand, saying: "I will die from a fall, as all men do – a fall from truth, as split in two."

"How, exactly, will you die, dear brother?" Gwendydd asked again.

Again, Myrddin stared at the leaf, answering: "I will be hung, and left for dead, to be unsung, my verse unsaid."

"Are you quite certain this will be the manner of your death, my confused twin? Tell us again." The queen persisted.

A third time, Myrddin stared at the leaf, arriving at a different answer.

"It is clear as night is day, I will drown, and pass away, to drown in lies without a breath, to drown in shallow mortal death."

"You see, sadly, my dear brother has lost all reason," Gwendydd stated, weeping between her words. "He has been silent, all of this time. And now, he reads a leaf, a leaf. I have never betrayed my king; but my brother has been betrayed, by his own mind."

Myrddin turned, looking up and out of the window again, silent, as before, as if he had said nothing. Rhydderch gestured to the guards and they took Myrddin away. Queen Gwendydd sat there on the floor, weeping, where her brother had just stood. She looked up for a moment, puzzled by Myrddin's fixation with the window above, questioning in desperation.

"Dear brother, what did you see? What, pray God is left of you?"

King Rhydderch reached down, lifting her into his arms, walking her out of the main hall. The guards escorted Myrddin back to his cell, stopping momentarily in the courtyard. His chains had been left off, because the befuddled bard seemed quite docile. Suddenly the quixotic vagabond bolted for the courtyard wall, scaling the stone and timber structure with the speed of a wild cat, quickly reaching the top and bounding over it, arms spread like the arched wings of a bird. The guards scrambled to make their way through the inner corridors to the outer ward, too late to apprehend the seemingly shape shifting bard. Myrddin landed outside the walled courtyard in a cat-stance, wily and feral in his every move, darting through the lanes and alleys of the fortress. Entering the crowded citadel beyond the walls, jarring voices and masses of people unnerved him, drowning his senses with chaotic impressions. In a panic, he ran to the river's edge, leaping with the gate of a bold stag, plunging into the waters, swept away by the current, disappearing from the view of the belated guards, just arriving, out of breath and astonished. Myrddin was carried into the stream across its wide expanse, before he flopped himself onto the southern shore emerging from an ebb within the chilling Clud waters. Nearly drowned and exhausted, he laid there for a moment on his back, watching the voluminous forms of clouds parade a menagerie of fanciful creatures before his vivid imagination. Rising to his feet, he looked around, setting his sights to distant woodlands in the southeast. He was not readily familiar with his surroundings, but latent memory or animal instinct led him into the forest again. The fugitive of courtly sanity soldiered-on until nightfall, finding comfort upon a dense bed of leaves, drifting off to sleep and dream.

Within his dream visions, he was king of the woodland realm again. Gathered around him were the creatures of the forest, attentive to his every command and motion. Great stags were his cavalry; wolves were elite troops, along with regiments of boars and badgers, the reconnaissance of wild cats, and swooping forces of birds of prey. The bard was not adept in ways of war; and yet a primal strain of natural survival now flowed through his nerves and veins, relating him to every cunning noble beast. He led his animal army, lined in herds and packs and flocks of their own kind to redress the wrongs of civilized human beasts, concealed within their fortified dens. Myrddin rode upon the back of a massive stag, a king among his own ilk, followed by the throngs of creatures up to the gates of the old Roman wall, where Gwenddoleu had once reigned. And here, the bard turned forest lord demanded his twin sister show herself, and exit from her illicit keep.

"The presence of the natural world calls you from your lair of deception, my adulterous sister!" Myrddin shouted.

She did not answer his angered call; but Gwenddoleu appeared instead, challenging the woodland bard to single combat. They met before the milecastle gate on the open plain. Spectators lined the walls to see the king astride his horse and Myrddin on his great stag. Animals of every breed rested still, watchful of the scene. Lailoken stood off to the side, observing this pending match of rivaled wills. King Gwenddoleu charged his steed toward Myrddin Wyllt, who charged his mighty stag as well. When nearing the clash of conflict, Myrddin stood-up upon the back of his wild mount, breaking free the wide pointed rack of his stag with both hands, shed as weapons of attack, hurling himself through the air to collide and pierce the fateful peat bog king with seven wounds running through his vile body. The bard removed the bloody rack of antlers from the impaled dying king, raising them above his own head, to crown himself as king of this frenetic liminal world. Lording over the fallen king he said, "You have severed all that is natural and good, a divide that may not mend. I end it here within myself, to begin again, in nature's realm." Then he turned about, shouting back to his sister within the keep, "I leave you again, Gwendydd, as I am now a King of Nature's State. The presence of this realm awaits you, beyond your faulty walls of conceit." With that the ethereal bard king retreated to the woodland groves again with his myriad enclaves of devoted fauna, only to awaken from his dream, on the forest floor and his bed of leaves.

Myrddin awoke with clear recollection of this vivid dream, pondering the role he played within his mind, his dual identity as Lailoken, standing there watching the conflict. "Who is the real identity of me?" Myrddin questioned himself. "Who is even there, within dream, other than me – whoever that is? Am I Lailoken, Myrddin the twin of Gwendydd, or the erratic Bard Buile Suibhne? I am no longer a man of the citadel, or of the court of kings. Am I a man at all? Or am I a beast, or an inflated lord of beasts? Is this forest who or what I truly am? Is the open space, my field of view, the true identity of me? Am I a person, or more rightly, the space that I occupy? I do not feel like any person: any person that I have been, or could be called by name. I cannot see a future as a person. Destiny, it would seem, is an imagined future, based on a vanished past. I took on an identity. This person that I insisted that I was . . . was an identity bound to me as if by chains, dragging along behind me, keeping me from freedom. What is the freedom of the forest? What is the purity of open space? Is this the identity of the unbound self? Why is there bloody conflict – conflict within and without? The dominant prevail, with sword or rack or sheer brute force. One foe lives, one dies or suffers – to what end? When I am dead, not anything but dry bones, who am I then? What was I? What continues on? Where does this life of mine go? Where does the blood, the pulse, the moisture of the flesh, the water of life, the fluidity that I was – to where does it all depart? Do I become the mist of the air? Do I become the breath of all life? What breath of saints am I breathing now? The person I was has been my own deception. My twin, a woman, also a deception, reflects desire. And her twin, this Myrddin, reflects the fear. I am neither person nor desire nor fear. I am neither a body, nor a body of thought. I am neither a sensation nor a perception. Personas have appeared, desiring, fearing, possessing, controlling, murdering, raping – clawing away to dominate others – to be lords of the beasts. What is this vile behavior? What is its end? Now, in the deep wood, I begin to watch this. I am watching everything, like Lailoken. I can see everything if I am not consumed by clawing at my own fate. I can see that I am nothing, not even shite. I can see and sense everything, even the shite. And yet, I am not consumed by it. It's all dry bones, piled-up in my mind. I have been building a self of bones and shite, a mound to crow upon. Each day I will awaken from sleep and dreams – or not – I could die tonight. Who am I to be then? Would I be anything? Would I perceive anything, would I be aware, or be anything that has awareness? Within the forest, I am as aware as the forest. I am awareness. I leave the person. I leave the past. I leave the future, alone. I breathe with the trees. I am rooted in earth; but I am reaching the sky."

Myrddin walked to the edge of the wooded grove and realized that he was still too close to the river running through the defended lands of Rhydderch's kingdom of Alt Clud. His sister the queen was sure to send out another search patrol to find him. He decided to head south toward Gallwyddel. Before stepping out of the woods, he saw a column of nuns and clergymen with a small force of armed warriors traveling north on the nearby road. They halted their progress while a small group of these

Christian nuns and another small group of these Christian monks departed from the ranks and began walking towards the woodlands. Myrddin retreated into the forest, quickly climbing into a tree. It seems that the clergy had chosen this spot to relieve themselves; sheltered in privacy from the rest of the entourage and its escorts. One clergyman came quite near Myrddin, stepping into the shaded woodlands, watering the very same tree where the bard was hiding, as Myrddin cracked a branch, almost falling from his perch. The startled monk promptly finished his business, looking up into the trees above, catching sight of Myrddin.

"Who's there?" The monk called to him, as Myrddin tried to conceal himself in the foliage.

"I see you. You might as well come down. What are you doing up there? Are you a huntsman or a thief?" The monk questioned him further, as Myrddin descended to the forest floor.

"No, Father, just a man of the wood."

"You live here then?"

"No, Father . . . nowhere . . . in particular."

"You have no home, do you have a name?"

"I am, uh, Lailoken."

"Lailoken?"

"Yes, Father . . . or sometimes Myrddin."

"Ah, I am Cyndeyrn, or sometimes called Mungo. You startled me, Lailoken. I thought you were one of God's creatures."

"I am, Father."

"Ha, ha, yes I suppose you are. And yet, we have dominion over the beasts of the forests and fields."

"Why is that, Father?"

"Because we are created in the image and likeness of God, as His children," Cyndeyrn asserted.

"Are not the beasts His children too, Father?"

"No. They do not have a soul, as man does," said the monk.

"If a man were to lose his soul, would he become a beast? And could a noble beast, find a soul of its own, becoming better than some men?" Myrddin asked the monk.

"A man can redeem his soul; but a beast cannot find a soul of its own," Cyndeyrn stated with authority.

"If God created the beasts, are they not part of His creation, and part of God, just as a man and his soul?" Myrddin questioned further.

"God created the world and all its creatures in seven days. He gave dominion to man, over the beasts, to name them and subdue them. Man was given dominion over all of the earth. There is an order of things. That is God's plan."

Myrddin pondered that for a moment, and then challenged the monk. "When a beast kills a man, or a man kills another man, becoming like a beast – is that God's plan as well?"

"It is not the proper order of things. A man must pay for his sins," Cyndeyrn responded.

"If a beast has no soul, and a man who lost his soul becomes a beast – how can a beast without a soul or a man without a soul commit a sin? Is not survival, or life and death also the order of things?" Myrddin debated.

"Who are you, Lailoken?" Cyndeyrn asked, seeming a bit perturbed, straining his patience.

Then one of his armed escorts appeared; and as Cyndeyrn turned away for an instant, Myrddin vanished into the forest between the light and shadows.

"Are you alright Father?" asked the escort.

"Yes, yes," answered Cyndeyrn.

"Were you talking to someone, Father?"

"No, no one, from nowhere in particular, or perhaps an apparition," Cyndeyrn responded with a puzzled look.

"I beg your pardon, Father?"

"Nothing, nothing my good man," Cyndeyrn muttered.

Myrddin kept well hidden within forest until the entire entourage moved on to the north. Then the bard continued his journey to the south, making great strides, hiding from view as best he could, settling into another forested bed after nightfall. Again, the imaginative bard conjured fantastic dream visions in his sleep, assuming a more peaceful version of his role as lord of the beasts. This time he was accompanied by a grey wolf, a raven, a tall crane, a lynx and a bear cub. Several creatures spoke to Myrddin within his mind, as if their thoughts and instincts were shared with his.

"We know that you believe yourself to be a man," conveyed the lynx, "and that is fine, if you wish to do so. But you must realize by now, that there is no division between the countless creatures and the upright walking beasts called men."

The crane stopped preening himself for a moment to interject, "I have been a cat in a forked tree. I have been a goat in an elder tree. I have been a crane well filled – a sight to behold."

The bear cub looked up at the tall and gangly bird, with a baffled expression and a curious tilt his head.

"We heard your conversation with that man of the Church, telling you that creatures have no souls," the grey wolf added. "It is more the case that he allows no creatures into his soul, cloistered in the confinement of his limited thinking. He clearly cannot tell the difference between where his body ends and his soul begins."

"As you know from your immersion into the woodlands," the raven continued the grey wolf's thought, "soul is as elemental as the air. It is the recognition within the ether that a voice or point of view can be heard or felt, as every plant, or bird, or creeping thing is part of the forest realm. A soul is part of one spirit realm: individual in awareness, but inseparable from spirit's wholeness."

"How is it then that you can fly and I can only walk?" Myrddin asked the raven.

"Ah, but in your dreams, you can fly, as easily as any raven. Just as I can speak to you now as a raven, or become a man."

With that the raven quickly transformed into a masterful druid, dressed in a black robe, his hair and beard raven black, except for a streak of white rising from his brow.

"Wonders of Awen – you are the Myrlyn!" Myrddin responded. "I had heard your countenance described, just as you appear right now. I see you here, somehow; and yet this is a dream. Emrys Myrlyn has been dead for many years. Are you a ghost of spirit, or an image within my mind, and nothing of the man that you appear to be? You could be Lailoken, for all I fail to know and understand."

"Yes, I could be Lailoken," Myrlyn said, as his image shifted momentarily into Lailoken and then back to Myrlyn again. "I have been Lailoken, within my own dream visions. I have had some heated confrontations with this Lailoken. All of this is a play of shifting images within the mind. A better question might be: what is this realm of the fluid mind, and what part do these images play?"

"I see. If mind and soul are fields of the play of images, then entities are the emanations of mind and soul, rather than bodies housing minds and souls," Myrddin realized.

"Brilliant, lad – this is why I speak to you this way. So that you may observe the conversation within yourself as a broader realm: that is in fact yourself revealed. This break that you have taken from what you knew of yourself, to become attuned to the wilderness, is a chance for you to see differently, to feel differently, and to be alive differently. I am a voice that you likely revere. And yet, I am not apart from you. The image of Lailoken was that same wise voice for you; but you did not respect him at first; because you did not respect yourself. Lailoken was the opposite voice for 'the Myrlyn' – a challenging counterpart appearing in a time of inner struggle. It is the wisdom that must prevail, not the assumed identity of anyone. You are beginning to see that now," Myrlyn explained.

"Where do I go from here?" asked Myrddin.

"Where were you going?" responded Myrlyn.

"South, I was going south," said Myrddin.

"Well then, it seems you were going just where you needed to be. There is a spring, far to the south. You will meet others there who will share your path, for a while," Myrlyn confirmed.

"Thank you. Can I call on you for guidance in the future, Master Myrlyn?"

"Any time that you ask for guidance it will be given to you. And although I am not apart from you, your guidance may not appear as if it came from this one you call Master Myrlyn. Trust your guidance. Keep listening. Keep watching. You will know what to do, and when to do it."

After rising from sleep the next morning, Myrddin traveled south, avoiding the main roads, taking his next night's rest in the woodland groves whenever he could. Each day he asked within his newfound sense of self for direction, with every turn or crossroads seemingly presenting an answer for him. As he forded any stream, brook or creek, or heard their fluid voices sounding nearby – he questioned these elemental sources.

"Tell me, babbling waters, where is this spring that Master Myrlyn spoke of? Lead me to that source – that well, that fount."

On and on he journeyed through the lands of Gallwyddel, onto a southern most peninsula, passing abandoned brochs and ancient Pictish forts in ruins and rubble. Questioning each turn, he wandered on; until he reached a sheer cliff edge, looking out to the expansive sea. "Journey on," was the perplexing answer he now heard within himself. He looked over the coastal ledge, surveying the precipice down to the narrow beach below, realizing: he could go farther. The cliff could be descended, with care.

"Alright then, journey on it is," he muttered to the elements of the ocean air. After a considerable time, he stepped down onto the sand, pondering the horizon spread out before him. "Don't ask me to swim to Eirenn now, my mischievous guides. I have been alright as a stag and a wolf, but not so well as a fish."

He walked the beach, less led by guidance than by the earnest exploration of a last resort. As he climbed around a rocky ocean-pitted crag of the shore, he observed a crevice leading into a coastal cave, marked by a growth of bright green moss. To his astonishment, a gentle trail of water trickled down. Myrddin moved closer, reaching out to touch the waters, tasting them by cupping his hand to his lips, exclaiming: "Wonders of Awen – a fresh water spring!"

He looked high above his head, now seeing the towering coastal cliff standing like a mountain above him, he, yielding at its foundation, its foot, its spring of life just steps away from the depth of the sea. The waters were one. The ascending cliffs and the ocean floor were one. Myrddin felt a fluidity of being rushing through him: the rising ocean tide, the natural flowing spring, the misted coastal air, and the clarity of guidance he had followed to the earth's very edge. The waters of the surf were increasingly moving-in with each set of waves, alerting him to return to the beach. Climbing around the rocks, he reached the sands again, walking with more joy than he had known in quite some time. As he gazed out to sea, he saw a small ship nearing the shore. It anchored off the coast, lowering a boat, with several people boarding and rowing their way to land. It wasn't long before they reached the water's edge; and Myrddin met them on the beach. He waded into the surf to lend a hand, recognizing two of the mariners, to his great surprise.

"Taliesin, Lady Vivianne – I am astonished! There is not a soul for miles around, and here you are," Myrddin called out to them as he neared their boat.

Taliesin shouted back, "Myrddin – what – how did you come to be here to greet us, brother bard?"

"Awen, brother, pure Awen!" responded Myrddin.

Myrddin and an oarsman pulled the launch in, helping Taliesin and Lady Vivianne ashore. Once on the beach, Vivianne's eyes traversed the coast, leading her to point towards the hidden coastal spring.

Myrddin looked at her with amazement asking, "Are you here to find the spring?"

Vivianne smiled with a look of wise recognition, saying, "Yes, my dear Myrddin, welcome back."

"Ha ha!" Taliesin laughed, "She told me we would find a revived spring here, one untouched by the recent tragedy – and that I might encounter an old friend: if he regained his wits and followed his true course."

"Well praise Awen and the saints, here we are," Myrddin responded with jaw-dropping awe.

"Quickly, the tide is rising," Vivianne directed, as she strode on towards the rocky cliffs, her gown soaked to the knees as she neared the mouth of the spring. She trudged in closer around the coastal crags, drawing a golden cup from her cloak as she reached the flowing source, filling the chalice with the surging fresh waters from the awakened fount. She took a drink from the cup, handing it to Taliesin who did the same, both of them briskly retreating to the beach before the tide could sweep them away.

"Shall we build a fire?" said Taliesin as they returned to the others.

"I've gathered some driftwood already." said the oarsman.

"Well Myrddin, it's been a while since we've seen you. It was at the Aenach Garman, I believe? We must hear of your adventures." Taliesin said to his old friend, laying a hand on his shoulder.

"Yes, it seems as if ages have passed by since then," Myrddin answered.

They built a fire on a broader section of the beach, warming some mulled wine for their refreshment. The sound of the waves created an underlying rhythm to the cadence of their conversation, as if tides of the vast sea were acknowledging their reunion.

"It is so miraculous that we would find you here at this time. Although I have grown accustomed to these rare encounters guided by Vivianne's visions. Tell us, what led you here to meet us at this precise time, old friend?" asked Taliesin.

"I have been on a journey for many months, though it felt like years. I had lost my way, my reason shifted into darkness, into light and shadows of mind and spirit. I . . . I was deeply affected by Arfderydd, mourning the losses in a disturbed sense of shock. I could not come to grips with my influence upon the depraved king, whom I had served as a bard for many seasons," Myrddin confided.

"You must not hold yourself to blame," Lady Vivianne consoled him. "Many of us had visions and cause to be alarmed; and yet we could not stop what did unfold. It was Gwenddoleu's madness that led to yours. You did not incite his insanity. It had festered within him long before you became his bard. Your woes arise from nurturing a serpent."

"Thank you, Lady Vivianne; it is very kind of you to share your clear insight. I believe all of these events led me to this moment here and now with you. I had become detached from any sense of what I knew myself to be: not a bard, not a prince, not a brother, not even a man. I had become a sylvan creature, merging with the woodlands as an expansion of my altered being. My senses melded with the elements, divorced from any identity. I struggled with my dream visions, confronted by a shadow of myself, or at times by an enlightened and awakening side of my fractured being. It had me most perplexed. Within the waking world, I was captured by men at arms of King Rhydderch, held in chains, spouting verse to my sister, coherent only to my own soul, in some vain attempt at honesty and revelation. I escaped from there, after cryptically predicting my own threefold death, which it appears I have endured and survived as a soul born anew. Then, strangely, I encountered a traveling monk. Cyndeyrn was his name. In that brief exchange, I challenged the nature of the soul of man and beast, innocence and sin, as if to debate these truths within my mind as a rational discourse carried on with this pious monk. Later, alone again in the wild, I had a dream visitation with your wise father Myrlyn, my dear lady. He helped me to discern the nature of my splintered self, and the character of Lailoken – a name I have since oddly claimed as my own – sprung from wisdom within internal strife. I now understand that I am neither Lailoken nor Myrddin, but spirit and soul guided through this life to learn, to love, to be . . . rooted, just as the forest is, without cause or reason not to be. At my lowest ebb I thought that I had died, immersed into the light of the sky. It must have been one of those threefold deaths. Your father, the wise raven – and he did appear first as a raven – awakened me to more lucid paths within my dream visions, aware of guidance most prescient and tangible. It was in that vein that I came to this beach, drank from the healing fount, and met you here this day – a man survived threefold, mending wounds of self turmoil and sorrow."

"We are happy to find you here, recovered from your inner turmoil," said Taliesin. "These waters surely gave you that final taste of a healing reality confirmed. And your retreat into the woodlands served as a necessary shift. The forest can be a revitalizing place, surrendering the troubled mind to the elemental world. The mind is not the best origin for a journey to freedom, crowding-in upon the privacy of soul. Everything in the forest has its own awareness that surrounds it. Finding this awareness is the true place where your journey began. You seem to have emerged from the mire of ideas, doubts and fears: that incessant thought stream of a tormented mind. That stream was not your freedom, but a form of drowning. You had fallen from reason into madness, as you described, to free yourself from your own mind. It was a little death, one of those threefold deaths that you spoke of."

"Yes, yes . . . and when I was captured by my own sister's liegemen – I was suspended within the very trees that I had been conversing with. I was hung between them, by foot and limb, caged and taken away to the fortress of Alt Clud," Myrddin related.

"You were suspended between ideas of yourself: your identity, your worthiness, and your understanding – dangling for your life, each idea another death or a clue to new life," Vivianne added. "Ideas are points of notice within the mind, landmarks of a convoluted journey. When ideas become a fortress of identity, they become a cell of bondage, bondage within illusion. Illusion is the ignorance of reality, portrayed by a dualism in the mind. The drama of illusion divides the mind, and the perception of the outer world becomes divided and fragmented as well. Only your deeper awareness returned you to the reality of wholeness, connecting to your guidance, to finding us here, to finding yourself, no longer a limited entity, here and now."

"I had escaped my captivity by leaping into a great stream," Myrddin reflected. "I did not know where it would take me; and I did not drown myself. And yet, something was washed clean, set free. Then I was free to drink of this pure spring. Something of me died, or was left for dead, so that an unfettered self could be born."

"All identities will die," Vivianne said, "sinking of their own dead weight; awareness continues to expand, born into life beyond death."

Myrddin rested peacefully that night by the fire, reunited with his dear mentors of Afallon. The following day they visited the spring one more time. Vivianne communed with the flowing energy of the fount, as she stood before the source waters, holding her raised palms high, enacting a mystifying preservation of the site. To his amazement, Myrddin perceived an expansive glow of light around the priestess and Taliesin, standing near her with his eyes closed.

Myrddin asked the oarsman, "Can you see that glow?"

"Glow? What glow?" The crusty oarsman replied, squinting his eyes and turning his head side to side. "They are often in prayer or trance. I try not to disturb them."

Myrddin just stood there, transfixed, the bard realizing he had so much to learn from this pair of mystics. He soon joined them on their return voyage to Afallon, directly south to Ynys Manau. The tides favored their departure and the short voyage. Upon landing, it wasn't long before Taliesin reminded Myrddin of their early practice of the movements of the mountains and the streams. Many of the bards mentored by Taliesin had failed to keep up these practices after they returned to their diverse tribes and kingdoms. Myrddin now began to absorb as much influence as he possibly could from the Afallon Ysgol. He moved about as if he had entered a different skin. His sense of time and space had shifted, with Taliesin, Vivianne and other mystics of the isle supporting his new way of being. Autumn merged with winter as he lingered there on Ynys Manau. Myrddin had much time to explore his awakening inner world with Taliesin and Vivianne. Members of his brotherhood of bards – cousins Llywarch of Rheged and Aneirin of Penllanw – had visited the isle and the court of Urien that year. But the life of a courtly bard had lost its vague appeal to Myrddin. He still loved words, delving into their invocations of spirit, their primal origins as extensions of his soul, and their expansion of his inner voice. It was a private conversation with his source, with creation, with creation of all he realized could be. Myrddin still found himself drawn to those environs where his inner growth of solitude had come alive – the abundant forests and wooded groves.

Taliesin and Vivianne had become Myrddin's outer guides to his inward search. Creation was the essence of his spiritual inquiry: what he created of himself, and how all manifested life came to be. Words, as he saw them, were the seeds of the mind, growing as conjured thought forms, expressions of the patterns of his being. What escaped his grasp was the underlying page or broader field on which these notions found their ground. This was the vast expanse of conceivability and possibility – the realm and wholeness of his source.

"The atmosphere that we inhabit is a world that I have just begun to explore," Myrddin began his question to Taliesin and Vivianne. "I have traversed seasons of storm and shift, which have brought me to a varied climate and regions of strange weather within my recovering soul. I wake each day to navigate this realm, rising from dream and sleep, which hold their adventures for me as well. Now, through eyes awake, I blindly grope the atmosphere of a new reality. Can you shed light on this field of being, on this ether of our soul's transit that would help me on my uncharted course?"

With a wry smile Taliesin said, "Vain attempts have been made by many before you and I upon the cosmos to capture in a cup of our endless stream of mind, a conception finding order within all of this that we observe and imagine, realizing that chaos is conceivable, yet any order to chaos is by definition inconceivable. So what then is the ground of being, as if being were as tangible as this body or this earth? The ether is a term, a word – we love words, don't we brother bard – ether is a term to vaguely connote all that is unmanifested, yet somehow ever-present. The elemental qualities of nature do not suffice to define the indefinable. Even as alchemy and metaphor, we find that we build a little box around a fragment of the infinite and say – 'Ah ha!' Only to recognize later, we missed something significant, or most everything significant. The images of our poetic forms are rich and beautiful at times; so we can only hope they bring the ether with them as they collect upon our ears, our hearts and our minds. The tree is one such enriching word that grows forever within the mind and the impassioned core of those of reason and sensitivity who open to its monumental girth. All imagined realities are expressed through the tree of life. We can conjure this tree as if to grow with it, as it lives on within us. This tree and its varieties are the crown and roots of our creation. It is here; but it is the concealed of the concealed. Only as imageless and formless growth, do we truly know it intimately. Its wisdom is shed in mercy of our ignorance. Its radiance is our strength. We cannot uproot it, because it is the foundation of our being. In our veiled understanding we glimpse its glory, to reach and extend what we believe ourselves to be. That is the path you began into the forest. Continue on, as you have been, and you will be led as a leaf turning to the light."

"You have discovered much within your forested retreat and refuge, my distant cousin," Vivianne added. "Now you are not so distant from my wise father, and all of his descendants of Afallon. I am sure the Myrlyn has further guidance to offer you, as he has for so many of us. You are welcome here as long as you wish; but first listen and respond to your own guidance."

"Thank you Vivianne, Taliesin, the Myrlyn told me that our paths would merge, for a time. He did not say it was you; but that is clear now. I will listen, and watch, and see what this new spring will bring to me," said Myrddin, bowing reverently to both of them.

At the first thaw of spring, Myrddin realized it was time for him to travel north again. He caught a ship for Dalriada, joining Gawain and

Morcades on their voyage to Dun Airigh. Morcades encouraged Myrddin to develop his attention toward his inner guidance, acutely aware of the opening of light and vision within the bard.

"As a bard you are adept at opening to the muses, keeping an ear to Awen at all times. The way of a seer is quite similar. I have seen you rising in this gift of vision. It is clear that you are a great soul. This recent shedding of shadows has allowed you a new freedom for your spirit to soar. Listen and trust that rising current of the ether, it will carry you far," said Morcades.

"You are a dear sister of spirit," Myrddin responded. "I have a twin sister; and I know that my departure from her is part of this new freedom."

"I can see that. She has been an emotional shadow to your soul. Your bond of birth with her is complex. Each of us can carry burdens begun even in the womb, twins often reflecting each other's burdens and struggles throughout life. You are breaking free, to find your own clear path, dear friend of Afallon," Morcades elucidated her impressions, embracing Myrddin, giving him much to ponder as they neared Dun Airigh.

Myrddin contemplated these things as he gazed silently towards the northern horizon. Suddenly he turned to the steersman requesting: "Good man, can you bring us to shore here, to the leeward side?"

"It's a mite shallow, but if you don't mind a bit of muck," the steersman answered, looking to Morcades.

"It's just me, my good man," Myrddin clarified. "Morcades, Gawain – I will meet Prince Aedan another time, perhaps. I hear the woodland groves of the north calling me to the solitude of forest and glade."

He quickly gave Gawain a Roman forearm grip and Morcades a glancing peck on her cheek. Bounding from the low draft vessel into the water's edge, sinking to his calves, turning with an abrupt wave of his arm, he trudged to the bank with joyous vigor, eager for his woodland refuge. Myrddin crossed marshlands and fields, resting at an ancient nemeton site: a small grove of oaks surrounding a ring of stones. He felt the rising current of the Sidhe within the circle welcoming him into the elemental atmosphere. By dusk he had reached kindred stands of trees: leagues from the lands he knew, yet greeting him like long lost brothers, embracing him with their majestic limbs. Every evening sound invited him to hear their ageless stories, collected in expanded rings of growth, resonating organic messages from bark-clad trunks he now understood, melodically lulling him into deep slumber.

Morcades and Gawain had arrived at Dun Airigh, greeted warmly by Aedan, Domelch and their four sons, with the youngest Eochaid Buide and Domangart now joining Eochaid Find and Artúr the eldest – as tall as Aedan, sprouting his first outcropping of a beard. The two oldest lads went out hunting the next day with Aedan and Gawain into the northern forested lands, which came to be known as Achnabreac for the speckled lineage of its ancient native peoples: from the Creones and Picts to the Cymri and Scotti. Large standing stones in these nether regions marked the mystic heritage of the distant lands. It was not an accident of fate that Myrddin wandered into these woodlands, or that Aedan's hunting party would meet him there.

"I saw a buck or something, father, behind those distant trees," Eochaid alerted Aedan.

"Oh you did now, before any of your elders? It must be your young eyes," Aedan humored him.

"I think he's right father," Artúr said, pointing to the deep wood and thicket. "I saw some movement there too."

"Alright then, let's move-in, slow and quiet," Aedan directed, while stringing an arrow on his bow.

Gawain had a sense of something else, telling the others, "Take care not to slay a hermit, a druid, or a pilgrim wandering in search of a hidden cairn."

"Very well, they don't roast-up very nicely anyway," Aedan jested, raising chuckles from his lads. "Quiet now, or no pilgrim pudding," he said as he silently pointed for the others to spread out in their slow pursuit.

Gawain scoured the branches of the trees with his eyes, accustomed to following his guide hawk leading him through the wilds. He was the first to spot the elusive forest dweller, Myrddin, perched in a tree, grinning with arboreal glee.

"Good day lad. Have you brought your Scotti royals out for a stroll?" Myrddin greeted him from the swaying heights.

"You really are a forest creature, aren't you?" Gawain answered back, shading his eyes from the flickering light silhouetting the bard in the upper branches. By the time Myrddin climbed down, Aedan and sons had joined them, following the voices of Gawain and the bard.

"Aedan, this is Myrddin, the bard of Penllanw. Myrddin, Prince Aedan of Dalriada," Gawain introduced them.

"These are my lads: Eochaid and Artúr. They thought you were a wild buck, if that was you moving through the thicket," Aedan said to the odd sylvan bard.

"I have been a wild buck, not so much of late. I was a tree, a moment ago, until hawkeyed Gwalchmai spotted me," the bard quipped.

"What kind of tree were you?" Prince Artúr played along.

"Well an Elder of course!" Myrddin proclaimed, drawing their laughter.

"I would have guessed an oak, high king of the wood," Gawain added.

"Ah, thank you lad – alas, I am them all," Myrddin stated, turning 'round and 'round, his hands reaching up to acknowledge his richly foliaged friends and mentors standing tall around the distracted hunters.

"You are welcome to join us tonight by our fire and share a meal from our meat of the hunt, bard Myrddin," Aedan extended the invitation.

"Thank you kind prince; if the spirit moves me, I will find your light."

Gawain, Aedan and the lads proceeded on their hunt, slaying a fine buck for their fire, making their camp less than a league away from where they met Myrddin. Eochaid had been especially curious about the mysterious forest dweller, having never encountered a hermit before.

"Why does a man like Myrddin live in the forest, Father, and not come to Dun Airigh?" asked Eochaid.

"Some men, hermits and monks, or druids, choose to live alone in the wilderness, believing that they will grow closer to their god or gods, away from other people and the busy life of a citadel or village. Many of them wish to be closer to the natural world, with its wild surroundings and creatures." Aedan explained. "Colum Cille had lived that way for a while in his early life, before he built churches and monasteries."

"Is Myrddin a man of the Church?" asked Artúr.

"No. He is a bard and a druid. He came to Afallon last autumn, spending time with Taliesin, Vivianne, my mother, and other druids on the isle," Gawain told them. "He is somewhat of a seer, as well; and has gone through some kind of great loss and change to his life. He joined us in the power of the mountains and streams while on Ynys Manau, appearing quite adept at the practice, having learned this training from Taliesin years ago."

"And Taliesin was a student of Lady Vivianne's father, the Myrlyn, famous druid and seer of the Cymri," Aedan added.

"Yes, Gawain has told us about him," said Artúr.

"Myrlyn spent many years in the forests and mountains before he opened the Ysgol at Dinas Emrys, in the southern Cymric lands," said Gawain. "The natural world was very much a part of the Raven of Awen."

The hunting party settled into their secluded camp in the forests of Achnabreac, preparing a hearty supper of roasted venison. Myrddin Wyllt did not show himself that night. Aedan and the lads slept comfortably around the fire, waking with dawn's light. Myrddin suddenly appeared at their camp, emerging from the early morning shadows of the woodlands.

"I thought you lads might start the day with the power of the mountains and the streams," the bard announced upon arrival.

"Why yes, of course," Gawain eagerly responded. "I have trained Artúr and Eochaid – Aedan has at least observed our training."

"It is an interesting art," Aedan acknowledged. "The warriors who have trained this way hold an edge over others. I have seen this fluid movement develop in my sons; and I will enjoy watching you lads train together."

Gawain led the lads and Myrddin in the familiar movements. Then he sparred with the two lads, applying these practices to their battle training, Myrddin and Aedan standing back, cheering-on Artúr and especially Eochaid. Myrddin was invigorated by the currents of power that moved through him and the lads. Something was born here with the sons of Aedan, and Myrddin knew it immediately. By late morning, the lads said goodbye to Myrddin and returned to Dun Airigh. Gawain and Morcades stayed-on a few more weeks in Dalriada before returning to Afallon. Morcades had been having visions involving Prince Artúr. She encouraged him to seek-out Myrddin, knowing that there was a mentorship about to be initiated.

Morcades met with Aedan and Domelch expressing her vision for their son: "There is a connecting line of spirit that must be recognized here. Lady Vivianne has seen this too. It is clear to us that your son Artúr will have an important place in events that will unfold. Myrddin of Penllanw has recently emerged from a period of awakening and is here to play his part in your son's destiny. It is a significant time for Artúr to embrace his future and be open to what this Myrddin Wyllt will be able to convey. The destiny of the kingdoms of the north can turn on this new alliance of souls."

Over time, Artúr and Eochaid would meet with Myrddin in the northern woodlands of Achnabreac. They would train in the powers of the mountains and streams; but more and more frequently Myrddin would attempt to answer their profound questions of life and spirit, especially with Artúr. Myrddin had become quite clear and confident in his wisdom and understanding, having learned to step aside within his mind and allow his inner voice of guidance to speak. There was a grandfatherly bond formed between Myrddin and the lad. Artúr had never known his grandfather Gabran mac Domangart, because Gabran died the year Artúr was born. Myrddin openly revealed to Artúr his struggle and transformation after the tragedy of the maidens of the wells and Arfderydd: his descent into madness and recovery, illustrating how someone could rise from the depths of despair and confusion into clarity. Artúr revealed his doubts. They talked about their dream visions, their ancestors, the Otherworld, their fathers, and their clans.

"You are heir to your father's legacy: the legacy of Aedan, of Domangart, and Fergus Mor." Myrddin recounted and elaborated to the lad. "The souls of our ancestors and great mentors watch over us from the Otherworld, encouraging us to be watchful and aware within this waking life. Even as great as our lineage may be, remember each and every soul is heir to the infinite and eternal. This is my realization arising from my internal leaps and stumbles beyond my own identity. It is important to know who you are, at your age this is just beginning. I hope that one day you will realize who you truly are, beyond any idea of identity, lineage or sovereignty. We share much in this waking life; and you share much with many great souls. My great uncle's name was like yours, only of the Cymric tongue – Arthwys, Arthwys ap Mor. His cousin Arthwys ap Maesgwid was a Pendragon, and one of the first five lads to be mentored by the Myrlyn, who was raised by the druid Blaise of Brycheiniog. The lad was named Emrys, after Blaise's uncle Emrys Ambrosius, an earlier Pendragon of the Cymri. Emrys Myrlyn's mother was of the Brychan clan, as was your grandmother Luan Ingenach. Emrys Myrlyn was the child of the rape of Ebradil ferch Brychan, daughter of Ingenach Hen, your great great grandmother. The rapist, Myrlyn's father, was Constantinus mac Fergus, brother of your great grandfather Domangart, the namesake of your younger brother. You and your brothers are of the same speckled lineage as Emrys Myrlyn, the Raven of Awen, born over a century before you, my lad."

Artúr sat silently for a moment, his mind reeling with the intensity of this legacy, and compounded by the recollection of a dream he had yet to share with his forest mentor.

"From what you have told me, I am of the same blood as Emrys Myrlyn, from both of his lines of descent – and, his grandmother's line as well, Ingenach Hen of the north?"

"Yes lad, that's correct."

"How do you know these things Myrddin?"

"I have studied as a bard and druid to know the lineages of the Cymric clans. I have also studied with Taliesin, who knew the Myrlyn well, and is wed to his daughter, Lady Vivianne. My dream visions have also involved visitations form Master Myrlyn, mentoring me as a druid, as a raven, and as entities that I know to be speaking for him. He has led me to you; after he prepared me; knowing that these are things that you should understand."

"I must tell you then, Master Myrddin, you have said these things at the most timely instant. I have had a recent dream vision, containing potent images I can recall from other dreams before. Within the dream, I am standing at Dun Airigh as a child, standing in the footprints of the kings etched into the stone floor. As I stand there, my feet grow into a perfect fit for me to fill these great impressions within the solid rock. I have grown to manhood, feeling my first beard rapidly covering my chin. I walk across the citadel of rock and step off onto the expanding grass covered plain. There I discover myself surrounded by a ring of kings around a ring of stones. In the center of the ring is the Stone of Destiny: the stone carried by my ancestors from the Isle of Eirenn to the Dalriadan coast. Then I hear great thunder sounding from tremendous clouds, billowing overhead, forming mountains of dark and light, like towering citadels growing ascending turrets to exceed its height again and again. I see the clouds reflected in a lake, creating a pool of shining surfaces, capturing the light. Rising from the lake, a priestess breaks through the image of the clouds as lightening arcs upon a sword she holds in her extended arm. A druid cloaked in a black robe takes the sword from her raised arm, walks across the reflective waters, placing the sword into the Stone of Destiny as flashing sparks of light bounce off the flinty surface of the stone. The dark figure waves his hand to me, drawing me near the sword and stone. Writhing serpents wrap the sword's grip, appearing as living dragons holding the pommel in their jaws, igniting sparks and flashes of fire jumping off their scaled bodies down to the hilt. I know what I must do; but I do not know if I can. The druid waves me on, until I grasp the sword in my outstretched palm, feeling its unearthly power coursing through my every bone and sinew. I pull the sword from the stone with startling ease – the scent of grinding metal, the ringing sound of an air piercing bell, my breath alive with the taste of steaming mist, my stance touching the earthen field rooting me and raising me all at once, and in a blinding glint of light upon my sight – I emerge within a solitary boat, drifting on a calm sea, to awaken aglow in the morning sun."

Myrddin smiled, and speaking from a centered calm he had only rarely known before, he said: "There is an ominous billowing that forms our destiny, born of expansion and contraction, within majestic imaginal mountains of darkness and light. These realities overwhelm our senses. And then we are called to choose, to know we can, to be rooted here and now, fully aware, awake at last."

Chapter Five ~ Hallows of the Grail

Our dream visions hold the soul's hallowed images. While we verbose wandering bards of legend, scripture and myth know well, there is an ignorance of sleep that has fallen upon humanity. Myrddin knew the nightmares of these shadows of mankind's stupefying sleep; and yet he also began to know of the awakening – the quickening of his soul. He had seen the fallen Eden, the defiling of innocence, the pain and desecration, the revenge, and the rising of the arcane flaming sword. It was his earnest hope that a healing could occur, with a new generation holding divine promise within their waking souls. The sword, with double-edge, had long been a conflicting symbol for renewal and release. Kings, queens and kingdoms bore outer and inner wounds of this ancient conflict. What was visible to the senses became divisive. What was invisible and elemental was by its nature hallowed and indivisible. This was true of both outer kingdoms and the complexities of the human soul. Dreams display the layers of mind and spirit hidden from waking sight, pried open to reveal the soul's imagery upon a mythic inner landscape. The manifested myths of kingdoms and cultures also display their artifacts, prompting our search and reverence for the unmanifested truth, imagined and demonstrated through these hallowed forms.

Taliesin and Vivianne, relying on their wisdom from beyond this world, set in motion events defining action by their charges, among the kings and princes of the north. The Celtic world held highly their well-crafted symbols, taking form as hallowed artifacts seemingly conjured by the gods. These were the connecting points to primordial worlds, handed down for millennia through the grasp and reverence of ancient cultures. A source, a spark, and a current of a greater reality spoke to the soul beyond dividing lines of clan and kin. Those who learn to feel and convey that source-current recognize the essence of hallowed forms, drawing forth that key found within them to open timeless avenues of spirit. It is in the convergence of the aware soul with sword, shield, lance, cauldron, cup and stone that sparks of immortal destiny meet an eternal moment within the shadows of time.

Born of flame, the metal of an iconic sword had been brought from ancient eastern lands to be created as a blade of balanced beauty by a gifted chosen sword smith on the isle of Eirenn. Ancestral kings of Dalriada carried this masterwork of weaponry to the north, along with the Stone of Destiny. Each was held secure, until the legendary sword fell into the uninitiated hands of southern princes who could not wield its elemental power. Cadel Ddyrnllwg of Powys possessed the sword for a time, until it was lost again and hidden from the world. Master Myrlyn rediscovered the wondrous blade, teaching his charges how to surmount and harness its power. Upon the death of Arthwys ap Maesgwid, Cai Hir and Owain Ddantgwyn – the mythic weapon disappeared once more, awaiting its time of destiny to be brought forward.

It was Taliesin, Vivianne and the wise souls of Afallon who were shown in prescient visions and rising impressions that the hallowed sword's time of return had come. The Pen Bard of Rheged journeyed south to his retreat at Llyn Geirionydd. This was the site of inspired gatherings of bards called the Gorsedd, where they voiced their imaginative words, creatively sparring within their band of talented peers. Master Myrlyn had recognized during his own youthful years that this secluded place would become a vibrant focal point of Awen. These bards were the active voices of the Cymric soul, speaking for the Gwyr y Gogledd, all of them descendants of the great Coel Hen lineage; except for their revered mentor Emrys Myrlyn, whose paternal bloodline was from Fergus Mor of Eirenn and Dalriada. It was Myrlyn's charge Taliesin, now an aging bard, who was to bring these strains of mystic heritage full-circle. After some time of contemplative solitude at Llyn Geirionydd, Taliesin travelled into the Llydaw, climbing to the peak of Yr Wyddfa. It had been decades since he had made this trek with Master Myrlyn, his master's timeless spirit embracing him there again. The fullness of the mountainous expanse, rich with the current of Awen, encompassed and joined these great souls. Through the mist wafting between the crags of Yr Wyddfa, Taliesin perceived the faint image and muted voice of Master Myrlyn greeting him, leading him on up the familiar mountain path. As Taliesin rested, drifting off to sleep, the Master was there, within the bright passages of deep vision and heightened imagination, telling him what to do.

"You and Vivianne know it is time for the return of the Sword Caladbolg. It is widely believed to be lost forever, into the depths of Llyn Llydaw. All of these years, it has been kept safe, within my private inner sanctum, where I had once revealed to you your journey of awakening. You and my dear Vivianne know the hidden sequence to open the secret chamber within this room. Go there, and retrieve Caladbolg. Take care with the sword. It is highly coveted by many who are ignorant yet envious of its power. Only you and your lads can wield it. Be wise with it, my son. I am always here for you, in the depths of vision. I will meet you at the mountains and streams," whispered the elusive and ethereal Master Myrlyn, sending the bard from that fleeting dream into the waking world, there to see with open eyes the startling grace of a mountain lynx passing by his camp through veils of the enveloping brume.

Vivianne had known what Taliesin was to discover; and his glimpse of the wild cat confirmed her wise presence. The mystic father and daughter were his guides, from within this life and beyond it. The Pen Bard dutifully took the next steps to complete his task, bringing the hallowed sword back into the wider world. Taliesin's return to the north was quite timely, leading him to proceed to a highly significant gathering of the Cymric Cylch at a stone circle ten leagues northeast of Caer Lliwelydd in the recently conquered regions of the former Kingdom of Solway, at Maen Gwregys, later called the Girdle Stanes, along the shore of Afon Gwen Esk. It once was a circle of forty-two stones, until the shifting tributary of the Esk had toppled part of the grand ring into the flowing waters. The original span of stones formed a perfect circle, fifty-two paces across, aligned with the rising sun of

Samhain on the morning before All Souls Eve. This was a time of the thinning veil between the mortal forms of human life and the immortal spirit realm of ancestral souls. And just as the seasons with the movement of the stars circled 'round the earth each year, the voices of kings, Wledig and tribal leaders were heard around this assembly of the Cymric Cylch. They stood within the ring of stones – stones mirrored by an arboreal ring of ancient Whitethorns, the bark clothed in vibrant lichen, forming feathered tiers on their northern faces, like cascading coverlets or tresses of the goddesses of nature's sovereignty, watching the proceedings in silent attendance from these arching wooden aisles.

Nearly thirty kings and princes, several bards and druids, seers, monks and the newly appointed bishop of Alt Clud arrived at the ancient site to weigh-in their concern for the future of the Cymric Kingdoms. Aedan of Dalriada was there, recently crowned king of the Scotti kingdom to the northwest, since his cousin Conall died in battle against the northern Picts that same year. Artúr, Aedan's eldest son joined his father, their presence initially challenged by some, namely Rhun Hir of Gwynedd. Rhydderch Hael opened the assembly, as it took place on lands acquired by Alt Clud after the battle of Arfderydd.

"Welcome kings and princes, Wledig, respected seers, druids, bards and our new Bishop of Alt Clud, Cyndeyrn. We have called this gathering to reunite the Cymric Kingdoms as threats from Pict Gwlad, Bernicia, and factions of Bryneich have increased since Arfderydd, likely attempting to drive a wedge into the Cymric Cylch, seeing we had been divided by inner strife. I have invited King Aedan and Prince Artúr of Dalriada because they are my Scotti neighbors, and we have not always been allied. Now, after the loss of Aedan's cousin Conall, battling our Pictish foes of the north, we have even greater need of these Scotti as comrades. We also welcome Rhun Hir and his son Prince Beli as our southern Cymric allies. They too stand with us against the Saesneg, and perhaps to quell the assaults by their Pictish kindred to the north. I should be clear: we do not choose to pit brother against brother or cousin against cousin again. That is what the Saesneg seek to exploit – edging-in upon us – attempting to divide and conquer these islands of kingdoms. We must unite under our current Pendragon, our chosen Protector of the Isles, Urien of Rheged, and prepare for his successor, as King Urien enters his aging years. I invite King Urien to speak to you now – Urien."

"Thank you, King Rhydderch, and thank you all: allies, kings and nobles from the north, south, east and west. I do not know how many years I will have as king, or may continue to hold the honor of Pendragon, our battle lord of vigorous command. It is clear that we must stand together, and embrace a leader that will encourage that cause. There are too many threats within our neighboring lands and abroad. Many of our kings, princes and Wledig are worthy of the mantle of Pendragon. My successor is to be chosen by the members of this assembly of the Cymric Cylch. As Pendragon I would choose the one king who has done more to embody the spirit of the Cymri, the allied, the descendants of Coel Hen, of Cunedda, of Brychan, of Cynan

Meiriadoc, of Magnus Maxen, and of Ceredig Wledig and Dyfnwal Hen. That king, my chosen successor, is King Rhydderch of Alt Clud. Whether your decisions are made today, or upon the time of my future passing, consider my recommendation. Watch and remember King Rhydderch's actions, and I believe his appointment as the next Pendragon will be clear to you all."

Rhydderch stepped forward again, addressing the gathering: "Thank you King Urien, for your vote of confidence and for your great courage and bold leadership as Pendragon. Any of the leaders here today may call for a vote at anytime. I shall stand back from that privilege, and allow my Cymbrogi to consider the many noble choices among us for the next Pendragon. But now, I call on Taliesin, Pen Bard of Rheged to address us all, Taliesin."

"Thank you, King Rhydderch. We have come through a dark and divisive time in our history, conquering our own brothers and cousins who defiled the most sacred and precious among us. The chalices of the wells have been tainted, stolen from their hallowed places, and their guardians murdered or scarred and wounded for life. We must protect the sacred devotees of spiritual life. We must retain our highest regard for those symbols sacred to our heritage. We must recover the lost chalice of sovereignty and all of the sacred cups of the fountains. All kingdoms must respect these artifacts as emblems of an enduring sanctity and sovereignty that we share as brothers and sisters of these islands of kingdoms. I have journeyed far in recent weeks to bring before you one such emblem of our diverse yet united people: the Cymri, the Scotti, the Romano-Britons, the Franks, the Gauls, the Picts, and the ancients who came before us."

Then Taliesin lifted-up a bundled cloak, wrapped with a leather tie. He stood it on end on the ground, rapidly releasing the tie and unfolding the cloak to lift and display a finely sheathed sword. Drawing the blade, raising its sharpened edge to the sky, he shouted: "Behold, the sword Caladbolg!"

Initially stunned, the gathering kings and princes quickly began to cheer and shout with excitement. Taliesin swung the sword above his head, as the crowd grew silent again, in awe of the otherworldly but subtle whoosh and vibratory tone emanating from the wondrous blade. The bard gestured with his head for Owain to come forward, handing him the sword. The Prince of Rheged had been Taliesin's longest student mentored in the power of the mountains and streams. Owain immediately felt the surge of the power of Caladbolg as he took hold of the carved dragons on the grip above the hilt.

Taliesin nodded to him, quietly saying, "You are grounded in the mountainous earth. Allow the vibrant streams of our ancestral masters to guide and carry your movement; because now, you are one with the blade."

Owain stepped directly into a warrior's stance, beginning a series of rapid movements, responding completely beyond himself, yet smoothly articulated throughout his highly trained athletic body. And then, the sword began to sing. A high pitch and whirring drone astonished the observing kings, even more than the prince's bold display of swordsmanship. Gawain, Llenlleawg and Peredyr stepped forward to try their hand at wielding the sword, and others soon followed. The lads of Afallon displayed skill and agility, with ease equal to their elder comrade Owain. Rhydderch's son Constantine could only hold the sword for an instant before being overcome with dizziness, taking-on a sudden sickly pallor. Taliesin relieved the prince of the sword, while the young princess of Alt Clud, Constantine's sister Angharad supported him.

"As you see, kings and nobles," Taliesin announced, "the sword Caladbolg cannot be wielded by just any prince or warrior. This blade seems to have a will of its own, only accepting the extended arm of those attuned to the sword's otherworldly power. Many of you may claim the right to carry Caladbolg into battle, but there are few here today for whom the sword itself will acknowledge as its bearer."

King Urien stepped forward again, declaring: "As the lineage of Rheged has long been the wedded and allied clan of Master Myrlyn – 'the Raven Kindred' – it is clear by display of skill and heritage, my son Owain holds claim to the sword Caladbolg."

This immediately raised a clamber among the other kings and princes, each claiming their right of heritage and precedent: King Loth bellowing above the others – "My sons have equal rights, Urien, being of your kin and clan! Gawain has already shown his affinity with the blade and its power!"

Rhun Hir claimed the sword as a treasure of Gwynedd, and his relation to Bedwyr and Owain ap Einion Yrth Pendragon. Maig and Cyngen of Rhos promptly argued their direct descendancy from Owain Ddantgwyn. Ceredig ap Gwallog claimed right by relation to Arthwys ap Maesgwid. Finally, Rhydderch attempted to regain order, suggesting that King Aedan of Dalriada held the greatest claim as both the descendant of Fergus Mor who brought the sword from the Isle of Eirenn, and being of the same lineage of Master Myrlyn: by Fergus, Brychan II and Ingenach Hen of Alt Clud. This only enraged the nobles further, many of them not even accepting the presence of Aedan at the Cymric Cylch.

Then, Vivianne, standing atop one of the sacred stones, shouted: "The Sidhe must decide! Our ancestors have given us this miraculous sword of kings. We must hear their voices and silence ours. Let us listen, listen to the sword itself. Let one man, blindfolded in the center of this great circle, be turned and guided by the sword's power to choose the future bearer of Caladbolg."

This alternative quickly gained a consensus of support. Taliesin was blindfolded, holding the sword, standing in the center of the great ring, the king of each kingdom standing just inside the sacred stones. Owain turned the blindfolded bard around a few times, abruptly stepping away into the outer circle. Taliesin held the sword at shoulder height, turning slowly to feel some sense of direction, stopping still, pointing into the ring of kings. It appeared to every observer that the sword pointed directly between King Rhydderch and King Aedan. Bishop Cyndeyrn of Alt Clud immediately challenged the haphazard proceedings.

"This is not even as clear as divining a well or hidden stream! I cannot condone these shady druid practices!" The bishop decried with fervor.

"Everyone remain standing as you are!" Vivianne directed. "The answer is clear. Who among you had any foreknowledge of the sword Caladbolg being presented here today?"

Vivianne raised her hand, as did Taliesin, Myrddin, Morcades and young Penasgell.

"Aside from these seers, has anyone had a dream or vision of the sword Caladbolg in recent days or weeks?" Vivianne questioned again.

After a moment of silence, Myrddin spoke-up, "I know who has had such a dream, Lady Vivianne."

"Yes, Myrddin, bard of Penllanw, how do you know this?" Vivianne questioned further.

"The lad has shared his dream with me." Myrddin answered.

"And who is this lad?" Vivianne asked.

"He is Artúr mac Aedan," said Myrddin.

A rumble of voices moved around the circle before Vivianne spoke again, "Everyone, please, remain where you are! Artúr mac Aedan show yourself to us all!"

The lad raised his hand, standing a few paces outside the inner ring of kings between King Rhydderch of Alt Clud and the lad's father King Aedan of Dalriada – precisely where the blindfolded Taliesin had pointed the sword Caladbolg.

"As you see now my lords, the sword has shown us what we could not see before," said Vivianne. "Come forward lad!"

Artúr stepped forward while Owain removed Taliesin's blindfold.

"Come, tell us of your dream, lad." Vivianne directed him with a welcoming lilt in her voice.

"I was standing as a child, within the footprint of kings at Dun Airigh, when my feet suddenly grew to fit the footprints. My beard also grew, as it has begun to grow in recent months. I walked across the northern plains to a ring of stones surrounding a ring of kings, just as we are here today. In the center of the ring was the Stone of Destiny brought by my ancestors from Eirenn. I saw a priestess rise from within a lake, as time and distance collapsed within the dream. She held a sword with two carved serpents above the hilt, handing the sword to a druid. The druid drove the blade of the sword into the Stone of Destiny, igniting sparks to fly off the edges of the blade. He beckoned me forward to the sword and stone. I drew the sword from the Stone of Destiny with one hand, and suddenly all my senses were overwhelmed by a blinding light; and as my sight returned, I found myself in a boat drifting on a calm sea. Then I awoke from the dream."

"Thank you, Prince Artúr. Prince Owain, would you lay the sword down on that flat stone near you, and then step away? Prince Artúr, walk over to the sword and see if you can pick it up." Vivianne instructed the lads.

Artúr walked over to the sword lying on the stone, kneeling down with reverence before it, reaching forward with one hand – he raised the sword Caladbolg above his head, smiling with honored exaltation. Then he stood up, as if the blade's motion had lifted him. He slowly rotated the sword with one arm; and as his movements increased, the sword began to sing its eerie song again. The gathering was silenced by the bold display of the lad, barely a man, yet somehow moving as adeptly as any mature and consummate warrior. When the lad had ended his splendid demonstration of such great affinity with the sacred sword, Rhydderch stepped forward, addressing the gathering again.

"I have a proposal for all the kings and Wledig, but especially for King Aedan of Dalriada and his son. It is clear to me that the sword has chosen its bearer in this young prince. To encourage a firm alliance with all of our kingdoms, I offer to foster Prince Artúr of Dalriada as a son and Prince of Alt Clud, for a period of four to seven years, binding the Cymri and the Scotti of the north as brothers in our Cymric Cylch."

Aedan stepped forward saying, "If my son agrees, and he remains the bearer of Caladbolg, I will consider this proposal."

Then Artúr spoke out, holding the revered sword Caladbolg high in the air – "I share this sword with my Cymric brothers, the lads of Afallon, to wield it with me, as our ancestors did, to engage in a bold new union of Cymbrogi!"

The lads of Afallon cheered their young brother-in-arms, the others soon joining them, King Loth then stepping forward, shouting over the crowd: "I call on us all to now choose our next Pendragon! I join my brother Urien in recommending King Rhydderch of Alt Clud! Kings, princes, Wledig, druids and priests of the Cymri – who will join me in electing Rhydderch as successor to Urien as Pendragon – say aye!"

"Aye, aye, aye!" the gathering resounded in loud response.

"And those opposed, say nay!" Loth shouted.

"Nay, nay!" a lesser faction responded.

"To all ears the ayes have chosen Rhydderch of Alt Clud! Hail Rhydderch, Pendragon of the Cymri!" shouted Loth.

"Hail Rhydderch, Pendragon of the Cymri!" the crowd answered back.

"Hail Urien, Pendragon of the Cymri!" Loth called out.

"Hail Urien, Pendragon of the Cymri!" The crowd answered back, as was the custom when the reigning Pendragon welcomed his successor.

The gathering continued for another day and night with feasting and reverie at their encampment. New and renewed alliances were formed, discussing plans of defense against invaders, the impending threats of the Saesneg and their own distant cousins. The sword Caladbolg had revived their united defense of all they held sacred, and an inspired search for the lost chalice of the wells. Even though the choice of Pendragon was not unanimous, they all were bonded together again by the sacred symbols of their joined heritage, manifesting a greater power than they could muster on their own, or expect through any chosen leader. They held certain forms hallowed: the chalice, the sword, and the rings of stone – reminding them of this timeless truth.

Aedan, Rhydderch and Loth had joined forces in the north to battle the Picts, who were comprised of two main factions: those allied with Bruide, Aedan's estranged brother-in-law, and the highland alliance of Miathi tribal kingdoms. This division among the Picts, as well as the remnants of the

Orcadians under the rule of Loth, allowed Dalriada to regain dominance in the north, after the death of Conall and the crowning of Aedan as King of Dalriada. Artúr received the benefit of battle training and strategy from both Rhydderch and his father, as foster son of Alt Clud and prince of Dalriada, while gaining wise mentoring from Myrddin the mystic bard and Cyndeyrn the new bishop of the north. Cyndeyrn's influence on the kingdom of Alt Clud was evident, with Rhydderch being one of the increasing numbers of Christian kings. He seated the new bishopric near a monastery that had existed since the time of Saint Ninian at Penprys, in the vicinity of an old fort, by an overgrown thicket at the head of the Afon Basses estuary above Solway Firth. Being less than ten leagues west of the battle site of Arfderydd, a new guardianship of sacredness was emerging in the north. Colum Cille continued his influence upon Dalriada and the Picts, even making missionary journeys into Bruide's northern kingdom. This was the new Christian frontier, as unlikely for converts as the eastern Saesneg settlements, who had broadened their invasion of the south up to and beyond the Severn. Horrific news of the rape of nuns and the murder of Cymric saints reached the north, still recovering from Gwenddoleu's rampage and Arfderydd's carnage. Catwg of Llancarfan was killed in his own chapel, impaled on a Saxon spear. Reverence had no home when the beast of war ran wild. Those who survived sought the sacred wherever it could be found. For some, it was the sacred vows of marriage, securing alliances with distant allies or old adversaries, as had been practiced for centuries.

Gwenhwyfar ~ Gwenhwyfach

Four years after the Aenach Garman of Llenlleawg's triumph, the King of Laigin wed his daughter Gwenhwyfar to the Prince of Dalriada, Artúr mac Aedan. When news of the betrothal reached Llen, he was struck by a blow harsher than any he had endured in combat. He believed that their continuing love was deep, but he was not a recognized prince, holding no kingdom, title or clear lineage of his own. He did not even hold the sword Caladbolg. The next blow to strike at Llen was the sudden invasion of Ynys Manau by the northern King of Eirenn, Baetan mac Cairill of Ulaid. Aedan, Rhydderch and Loth were heavily engaged in conflict with the Picts, the newlywed Artúr among them, brandishing his sword of divine right. Gawain took part in that northern campaign, protecting his maternal ancestral lands of the Orcades. It was up to Owain, Peredyr, Llen and the warriors of Rheged's "Raven Kindred" to defend Ynys Manau, and secure the sanctity of Afallon and its priestesses. Recently wed Gwenhwyfar was there at the time of Baetan's first landing. Vivianne, roused by a vision, alerted Llen and others before the ships arrived. She had also foreseen the romantic tension posed by Gwenhwyfar's visit while her new husband was off fighting in the far north. Now it was Llen, not Artúr who would become Gwenhwyfar's protector. The king of Laigin was incensed by Baetan and the Ui Neil attacking Ynys Manau, when he had just secured a greater alliance with the Cymri and the Scotti of Dalriada. Even Colum Cille stepped-in to negotiate with his former countryman King Baetan, before a civil war of the Scotti could ignite throughout Eirenn and the western isles. Baetan expected tribute to be paid to him by Dalriada; but Aedan refused, seeing his kingdom as independent from the High King of Eirenn's rule. Baetan saw Laigin's marriage of alliance to Dalriada as a threat to his control of Eirenn and his status as High King; while Baetan's son Mael Umai was among the many princes desirous of Gwenhwyfar for his own bride. Mael Umai led the incursion of the island toward Afallon, while Baetan fortified the western coast. Under the guise of truce, Mael Umai met with Llen and a troop of warriors to discuss Eirenn's annexation of Ynys Manau.

"Greetings from Eirenn, honored champion of Aenach Garman," Mael addressed Llen.

"Greetings?" responded Llen. "Your father lays siege to this peaceful isle and you offer greetings?"

"I do, and I offer peace. Afallon need not be affected by which king holds claim to this peaceful isle. You are an honorary 'Man of Eirenn', are you not, Llenlleawg?"

"Yes, and therefore, honor is the question here," Llen answered. "Is it honorable for the High King of Eirenn to invade the protectorate of Rheged over a dispute with Dalriada?"

"First Dalriada takes the Stone of Destiny," Mael fired back, "and now I understand, also holds the sword Caladbolg, and weds the sword bearing prince to a princess of Laigin – this does not appear honorable to me, but rather a legacy of thievery."

"How does one steal what one already owns?" Llen questioned further. "If a king of Eirenn held a sword or stone, is it not his right to move them about as he chooses? Fergus mac Erc held that right, as do his heirs and descendants."

Mael continued with a fervor in his voice – "Manannan mac Lir and the Tuatha De Danann held this island too. We, as their descendants, claim it as our own, and our sisters and daughters as our own."

"The king of Laigin may wed his daughter to whom he chooses. Even the daughter has little say in that fact. As for the priestly sisters of Afallon, they are daughters of spirit, not daughters of the land or earthly kingdoms. Your ancestors must hold this sacred, whether newly baptized as Christians or not," Llen declared.

"You have a choice here Llenlleawg," Mael Umai continued: "to be an honored 'Man of Eirenn', or to become an enemy of Eirenn. We will await your choice until dawn of the morrow – Good day!"

Prince Mael and his troop retreated, as Llen and his men went back to the Afallon Ysgol, awaiting support from Rheged. Owain and his cousin Peredyr had just received word of Baetan's invasion and were marshaling a force to set sail with the tide. Ynys Manau was not fully fortified around the Ysgol. Ports to the north and south near the Ilo, or calf of Manau held forts since the druid exodus from the Romans, centuries ago. Christian settlements existed peacefully farther north, established by Saint Patrick and Saint Maughold. Baetan had taken a fort to the west on an offshore island with a treacherous access called "the sword bridge". Main entry to the fort was by docking from the Sea of Eirenn. Baetan could house his force for landings on Manau or retreat to Eirenn with ease from this secure location.

While the troops of both forces slept that night, Mael Umai led a small party back to Afallon to prepare a plan of attack, before the Cymri could gain reinforcements from Rheged. Bercnaf and Llen led the night watch of the grounds. In the late hours past midnight, Gwenhwyfar slipped out into the darkness, drawn to Llen by an irresistible desire to be alone with him. Bercnaf's hounds began to bark as the princess approached.

"Hush you – it's only the Princess Gwen!" Bercnaf silenced the hounds. "My Lady," he said, bowing.

"You should not be out here," Llen abruptly told her.

"I know," she answered, smiling coyly. "I couldn't sleep. Can we walk?"

"Ah, perhaps, for a bit – then you must return to the Ysgol," said Llen.

"Thank you," she answered, holding his attention with her eyes.

"Oh shite," said Bercnaf, under his breath.

Llen and Gwenhwyfar strolled along the garden path leading away from the grounds of the Ysgol.

"I have not had any time with you alone since I arrived at Afallon," she said to him.

"It is probably for the best, now that you are wed to Prince Artúr," Llen responded curtly.

"Best for whom – Artúr?" the princess snapped back.

"Best for everyone!" said Llen, pulling her into his arms and kissing her passionately.

After extended moments of rapturous embrace, she caught her breath, saying: "This is best, for our souls – too long torn apart by kings and their kingdoms."

"I agree in my heart, but we are duty bound; and may suffer death or worse for one moment of passion," Llen answered.

"Then are we to live without passion? That seems to be more of a suffering life, or worse, my dear Llenlleawg."

Just then the hounds barked again; and Llen put his finger to his lips, silencing their conversation. He stepped off the path, listening for any sounds beyond the hounds, looking intently across the moonlit terrain. He heard a short gasp from Gwenhwyfar as she was grabbed from behind, he bounding towards her, only to be struck on the back of his head, left unconscious. Mael Umai had seen the two lovers while spying form a nearby knoll, moving-in and seizing the moment when Llen stepped away from the princess. When Llen came-to she was gone. Prince Mael had his prize hostage. Llen had lost her again – or worse. Bercnaf, concerned over Llen's delay, but assuming a romantic interlude was lingering-on, discovered his good friend on the garden path, dazed from the sudden ambush.

"What happened? Where is the princess? Did she knock some sense into you with a stone?" Bercnaf grilled him.

"No – someone took her, probably Mael and his men," Llen answered, rubbing the back of his skull.

"Oh shite, you really stepped into it this time," Bercnaf scolded him.

"Yes, deep my friend, deep," Llen sullenly responded.

"What now?" Bercnaf asked.

"Before first light I move on Ynys Padrig," Llen declared.

"Are you mad? Baetan's full force must be there," Bercnaf cautioned.

"I'll go it alone, across the 'sword bridge' at low tide. No one there will expect it," Llen calmly stated, with a look of determined intention.

"You are mad. Why not wait for the arriving troops of Rheged?" Bercnaf questioned further.

"They won't arrive until well after dawn. If I don't succeed before dawn, I will be dead or captured or worse," Llen answered.

"Or worse – it sounds worse already," added Bercnaf.

"Her capture means the battle is on. I will bring her back or die trying. Owain and the men of Rheged will come 'round by sea, occupying Baetan for my safe return," Llen reasoned.

"Your blind confidence is baffling. If I ever fall for a woman like you have, please, slit my throat – because my mind would be, like yours, turned to jelly."

"You can count on me friend, if that time comes. Today, the princess can count on me. You will see," said Llen, as he prepared to depart.

The princess had been taken to Ynys Padrig, the western tidal island of Ynys Manau, now held by Baetan mac Cairill. Its rocky cliffs made the fortress atop its ledges nearly impregnable for an armed siege. Only a stealth attack by a few warriors could breach the walls and towers. Mael Umai believed he was quite secure there with his desirable captive. The night raiding prince and his men brought Gwenhwyfar into the main hall of the fortress, his father Baetan asleep in his bedchamber for hours by the time they returned from their covert mission. Mael untied the princess, shoving her into a chair, as she scowled back at her arrogant captor.

"Well, Princess of Laigin, finally I have you to myself," boasted Prince Mael, as he dismissed his liegemen with the wave of his hand.

She just stared angrily at his freckled face and fiery red hair. He reminded her of her uncle – whom she also detested.

"You don't have me," she defiantly responded to him.

"I soon will, now that you are a ploughed field, wed to Artúr the imp of Dalriada," Mael snarled back. "But first we must drink to celebrate our own union, before I bash the bride."

He handed her a cup of wine, which she promptly threw into his face. He slapped her. She then swiftly raised her leg, kicking him in the groin. A bit off target, this angered him even more, as he grabbed her throat with both hands, pinning the princess and the chair she sat upon against the wall.

"Enough delay, little wren, I could snuff the life from you this instant. But then I would cheat you of the pleasure of being mounted by a real man – not some boy prince of Dalriada."

She gasped for air as he released her throat, grabbing her by the hair, pushing her face-down over a table, lifting her garments to forcefully take her. She held the table tightly, gripping its edges with each hand.

"Now I have you – Gwenhwyfar," he growled as he entered her flesh.

"You have no one. I am Gwenhwyfach. Do what you will. No one is here," said the princess, succinctly, in a voice unlike her own, resolutely calm and chilling, even to this brute of Eirenn.

Mael Umai finished his brief assault and guzzled a cup of wine. The princess remained prone on the table, hardly moving. Mael sat in a chair, drinking another cup of wine, just looking at her bare behind. Finally she stood up, pulling her garments over her body. She then sat down at the table facing him, staring emotionless, as if looking through him at an empty chair.

"What, no gratitude for sparing your life?" he said, attempting to rattle her stolid gaze.

Her eyes appeared to regain focus, looking at him, seeming to just then notice he was there, saying: "Which life?"

"You are a mad woman. If not for your beauty or a ransom, I would have no further use for you." With that, he took her by the arm up two narrow spiraling flights of stairs to a room within a tower facing east, throwing her onto the floor, and saying: "Do not try to leave. You cannot escape this fortress or this island. Soon we will bargain for your life and find your worth, if anything."

He closed the door and left her there. She lay curled-up on a patch of straw, falling asleep for a short time to awaken startled, not sure of her surroundings. Standing up, she walked over to the window, looking east at the moonlit terrain. She thought: "I am on an island, in a tower. There is a mainland or another island out before me." Looking down, she saw the low tide exposing a jagged row of stones connecting the fortified island to the other land. Sharp spikes of steel rose up from the jagged rocks, creating a perilous causeway for any ships or men attempting to cross over. She saw something moving down there across the rocks. It was a man, carefully weaving his way through the dangerously sharp obstacles protruding throughout the causeway. The man looked familiar to her. It was Llen. Her heart raced as she realized he was coming for her. Gwenhwyfar went to the door; and to her surprise it was unlocked. She quietly crept down the steps of the tower, not seeing a soul. Outside a lower floor exit, a guard was huddled asleep under his cloak. She gingerly stepped by him and made her way towards the parapets above the sword bridge causeway. Llen was nearly across by this time, looking up to see his beloved peering out between the parapets. Reaching the base of the wall, he removed a coil of rope hung diagonally across his chest. Carefully loosening the coil, he tied a loop in the end, tossing it up to Gwenhwyfar, gesturing to her to wrap it around the parapet and to lower the loop down to him. Slipping the end of the rope through the loop and pulling it up snug to the top of the wall, he slowly climbed the wall to reach her.

Embracing her firmly, she kissed him passionately, until he stopped her, whispering: "Keep holding tight as I climb down. Stay silent until we are across the causeway. Be careful of your gown; the passage is treacherous."

They descended together, slowly, pausing at one moment when they heard footsteps above the wall. Shadowed by the waning moonlight, the rope disappeared into a crevice between the stones of the parapet. When the footsteps faded away they continued down the rocky cliff. Making their way through the shadows, they reached the sword bridge. Again, Llen whispered to her to be careful of her gown. Partway across, the blades caught her garments; so she used the sharp edges of the blades to cut them from her legs, letting the fabric wash away with the rising tide. Her bare legs became bloodied by abrasions from the jagged rocks and slices from the steel blades. She proceeded unaffected. Llen looked back, noticing an expression of near pleasure on her face as she felt each cut of self wounding. By the time they reached the other shore, her legs were lacerated from thighs to ankles. She just smiled lovingly at him, showing no pain or discomfort. It was approaching dawn, and the tide was rising, soon to obscure the sword bridge.

They hastily followed the edge of the road through the shadows, until the grounds of the Ysgol were in sight. Llen helped wash the wounds on her legs at a spring, tenderly, as she lay upon his cloak, which she had been wearing since they left the causeway. While he tended to her, touching her bare legs and thighs, he soon began kissing the soft skin of her lower body, she holding his full head of hair gently in her hands. After his loving lips and tongue had aroused her pleasure for some time, he lay with her face to face, as their passion met its culmination, there at the center of Ynys Manau, at the center of their island world, free of all sense of loss, free of all sense of wounding, free from betrayal.

Llen helped the princess to slip into her bedchamber unnoticed, as dawn light was just beginning to illuminate the landscape. Bercnaf and his hounds were the only souls aware of the daring couple's arrival.

"Well, you survived, none the worse, it seems," said Bernaf.

"Yes," Llen answered in a contented daze.

"What . . . you saved her and bedded her too?" Bercnaf questioned him.

"Love, my friend, in its fullest; I did not believe it possible," Llen said softly, through a dreamy smile.

"Huh, it is impossible, even that it happened. You are a dead man, if ever discovered to have violated even a willing and wed princess. Your life is now the sword bridge – one false move or loose step and you're cut to ribbons!" Bercnaf chided him sternly. "By the way, we still have an island to defend. Hopefully we see Owain's army before Baetan's."

With dawn light reaching the west side of Ynys Manau, Mael Umai had awakened to discover the princess gone from the tower. He and a handful of men searched the rocks at the base of the fortress walls, puzzled by her disappearance. One man found the remnants of her gown, cut to taters by the sword bridge blades, with traces of blood on the fabric. Mael held it in his hands, shocked by her apparent desperation, believing she had perished in the tide. Baetan soon became aware of the calamity, seeing his son holding the princess' garment.

"What is this?" Baetan asked.

"An accident, father," Mael replied.

"This garment is the color of royalty. What have you done?"

"She has done it, not me."

"Who?" Baetan angrily asked.

"Princess Gwenhwyfar of Laigin," said Mael.

"What? How did this occur?"

"I was on reconnaissance near Afallon, when I saw her on a path . . . and took her hostage. She escaped in the night and . . . and drowned herself," Mael haltingly explained.

"Drowned? Have you found her body?"

"No, father, just this tattered and bloodied garment – she is no doubt lost to the sea."

"You have put all in jeopardy with this rash move. Now, we dare not take Afallon, with one princess dead and vanished – lest we incur the wrath of all the Cymri. The stain and stench of Gwenddoleu still lingers. Afallon must remain untouched and held sacred. You tie our hands, stupid lad. Now we wait and see if Aedan and the Cymri advance," said Baetan turning away from his son and furiously returning to the fortress.

Back at Afallon, no one was the wiser, except Vivianne, of course. Her keen awareness knew something had occurred in the night between Llen and Gwenhwyfar. She went to see the princess in her bedchamber. This bard, raised at Afallon by the priestess Claire, recalls that day as one of my earliest memories. I must have been nigh four years of age or younger, when Claire was asked to bring warm water in a basin and a balm to Princess Gwenhwyfar. I remember seeing the princess, her legs bare, with cuts up and down them. Even at that age I was stunned by the contrast of her beauty and the wounding. Claire whisked me away, telling me never to enter a lady's bedchamber, and not to utter a word about what I had seen. Soon after that incident I remember seeing Vivianne enter Gwenhwyfar's room, closing the door as I spied down the hallway.

"You can confess to me of your encounter with Llen, my troubled child." Vivianne directly addressed Gwenhwyfar. "I already know you have broken your vows. Don't worry; all of your secrets are safe with me. My visions have shown the torment that you have struggled with for so many years."

Gwenhwyfar broke down in tears, as if Vivianne had opened a deeply submerged door into the shadows of the dear lass's soul, allowing the flood gates to free her from a hidden pressure and near drowning.

"I, I," Gwenhwyfar began, weeping heavily between her words. "I lose time, when I, I cannot remember what has taken place for hours at a time."

"Have you had this happen recently, or as a child?" asked Vivianne.

"Both, it seems most of my life."

"What did that feel like?"

"As a child, I felt as if I had a hidden friend, who would visit me and protect me."

"Protect you from what?"

"I don't know."

"When did you first have this feeling?"

"After my mother died, and I went to live with my aunt and uncle for a while."

"How long did you live with them?"

"For a few years, I believe" said Gwen, trying to recall lost time.

"And it was then that you began having these lapses in your memory?"

"Yes, I think so."

"Why do you think you went to live with your aunt and uncle?"

"At first I did not know. I was sad. My mother had died, and my father was very distraught. I thought he didn't love me anymore."

"Do you still believe that?"

"No, but then, I didn't understand."

"How was life with your aunt and uncle?"

"It seemed good, but strange."

"How was it strange?"

"Well, I went from losing my mother and missing both my mother and father, to being showered with love and attention."

"What made it feel strange to you?"

"Hmm, well, it didn't seem real. I found myself living in a world that was made-up, not me, not my world, or the world I had known, but like I had become someone else."

"Is that when you began to have the friend to protect you?"

"Yes, I think so."

"I would like to try something with you, to help you remember some of those times that you forgot, when you say that you lost time. Would that be alright with you?" Vivianne asked.

"I suppose. What do I need to do?" Gwenhwyfar replied.

"All that you need to do is relax, close your eyes, and I will do the rest."

"Well, alright."

"Just listen to my voice. Feel it as a soothing voice, a loving voice, knowing that this voice is one you feel completely safe with, protecting you, nurturing you, and helping you to be the complete loving soul that you are. Feel yourself utterly relaxed, drifting upon a cloud of love, peace and security. You are free of any sense of your body. You are weightless, floating in perfect ease. You are as free as the air that surrounds you. Deep within you is vast space: space to see all that you can be, all that you can know, all that you have been. You know who you are. You are love itself. You know love. You know your mother's love. You know your father's love. Now, remember a time when you forgot that you were loved, when you thought you lost your love, or lost those who loved you. What do you see?"

"I see my father. He is very sad. He does not want me to see him sad. So he sends me away."

"Where do you go?"

"I go to live with my aunt and uncle."

"What happens there?"

"I am confused. My aunt and uncle try to love me; and I want to be loved, but something is wrong. It feels strange."

"How does it feel strange?"

"Creepy . . . my uncle does things to me."

"What things does he do?"

"Secret things – he says it's our secret, secret touching, hurting, ow, ow, ow – it's not me." Gwen's response suddenly shifted to a harsh tone, the character of her voice changing as she spoke. "I can't be hurt. There is no pain. It's fine. Nothing is happening. I will protect you."

"Who is speaking now?" Vivianne asked.

"I am Gwenhwyfach. She cowers. She cannot protect herself; but I can. The red-haired bastard is scum, a worm. One day I will kill him."

"It is alright now. You are safe. Let go of him. He cannot hurt you anymore. You are free. You are at peace. You are relaxed. Remember that you are protected. Remember that you are loved. When you awaken, you will remember everything that you have told me. You are strong. You are whole, undivided. You are love itself. No one can hurt you. Return to this place as Gwenhwyfar. You are safe. You are safe here with Vivianne in Afallon. Slowly open your eyes, awake and clear."

Gwenhwyfar opened her eyes and immediately began weeping, holding her head in her hands.

"It's alright dear. You are safe," Vivianne said, holding Gwen in her arms. "You are stronger now. You know what happened to you. You are protected. You are love, pure, strong, love."

Vivianne held her and rocked her in her arms for quite some time before Gwenhwyfar finally spoke.

"I don't know what to say."

"What do you feel?"

"I feel shock. I feel horror. I feel shame. I feel your love." Gwen said, weeping again.

"There is no need to feel shame. You were a child, an innocent. It is alright now. You are safe. You are love. Love is your strength. All of the strength that built your friend and protector, Gwenhwyfach, is within you. You are that strength. You are infinite love and strength."

"My lady, I, I see so much more now," Gwen responded, then silent, pensive, taking it all in.

"What do you see?"

"I see what happened back then. And," she began weeping again, "I see what just happened."

"What just happened?"

"I was abducted and Mael Umai raped me," she wept and wailed.

"Oh my dear, dear lass, you are strong. You are safe here. Your strength and love are now together, bonded in the infinite power of love."

"Thank you, Vivianne, I lost myself when he attacked me; just as I did as a child, when my uncle . . ." she wept again.

"You protected yourself the only way that your soul knew how – by becoming a fierce and stronger you – Gwenhwyfach. But in truth, she is not greater, but smaller. She is your hate. She is your anger. She is the false Gwenhwyfar. Now you are stronger, more complete, undivided and aware," Vivianne reassured her.

"I love Llen," Gwenhwyfar began weeping again.

"And he loves you – I am certain."

"We made love after he rescued me. It was wonderful. But it was only half of me. I had forgotten what happened with Mael. Llen won't love me now. Llen won't love me anymore."

"Yes he will. I know him. I love him too, as much as if I had given birth to him myself. He is steadfast."

"It is so complicated," Gwenhwyfar shook her head in disbelief. "I am married to Artúr!"

"This is the trial of a princess: to love, to honor, to become a queen, but also to know and protect the sovereignty of her own soul."

"I now remember how cruel I was to Artúr. He is almost as innocent as I was as a child."

"How were you cruel to him?" Vivianne asked.

"Our wedding night was mutually unfulfilling," Gwen answered.

"That is not an unusual occurrence," Vivianne commented.

"I'm sure of that," Gwen continued, "and was to be expected, with my confused childhood, then becoming betrothed to a stranger, rarely seeing each other until the wedding night. Artúr was clumsy and inexperienced; and then he was still further disappointed and shocked to discover that I was not a virgin."

"He knew that much, it would seem," said Vivianne.

"Yes, he said, 'I do not claim to be a man of the world, but I know enough to see that I am not your first lover.' That brought a response out of me from my protector, saying – who are you to question me, from your small world? You are not a man, but a boy with a sword and a title – 'hard lighting' fitting you – as it was over quickly without any thunder to move me to love."

Vivianne raised her eyebrows, giving the princess a look of moderate disapproval, as Gwen went on, "Then I told him that we are a bargain between kings, not impassioned lovers. And, that I could not hide my experience from a boy (knowing inside that I had been forced into womanhood years before my first blood moon) saying to him – a woman is a woman at her first blood moon; you have not drawn your first blood in battle. Go then to the north with the men of your clan, and maybe you will come back a man."

"How did he respond?"

"He slapped me across the face with his open palm."

"What did you do?"

"I smiled, staring at him coldly, like I had with my uncle and Mael Umai, as if by raising their anger, I held the power."

"How did he react?"

"He seemed disarmed," Gwen described him, "uncertain of how to handle the she-devil I appeared to be. Then he left, off to Pict Gwlad,"

"How did you feel after he left?"

"I felt numb, laid back down, fell asleep, and did not recall the entire episode until today. I supposed and believed he had bedded me that night. That was what was supposed to have happened; but at some point it had vanished from my mind, until now," Gwen explained.

"Now that you understand what happened to you, it will take time for you to heal, and fully see yourself as whole and complete, returned to the loving innocent soul that you are."

"I am?"

"Of course – you love Llen. You still love your father. I assume he knows nothing of your uncle's abuse."

"No, he would have killed him. My uncle had told me, if anything happened to him, if he were killed because of our secret, that I would be tortured and killed by my uncle's men."

"Oh my dear Gwen, it's over – you are now aware, the healing of your wounded soul begins."

"I am ready. I will need your help. It may help me that my uncle recently died. I heard that he choked on a bone or something, while stuffing himself, like the sick old dog that he was."

"Well, as I said, it's over. I am here to help you. You may stay in Afallon as long as you need to."

"My husband will want heirs."

"In time, my dear, in time," said Vivianne, hugging Gwenhwyfar again. "Come to me anytime. You are strong. There is a wise woman emerging within you. I am here for you. Love is here."

"Thank you, dear Vivianne, you are love," answered Gwen, her eyes welling-up again as the high priestess kissed her forehead before leaving the bedchamber.

Vivianne left the young princess alone to contemplate all that she had revealed within the lass, seeing the resilient strength within Gwen's embattled soul. All around this sanctuary of inner work, the grounds of the Ysgol were bristling with the activity of men at arms, building timber ramparts to prepare for Baetan's impending attack. Owain, Peredyr and the troops of Rheged arrived to assess the situation, Llen conferring his strategy and the defensive status of Baetan at Ynys Padrig. They resolved to send a force by land, to hold the shore from further invasion, and place ships near Ynys Padrig to attack by sea, limiting Baetan's naval assaults. Baetan was quick to assure the Cymri that he had no intention of attacking Afallon; and that he considered the Ysgol there as sacred as any monastery. This was a great relief to Vivianne and the priestesses that their sanctuary was secure. Baetan still held other ports and coastal fortifications, effectively controlling Ynys Manau. Aedan, Artúr and the Cymric forces of the north remained occupied with battles in Pict Gwlad for many months. A stalemate withheld for three years before Baetan's forces retreated back to Eirenn, releasing control of Ynys Manau to Aedan of Dalriada. Aedan had been battling on two fronts: in the sea of Eirenn and in Pict Gwlad. Owain and Peredyr had returned to Rheged and eastern Cymric lands, as Dalriadan and Rheged ships policed the western shores.

Owain still held the position of guardian of the founts, even though most of them hand not recovered since the tragic assaults by Gwenddoleu. Many of the wells across the land had run dry. Only powers beyond this world could discern whether these were inevitable seasons of drought or evidence of the wounding of the sovereign earthly goddesses. Owain and Peredyr sought to restore the sacred sites, recover the chalice of the wells, and revive the ancient sovereignty of the land. This was a daunting task, bridging otherworldly realms, and expanding the human limits of each questing warrior who would join them. Peredyr also endeavored to rebuild the legacy of his father Eliffer's great javelin armies, harkening back to the ancients, trained both on the left and the right hand. It was Peredyr's calling to lead them, and understand more deeply the revival of the ancient legacy of the javelin and lance. He had remained close to his sister Penasgell during those years of defending Afallon and his bonding with his new band of brothers in the north. Penasgell had become more adept in her gifts of vision and the interpretation of dreams. Peredyr's mastery of the javelin and lance took on new dimensions within his dreams, inviting his wise sister to shed light on his inner world. He met with Penasgell, describing a vivid dream vision to her.

"There is a troubled warrior. I am observing him, and yet I feel that I am a part of him. This warrior has two swords. He is in search of his lost brother: a twin that he believes he may have killed. This brother warrior is armed with a lance, but cannot be seen as long as he desires to hide himself. When he is armed, he vanishes. When he is unarmed, he may be confronted; but to harm him is an act of cowardice. The warrior with the two swords stands before a Frankish king and his court, where a feast is being served. The warrior is staring into space, distracted by his thoughts, trying to understand his own sorrow and inner turmoil. He does not partake of the feast, and feels judged by the overcrowded court, seeing his behavior rude for not gratefully receiving their hospitality.

"The brother of the king, a warrior named Gorlawn, strikes the visiting warrior across the face, saying, 'Raise your head! You bring ill-will upon yourself by rejecting what is given, to do nothing but think, lost within your own thoughts.'

"The warrior responds, 'Gorlawn, I also reject this injury; and it is not the first time.'

"'Defend yourself!' shouts Gorlawn, raising his sword.

"The warrior of the two swords blocks the blows of Gorlawn with one sword, and with one violent blow of his other sword, splits the helm and head of Gorlawn in two. Then a vision of his twin brother appears, without his lance, only to disappear, leaving the lance standing on its own. The warrior with the two swords watches the lance begin to draw the blood from the fallen Gorlawn, as streams of brilliant light ascend from the stricken body. Everyone in the overcrowded court marvels at the lance standing on-end, drawing the blood as if siphoning wine from a cask. The king rises from his place at the table to assail the warrior who had just killed his brother, striking the warrior's sword, shattering the blade just above the hilt. As he backs away toward the hovering lance, the warrior drops the remnant of his shattered sword, takes-up the lance, throws it at the enraged king, piercing the king through both of his thighs as he tries to turn away to avoid the lance. Suddenly the entire palace begins to shake, as a violent tremor rocks the whole land and the foundations of the citadel. It seems as if all the kingdoms of the north had begun to shake, with brothers avenging brothers in battle after battle. The wells run dry. People mourn the dead. Two-hundred warriors lay dead in the citadel. I am aware in the dream that the lance now holds the blood and the light of life and death. But I cannot find the lance. I cannot find the wounded king. What I do know is that I must find you, my sister, to understand what I must do. Then I awoke."

"We have lost too many brothers; and we are twins to each other," Penasgell began to interpret her brother's dream. "We grew up sheltered from the warring world by our mother. Our father, who was our king, and our brothers, were lost to us in battle. Warfare is a conflict of will – ill-will at its worst. The twins, one of the flesh and one of spirit, are observed by you; but they also are you. The spirit is elusive, maybe lost; maybe we feel we have somehow killed him or her – that other part of us. The lance – direct shaft of insight, or of revelation, or of pain – pierces the veil of realities between the living and the dead, between the blood and the light. It is cowardice to attack the soul. This is self-wounding. To live from the spirit rather than the taunting of the crowd requires courage. Gorlawn is the overcrowded outer voice, which strikes-in, as the inflated king, shattering our defenses. Thoughts are as much an outer weapon used against us, as they are an inner language or tools of contemplation and understanding. Life is a feast. The question is: how much do we partake of it? The ascetic monk avoids it. The hedonist wallows in it. You must 'raise your head', or lift your thoughts. Their injury upon you is not the first time, and certainly not the last. The attacker is split in two: his head split between the dual nature of experience. One violent blow reveals the twin nature of being. The lance, however, stands alone. It represents a vertical center, and a will beyond our own. Everyone marvels, yet few understand, as a phenomenon that intoxicates the masses like a cask of wine, siphoned from spirit into matter, where once manifested – confounds us. The king, our aggrandized self, rises to the conflict to strike-out; but is pierced by the lance of profound truth, even as he turns away from it. Within dualism, one of the two swords is always shattered, in a perpetual clash of opposites. It is a dolorous stroke. Our foundations are rattled. Our land of dreams is in turmoil, with only respites of peace. Progress seems crippled, pierced through the thighs, impeding forward movement. The wounded king or queen is us. We continue to search for the lance for some sense of healing. The love that we know and share as brother and sister, observing the battles without perpetuating them, is our solace of understanding. What you must do is find your way to be the love within life and perpetuate that, dear brother."

"As always, you bring me back to that clear place of spirit," he told his sister. "You are still my peregrine guide."

"You are that lance of power and healing love to me as well, dear brother," she responded, embracing him.

Penasgell had learned well from Vivianne during her time at Afallon. Observing the high priestess share her visions and revelations, Penasgell understood these things natural to herself. She also helped Gwenhwyfar to find her way back to greater stability of spirit, encouraging another strong woman of her generation. Gwenhwyfar performed her duty as princess of the north and wife to Artúr, growing in her wisdom with mentoring from Vivianne and support from Penasgell. And yet, she secretly met with Llenlleawg, keeping their passion dangerously alive. Llen frequently sought counsel from Vivianne and Taliesin, and quite often with Vivianne concerning his illicit love affair with Gwenhwyfar, receiving cryptic and cautionary advice from the high priestess for the challenges he faced.

Vivianne explained to him, "Your Gwenhwyfar has three fathers – her father the king of Laigin, her father-in-law the king of Dalriada, and Manannan Mac Lir the king of the turbulent sea – tossing her between the rivaling seasons of winter and summer: as the flowering bride of a dynastic alliance consummated in spring, bringing the early dawn of yet another season of battles and wounding into the dusk of the fall. She recovers from battles within herself. When her mother died, her father was so distraught he allowed her to be fostered by an aunt and uncle. The child, your Gwen, was abused for years. Her soul built a fortress of defense, assuming other identities of strength to survive a siege upon her innocent soul and body. I'm sure that you have seen her capacity to endure pain. At times she may even seek pain, believing that is what see needs or deserves. She also has an untapped visionary gift that allows her to conjure and relate to other entities and realities, which have been used for her defense, potentially waiting to be developed as she may mature into a priestess. The powers that live within her are elemental: winters could be harsh; but summer may bring inner battles – torn between her shaded duty to a kingdom and the bright sun of radiant passion for her soul. These inner torrents paralleling nature can allow a budding calm to become the atmosphere of duplicity, tempting this daughter to embrace the immensity of the natural world, or be lost in the diminished identity of survival and desire. She is a listing ship that can only right itself by will, reason and intention. She loves you, and sees you as the only man to master the wild tides that she knows are churning within her, tipping the fragile vessel she still is."

"I love her too, deeply and madly – but am I capable of sharing her torment?" Llen asked.

"Only you can know this. I see the strength within you to conquer any and all adversity. Now you know that what you face is more than a lover wed to a prince of Dalriada," Vivianne answered.

"Why are we so drawn to each other amidst this conflict of destinies?" Llen struggled to understand.

"Your inner destinies are aligned: both of you struggle with a sense of identity undefined. There is a need to prove your selves worthy: she of love, you of title, honor and recognition – both for recognition of the great souls that you are. You may believe your quest is for your identity; but your quest is really for love, and some sense of healing all the wounds of lost or unfulfilled love. This sense of identity turns the veil of immortality into a wall, a fortress built around yourself, accessed only by a sword bridge. Your quest is a quest of the heart, to reveal the love beyond the veil. It is the love and joy of your being. This is the only seemingly lost love, a love living inside you, covered by an armored identity and its fortress for a false king or queen. Armored for war, endless battles will hammer away at the core of love, the innocent foundling that you once were, and the innocent child Gwen once was. They both live inside of you, as the love you join together. Love is your immortal life – which can be lived right now. A prince who does not recognize his sovereignty will remain in exile. However, if he embraces his divine sovereignty, he will realize who he truly is – a divine heir wherever he dwells."

Dolorous Gates of Dream

"Thank you Lady Vivianne, my sovereign mother on this earth," Llen acknowledged. "You have led me to that heaven of love and understanding all of my life. I continue to attempt to grasp all that you and Master Taliesin have taught me. I know the inner life of my dreams is a window of my soul and a door to the Otherworld. With all that has happened within the heights and depths of joys and sorrows, I must share with you a recent powerful dream. It touches on much of what you have said to me today.

"I was following a hart buck down a path through a dense wooded grove the path no broader than the expanse of my hand. The buck seemed to be that same great spirited beast of my first kill. Suddenly the forest opened near a coastal cliff, and the hart buck leapt from the towering ledge toward an island closely offshore. The sunlight glared against my vision, as I tried to discern the image of the island and the direction of the hart. I saw the island heavily fortified at one instant, and then as supportive of an enormous tree in the next instant. The tree was shifting within my sight from a bourgeoning gigantic form, branches reaching to the limits of the sky, into its own reflection on the still waters, inverted and fully formed, growing towards the horizons of the earth. The roots were alive and rising above the island realm, forming a maze of double walls and corridors of the fortress, building itself larger and larger upon this secluded isle. The roots and corridors are both paths and gates that I know I must enter to explore, confronting an ominous power guarding against me, threatening my intrusion into this foreign realm. There were ships nearby that seemed to be awaiting my endeavor, to enter and claim the fortress, or island-tree, as it were. There was a doleful air about this place – a foreboding tension building – as I heard the creaks and moans of the living walls and corridors, formed of roots and branches of the all-encompassing tree. I also heard a voice of a mysterious seer, a priestess of Afallon, advising my advance, telling me of the odd conditions that I would face ahead.

"As I stood at the outer gates, the voice of the priestess said to me: 'Every warrior who has entered this place has perished here, either by combat, or the wounds of conflict. Only the one who can confront and conquer ten seemingly impossible opponents will endure and survive, finding true fulfillment from his endeavors, and freeing this citadel of its torment. The challenger must remain for forty days, if he can fight his way through the double-walls, the gates, and the maze of passages. Above an inner gate, a colossal copper warrior stands with a double-headed axe. When this warrior falls, the challenger will know that the inner gates may be opened to him.'

"I accepted the challenge, the priestess appearing for a brief instant – veiled, but beautiful – then vanished from my sight as a warrior emerged from the outer gate. He stood in a formidable battle stance, confronting me at the rocky foot and foundation of the fortress. It was past midday as we engaged in a clash of wills, his skill and strength equal to mine. Even as the blows of his two-edged sword seemed to appear from nowhere, I saw them in the precise instant to shield myself from each flashing strike. Our eyes were on each other's every movement, both of us enduring minor cuts upon the flesh – a slice here, a gouge there – until a glancing thrust of my blade took his right eye, blinding him with the flow of blood across his face. He yielded, asking to be spared as my prisoner.

"Just then another warrior appeared from behind me, while I keenly heard his footsteps approaching in time to block his quick assault. He too was equal to my skill, agile with sword and dagger, clashing with my blade in a rhythmic ringing of steel against steel. Again, I was able to thrust my sword, this time through his two-blade guard, slicing-off his left ear, clearly paining him; yet he fought undaunted. Finally, at a moment when his focus was distracted by profuse bleeding across the side of his face, I delivered a deafening blow through his right shoulder, leaving him powerless, yielding, and begging for mercy. Before I could audibly acknowledge his capture, a loud horn sounded over my voice, and another adversary burst out of the fortress.

"This hulk of an axe-wielding attacker ran at me with bloodthirsty fervor, prompting me to dodge his broad swing, nearly stumbling over my last captive opponent. Swordsmanship was more to my skill and preference, having no taste for axe-wielding, mace or cudgel, finding this new foe to be a barreling bear for me to confront with my delicate cutlery of defense. It was an awkward dance with this enraged bear of a man, taking care not to get bit or mauled, while making tasteful turns in my footwork, allowing quick jabs or slices to dice the beast before a final skewering, after he had been well basted in his own blood. His final moment occurred when he followed through on an overhead swing, leaving himself extended forward, exposed to an adroit cut through his jaw, opening his neck, dropping the ursine warrior to the ground, choking on blood with his last breath.

"The scent of a fire arrow introduced my next opponent, who began his attack from behind the outer gate. As he approached, he set his bow aside and continued, sword drawn, grinning with a simmering pleasure aroused by the fragrance of his smoldering advance arrow. Every troop of warriors seems to have some fire-crazed contingent, eager to smell something burning. He may have fared better with a hot iron, rather than a sword; because it wasn't long, even after the fatigue of battling the first three that I secured another surrendered prisoner, slicing through the fire-loving archer's grinning face, taking away a large portion of his nose.

"Relentlessly, a fifth warrior arrived, announced by the sudden feeling of a laceration across my back through my leather hauberk, just enough to draw blood. Number five was an adept swordsman, challenging my prowess into the twilight with his highly advanced handling of the blade. He had a touch and accuracy that I have rarely seen, truly keeping me in a heightened sense, to feel his moves before they arrived. It was my bolder actions that were his undoing: when I defanged the darting serpentine action of his blade-work by severing several fingers of his best hand. He immediately yielded, joining the other three prisoners and the slain brawling bear.

"As I gathered myself, preparing to face another assailant, I could see the gates of the fortress had been sealed, and now had torches lit on each side of the barred entry. Suddenly the veiled priestess appeared again, telling me: 'There will be no more combat tonight.'

"'But I have not defeated ten warriors this day,' I replied.

"'Tomorrow you will face ten more, starting again as if you had done nothing,' she informed me.

"'How can this be? I saw them. I heard them. I felt their blades. The scent and taste of their blood is upon me. I know these conflicts happened. I know what I have done. The body of one and the other four prisoners are here for any and all to see,' I protested.

"'Where are they?' she asked, gesturing with her hand for me to look around, leaving me baffled, to see no one else there.

"'But, they were here,' I claimed, franticly looking about for evidence of my opponents. Then I showed her my wounds. 'Here, see these cuts and bruises, lacerations to my hauberk and shield – I could not have inflicted them upon myself.'

"'Who else could?' She dismissively answered. "Night has fallen. It is time for you to rest, to heal your wounds, to face another day.'

"I followed her, dumbfounded, as she led me into a village, entering a fine cottage. It seemed that everyone had gone to sleep. Although a fresh meal sat on the table for me to eat to my contentment. The veiled priestess showed me to a nearby room, where she washed and dressed my wounds, while I stood nearly asleep on my feet, soon collapsing into bed, unaware of her departure.

"Strangely, I dreamed within the dream, realizing that my wounds were completely healed. My white battle-shield was unscathed. The priestess was there again, telling me: 'Your shield is without mark, or sign of conflict, or any heritage. When you wake, you will carry this shield again; but you will carry other shields with you as well. These three other shields will not be seen; but you may call on them at any time. With each shield, you will be able to interpret each new conflict that will arise. You will know with your mind; you will know with your heart; and you will know with your soul through the power of each shield what you must do. In this way you will regain your strength as the drama and fatigue of combat assails you.'

"The next thing I remember, I was standing on an open beach, at the rocky foundation of the fortress. My body was unscarred, without a mark or slice upon my hauberk, shield or leggings. A woman stood at the foot of the first gate, dressed for battle, crowned and armed, with a throne and double altar visible behind her within the fortress. She said, 'This is the gate of the shadow of death. It is also the gate of life, the gate of tears, and the gate of justice. Here, your balance is challenged. I am the daughter of the mighty ones. I am the exalted intelligence. I am the virgin queen and bride to all that is. Through me all futures are born, and all that was of the past dies. You must first engage me to continue.'

"'I cannot attack a woman,' I replied. In response, she began hurling daggers at me with the speed of a hundred bats rapidly emerging from the depths of darkness. I crouched behind my white shield, points of daggers piercing through, each tip jarring my resolve; until the thunder of repeated impact stopped. Peering around my shield, I could see that she was no longer in front of the gate. I set the dagger-littered shield aside, approaching the gate, only to have this bizarre female warrior strike at me from out of the corner of my eye. Reacting instantaneously, I blocked her sword with mine, engaging in a rigorous battle of blades equal to any man I have ever fought. She was brilliantly agile, keen to anticipate my every move. After what seemed like hours of intense swordplay, I was able to raise one thrust that would surely have penetrated her body; but she vanished from my sight, the gates of the citadel opening behind her, exposing an interior garden equal only to the Biblical Eden.

"I entered the gates, gazing high above to the limits of my vision to see the cascading of blossoming vines of diverse forms, hanging from the crowning entablature of three triangulated columns. Although I walked directly into the scene, I felt as if I was drawn-in by some otherworldly force overcoming all earthly inertia. Entranced by the setting, I was soon greeted by a strong young Adonis, standing upon broad marble steps, utterly naked except for his fine sandals. He was the most handsome man I believe I have ever seen: muscular in his torso and every limb, well endowed, with veins evident on his hands and arms that seemed alive with the currents of the rivers flowing from all creation. His eyes emanated an intensity that stupefied any semblance of words I could attempt to speak. As he walked towards me, he did not speak either – although his mind of pure intelligence somehow entered my own, holding my attention to the point of freezing any motion across the nerves and sensations of my stunned human form. As his mind momentarily merged with mine, I could perceive the workings of the cosmos. In a flash of realization I now understood him to be master of the mill of time and space, turning its eternal action with powerful brute strength and harnessed equilibrium. When he withdrew his overshadowing thought from mine, I immediately felt inept and vulnerable to his innate power; suddenly realizing that I would soon battle this superhuman entity for my life. It was then that he drew forth a razor-sharp Roman gladius; and I was forced into conflict with this god-like adversary. My strange mental encounter shifting quickly into combat was oddly accompanied by the rich fragrant perfume of the floral vines hanging overhead, keeping me aware of these surroundings and my connection to all elements of the scene, being in a scene within my own dream and of the interior of my mind. Now I saw my opponent, who possessed the strength of ten warriors, was in fact an aspect of myself and reservoir of my own strength, at one with all elements of this conjured reality. His prowess was my prowess. Therefore, I was invincible within the realm of my own dream awareness. With that encompassing notion, I drew my sword, not to strike against him, but to release the vines meandering around the pillars, which soon encircled the struggling naked body of the iconic warrior, lifting him from the scene to a place beyond perception. It felt as if I had called upon one of those miraculous shields, without even knowing so: the shield being a shift in my awareness and interpretation of the events appearing in this strange world.

"To my shock and amazement, another warrior emerged from the atmosphere into view – one of the strangest creatures that I have ever seen. He or she was both male and female, lightly bearded, breasted like a woman, but also clearly endowed like a man. His or her features were rather severe and angular, with very muscular loins and legs. I have heard of these hermaphrodites described by the Greeks; but this entity was beyond any previous imagining. Yet there I was face to face in my own dream with a creature that defied the opposites of nature. And after battling the earlier warrior queen, I had no resistance to fight a breasted opponent, yet without a clue how to interpret this apparition. It was akin to battling two warriors at once, confusing my perception and sense of reality. In the end 'they' fell to my blade and vanished like the others.

"Another combatant arrived almost immediately, jarring my sense of fair play again, in that she was an extremely beautiful woman, standing stark-naked in front of me, arousing both my mind and lusting heart with her obvious allure, clairvoyance, and spiritual presence. Her loins, hips and legs were unquestionably feminine. Her lips pursed with the subtle color of a budding rose when she spoke. She could have slain me with a glance, before any conflict began. The fight was brief but intense. Surprisingly adept at her use of a long dagger, she was able to quickly best my swordsmanship, nearly cutting my throat, only to disappear after whispering one enticing word into my ear – 'Mercy'. At that moment, I dropped to my knees in utter gratitude to all the powers of the cosmos, looking up at the towering copper warrior, his form rising above a wall of the inner gates. He slowly began to rock to and fro, until he completely toppled to the fortress floor, bursting into a shambles of tubular fragments and panels of copper shapes, shattered apart at the seams.

"Climbing around the hammered forms, I discovered another path leading to a garden cemetery. I wandered there among the stone markers and crypts until I came upon the tomb of a king and queen. When I read their names I was struck with a rapturous chill that rose up my spine. It was not the specific names that overwhelmed me; but it was the stating of their lineage and legacy. Carved there in the stone it read: '. . . of the line of Benoni, Gilead, and the sons bearing the name of Galahad'. With the reading of that inscription, I awoke in tears of both sorrow and joy, not certain of who I was, or who I was to become – but I knew somehow these words and names held an answer."

"Words and names speak to the mind; images speak to the soul," Vivianne began interpreting his dream. "This is a most profound dream vision. Dream-life conveys a story of images, displaying the paths we take: the paths we have taken, and the new paths we may explore. These paths are living branches of a tree, describing our soul. You are the island and the tree, on a hunt or search for the self, following the 'hart'. The fortress is the fortification of your heart against your own heart's desires. You followed the 'hart' to discover the island fortress of your own soul, all at once a fortress and an unfathomable tree, the Tree of Life. The Tree of Life is the tree of our source and origin as a people, describing the cosmic path of the spirit of all humanity. All souls dream their own pathways; while each soul's pathways are individual reflections of the infinite Tree of Life: just as a seedling is a reflection of a giant tree whose seed has fallen to earth. The seed enters the earth as each soul enters a life to find their way, through a maze of experience, double-walls and corridors, in a seemingly secluded isle of self. The earthly experience is one of duality, dualism, challenge, and conflict – if we engage in the drama, the nearly unavoidable battle. Our own roots form corridors, patterns of paths – some we create, some we inherit – from our parents, from our ancestors, and from humanity as a whole. Dreams display a layered story within the mind, reflecting both the waking life and the awakening soul. You are challenged to be aware of the mind, observing it as an avenue of adventure, realizing that the reality behind it, beyond it, and encompassing it – is timeless and infinite. All adventures are waking dreams: when you are within them they seem incredibly real. But as you awaken, you realize how asleep you were for a time. You have your own sense or intuition of what awaits you on an adventure; and you may receive guidance from a seer or guide. They all reflect your own inner guidance.

"You were told, 'every warrior who has entered this place has perished here', as all identities, all physical bodies die. This death is a death from the reality of the five senses, which is where your battle began in the dream. You are challenged at the outer gates five times, each opponent being an outer sense overcome before reaching the inner gates of awareness. They become prisoners to your advancement, as you had become a prisoner to the limitation of your own sense impressions, illusions, and false beliefs. What you taste, swallow and ingest becomes what you are. These embodied impressions must be terminated. The other factions of the senses survive as prisoners to serve your interpretation of reality. The final sense and arbiter is what you feel, what touches you, as intuition, as prescience, as deeper vision and awareness.

"That is the end of outer conflict, 'as if you had done nothing', as if all before was an illusion, or misperception, or misinterpretation. You were affected. You carry the wounds; but they can be healed. It seems that everyone is asleep, as you were, and are, in a dream within a dream. Your shields are your modes of interpreting your experience. How you feel it and interpret it becomes your reality. From this awareness, you are prepared to enter the inner gates of experience. Ultimately you become aware that all dreams and adventures are happening within you, allowing you to become lucidly awake and aware beyond them. The ten opponents are one opponent – you – your sense of self emphasized and expanded as your imagined reality. The period of 'forty days' represents the four walls and four shields as your own barriers or protections to be understood and interpreted for a new Jerusalem – your newly founded peace.

"At this point in the dream you have entered the gate of self mastery. 'This is the gate of the shadow of death, and the gate of Life. Here, your balance is challenged.' You face your opposite, your desire, your fear, and your sense of justice or moral standing. Oh, and the daggers do come at you! This is an ancient path, as ancient as Eden, as ancient as all creation. It is the path of return to the source of our being. The intricacies of this understanding are displayed within your dream imagery in a phenomenal way. I believe it is because it links directly to our shared heritage of ancient wisdom from the Fisher Kings and the Sicambrian Queens, and from the Merkabah and other ancient paths of understanding. The warriors beyond the inner gates of your dreams are otherworldly. The copper colossus collapses because it is a shell, a fabrication, a false idea of some towering being. All of your notions of strength and weakness, of male and female, of vengeance and mercy are shattered through the voice of your own inner imagery. Gratitude for this depth of mercy and equilibrium is all you can see; and in that you know you are part of an ancient line of understanding. The paths of your adventure and its gates for you to open to know who you truly are, is realizing the beginning and the end of every path exits only in your mind. There is a source; an origin of who you are that compels you to embark on a path to discover that which has always existed inside of you. It is not within the colossus that stands before you, to be conquered or to collapse. That is of the mind's making. Creation is more than a path, or an object, or a conjuring of the mind – it is realization of being. Our ancestors traveled this path of creation and realization, as our descendants will too; whether they are descendants of the blood or not – they are descendants of the Light. My visions are confirmed by your dream that you are a descendant of the line of Benoni and Gilead, as son of Ban of the Benoni. His father was Galahad, from the line of Fisher Kings, reaching back to the tribe of Benjamin – son of his father's sorrow, become son of his father's joy – son of Jacob ben Isaac, patriarch of the Stone of Destiny, whose dream of angels ascending and descending is our dream of awakening."

Chapter Six ~ Wheat of Song

Souls ascend and descend as echoes of their own angels. The minds and bodies donned in this life for a span of time vanish from recognition, unless they have left some mark on form and memory. The bard chants his verse. The king amasses and retains property, leaving a legacy to his heirs. Words and deeds impact others and patterns of living perpetuate themselves as if by sheer inertia. Bards attempt to stand at the edges of battle to observe and reflect insights; more often, they aggrandize the avalanche of human events. I must have descended into this life from some other sense of being; because I am repeatedly perplexed as an outsider to the world that I inhabit. An odd word – inhabit – so much of what I do or assume is by habit. Had I not been raised by bards and mystics would I see things as I do? I believe that I am where I was meant to be; but is that because it is what I have known and lived? My accident of birth seemed aligned with a greater intention. That is where I live and express from – my greater intention.

Much like the words of verse, living comes from this innate intention followed, not as manufactured will, but as listening in cadence with inspiration – inspiration received in open awareness – in a word: Awen. The wise bard realizes the balanced power of an innate will that exists as a guide within the flow of events. On the contrary, there is a reactive will within mankind that tries to control events. Reactive will and its battles of mind and form leaves the earth littered with carnage of unfulfilled vision, marked by bodies piled up from generations of justified ignorance. Even a warrior's dreams are illustrated with images of bloodshed, while still displaying the imaginative convolutions of mind and soul. How did we arrive at this point where suffering is the metaphor of truth? Sons of gods sacrifice themselves as heroes within our myths and dreams; and we hold them up as exemplars of truth. Bards have told and retold these tales, many written down to linger in time. We bards have continued to paint a false picture of a habitually suffering world. Maybe we can open our words to reveal the Otherworld, the world of the expansive heart, and rise from sleep and dream as ascending angels, lifted above the repetitive lines of the gravestones of destiny. What are we destined to be? Are we merely destined to repeat what we do, what our ancestors did? They observe us and speak to us from the Otherworld; but most of the time we do not listen.

There is wisdom within our virtual being. Master Myrlyn and his foster father Master Blaise knew of the coming of Taliesin. They were aware and looked for the lad's arrival. He was a child destined to be a bard, fostered by the wisest souls of these isles. Decades later, I was born and brought to Afallon to be fostered by Claire and Morfyn under the guidance of Vivianne and Taliesin, the wisest surrogate grandparents any bard could dream of having. Beyond our earthly teachers there is a field of knowing that surrounds us. We are planted here within a manifested life to sprout and flourish on the earth. Every potential experience is a burgeoning shaft of life.

Through our re-awakening innocence we learn to discern between the tares and the wheat within the fields of our souls. A seed grain lives in our depths, cast from our greatest source of origin and truth. We are here to cultivate that staff of life, our center of being – our art of living. This is what I learned from my mentors of vision and song. Taliesin taught me to see from the eye of origin; as he was taught by Master Myrlyn; and as he taught Aneirin and other bards. There is an eternal harvest of vision that any soul can realize. I have made it my constant intention to bring forth the wheat of song.

I sprang into life as a wild weed: sired by violence unknown in my innocence. I was fascinated by Taliesin early on, somehow knowing he held the magic that I would desire to master for myself; even though he was aging by the time of my birth, after the battle of Arfderydd. Both he and Aneirin, his gifted student and distant cousin, saw something in me to be cultivated and revealed. Well before I understood language, I was drawn to their voices like a fledgling bird to its parental song. Although it was Claire and Morfyn who witnessed my first utterance of speech, it wasn't long before Taliesin encouraged a rhythm and metre for my babbling sounds. I was being trained in the mimicry of rhythmic patterns before I had acquired speech. The subtle vibrations of deeper resonant elements were without a doubt also embracing me as a child of Afallon. I recall early dream visions where Master Myrlyn would appear with my mentors Taliesin and Aneirin, before I ever studied with Aneirin. They would lead me to the summit of a hill, prompting me to fly, which I did again and again in my childhood dream visions. The Flight of Icarus was an early favorite myth, likely because of these soaring dreams.

As I grew older, I experienced a continued teaching infused within these flying episodes, paralleling my waking life at the ysgol. A vast amount of memorization and recitation of verse was required from me to be accepted by these wise mentors. I learned the classical languages, while enhancing my vocabulary with each passing year. History and philosophy gave a context for the language skills; but what drew me deeper was that vibratory sense emanating between thoughts and words. Aneirin saw this in my early verses, swaying him to take me under his charge. It was a rigorous training and a disciplined study, keeping me terribly busy, concentrated on my study in my youth, inspiring these early lines.

Beirdd Diwyd	Busy Bard
iawn diwyd	very busy
bod y beirdd	being the bard
y beirdd bod	the bard being
y gwenynen	the bumble bee
mewn hediad	in flight
am droglau	'round the scented
o' gair blodyn	flower of words
troi yn golau.	turned to the light.

Taliesin and Morfyn also trained me in the power of the mountains and streams, guiding my cultivation of that source of the flowing energies of life.

I saw how warriors like Llenlleawg, Gawain, and Owain the Prince of Rheged held the power of that primal source from their years of practice. Taliesin taught me that whether the energy of creation flowed into a warrior's sword or a bard's words, the source and essence of gifted power was the same. Awareness is the central element of the creative spirit. Taliesin said Master Myrlyn called it the "sparked observer". It could be felt rising up through the soul and into the finger tips of the initiate, allowing the words of one's otherworldly voice to be heard. This "swyn bys asgwrn" or "charm of the finger bone" could be developed and called upon to enrapture the expression of the bard. "Be open to the current and feel the flow," Taliesin would tell me, as he had told Aneirin, well known for his "flowing verse". They both reminded me again and again of the words of Master Myrlyn that, "there are avenues of the mind that allow a higher listening". The bard learns to hear, speak, and inspire from this place. The power of the mountains and streams enhances the vibration of song to resonate with the source of all creation. I was blessed with the gift of these mentors to carry that creative source into the world in my own way.

After my foster father Morfyn died, I began to travel with Aneirin, from the courts of Rheged, Dun Barton and Lothian to the Gorsedd gatherings at Llyn Geirionydd. He affectionately called me "Cian", his pup-bard in training, a name first giving to me by Morfyn and adopted by Taliesin. But as my skill grew, I became known as Cian "Gwenith Gwawd" or "Wheat of Song", because I endeavored to instill that seed of the truth creation within my inspired words. Within every living being the truth of creation exists and expands as each individual entity, at one with the whole expanse of creation. Even a speck of an insect or a tiny bird wriggling full of life reaches out into their vibrant reality, struggling to live, to grow, and to learn. Somehow even the smallest creatures discover their path of survival and guided movement into an increasingly broader reality.

Icarus Jay

One time as a lad, I rescued a fledgling jay, lost from its nest, abandoned by its parents, left alone on the ground as an approaching late spring storm closed-in on the fragile being. First I tried to protect it with a make-shift nest of leaves and dry grasses, hoping the parent jays would return; but they never arrived. So, I brought the little being into the ysgol, keeping it in a small crate packed with leaves and grasses under my bed. I managed to scrape together a little mix of wheat and oat porridge with mashed poultry scraps, feeding the tiny puff of downy tan, grey and blue feathers with the end of a stick. It devoured every bit I fed to it, chirping with gratitude, with beak and throat gaping open to expose a strange pointed tongue, uniquely suited to swallow every moist dab of nourishment.

Each day the fledgling got stronger; its wispy grey and tan down turning to more layers of blue striped feathers. Eventually the little fellow ventured out of the crate, hopping about, curiously inspecting my short boots and wool leggings. I couldn't keep my miniature roommate a secret for long. Taliesin and Morfyn both told me – "He's a wild creature lad, and to the wild he must return." They were right, of course; but it did not know the wild, and had no parents – just like me. I was its foster-father-bird, feeding it several times a day.

The day before I found the little thing, its nest had been attacked by a predator. There was a great commotion outside my window: two jays chasing a hawk into the distant trees. Any siblings of the lone fledgling were likely killed. I never saw the parents again. So I stepped in. After about a week, the little bird advanced from short hops to ascending flutters, not quite flying, but close. It would jump from the floor to a stool, to a small niche in the wall. I brought in a dry branch from the grounds, which it took to straight away, never returning to the crate of leaves and grasses again.

The little being seemed to know it was time to grow up, to perch, and to attempt to fly. It fell on the floor numerous times, trying to reach new heights to perch, or to land on my hand, arm, or shoulder. I knew it would have to fly and fend for itself before I could let it back into the wild. Somehow I believe it knew this as well. I could not teach it a thing. Instead, it was teaching me to step-up to its new level of independence. This winged and leggy lad was going places, any day. All that I could do was watch. There was something within that tiny being that knew what to do, and when to do it. Creation and freedom were bristling inside that minute form, building to take flight and soar. No one had to tell it how. I learned from that little spark of life that giant leaps are bounding within us, if we can only let them go, to be completely free. There is a will of creation that sets each being on its way into the world: the will to live, pooled and flooded into action by the raw power of creation. Gradually each new entity becomes aware of its surroundings, rising to meet an innate pulse of survival. All creation is reaching out for its instinctual source of life, carried deep within it, finding expression in the manifested world that we persist to inhabit.

As the jay grew larger and stronger, it shifted from short fluttering to flight – darting across the room over my head, strafing the upper wall above my window, frantically reaching for some way out. I knew I must let it go. It needed to know the world, for good or ill will, discovering its own mighty little destiny. It, I called it – not knowing the bird to be male or female. It, not knowing me to be human or a non-feathered friend, I suppose; and yet knowing that I would feed it. What would it do when facing beak to beak another bird? Soon, I would find out.

I had a rare day without needing to be the busy bard, so I sat with the bird the better part of the day, outside, near the bush it was born in, the nest still there. It never entered that empty nest, the nest where its siblings had been killed a little more than a fortnight before. The bird stayed in the bush most of the day. I fed it every couple of hours, giving it drops of water from a wet bit of cloth at the end of a stick. I could barely reach up to the branch that the jay perched upon, to allow each morsel to slip into the open mouth of the well protected feathery creature. It moved about the bush numerous times throughout the afternoon, quietly peering out to view other smaller birds flitting about on their daily routines. A pair of older jays was in the vicinity, also quite busy, neither one seeming to notice my fledgling friend. All day long the bird never chose to hop onto my hand, as it had done so many times during the past number of days. Just two hours before sunset, I fed it a hefty portion of the porridge and poultry mix, which it devoured with the usual delight. Then suddenly, it flew out of the bush and into a small tree across the walkway from my window. I went over to my tiny friend, offering my hand again, but it declined. So I stood back. Soon it ventured over into another tree: a tall cedar. Quickly it ascended, limb after limb until I couldn't see its tiny form anymore, high above me in the tree.

Wow, I thought, it's on its own now, out of my reach, free to find its own way. The next thing I knew, in a sudden flash of golden and spotted feathers and a chilling tiny shriek, a hawk rushed through the upper limbs of the cedar, snatching the innocent young jay from its perch. The elation of the tiny jay's success and freedom was abruptly dashed by its horrifying cry of capture in the talons of the hawk, followed by the alarming screeches of two adult jays, desperately attempting to stop the violent abduction. I followed the calamitous cries into the woodlands, the jays battling the hawk, the hawk clutching the lifeless puff of my tiny friend, unhampered by the jays' aggressive harassment. The brief life of the fledgling jay was over. I stood in shock, heartbroken. My rescue had ended in violent tragedy. I could not fathom how cruel that immediate reality was, ending the life of a truly innocent being, taken by the wild force of nature, taking part of my innocence with it, leaving a wound upon my young heart, where I had let the tiny bird in.

Around that time I first learned of the events of my violent conception, the desecration of the sacred wells, and my mother's death at my birth. My dear foster father Morfyn was to die a few years later, after I became aware of these harsh truths. Even in the idyllic setting of Afallon, I saw that death was always at the edge of this tenuous life. My innocent perception was alive within that tiny jay. I have endeavored to keep that innocence active in my heart ever since, in the face of cruelty and carnage, seemingly inseparable from the stark reality of life in this world. It is the higher aspiration that I must keep vital, knowing that otherworld of spirit lives here within me to fill my moment by moment inspiration. My little jay friend was like Icarus, climbing too high too soon, unaware of the fragility of his reality. Taliesin and Aneirin helped me to realize that I must let the jay soar within me; because that jay never had the chance to soar for itself. There is risk in being completely free, requiring a cultivated wisdom, usually absent in youth. If we can more freely access the innate wisdom of spirit, our souls can soar more readily, without fear or an encroaching sense of loss. A dual nature of tragedy and joy seems to haunt us or lift us through this life. But in our deepest awareness, the Otherworld awaits to remind us that a divinely born spirit is the primary reality of each soul. It took time for me to reflect on this early incident with the jay. As a lad, I cried for days. It was a brutal experience that did not make sense to my innocent understanding of life.

I had many dreams about the jay back then, and still do sometimes, that innocence barely surviving in this old bard. Taliesin and Vivianne counseled me as a young lad, regarding my early dream visions. In a recurring theme I recall, I was approaching the edge of the woodlands, searching for my Icarus Jay, believing he may still be there, somehow surviving on the forest floor. Then the chase of the hawk by the two adult jays began, as I frantically ran after them, desperately trying to save my little friend. Reaching an open field, I also leapt into the air flying in pursuit of the hawk around trees and through branches. Suddenly I saw a young woman, lying on the ground, badly beaten with her dress torn and bloodied below the waist. I believed she was my lost mother that I never knew. I felt as if the hawk had killed her, conflating two villains into one, having faced the knowledge of these tragic realities near the same time in my young life. Within the dream, I believed if I could stop the hawk, I could resurrect both my mother and the jay, saving them from earthly mortality. I leapt into the air again, racing through the treetops after the hawk, soon seeing the jay, more mature now, flying right there beside me. The hawk eventually evaded us; and I landed with the jay in a meadow. There was a silent communication between us. The jay thanked me for the loving kindness I had given, allowing it to live long enough to fly. I asked why it took that great risk to climb the cedar. It conveyed to me that it had to keep ascending, with an essential nature to persevere; and further, that I must find my own way to also ascend. I felt that the jay was part of me: as if my soul had merged with its own as the ascending bird departed. Even though I looked for its tiny feathered form to appear again; and although it would not show itself in my waking life – I knew the essence of that being would always be with me. It flew out of sight within the dream, and I stood there, a tearful lad, still full of many questions. At that instant, I thought I saw a raven fly past me within the shadows of the nearby wooded grove, as a druid in a dark hooded cloak suddenly emerged from the wood. He dropped his hood and I immediately recognized him as Master Myrlyn.

"What is it that you want to know lad?" he asked me.

"I want to know why this happened to the jay, and why it happened to me," I told him.

He smiled, with a wise and loving sparkle in his eyes and said, "When you expect each path to be traveled within you, rather than an adventure all about you, you will find it to be an adventure into the unknown, reaching to ascend heights unimaginable within you, as an awareness of something incomprehensible."

After he spoke those baffling words, he vanished, and I awoke. I told Taliesin what he had said as soon as I could, as not to forget a word. We have discussed this dream many times since then. One of the first things Taliesin told me was: "No matter how long you may live, what takes place is the unfolding of consecutive moments, each a present instant, most of which are forgotten within this dream of perceived time. Only those moments in which you are fully present touch something incomprehensible; because they are timeless, boundless, and eternally relevant. Apparent time within the dream rambles on, while these moments of awareness remain as the foundation of your being. The jay is the nature of your spirit. It is your totem. This is an element of your foundation of being. Deep experiences build this foundation within you, beneath the appearance of outward events, seemingly happening of their own accord, or often in discord, in the material world. The manifested world is dualistic."

"What does that mean?" I asked my old mentor.

"This is a world of opposites and extremes," Taliesin continued, "because it has a wide range of experiences. It is the nature of appearances to be dualistic: night and day, man and beast, you and I, us and them, good and evil, cruelty and kindness."

"Is all life this way?"

"No, but nearly incomprehensibly, the deeper life of spirit is beyond opposites, beyond time, beyond appearances, as an eternal life, inseparable – therefore incomprehensible to the dualistic mind."

"But why then Master Taliesin is there so much tragedy and death in the world, like the jay being killed by the hawk, if spirit is inseparable?"

"The tragedy, dear lad, is in the severity of the outward event: first exaltation, then annihilation – a harsh illustration of dualism in one instant. It was a shock to the tenderness of your heart. Be grateful for that tenderness. There is much too much callousness in the world."

"Is this why I became so connected to the jay?"

"His character and qualities are directly suited to you. He is your aspiration as an image of experience, manifested in you and from you. In truth, you are inseparable from spirit and love: although, in dreams and in the waking world, spirit and love appears in many forms. In life you express and receive the current of love with others, even a helpless creature. In this case the outward life mirrors the inward symbolic significance inspiring you. That inspiration within the experience of outward life is fragile. Your human loving nature is impacted and challenged when expectations and hope are struck by disappointment."

"Why is there such violence and evil in the world?"

"Do you believe that you deserve complete freedom of choice in your life?" Taliesin questioned me.

". . . Yes," I answered with hesitation.

He queried further, "Even if that choice can harm you or someone or something else?"

"Well, no – there is a sense of safety, and right and wrong," I muddled a compromise.

Taliesin continued: "One has the choice to be peaceful and loving. If there was no choice, but to be peaceful and loving, would one be truly free?"

"One would, I suppose," I pondered, with a puzzled expression on my young face, "one would know nothing else?" I concluded with a shrug.

"Isn't complete freedom the ability to choose to be peaceful and loving, while realizing that there are other seemingly endless possibilities?"

"I suppose so," I agreed.

"Then with this gift of freedom, there is choice; and, as you have said, awareness of right and wrong – an ethical choice. Within each moment one can choose to be peaceful and loving, realizing love is the only true freedom."

I sat and mulled over my choice to raise the jay, and whether I released him into freedom too soon. Then I asked Master Taliesin: "Did I overstep with my choice to raise the jay?"

"You made a loving and innocent choice. Innocence does not overstep. Innocence is open, potentially unaware of a dangerous pattern of events, but innocent. Duality in manifestation can close-in abruptly, catching innocence in its claws. That is the collective calamity of this manifested world. Innocent souls inhabit a shared space of diverse intentions, desires, fears, and events within outward reality. As spirit becomes form, form may respond to its own habitual patterns. You, as a spiritual being, feel torn between bad experiences and good experiences, believing there is a separation between spirit and form. The essence of spirit lives within everything. Both the jay and the hawk aspire to live. Even after the jay died, its essence lives on. It lives in you: in your love, and in your memory. The jay is the spirit totem creature that readily ascends. Your jay ascended the cedar – tree of the gods. He epitomized eternal life in his final act. You joined him in the land of the Otherworld with our Master Myrlyn. This is a great gift, demonstrating an ascension that lives on within you, and will live within you all the days of your life."

Wellspring

Ascension lives within all the great warriors of the Cymri, and it lives within the most adventurous bards, druids and priestesses of this island world, as the desire to soar lives within every soul. The mythic story of Icarus illustrated that unguarded desire to ascend, cautioning against the risk of bold leaps of discovery. Some may find ascension difficult to discover; while others never attempt to search for it. Too many souls struggle just to survive, like the jay, most of their breed rarely reaching maturity. Brutality rages across these isles, threatening this age of Afallon and its wise heirs, with warring hawks continually stalking peaceful doves. We bards and druids were taught to listen for the inner song: the harmonious pulsing cadence of inspired life that exists beneath the surface reality and surrounds all existence. It is the flowing waters beneath the waters that gives rise to every well and spring. There is a fluid table of being that is the source of Awen, a realm of awareness and guidance. This is the forge and foundry of the Grail Hallows, releasing essential truth into manifestation. Just as each well is filled from rising spills into a fount from deeper source waters, visions and forms find expression in the receptive mind and adept hands of the wise initiate. The bard sings his song to carry that innate tuning of being into an embattled world. The warriors and explorers of the outer world search for answers, traversing obstacles and conquering their foes in an outward quest for inner freedom. The bard, the druid, the seer and the priestess takes the inward journey to find that wellspring of freedom, rising in unseen pathways. Years after the loss of my Icarus Jay, I wrote of that pursuit of inner freedom, beyond life and death, beyond dream and desire.

Wellspring

Archival waters settle deep
to form fluid memory in sleep,
flooding visionary quest
for each latent soul's behest.
Ever flowing scenes emerge,
displaying every passion's urge
recounting hearts and tears defined,
as collective history refined,
that in this mythic inner play,
a stumbling traveler finds a way
to re-illuminate his sight,
with cascading showers of this light,
a light that streams within the mind
to shine on images, self-designed
in conversations of the self,
unearthing cavernous inner wealth.
And in the outward journey, sealed
to be eroded and revealed,
the puzzled pilgrims of the grail,
shift a course, in which to sail
emerging from doldrums and storms,
to see the heart and mind reforms,
taking shape, as vessels of light
as the Otherworld renews our sight,
and in that seeing, washed and new,
all this matter is seen through

as fluid forms resuming course,
directly from their deepest source,
no longer islanders marooned,
to cry a song among the doomed,
vision comes ~ not from the seeing,
but from the unencumbered being.

The traveler takes on the weight of an inherent satchel, and the warrior dons outer armor, weaponry and shield, entering each new battle or quest. Often the quest finds the seeker suddenly detoured from an outward intention, as if the odd narrative of dream has now redirected waking life. The movement of each scene becomes an unfolding tableau of guidance, or distraction, challenging awareness. The warrior is armed and masked for confrontation. This is what he knows. Defense has become identity. Self protection must fall to self revelation or each encounter will be another confrontation. Ultimately, the warrior or seeker confronts himself. Along the many hidden paths, realities are shifted; and the Otherworld becomes the realm of discovery. From the perspective of the Otherworld, the initiate walks the balance between worlds. The wise seeker knows that there are layers of paths being tread beneath the dramas unfolding in plain sight, dramas between individuals, and dramas between kingdoms.

The Cymric kingdoms were held together by the Cymric Cylch and the integrity of its kings, druids, clergy, priestesses and individual warriors. There were factions among the Cymric dynasties that sought to undermine the kingdoms of Rheged, Alt Clud, Dalriada, and the sanctuary of Afallon. It is strange how jealousy and rivalry can simmer and stew for generations to boil over from suppressed resentment born into its descendants. Who knows how far these undercurrents seep back in time, possibly to the daughters of Gwyrls and Ygerna, over a century in the past. Now their great great granddaughters being the namesakes of Marganna and her sister Morgause have become descendants of that heritage of wronged women, or the notorious "other women" of dynastic intrigue. The elder Marganna had wed the druid King Afallach in the late fifth century, gaining power and prestige as Queen of Gallwyddel; yet denied the opportunity to become High Priestess of Afallon, losing that honor to Nimue the wife of Master Myrlyn. Marganna's daughter Gwallwen became one of the mistresses and then one of the wives of Maelgwyn Gwynedd, who defeated Arthwys Pendragon and Marganna's half-brother Owain Ddantgwyn at the battle of Cwm Llan. Gwallwen's daughter Modron, rumored to have been sired by her own grandfather Afallach, was the mistress of Urien of Rheged. While Gwallwen's son Rhun Hir became King of Gwynedd after his father Maelgwyn died of the plague. The female descendants of Marganna found ways of skirting the thrones of power without actually holding sovereignty of the land through matriarchal inheritance. Modron's daughter Morfudd, sired by King Urien of Rheged, married Morcant Mwynfawr, nefarious brother of King Rhydderch of Alt Clud, known as Mynyddog Mwynfawr for his mountainous wealth, gaining his fortunes through mining, conquest, and skullduggery, described by his adversaries as leaving a path behind him where neither grass nor plant would grow for a year. Morcant and Morfudd had two daughters, named after their great great grandmother and her sister: Marganna and Anna Morgause. Anna Morgause became the Queen of Lothian, as wife to King Loth, reigning at Arthsedd, also known as Caer Morwynion, where maidens had historically held matriarchal sovereignty until the dynasties of patriarchy dominated the north. Marganna the younger brokered an alliance by marrying King Coleduac of Bryneich, bearing a son to him named after her father – Morcant. This line of kings descended from Garbanion ap Coel Hen, a faction of the Gwyr y Gogledd chronically contentious for the power, property, and prominence of their western cousins, earning the frequently repeated characterization – "nothing good ever comes out of Bryneich".

It was in Bryneich where Llen's parents had been killed and he was rescued as an infant by Lady Vivianne. Assassinations and abductions only seemed to spread from Bryneich, continuing throughout the kingdoms to the west. There had always been kidnapping and murder across the isles and the continent: sometimes assassins hurried along the line of succession; and often a bride was openly abducted just as part of the wedding ceremony. It was much easier to abduct an heir or bride in transit than to battle an entire kingdom to capture a valued hostage. The careless adventures of royal heirs became the target of would-be kidnappers and cutthroats. Reckless lovers Llen and Gwenhwyfar repeatedly met by planning travel where they could easily cross paths, to steal away for romantic interludes between kingdoms. One early autumn as the first leaves began to turn, the two lovers met in Gallwyddel when Gwen was on her way to Dalriada. They met at a secluded cottage, letting their passions be satiated once again, each departing their separate ways after two sexually charged and enraptured days. Following this illicit rendezvous, Llen traveled with his old mate Bercnaf into eastern Gallwyddel and Alt Clud to collect some hunting hounds to bring back to Rheged and Afallon. They arrived in a market town known for its sulfur springs and as the trading place of wool and livestock, north of the Solway, up the River Annan – called Maghfada by the Scotti and known as Gwastadmaith by the Cymri. Resting from their day's ride in a bustling tavern, Llen and Bercnaf overheard three huntsmen, well into their cups, laughing about the kidnapping of Prince Artúr's wife, Gwenhwyfar.

"He's off in the Orcades and Pict Gwlad with his father, while his bride waits for the next wild ride in the wood," said the boisterous huntsman.

"She likes it rough, I hear," chimed-in his drunken mate, nearly falling off his stool.

In a lowered voice, the third huntsman leaned-in saying, "She's just been taken again – off to Coed Celyddon this very night."

Hearing this, Llen rose from his chair, with Bercnaf following close behind, Llen grabbing the third man by his collar, dragging him out of the tavern door. With a blade to his throat and an eye on the door to see his stumbling mates tripped-up by Bercnaf, Llen grilled the shaken huntsman.

"Speak the truth now or lose your life. Do you know for a fact that Princess Gwenhwyfar has been abducted this night?"

"I swear sire, I saw a band of men riding nor' east, with a woman bound on horseback, straight past my hunting blind. I heard one man mention Gwenhwyfar by name," the huntsman answered in a panic.

"Do you know it was Lady Gwenhwyfar?" Llen pursued the questioning, as his knife blade scraped against the stubble on the huntsman's neck.

"I've never seen the lady before. All I know is what I saw and heard today. The woman was gagged and bound; and the men were in a great hurry. Please sire, spare my life. I've told you all I know."

"Which road were they on?"

"The north road toward the Tweed and Celyddon, sire."

"How long ago was this?"

"Near dusk, sire?"

"Alright," Llen responded, drawing his sword while releasing the man, as his drunken mates approached. "Stand fast, we are skilled and sober. Your friend is unharmed and we'll be on our way." With that, Llen and Bercnaf mounted their horses, turned abruptly, and were gone before the huntsmen could answer.

The drunken huntsmen helped their friend to his feet, asking: "Are you alright mate?"

"Oh, yah, though I nearly pissed myself."

"Did you really see Gwenhwyfar taken away?"

"I don't know. It appeared that way. Who the bloody hell was that riled swordsman?"

The portly old tavern keeper walked over and said, "That was Llenlleawg Gwyddel, three time champion of Aenach Garman."

"Oh shite!" the accosted huntsman exclaimed, falling into the arms of his mates.

Llen and Bercnaf rode fast to the junction of the northern road, before the River Tweed, where Bercnaf stopped. "Hold up a moment Llen! Don't you think you're taking this a bit hasty?"

"I need to know if Gwen has been abducted. Haste is the only hope we might catch-up to this band of rouges," Llen answered.

"You have no idea if it's true, or if you'll find them," Bercnaf responded.

"If we move now, I will know sooner," Llen declared, starting off again at a gallop.

Bercnaf shook his head, following right behind Llen up the northern road. They rode well into the night, wary of any campfire light or the scent of lingering smoke. By dawn they caught the smell of a fire, approaching slowly toward a clearing, not too far from the road, seeing the abandoned site of a small camp.

"It looks like there were half a dozen horses, five men and likely a woman, by the smaller footprints and shorter stride," Bercnaf said as he examined the tracks around the site.

"They're not far ahead, probably left before first light," said Llen, inspecting the ashes of the campfire.

"Where do you think they're headed?" asked Bercnaf.

"I would guess toward the Tweed Valley, but from there, I don't know. Who they are and what there about, is any man's guess. If we see them turn towards Bryneich or Lothian, it might reveal more," answered Llen.

"Do you believe two of us can get the jump on these bastards?"

"First we need to get close enough to see if it's really Gwen that they have. Next, we have to find an opening to snatch her back, when she's unguarded or less guarded, possibly picking-off one or two of them to even the odds," Llen explained. "For now, we need to stay on their tracks. Let's keep moving."

By the time persistent Llen and Bercnaf finally caught up to the band of kidnappers, the five men and their captive had increased to a troop of near twenty, with another woman among them. The second woman seemed to have some authority over the men, Llen and Bercnaf seeing from the cover of the wooded grove her arm motions as she spoke to the troop, directing them toward a crossroads in the distance.

"What now?" Bercnaf asked with concern in his voice. "Their numbers are four times what they were."

"Yes, and I still can't tell if that is Gwen with them. I think I'll just ride right out there and greet them face to face," Llen mused with a grin.

"Oh no, you're mad! That woman has taken your mind. I've seen it before. They'll strike you down on the spot," Bercnaf responded.

"You stay here, out of sight, and follow later if I don't return," said Llen.

"If you don't return – do you mean if you don't return to your senses, or are you asking me to return your body to Afallon for a fool's funeral?" Bercnaf snapped back.

"If I don't take the risk, I may not have another chance. I'm going out there," Llen declared.

"You're impossible. You've lost your head already – so it won't matter if they take it. Goodbye mate. I'll see to your remains, if I can find them."

"Thanks mate. I knew I could count on you," Llen said, as he mounted his horse and slowly rode out to meet his destiny.

He was spotted by one of the troop, who alerted the others. They all turned and faced Llen as he approached. Once he came closer, Llen could see that Gwen was the captive; but he didn't recognize the noblewoman in command of the troop.

"Good day, my ladies, it appears one of you is an unwilling companion," Llen boldly addressed them.

"You must know sir, that it can be difficult for a man to know if a lady is willing or not," the noblewoman said.

"Perhaps you could explain to me why a woman bound by rope, on a horse led by its reigns, is a woman somehow willing to be taken," Llen bantered in response.

"Ah, clearly this lady is divided in her mind, and has not discerned her heart. So, we are guiding her until she finds her way," said the noblewoman.

"That leaves me divided as well: with her eyes showing her obvious distress and her mouth gagged, unable to speak for herself," Llen replied.

"Un-gag her!" the noblewoman ordered, gesturing to one of her liegemen to promptly do so.

"What are you doing here, you mad fool?" Gwen frantically asked Llen.

"It appears you need a more proper escort, my lady," Llen quipped.

"I can see there is a bond here. You must be the reason our princess was such an easy target, unprotected in Gallwyddel. And, I know that you are not her husband. Certainly, you must be her lover," the noble woman surmised. "Who are you, 'you mad fool' and would-be escort?"

"I am Llenlleawg of Afallon."

"Well, I should have known. Few would be so bold. I am the Queen of Bryneich and the true heiress of Manau – bind him!" She ordered her men.

Llen offered no resistance, being clearly outnumbered. He now knew Gwen was under his protection, even as he wås bound. His unfailing belief was that an opportunity would arise, affording them an escape to freedom, motivating his headstrong intention. The kidnap party traveled northeast through the Tweed Valley, as Llen had expected. Bercnaf cautiously followed after them, keeping his distance, while bemoaning his undying loyalty to his love-struck brother of Afallon.

"What does he imagine? Another man's wife! The Prince of Dalriada, no less – he's dead by any outcome, dead. I'm tracking a corpse and his sweetheart – bloody shite!" Bercnaf muttered to himself as he plodded along the Tweed River Road.

The terrain was varied for the kidnap party and the dogged tracker following the old course cut through the eastern hills between the Lothians and Bryneich. One winding passage spurred Llen's plan for a quick escape with his beloved. He knew of a trail that cutover to a road leading to an old roman fort held by the Cymri. The road they followed east had narrowed, leaving Llen and Gwenhwyfar led by a single rider. Llen saw his moment, knocked the rider off his mount, while guiding his own and Gwen's horse away from the troop. It took the others a bit of time to notice the escape and reverse their course along the narrow trail of a steep ledge. Llen had found the diverting path, gaining a good lead for him and Gwen, leaving the disordered party searching for the obscured cut-off to the southwest.

Eventually one shrewd rider caught up to the fugitive couple, jumping from horse to horse, unhorsing Llen, and sending both men tumbling down a steep ravine. By the time the rest of the party reached them, Llen and the other rider were lost. The Bryneich rider was in sight from the trail, his head crushed against a bolder several fathoms down the ravine, with his body strangely twisted around a tree cropping out of the cliff side. Llen was nowhere to be seen, below the dust, rubble and the debris created by the descending conflict off the trail. Gwen wept profusely as she peered down into the ravine, seeing only the other rider staring lifelessly into the dusty air. Llen's horse had kept running, as if he was as intent as his master to continue on to the old roman fort. The kidnap party retrieved their captive Gwenhwyfar, pulled-up the mangled rider, quickly burying him without ceremony or ritual beside the trail, turning back to the main road heading east toward Bryneich.

When Bercnaf came to the intersection of the side trail, he could easily see the confused tracks, leading away and then returning. His gut instinct told him to follow the side trail, so he did. He stopped where all the tracks ended, except one. Then he saw the fresh grave and the blood-covered rock down the side of the ravine. He looked at the grave, and then down the ravine again. "Oh shite," he said as he began to dig up the unknown body. It wasn't long before he exposed enough of it to see it wasn't Llen.

"Bloody hell, brother Llen where are you?" Bercnaf said, looking down the ravine again; then deciding to follow the trail farther. Soon he met up with Llen's horse, the sole witness to his master's recent conflict.

"Hey, hey old boy – where's Llen? Take me to him boy."

The horse led Bercnaf back to the grave and moved his regal head with a whinny, pointing down the ravine. Bercnaf secured a rope around a boulder near the trail and started descending down into the ravine. About halfway down he saw something beneath the brush, quite a bit farther down. As he got closer he could see that it was Llen's body. Hurriedly he made his way near to him, turning the body over, putting his ear to his dear friend's mouth – he was breathing.

"Oh you love-mad bastard – hold on," Bercnaf said as he looked into the face of his unconscious friend.

He poured a little water from a goatskin bag into Llen's mouth, unsure how close his mate was to death. Then he looked over Llen's arms and legs for broken bones, opening his hauberk to look for any protruding ribs or gouges to his flesh.

"You seem to be in one piece mate, aside from that nasty rap to your bloody hard head. I guess that explains your silence. I suppose that puts me in charge, for once. Since you don't seem to be in such a hurry anymore, I will climb back up to the trail, build a make-shift litter for you, and return to cart your sorry ass back to the nearest village, if that's alright sire. . . . I hear no argument, so I will proceed under my own direction."

Bercnaf constructed a narrow litter from cut branches that he could mount behind Llen's horse to carry his unconscious master over the winding trails. He was able to ease Llen onto the litter at the bottom of the ravine, secure him with rope and straps, and then hoist him with the rope up the steep incline to the trail.

"Alright mate, you're bound for travel again," said Bercnaf, securing Llen and the litter to his horse. "It could be a bit bumpy, but I haven't heard any complaints so far."

After a few hours of slow travel down the side trail, chosen to avoid the route of the kidnappers and to move into the safest direction toward Cymric lands, Bercnaf could hear the sound of someone chopping wood. Soon he saw a cottage in a clearing, where a woman was carrying firewood into her modest home.

"Hello to the house!" Bercnaf announced his arrival, "friendly traveler with an injured man!"

The woman came out of the cottage, approaching Llen as he lay there silently on the litter. "Can he speak?" she asked.

"Not lately," Bercnaf answered.

"I can see that he's had a blow to the head. He could be in a stupor," the woman said, reaching for a damp cloth near a bucket of water by the woodpile.

"He took a fall down a ravine. I checked him for broken bones. He seems intact," Bercnaf explain.

"He could be bleeding or ruptured inside. Let's get him into the cottage on a proper bed, and wash him up. His skull could be cracked, or bruised badly enough to knock him out. If he can take food and water, he may recover," the woman said with authority.

Bercnaf and the woman carried Llen into the cottage on the litter, transferring him gently to a bed. They took off his hauberk and leggings; then the woman began washing his body.

"You're right. He doesn't seem to have any broken bones."

"Are you a midwife or healer?" Bercnaf asked her.

"No, not by trade; but I've tended to a husband and sons, now gone, rest their souls – so I know a thing or two."

"Thank you for caring for Llen; and I'm sorry for the loss of your husband and sons. My name is Bercnaf."

"I am Lady Malenhau, or was, when I held property and had a husband and family. You can call me Mala."

"Thank you Mala. Again, I'm sorry for your loss. This life can be brutal."

"Illness or war strikes us sooner or later," she replied with a sigh.

"Or just the passage of time . . . it appears you have managed well enough on your own here."

"Yes, the village of Strathgwair is nearby; so I can get help when I need it. There is a holy well there, said to be founded by Saint Bridget. Waters from the well may help your friend to recover."

"I will retrieve some, and anything else I can bring to you. I can hunt some game for our supper, or add thatching to your roof, anything you need, my Lady Malenhau."

"Oh please, just Mala is fine," she responded with a giggle. "Why don't you stay here with your friend, in case he awakens. I'll go into the village. I had intended to go anyway. I'll be back soon."

Mala left the two men at her secluded home, as she walked less that a league into the village of Strathgwair. Meanwhile, Gwenhwyfar had been taken far to the east into Bryneich, despondent in the belief that Llen had perished in the failed rescue attempt. She had been kidnapped as part of a plot by the Queen of Bryneich and Morcant Mwynfawr to boost his appearance of loyalty to the Cymric Cylch. Once a ransom had been demanded by the kidnappers, Morcant volunteered to provide the ransom and retrieve the princess from the dangerous lands east of his own subkingdom in eastern Lothian. The ransom, in fact, would be of no loss to him: because his own liegemen and his daughter Marganna were the kidnappers. Marganna wanted the chance to taunt Gwenhwyfar in captivity.

"Perhaps there would be a greater ransom for your husband to know the truth about your dead lover Llenlleawg," Queen Marganna suggested, cattily irritating Gwen's emotional wounds.

"Now that my lover is gone, the threat to my marriage has died with him," Gwen replied.

"I'm sure Artúr would never let you go unpunished for your years of infidelity. How long ago did it begin, perhaps one of those years at Aenach Garman?" Marganna questioned, reading the reaction in Gwenhwyfar face. "Yes, of course, I bet it was that first time, when you awarded Llen his prize, bedding the hero then and there," the queen continued as Gwenhwyfar defiantly glared back at her. "You didn't want to marry Artúr any more than I wanted to marry Coledauc. We are both the whores of our father's kingdoms: our virginity traded like a common hen for a stretch of land or an army of angry cocks needing to crow and conquer. But you were living under the illusion of love, for a time. Back to the bridal bed, my dear, to drop the egg of another prince out from between your dynastic knees!"

"What has made you so bitter? Is it the taste of your own father in your mouth as he broke you in, before selling you to the highest bidder?" Gwenhwyfar fired back. "At least I have known love. That is something no one can take away. You have resigned yourself to be at best a bitch in heat, unable to know any more than the dogs you lay with."

"Well now, you have more fire than I would have guessed." Marganna responded. "But don't test me princess, or I'll set my dogs loose on your skinny royal ass."

Gwenhwyfar was held in Bryneich for several weeks before the sham ransom exchange was complete. During those weeks of Gwen's uncertain fate, Llen remained at the secluded cottage, cared for by Mala and Bercnaf. Waters from the holy well didn't seem to revive Llen to his former self, but he was still breathing and taking-in water, holy and otherwise. They spoon fed him oat and wheat porridge, relieved him in a chamber pot, and swaddled him like an infant. Llen appeared to be asleep or utterly unconscious all hours of the day and night. Mala could only speculate about his recovery.

"I've seen men bounce back before – suddenly one morning they're wide awake – others, sadly, just never wakeup, after weeks or months of silence."

"He's a fighter," replied Bercnaf with urgency. "Llen here is the most resilient man I've ever known – stubborn bastard, but strong as a wild buck. He's a champion among men, and of a determined heart. This man would come back from the grave to rescue his love from capture. I know he will complete that task, whatever it takes."

"I hope you are right. This is the fight of his life. It will take a strong will to live," Mala responded.

Llen lay there, still; the only visible motions were his rising and falling breath, and his closed eyelids appearing to twitch at times. This was a man who had been active in adventure most all of his days. It was inconceivable that he could simply stop. The mind and spirit are very mysterious aspects of a human being. We do not understand their depths. I can only relay what has been revealed to me about this starkly unusual time in the life of Llenlleawg. Somehow he had slipped into the Otherworld beyond life and death, experiencing a movement of being within the immovable, transforming beyond form, living for a time in a reality entirely real, yet outwardly unmanifested. His body remained motionless, yet his adventures within a body of appearances continued, with all his sensations felt to be completely real. Within this state he was at once asleep and aware, being everything he had ever been, seeing everything he would ever be, his outer faculties silent, with his inner faculties vibrantly alive. What he knew was not bound by the rising and setting sun or the shifting seasons; it was an inner occurrence, witnessed and enacted as the continuous movement of soul, without beginning or end. From this place he could delve into all manner of the dramas of life, as his mind and soul might conjure them.

Llen found himself wandering within a garden within a fortress. It was a scene he had experienced within dream before, where he had seen the gravestones of his ancestors. He was there again; but this time he saw all the grave markers of his brave companions: Bercnaf, Owain, Llamorhad, Baedd, Llew, Gawain, Peredyr and countless others. He saw the graves of his mentors Taliesin, Galehaut, Rheu the huntsman – mentors he never knew – Myrlyn, Blaise, Llalwc, Lamech, Nascien of Narbonne. Gawain appeared there, kneeling before his own grave, weeping. This struck Llen oddly; because he had never known Gawain to shed a tear. Then his friend stood up, turned and vanished from his sight, along with his gravestone. Llen wandered farther into the garden where he saw a woman weeping. She turned towards him, wiping her face.

"Forgive me," she said. "I did not know anyone else was here."

"It is quite alright," Llen replied. "I didn't mean to disturb your sorrow. Are you mourning the loss of a loved one?"

"Oh yes, many, many have been taken to some unknown dolorous place. My Master, it is so strange, he was here and then he vanished, as if his body was not flesh but spirit. All of his men have disappeared as well. They seem to have been captured," the woman explained.

"Who is your Master?" Llen asked.

"Gwalchmai," she answered.

"I know him," said Llen. "Where was he taken?"

"I don't know. I believe he is still here, although I know that he is gone. Does that make any sense? I'm sorry," the woman expressed her confusion.

"Yes, somehow it does," Llen reassured her.

"Are you here to mourn someone?" She asked Llen.

"I don't know. I thought there was a king, or a child that I was suppose to find here, when I came through the gate. But now, I'm not sure why I am here. You see, I can't quite make sense of myself either," Llen confessed.

"Is there a name that you can remember? Perhaps I have seen it on a stone. I wander this place often," the woman offered.

"If it comes to mind, I will tell you. Why do you come here so often," Llen asked her.

"I find it peaceful. It is a place of center and balance, between the living and the dead, between time and eternity. There is a sense that everyone who has gone from here has sacrificed something, either by being born or dying, as either lost gods or discovered souls."

"You sound like my mother Vivianne. She is a very wise woman."

"Thank you, I find that most endearing – a sincere compliment."

"It was meant so. Oh – I remember that name: Mala, Mala something!"

"Ha ha," the woman laughed, and at that instant she appeared completely naked, saying in a flirtatious tone to Llen: "I am Mala, but known as Chwim," then vanished.

Llen was spellbound, believing this was that same woman from his earlier dream who showed him mercy. Suddenly his attention was captured by a child running through the gravestones. He immediately knew this child to be his future unborn son. At the same time he believed this child was all sons and daughters yet unborn – a thought that perplexed him. At this point, Llen had to sit down for a moment to collect himself, reeling from these encounters, knowing somehow they were as much within him as appearing before him. The idea dawned on him that he was expanded as the totality of his perceived reality, all the while also within his apparent body. He had sensations and sense perceptions; but there was some manner of his own existence of which he was not fully aware. His physical body, as it seemed to him, had been an inconsistent state of his outer senses. His reality was apparently not of his senses, but a confluence of thought. He needed to make sense of things to move forward. The sudden appearance and disappearance of Gawain, the woman Mala-Chwim, whatever she called herself, being that angel of mercy, mourning the capture of "Gwalchmai" – Gawain, he realized, needed him. His next course of action was to find Gawain and release him from captivity – wherever that would lead.

As soon as Llen had thought of that intention, he found himself wandering through dense woodlands extending beyond the garden and graveyard. Finally discovering a path in the wilderness, he followed it until he saw a crude dwelling built of thatch and timbers where an old hermit lived. The hermit was sitting beneath a massive gnarled oak, chanting verse in an obscure language that Llen could not quite understand. The old man opened his eyes as he heard Llen approach, continuing his chanting. Llen stood still until the hermit stopped.

"Good day, I am sorry to have disturbed your prayers," said Llen.

"Not at all, the point of prayer is to open to that space which is undisturbed." The hermit answered.

"What enchanting language was that?"

"Chaldean."

"It was quite beautiful. Forgive me, I am Llenlleawg of Afallon. I seem to be lost. Do you know of a fortress near these woodlands?"

"Near? No – distant? Yes – although the forest is its own fortress of nature."

"Yes, I would have to agree. I seem to be its captive."

"You are free to go, anytime," the hermit said with a smile.

"Thank you," Llen responded with a laugh. "What is your name, if I may ask?"

"I am called Gwybodor."

"Are you comfortable here in these severe conditions?"

"Severity is only a perception, a path less taken, requiring strength and an independent nature."

"Yes, I'm sure; I just thought a man of your years would find greater comfort in a village."

"My comfort is within my soul. The sheer density of spirit embraces me here, away from the clamor of a village, fort, or citadel. Many cannot readily see this. As one acquires an inner silence, a space of silence is very appealing. It first requires a radical intelligence, and then surrender into the immutability and inseparability of one's elemental being."

"How did you come to this place?"

"I had a family. My wife and twelve sons all died within a year. Then I became a monk; but sought-out a deeper experience alone, immersed in the essence of creation. What are **you** searching for, young man, other than a fortress?"

"I became aware that my comrade Gawain had been taken captive. I seek to free him, if I can."

"Is this Gawain also called Gwalchmai?"

"Yes. Do you know of him?"

"There is a citadel of many gates, with many inner paths and corridors, built by a cabal far to the east of here, on an island called Ynys Medcaut. I have heard that twenty-two have been taken there, and Gwalchmai was among them. This citadel has been called Din Bran; others call it the dolorous fort. Its inner paths seem to grow and recede, as if it were a living thing – difficult to surmount."

"Can you tell me how to get there?" Llen asked.

"Getting there becomes more of a journey when you think you have arrived. Entry will be gained by a shifting of form, as if climbing within the form of a tree, realizing each branch goes deeper, as roots do, taking you into its center; where only after following a labyrinth of passages will you find the release you are seeking."

"Can I make it alone?"

"That is the only way you can. A force of arms would announce a battle. You are a bright warrior of light. Open your vision and your light will be seen, beyond this young man that you think you are. Follow the path in front of you," said the old man, pointing to the east.

"Thank you, Master Gwybodor. I will heed your advice," said Llen as he set out down the path.

It wasn't long before he saw a hart buck dash out in front of him, swiftly prancing down the trail ahead. Llen picked up his pace, running after the buck, strangely feeling as if he was rapidly moving along and within the body of this graceful creature. His exhilaration carried him across vast stretches of rising and falling terrain, over mountains and streams; until he reached a shoreline of steep cliffs towering over the sands below. In a sudden moment, as the fleeting grace of the hart buck leapt from the staggering cliff edge, Llen became that soaring creature, gliding in freefall, his sinewy legs moving in suspended time through a stillness of space to land surefooted onto the beach of an offshore island.

His vision felt odd: with poor distinction of color, yet an expansively wide view to either side, without even turning his head. He could see on the far edge of the horizon a horse drawn chariot leading a vast troop of three-hundred-twenty warriors, wrapping 'round the steep walls of a fortress built of stone and living timber. Crows rose-up in the air above the walls, crying their discordant song, stirred by the thundering army charging out from the many gates of the citadel. Ships awaited the troop's boarding beyond the distant edges of the wall to the other extreme reach of Llen's suddenly discovered ruminant vision. The warriors rode and marched right past him, led by the mighty charioteer, wielding a spear and chain, creating a din even above the cacophony of hooves, crows, and pounded shields. As Llen's vision focused through the eyes of the hart, the chariot driver appeared to be a youthful likeness of the old hermit Gwybodor. Once the throngs had passed by, Llen as the hart buck pranced right up to the base of the wall unnoticed, entering a gate; at which point he resumed his human form.

Standing up straight from his prone position of all-fours, Llen noticed a stairwell, just inside the gate. He felt a bit dizzy for a moment, not recalling being a deer before, belching a remnant of released gas, and hoofing at the first step with his right toe. After a quick snort and a rutting-like shake of his head, he climbed the stairway on two legs. The stairs wound in a spiral fashion up to the top of the citadel wall, where he found another corridor winding downward with a branch of stairs that appeared to be entering the depth of the citadel. It was damp, with roots emerging from gaps between the stonework, dripping an odorous water and slime onto the uneven floor. Each path or corridor led in disorienting directions, leaving Llen confused by the winding inner avenues.

At one point he heard voices, easing slowly ahead to observe or hear anything discernible. He surmised that there was a guard station or jailer's post just around the next turn. One man seemed to be departing, while another had just arrived. As soon as the one guard was alone, Llen was able to get a jump on him, silencing his voice for good, positioning him in a chair, face down on a table, giving the appearance that the guard had fallen asleep. There was a large ring of keys sitting on the table, which Llen quickly snatched-up. Looking at the torch mounted on the wall, Llen realized that he had been able to see in the darkness of these corridors, ever since he entered the fortress, thinking he held some of the buck's night vision, and then suddenly noticing a glow emanating from his own bodily form. He moved his hand into a dark corner, feeling the vibratory sensation of light coming from within him to illuminate the shadows.

Putting aside this puzzlement, Llen continued his search for Gawain and the other survivors of the twenty-two mention by the old hermit. He looked at the ring of keys in his hand, wondering what gates, doors, or cells could be opened within the depths of this convoluted passage. These tunneled paths seemed to extend as he wandered through them, as if they were alive and growing. The first gate he came to held two copper-clad warriors, facing-off against each other, about to do battle. They turned towards Llen as he approached, drawn to the glow of his ethereal form. Stepping through the gate, the copper-clad warriors confronted Llen, attacking him from both sides. Down the tunneled path beyond them, intense light shined around them and between them. A shield suddenly appeared on Llen's arm, which he held up above his head, holding the ring of keys out with his other hand, causing one key to glow, merging with the light within the corridor, creating a wedge of light between the copper-clad warriors, allowing Llen to pass through unaffected by their battling blows.

Llen proceeded into the brilliant light, seeing the image of a mighty king, crowned and throned, holding a glowing orb in one hand, and a gilded shepherd's crook in the other hand. The king was welcoming Llen: not by gesture or speech, but with a receptive intelligence, his expression of mind and heart instantly opening Llen's understanding. Within that embrace of light Llen could see the king's daughter, who he knew he was to marry, giving him a son who would be named Galahad. Along with this revelation, Llen immediately recalled the inscription he had seen on his ancestral tomb, mentioning "the sons bearing the name of Galahad". He knew that this king and his daughter were also of the line of Benoni from ancient Palestine, ancestors of the Fisher Kings.

Charged with a vibrancy of divinely imbued energy, fully absorbing this experience, Llen continued into the corridor of light, aware that he was moving closer to the place where Gawain and the others were being held. As he saw them ahead, behind another gate, he called out to Gawain.

"Gawain, I am here to release you!"

But Gawain did not recognize him, asking with joy and awe: "Are you of the flesh or spirit?"

"Don't you know me?" Llen responded.

"No, but I see that you carry the keys to our release – white warrior."

As he spoke those words, the key to their cell began to glow. Llen unlocked the gate and the entire subterranean scene instantly vanished from his vision. He suddenly found himself in the garden cemetery of the fortress. Night had fallen, with moonlight illuminating his expansive view of the citadel from a garden knoll. He could see three pillars and a vine covered entablature near the steps leading to the garden of tombs and gravestones, reminding him that he had been in this place before within a dream. Llen reflected on the fact that Gawain had not recognized him. How is it that a comrade he had known since he was a lad could not know him? Standing among the crypts and headstones, he thought about all of the identities, known and unknown, etched in stone, marking a place in time, hiding faces never to be seen in the waking world again. What was the value of these temporal identities? He had been the hart buck. He had been the key to his comrade's release – Gawain calling him the "white warrior" – the luminous glow still emanating from him. It suddenly struck him that he had forgotten about Gwen's abduction and his mission to save her. But now, he had glimpsed into his future, married to another woman to sire a son to be named Galahad. His head was reeling with conflicting thoughts of duty, honor, desire and destiny. Who was this person that he sought to define, to understand, and to have recognized? Was this person just a mask worn in waking life for a lapse of time to manifest an identity formed of unfulfilled desires? Was his destiny laid down generations before? Or was he being swept up by the inevitable momentum of worldly desire? But here, now, was this glow of lighted being that he carried, diffusing the identity that he thought he was. His sense of time and intention had been shifting into something newly unfolding within the present moment. He had been living his life in the waking world of time and manifested reality, all along carrying around an inner world, hidden from him, while announcing himself to the cosmos as a person separate and apart, combating or attempting to save other separate souls. From this Otherworld of dream visions that he found within himself, he perceived a divine estate, which was only forfeited by his ignorance of its infinite expanse as his own unbounded being.

In the moment he realized that this was who he really was, he felt no fear. This alternate cosmos of kingdoms was his own being, his deeper imaginal self displayed. It was his innermost expression, a creative tool, and an extension of his soul illustrated within him. And yet, everything seemed to be happening of its own inertia. What he was imagining was his reality; but he could not see this reality as pure imagination while he was living it. His imagined world held the specter of the duality he lived within the waking world − cruel and kind, wise and ignorant, heroic and mundane − even though there were clearly supernatural occurrences defying the limits of physical reality. When threats appeared in his imaginal visions, he could easily defeat them with a shift in his awareness. An innate love existed within him, dissolving the specter of fear. He had been longing for love, truth and joy in a world threatened by terror, duplicity and sorrow. Even as a revered son of Afallon, he had been searching to find who he was, how he came to be, and if the gods or a god truly existed. A god of fear and desire born of an imaginal world could not, in his mind, be the heart of the cosmos. Now his search became an inquiry into a timeless world to discover what remains and what departs; what is intangible and what is real; what is the song of experience and the wheat of its nourishment, learning all that is dolorous ends − to reveal joy.

Llenlleawg had thought Gwenhwyfar was his joy, for a time. Now he questioned that forbidden love. Why should it be so difficult? Why should it be denied? Nevertheless, she needed to be freed from her captivity. He had to find out where she had been taken against her will by the Queen of Bryneich. Could anything good come out of Bryneich? Llen's mind was encompassed by the persistent feeling he had been traveling to a destination continually being recreated as he went. Impressions and intentions that he held in the waking world still existed in the Otherworld; but the nature of reality was now much more fluid. His path was created by each choice he made along the way, while at the same time he felt caught by an irresistible current. There was a flash flood of thought and emotional upheaval within him, as an elemental force pulsed deep beneath the surface adventures. All of the contents of his mind seemed to be colliding, like the rocks and debris from the ravine. He found himself plummeting down that ravine again, wrestling with a man who was not there anymore. Then, strangely removed from the event, he observed his own body, lying at the bottom of the gorge, and his attacker's body mangled with a broken neck upon a twisted tree. Queen Marganna looked-on as her liegemen descended to examine Llen's seemingly lifeless body.

"He's alive!" One man shouted back.

"Can he be moved?" asked Marganna.

"Yes, with care . . . on a litter," The man answered.

"Bring him back!" ordered Marganna.

The Queen's liegemen built a litter and towed Llen's body from the ravine as Llen watched-on, unseen and unheard by anyone. He tried to get Gwen's attention, but she just looked down at Llen's silent body, weeping. He felt the frustration and helplessness, unable to be recognized by the woman he loved, to care for her. So Llen attempted to lie down with his motionless body on the litter to return to his life with Gwen, closing his eyes, only to fall into a deep sleep.

Startled – Llen woke-up in a dark pit within the cool earth, bound with ropes, unable to move or speak – veritably held in a sense of terror. Quickly he realized he could return to sleep and wake to a better dream. With that notion, he immediately fell asleep, dreaming again, this time unbound, walking slowly with sword in hand within a mysterious cave. He carried a torch in the other hand as he explored the cavernous tunnels winding through the darkness. There was something in there with him. He could hear it breathing. He even began to smell a beast; when suddenly a wild arm lashed-out at him. Llen struck swiftly with his sword inciting the deafening screech of the creature's pain as a reptilian claw fell to the damp cave floor. It lunged forward again in vengeance from the darkness, exposing itself to Llen's torchlight. A monstrous dragon blocked Llen's passage with a ferocity born of Hades flashing from its frighteningly intense serpentine eyes. Llen dodged another swipe of the beast's claw, by bending down low and then lunging upward to drive his blade into the belly of the monster below its ribcage. As Llen retrieved his sword the creature fell forward, nearly falling upon him, the dragon exhaling its last breath. Just as Llen felt a sense of relief, proceeding on through the cave, another dragon lunged out from the darkness. Quickly Llen ducked into a small crevice within the cave wall, avoiding certain annihilation. The dragon tried to reach its claws into the crevice, as Llen slipped deeper into the narrow passage, noticing an opening into another tunnel. He made his way farther along the other deep corridor, finding a larger cavern beyond it. There was daylight filtering-in at the far end of this darkened space. Llen moved rapidly towards the light. Rounding a corner, he discovered a barred gate, secured with lock and chains. Then he heard men's voices approaching. Soon three men faced him on the other side of the gate. One of them held chains and shackles. The others were well armed.

"Well mate, if you hand over your dragon sticker, we'll let you out," the first man said, "unless you'd rather take your chances with the beast. It has your scent already, or will mighty quick, to make a messy meal of you, Llenlleawg."

"Unlock the gate and I'll hand over my sword," Llen answered.

"Hilt first, and don't try to get one over on us, or we'll cut you up in bite size pieces for the cave beast."

"Understood," Llen answered as they unlocked the gate.

He promptly surrendered his sword. They let him out, locking the gate behind him, with their eyes darting into the caverns for any sign of the beast. The third man shackled Llen's arms and legs.

"We aren't taking any chances with the champion of Aenach Garman," the third man said as he gave the chains a tug.

They took Llen out of the cave, up to the keep of a stone and timber fortress. Large double wooden doors with iron hinges were opened as they got closer. After entering the main hall, Queen Marganna soon appeared.

"Leave me the key. You can go now," Marganna ordered her liegemen.

"Are you sure my Lady?"

"Yes. He won't hobble far," she responded, dismissing them with a wave of her hand.

"Where is Princess Gwenhwyfar?" Llen asked.

"Oh Llen, I'm crushed. What about me? Here we are alone at long last and you bring up your former lover. Can't you see? You're all mine now," Marganna toyed with him, running her fingers along his bare arm.

"Where is Gwenhwyfar?" Llen persisted.

"Oh you're no fun. She's gone back to her husband. Isn't that the way it is with her? I know: I have a husband too. But that won't get in our way. Forget about Gwenhwyfar. Give us a chance," Marganna teased him, reaching for his groin, as he turned away.

"Is she safe? At least tell me that!" Llen demanded.

"She is as safe as any girl worth her weight in gold. Her ransom was paid and she is safe at home making little Artúrs, I assume. She was set free. If you want to be set free, you will need to do something for me"

"I have already killed one of your dragons. Isn't that enough?"

"There was more than one? Well I guess you have more to do Llenlleawg Gwyddel. Those dragons are the best guard dogs; except that they just don't care who they have for dinner. No Llen, the dragons are fine. I want you to bring someone to me: Gwalchmai. I have heard so much about him, and his manhood. I know that you want to rescue him. If you do that and bring him to me, I will set you free. I know that you are a man of honor, other than adultery, of course. I understand passion. Your secret is safe with me – for a price. Bring the great Gwalchmai to me, and he can make up his own mind. He's a big boy."

"You are right that I wanted to free him. And if I find him, the choice is his, whether he will come to you or not. He is his own man; that you know as well. I agree to your terms. You have my word; but I cannot guarantee what my friend will choose to do."

"That is fair and noble of you, Llen. I expected nothing less. Now, one more thing: I insist that you bring an escort of my choosing with you," said Queen Marganna.

At that moment a beautiful young woman entered the main hall, scantily dressed in a revealing gown, with her eyes focused on Llen as she approached at a sultry pace.

"This is Hanna, Llen. She will accompany you all the way. Bring her back with Gwalchmai. She knows where to find him," the Queen directed.

"I hope that she can ride, and will dress for travel," Llen answered, with a look of skepticism.

"Oh, she can ride! Hang on to your reigns, Llenlleawg," said Marganna, with a mischievous tone to her voice.

Llen reluctantly embarked on this adventure with Hanna as his guide, soon to realize this escapade was just another test of his fidelity to Princess Gwenhwyfar. The tantalizing Hanna was continuously flirtatious with Llen on this ill-advised journey.

"Is this wanton behavior ever going to cease?" Llen questioned with an obvious tone of aggravation.

"I was born in the village of Chwanton. It is in my blood. Aren't you here to see to my every desire?" she persisted with her prurient feline aggression, moving as close to him as her horse would allow.

"No, I am not. Must you slither so, whenever you come near me? The horses may be spooked by your reptilian advances," Llen cautioned her.

"I am here to direct you," she responded.

"I know the direction you are headed; and it is a distraction and diversion. Now, ride that horse – because you won't be riding me," Llen said abruptly as he guided his horse to a gallop.

As nightfall neared, they came into a clearing within the woodlands where a bright colored tent stood, as if prearranged lodging awaited them.

"What is this, more of Marganna's enticing traps?" Llen suggested.

"You are already trapped, Llenlleawg, by the Princess of Dalriada. I am here to set you free," Hanna pestered him again as she dismounted her horse with a sliding descent.

He watched as she gracefully strolled into the spacious pavilion. A table with a buffet of food and drink was set for their dining pleasure. Centered within the pavilion stood a finely adorned bed, which Hanna proceeded to immediately, stripping-off everything that she wore, sprawling naked upon the bed, awaiting Llen's entry. After he saw to the horses, he stepped into the grand tent, seeing Hanna spread-out with loins and legs open to him. He walked directly to the dining table, poured a tankard of ale, grabbed a leg of roasted fowl, and exited the pavilion to eat his supper in the field. Hanna rolled over on the bed, smothering her laughter in the plush feather pillows. She wrapped herself in a blanket, dining alone bedside within the pavilion. After he finished eating; Llen bedded-down on the ground outside, falling fast asleep. In the middle of the night he awakened to feel Hanna's hand upon his aroused body, quickly pushing her away. She fell back, hitting her head, appearing to be out cold. Llen leaned over her to see if she was alright, when she surprised him with a passionate kiss. He rolled over on his back as she continued to molest his non-responsive torso with more unwanted affection.

In frustration, she slapped him, shouting: "You're not a man!"

"What am I then?" he asked.

"You're a ghost!" she declared, standing up and storming off to the pavilion to sleep alone.

Pondering her departing words, Llen drifted back to sleep. He dreamed within dream that he continued his journey. From a rise at the edge of a valley, he saw a broad flowing stream. As he drew near, he could clearly see the bodies of a man and a woman lying within the rushing waters, beneath the surface, fully clothed in the regalia of grand nobility, preserved in a still, funerary posture. Llen was shocked to recognize that these two people were Gwenhwyfar and himself. He walked into the stream and they disappeared, as he trudged and splashed the water in a frantic search for the bodies he believed to be so very real. Overwhelmed, Llen experienced a sensation of sinking into darkness – an imageless, faceless, and formless abyss. He instantly recalled being swept-up into the arms of Lady Vivianne as a babe – then, abruptly shifting to seeing her as a mature woman, the matron of Afallon, shining as a beacon of primordial wisdom. He felt comforted. No longer an orphan, no longer an orphan to wisdom and understanding, but now embraced by a sanctifying intelligence. At that moment, Llen awakened at Lady Malenhau's cottage, strangely aware of his physical body again, immobile, as if tied firmly to the rough hewn litter of his rescue.

"Llen, Llen, are you awake?" Bercnaf called to him.

Llen struggled to speak, but could only utter unintelligible sounds. He tried to move his arms, feeling bound to a wall of physical restraint, seemingly buried within the solid form of dense space. He could see. He could see Bercnaf and the vague surroundings of the cottage. His mind was emerging from a mental fog, wondering what had happened. Where was this place? How did he come to be here?

"Llen, you're alright. You fell, but you're back. I'm right here with you," Bercnaf tried to reassure him. "Mala! Llen's awake! Mala!"

Llen could vaguely recall this name, Mala, questioning himself, how he knew her, and from where.

"Llen, Llen, I am Mala. You're going to be alright. You hit your head. Bercnaf and I have been with you. It may take time, but you'll get better."

"We'll get you back. Don't worry. We'll get the power of the mountains and streams moving through you again."

Llen looked up at his dear friend with gratitude, exhausted, trying to mouth words of thanks: words not heard, but clearly seen in the depths of his eyes. Then he fell back to sleep, to rebuild from the inside what seemed broken, and perhaps to dream once again.

All of this time Vivianne had been aware of Llen's fall and the deep stupor he was mired in: first through her visions, and then through the messages Bercnaf was able to send to Afallon. It had been several weeks since Llen's fall. He showed some movement in his arms and legs while within dream, indicating a good chance of full recovery. Bercnaf moved Llen's arms and legs in some of the limited motions of their regular practice of the power of the mountains and streams, recalling their early lessons as lads. He talked to Llen, telling him stories of their youth, and tales of battle and bravery. Each day he worked with Llen, sometimes just a few movements until Llen became tired. With help, Llen could sit up in bed and move his upper body. His speech remained halting and slurred for some time, driving him mad with frustration. So much so, he threw a wooden bowl across the room in anger one day, receiving a vigorous round of applause from Mala and Bercnaf, as Llen finally demonstrated his first burst of powerful strength. It was a great day when they got Llen to stand at the side of the bed: Llen mustering the vigor to utter in a slightly distorted tone – "Aenach Garman, here I come" – arousing both laughter and applause from his attentive and dedicated friends. With daily training and practice, Llen soon walked short distances, continuing to move the power of mountains and streams through his body as he sat in a chair or lay in bed. It wasn't long before Bercnaf started working with Llen's reflexes, sparring with a wooden staff. From there, they finally got Llen on horseback for a brief period everyday: Bercnaf holding a lead off the bridle, running him around in a circle. One of Llen's greatest hurdles of recovery was his surprising episodes of violent mood swings, quite different from his even tempered nature of the past; appearing to go utterly mad for a while, into an odd lapse of fury and then becoming strangely detached from outward reality.

His ever loyal friend Bercnaf would say, "Heel Lad! We'll train that rabid hound right out! It's not taking over!"

"Is all bark, hound-master" Llen would answer. "I'll shovel my own shite out of the yard"

By the time of the spring thaw, Llen was nearly back to his former physical strength and agility; and yet, his sense of self was forever altered in ways he would reflect upon the rest of his life. He had lived another life in the Otherworld during those weeks of his bedridden stupor. Llen and Bercnaf returned to Afallon that spring before Beltaine. Vivianne told Gwenhwyfar of Llen's recovery weeks before his return. The Princess of Dalriada had almost completely resigned herself to a life with Artúr mac Aidan, after Morcant Mwynfawr spuriously negotiated her return.

Llen remembered many of his dream visions from those long weeks of astounding inner travel. He could not forget that brief glimpse of his future wife and son, knowing that his conflicted love for Gwenhwyfar was certainly doomed. Once again, Vivianne acted as his confidant and wise guide through the depths of his soul. He told her as much as he could recall of those turbulent adventures in the Otherworld.

"What is it that compels the soul to carry what seem to be two lives: our waking life and the Otherworld of dreams and visions? I suppose I could have never come back, lost in that other realm or embraced by death. At times I still think that I have lost my mind, altered somewhere in those labyrinths of vision, while a new strength has also been enlivened, continually coursing through my soul," Llen confided.

"The mind is restless," Vivianne began, "even as the body is still, whether in sleep or stupor. It may depart to another world, as you well know, to remain active, to fulfill desires, and to confront fears. The mind can also be opened within this inner realm to receive communication of a higher order, from that space inseparable from all wisdom, strengthening and enlivening the soul. The outer vessel of mind and body is fragile, because it is an artifact, or an artifice of thought. We make it this thing to claim as ours – a name, a face, a character, and an identity to cling to in our imagination. The mind may be lost, but the soul is never lost: only temporarily captured by the mind. A state of mind can be certain, rigid, immobile – until moved beyond its captured understanding. Then the soul may be free to know itself unbound. This body is bound within time, unaware of dreams and actions in the Otherworld. The perception within dream continues as body, mind, and emotion: yet the spirit is beyond life and death, beyond body and mind, eternally aware and accessible within the Otherworld of dream. Do not fear the loss of your mind. The mind can create dark dreams; but you are the light within them. Your compassion for yourself is to awaken from your own self-created nightmares."

"After this time of being . . . well I guess, stepped out of time, I question this conflict between what seems to be inner and what appears to be outer. I could have died. How much time do I have? What is my destiny in time? What is the destiny of my soul, in time and beyond time? These questions are much more important to me now," Llen questioned further.

"If you're looking for answers in the field of time, you will not find them buried there." Vivianne continued. "The passage of events in time displaying achievement, progress, or stagnation and regret is not the greater reality. It is only real as a perception or an interpretation. You can begin to observe this within time and space, avoiding the pitfalls and obstructions barring you from yourself. Then you may become aware of a deeper sense of yourself – a light emanating beneath or within your observation, as you experienced within the cavernous labyrinth of your dream. Your visions and experiences illustrate something beyond them. There was no process in time, other than your own stepping out of your own mind. The waking world as perceived is a manifestation of the mind; while your dream life is an unmanifested world of the mind. It is all an apparent life and identity, inward and outward, but as a temporary expression for deeper life and identity to be made known, beyond an individual life and its dreams. This is the only true destiny – to realize the greater reality that you are."

"I have learned so very much from you, my dear mother of wisdom, and Master Taliesin my father of great knowledge; while this recent experience has opened a much wider door to the Otherworld inside of me that I had only briefly stepped through in dreams before," Llen added.

"Even though these visions of the Otherworld and of dreams carry the symbols of generations of knowledge and wisdom, everything to be realized or attained is within you," Vivianne reaffirmed. "No one can confirm this to you except yourself. What is timeless is within your own awareness. It does not come from anywhere else, or anyone else; and you do not need to go anywhere else to find it. All of this hinges on your own readiness and willingness. It is not in the future: but can be held back by your own attachment to the past – that which you cling to, and that which haunts you. Your world of thought has been turned inside-out. You became unable to move outwardly, and moved into worlds inwardly, to see that there is an immovable stability that is not affected by outward circumstances, except in your limited awareness of your very own center. That center is everywhere and nowhere. It is infinite, without occupying tangible space, yet felt as immensely present. This elemental power is our potential, touching the infinite from an eternal immutable point of awareness, balanced as a subtlety of being. It is a veiled reality; because it is known only by being within it. Therefore, it goes unperceived within the waking world, but active within the Otherworld, the world of dreams, and at the core of being. What I am saying probably would not make any sense to you until now. Your sense of reality is now very different than it was before your fall and your recovery. Be patient with yourself. There is no inner versus the outer. There is only being: as the conscious heart, as the seed of eternity, as the wheat of song.

Chapter Seven ~ Grail Visions

In the early years of my youth, I, Cian Gwenith Gwawd began to see the turning of the world I had known. A young bard is trained to witness what happens around him, and perceive the shifts within him, and within those he observes. All of my life was impacted by the events just prior to my birth: Gwenddoleu's evil assault and the battle of Arfderydd. A wound lay open in the north, infecting all of my Cymbrogi, my fellow countrymen seeking ways to recover. The soul of the Cymri was scarred; and I was born from that gaping wound. Sacred wells were no longer the centers of inspiration, tragically becoming grave markers of sorrow. A theft of spirit had taken place, where one self-obsessed king had incited his cohorts to commit crimes against humanity. A healing needed to occur. While at the same time the Cymri needed to defend themselves from internal threats and outside invaders. The idealized symbol of a chalice of the wells arose in the hearts and minds of the Cymri as their sacred cup of recovery. So they sought to find it. This cup or chalice was the natural descendant of the cauldron and platter of ancient times. What these vessels had held varied with the customs and rituals of diverse ancestral cultures. It seems that the people of all clans, cultures, and kingdoms desire some otherworldly form to cradle their collective sacrament of soul and spirit, lest it be spilled to run loose among the elements. Wiser pilgrims may eventually realize, we are already imbued with sacred contents, elementally infused within each dreaming soul struggling to awaken.

Penasgell

The dear sister of Peredyr and Gwrgi, self-exiled princess of Ebrauc, grew into the gifted spiritual heir of her mentors of Afallon, Vivianne and Morcades. Penasgell had known many of the maidens of the wells murdered and assaulted by the ravagers of Solway led by Gwenddoleu, devoting much of her time and energies to caring for the survivors and their children, along with Claire and Morfyn, who cared for me as an infant and lad. There were many who suffered during those years of loss. Poverty and disease rose out of the deaths of fathers and brothers, and the failing crops of seasons of drought. Shortages of fresh water added to the spread of leprosy among some of those poor souls already suffering. Penasgell assisted Colum Cille in establishing a leper colony on a western isle. Her devotion to alleviate this scourge led Penasgell to give her own blood to help a severely ailing woman with two young children. There was a belief that bathing the affected area of the flesh with the blood of a virgin would induce a purification that would halt the spread of the disease. This generous gift of love left Penasgell in a dangerous state of ill health, lowering her pulse to nearly imperceptible signs of life. Prayers of Colum Cille and attending sisters of Afallon surrounded her as she balanced at the edge of survival.

The courageous lass soon found herself deep within otherworldly visions. In the depth of surrender her apparent deathbed became a sailing vessel for her soul, drifting on the open sea of vast awareness. She arrived at a shining citadel upon an imaginal sacred shore. There, rising and disembarking the ship, she was greeted by her mother Erfiddyl, who had passed away more than a decade before. Her mother embraced her and then they walked on together into the citadel. Erfiddyl led Penasgell to the expansive cemetery, where wrought iron letters above the entry read: Caer Marwol, meaning, fort of the mortal. They walked farther in, between the massive tombs and headstones, until they reached the graves of their own lost family, Penasgell's father King Eliffer and his sons, and her mother's own grave. At this point, Erfiddyl kissed Penasgell on her brow and vanished from sight. Penasgell began to shed a tear as her heart and breath were startled by her mother's quick departure. Looking closely at the grave markers, she read the names of the five brothers that she never knew – stunned again by the graves of Peredyr and Gwrgi.

"What is this? How can this be?" She questioned, immediately witnessing a vision of their deaths in battle, out-numbered and surrounded. Penasgell began to weep, realizing that she was or would be the lone survivor of her family, if she could not save her remaining brothers from this fate. At that moment, she was immersed and overwhelmed with an immense and expansive wave of love: love for her family, love for all humanity, and love for all those suffering souls she dearly cared for in her life of service to others. Then suddenly before her eyes, out above a distant tomb, Penasgell saw something hovering in the air. She could not quite make out what it was – perhaps a bird. As she moved forward, marveling at its enigmatic motion, she thought it to be an otherworldly spirit of indiscernible semblance, fluttering within this illusory atmosphere. Moving nearer to this apparition, she could clearly see that it was a swath of fabric, pale in color, yet emitting a subtle radiance of light. This captivating form was drawing her to come even closer, revealing the shadowy impression of a human image upon its wavering surfaces. She realized that it was a shroud, bearing the latent image of a bearded king.

Astoundingly, this entity's voice spoke to her within her own mind, saying: "This is the threshold of the Marw Mawr, the Great Dead, the Fisher Kings, the Meira, and the Maré. No earthly vessel can hold what permeates all being. You give your blood and embrace your light. This well of giving is infinite. Searching for a palpable presence to grasp will no doubt continue in the waking world; but here, now – know what it is to know what you are."

With that, the scene vanished, the shroud gone, the cemetery and all earthly appearances transposed into an ever-expanding realm of light and color, thriving with an effulgence of love, each ambient nuance seeming to convey the exaltation of an immeasurable sense of completeness. Penasgell felt unbounded fulfillment opening her every breath to a pulse of life infused with a satiating purity of joyous love. And then, she woke up, surrounded by her sisters of Afallon.

"We thought we had lost you, sister. How do you feel?"

"I, I feel embraced and enrapt by love itself."

"Did you have a vision while afflicted?" asked one of the sisters.

"Vision does not justly describe what I saw – or what I now see."

"What do you see?" Another sister asked.

"I see that love is all. I see that nothing is truly apart from this love."

"Surely there are dangers in the world," a third sister asserted.

"Whatever we continue to believe and fear will continue to appear," responded Penasgell.

"What appeared to you during this rapture of healing?" a fourth sister asked.

"It is not so much what appeared, as it is what was conveyed. We are sisters of a light that permeates all life. I was born into a human family, but there is a greater intimacy of love, beyond my blood. What has appeared to me is guiding me to see my family from that place of greater love. And so, I will journey to Ebrauc soon, where my family has lived and died, to find out what else unfolds in this waking life," answered Penasgell.

Within a few days Penasgell regained her full strength. The woman with the young children whom she had sought to help also fully recovered. Penasgell was sure it was not because of the blood, but because of the light. Now she needed to return to her family, for a time. She traveled east on the journey of more than thirty leagues with her cousin Gawain, to reunite with her brothers Peredyr and Gwrgi. Her bond with her brothers was formed in her mother's womb, each one of them born only minutes apart, now having been leagues away for months and years. Her brothers had become joint rulers of Ebrauc, after decades of rule by their elder cousins Gwallog ap Llaennog, his uncle Ceredig, and Gwallog's son Ceredig – heirs of the neighboring kingdom of Elmet. Peredyr had married Princess Blodgwyn of Powys, who was at that time with child. When Penasgell and Gawain arrived in Ebrauc, Peredyr was preparing to depart on a quest for the lost chalice of the sacred well. Gawain and Penasgell were greeted warmly by her sister-in-law in the grand hall of Caer Ebrauc.

"Dear sister, you are radiant with the love burgeoning within you," Penasgell said to Blodgwyn, kissing her on both cheeks.

"And you are as well. Is there a love in your life that we have not been introduced to?" Blodgwyn responded, glancing over at Gawain.

"Oh, ha, ha – no – this is our cousin Gawain. He was kind enough to escort me here from the western isles." Gawain remained silent, bowing his head slightly to Blodgwyn. "But as for love," Penasgell continued, "the love of spirit has filled me even more, lately, with gratitude and awe. But no, I have no other love to confess, or unrequited desires to fulfill."

"What brings you to Ebrauc?"

"I knew your time was coming soon, and I wished to see my dear brothers."

"Ah, well, I'm glad you arrived when you did. Peredyr has planned an expedition in search of the sacred chalice, or grail, or whatever this artifact is that has captured popular imagination. I do not see its value; but he is restless. Peredyr assures me he will return before the birth of our child."

"He always was the restless one. I'm sure Gwrgi will be content to rule alone in his absence. Gwrgi has probably impressed upon Peredyr the symbolic value of the chalice, as an inspiration to the people. As you know, much recent misfortune has been attributed to a dark shadow of fate falling upon the Cymri since the assault of the maidens of the wells. The return of the chalice would be perceived as a sign of recovery," Penasgell explained.

"You see things so clearly," Blodgwyn responded, clutching her arm and pulling her close. "I'm so happy to have my wise sister back home again."

Peredyr and Gwrgi entered the hall, immediately embracing their triplet sister, and greeting Gawain with a firm Roman forearm hand shake. Peredyr caressed his expectant wife, she absorbing each and every moment with him before his departure.

"You have surprised us sister. I saw no peregrine circling before your arrival," jested Gwrgi.

"You would have to leave your library to even notice, dear brother," Penasgell retorted.

"He does step out at least once a week, truly – I have witnessed him squinting at the sun," Peredyr joined-in.

"It is grand to be here with you both," said Penasgell, an arm around each brother. "And now our family grows again, with this beauty and her child," she added, acknowledging Blodgwyn.

"Thank you dear sister, I believe this child is urging me to my chamber," said Blodgwyn. "I'll leave you three to catch-up while I rest – so glad you're here," she added, clutching Penasgell's hand before departing.

"Your dear wife tells me you're off soon on a quest for the lost chalice," Penasgell addressed her brother.

"Yes, we have a good chance of discovering a trove of looted treasure from the wells, ferreted away in some of the caverns of Penllanw," Peredyr responded.

"I have heard rumors of these hidden caches. Do you have some promising leads," Gawain questioned.

"We do. Our scouts believe they've found a route to at least one possible hidden location where Gwenddoleu's allies had taken flight east of a prominent ridgeline," Peredyr replied.

"I know your search is intended to rouse public inspiration, if in fact, you can recover an artifact that captures common belief. I only question the timing: your wife with child, and the potential threat of Bryneich or Bernicia at your borders," Penasgell counseled him.

"In my mind, this is the ideal time for such an inspiration to refortify our borders and our internal strength, here in Ebrauc and across the Cymric kingdoms," Peredyr said, his arms crossed over his chest.

"I must concur that sooner is better than later – with the threat of invasion building. We rally the Cymric spirit with symbol, be it cup, cauldron, sword, lance or whatever else grips the imagination of our people and urges them to band together. Although, we do respect your insights, as we have since we were lads. Have you had any visions or premonitions that have raised your concern?" Gwrgi questioned Penasgell.

"Recently, I had fallen ill, after giving a large amount of blood to assist in the healing of a woman in my care."

"We all feared for her life. She hardly had a pulse." Gawain interjected, gently touching his dear cousin's shoulder, she touching his hand.

"I became so weak in my body that I departed from it for a time, entering the Otherworld," Penasgell continued. "The spirit of our mother greeted me; and we walked among the graves of our family, our father and our five brothers. But I also saw the graves of both of you. My vision showed me a battle, where you, Peredyr and Gwrgi were together, surrounded and outnumbered. I do not know where it was, or when it might take place, but it seemed to be your last fight. Then suddenly, in the seemingly disquieted yet tranquil air, I saw a shroud hovering above a distant tomb. The shroud held an image, a shadow of the face and body of a radiant king. His voice spoke within my own mind, saying: 'No earthly vessel can hold what permeates all being.' Then all worldly appearances vanished, as his voice commanded me to: 'know what it is, to know what you are.' From there, I was carried beyond any sense of time, place or person housing my soul. I was immersed in boundless love – more fulfilling than anything I have ever known. I awoke completely revived, with my sisters of Afallon around me. I knew then that I must come here to tell you both what I saw and what I felt. I don't know if we can alter fate, or the ultimate course of our future; but I know that we can alter our own awareness of what we perceive, here and now. I have not been the same since I had this vision – feeling forever changed. It is not because I know things that I did not know before: it is that I feel more fully beyond what I know, and what I thought I knew of myself, of my soul, of all being, and of love itself. So I share this with you out of love, not out of concern, or as a warning. I know that you are wise men, my brothers. You will do what you see fit with this knowledge. I love you both so very much. That is why I am here, to see you now."

"Thank you dear sister," said Peredyr. "That is an extraordinary vision. We come to expect nothing less from you, as you have always opened our eyes to the greater realms of our souls."

"I felt that presence with you, the moment you arrived," added Gwrgi. "And I believed it was because it had been so long since we had seen you. Although, in my mind I knew there was something more that you had to share with us, more significant than ever before. When you spoke about feeling things deeper, or beyond what you thought you knew, I understood immediately in my heart what you meant. I am a man of letters and learning, much occupied in my mind; but I have come to know vision far beyond symbol. That is what I felt from your vision as you described it. Our souls are bound to each other; and you are that aspect of our shared soul that allows us to reach past what we think we know."

"It is so very wonderful to be with you both again. I will stay for a while this time, certainly until after the child is born. It is a powerful thing to be born as three into this waking world, our bodies and souls formed together yet carrying our own independent identities. There is a love here eternally connecting us. It is so very good," said Penasgell, embracing them again.

Peredyr

The following day Peredyr and a small patrol of ten men departed as planned into the mountainous region of Penllanw. Gawain decided to go along, relieving some of Blodgwyn's concern, and satisfying his own curiosity. Their excursion was intended to last ten days, returning well in advance of Blodgwyn's expected delivery. Journeying through Elmet, signs of warfare and destruction still lingered across the landscape: some of it reaching back to the Roman occupation, but in more recent decades from battles with the sons of King Ida and the Angles encroaching from the eastern shores. Once Peredyr and his men reached higher elevations, their scouts conferred with local villagers on the route they had intended to take. After receiving some conflicting information, Peredyr and Gawain decided to divide the patrol into two groups of six, one headed southwest and the other headed northwest along a trail that traversed the eastern face of a prominent ridge.

"We'll meet back here in seven days, after seeing which lead plays out best," Peredyr determined.

"If events turn against us, and we can't return to this point, I suggest we find our way to Loidis, meeting there in eight to ten days," Gawain advised.

"That sounds like a wise back-up plan," said Peredyr. "These are the lands of my ancestors, so I don't anticipate any trouble. But then, we didn't expect the troubles leading to Arfderydd either."

"Safe travels and good luck to all," said Gawain, giving his younger cousin a hearty embrace.

The two parties headed out in opposite directions along the same trail. Peredyr's patrol encountered some rocky terrain to the northwest, following the sketchy description of abandoned mines and hidden caves that they had gleaned from the local villagers. After a sudden storm hit during their unfruitful rummaging of the rock-clad slopes, they took shelter in a cave. Storm activity was quite surprising, breaking the drought pattern of recent years. The shifting air held a mysterious foreboding of anticipation and caution, as if something may soon be revealed. Rain appeared to be the greatest revelation, making the craggy surfaces dangerously slick. One man fell, injuring his leg, requiring a splint. When the storm passed, he and another man to assist him would return to the nearest village.

The wind echoed and moaned through the entrance to the cave in the night, creating a haunting murmur between the sounds of distant thunder booming across surrounding peaks and valleys. Peredyr began to question in his mind the wisdom of this adventure, while maintaining a brave face for the men. The outer storm reflected the inner turmoil of Peredyr's sleep and dream visions that night. He found himself wandering alone through a desolate landscape, reminiscent of descriptions of ancient Elmet, after the Romans had scorched the abundant elm forests to the ground, burning with fire a strategic barrier between their settlements and the Picts to the north. Peredyr stepped through the ash and rumble of this wasteland: all of the trees burnt bare, seedlings uprooted by flooding. Ruins of old Roman garrisons, long abandoned, dotted the empty hillsides, the war machine of another time leaving a godless path across the land. As he walked on, Peredyr neared a wide and treacherous river, the relentless force of water demonstrating an insurmountable elemental power. Scanning the horizon with his eyes for any sign of a possible crossing of the turbulent river, a howling wind pounding his body and face, straining the ability of his vision to clearly discern what lay ahead, he saw something way out in the center of the stream. At first he thought it to be a small island or a rock, some bit of risen earth holding its own ground within a deluge of natural forces. Then he finally saw that it was a very small boat, holding one solitary fisherman within a miraculous point amidst the tumultuous waters, rapids raging around – and yet, the modest boat sat steady and centered within a calm eddy. Peredyr walked down to the river's edge. Bracing himself on a rock at the shoreline, he called out to the fisherman.

"Where can I ford this raging river?"

The fisherman replied: "nowhere today or tonight. You can stay the night at Caer Grail," pointing to a fortified hill.

Peredyr waved and nodded with gratitude. Then he proceeded across the windswept lands to the distant citadel. After climbing the winding road up to the top of the hill, he arrived at the dimly lit gates of the fort, alerting the guards in the gatehouse.

"Who goes there?" A voice from the tower cried out.

"I am Peredyr of Ebrauc. The fisherman on the river said I could shelter here for the night at Caer Grail."

The gates opened and a guard approached Peredyr, searching him for weapons. Seeing that he was unarmed, the guard led Peredyr into the citadel, up the central pathway to the doors of the main hall. Doormen opened both doors wide to reveal a festive court filled with light, music and boisterous sounds of merriment. As Peredyr walked in he saw a great bed in the center of the hall, off to one side, where an old lord reclined, his legs supported by lavish pillows. He appeared to be the same man as the fisherman who sent him there. Soon a procession entered the great hall, while Peredyr stood aside observing the grand display. The crowd had become silent as a young lad came forward carrying the most otherworldly white lance, stretching so incredibly far into the distance that it seemed to reach into the distant past, more than any conceivable form, existing as an intangible beam of light. From the leading tip of this extraordinary white lance, a steady flow of bright red blood ran along the shaft toward the raised arm and hand of the angelic lad holding the lance above his head. He passed by the old lord, bowing his head slightly to acknowledge him, the light of the lance trailing behind the youth, as he and the lighted lance merged with a field of brilliant light at the far end of the great hall.

This illumined exit was followed by the entrance of two more youths, both lads blindfolded, carrying golden candelabras: one holding nine candles, the others holding ten. The lad with the ten candles held his candelabra upside down; while strangely, the flames burned downward, contrary to natural order, as drips of wax ran upward to the inverted base.

Following these two lads, two young maidens entered carrying a silver platter with the severed head of bearded king resting upon it. The animated visage of the king altered form between a regal human face and a cawing raven, and then reverting back again. Suddenly, a dozen black songbirds swooped down from the high rafters of the hall, alighting on the edge of the silver platter to sing the beautiful melody of a familiar ancient tune. As the birds completed their song and flew aloft again, the severed head of the king announced himself.

"I am the blessed king of every time, remembered or forgotten, believed or disbelieved, reborn or dead to all. I am of the otherworldly mind, entered from a door that all may close to the common world of Prydain – the place of forgetting. Again and again the waking world forgets, and the old lord lies wounded. These youths carry wonders. Their hearts do not age. And their bodies walk in light."

With that, the two lads with the candelabras and the two maidens carrying the silver platter walked into the intense light at the end of the great hall, all aglow with the regal head, disappearing from mortal sight. Images of Peredyr's father King Eliffer, his mother, and his five departed brothers appeared momentarily within the radiance, only to merge with the light.

As soon as this had occurred, another maiden entered at the other end of the great hall holding a chalice out in front of her as she walked slowly toward the light. Miraculously, she carried the light. She moved with a gliding flow of weightless conveyance: hovering no more than a breath above the surface of the floor. Light emanated with such intensity from the chalice that she carried, it out-shined the immense light at the end of the hall. The maiden and the chalice became infused with light so brilliant that the image of their forms were barely discernible as subtleties within the encompassing luminescence. As she became fully absorbed by the light, the crowded hall remained still. But when the radiance finally diminished into natural light, attendants carried the old lord from the hall to his chamber, while the court resumed its activity, with music, feasting and frivolity.

Peredyr walked over to the great bed, sitting on the edge in awe of what had just occurred. He looked around at the chatter, the feasting, and the immediate resumption of worldly behavior after such a profound and otherworldly series of events. He wanted to shut-out the noise of the hall, to return to the blissful silence that was there moments before. He curled-up on the great bed, pulling pillows around his head, searching for that embracing quietness of the otherworldly light. The sacred space of the great bed was transported to an expansive plain, stretching to boundless horizons, illumined by the faint light of the gentle rosy hues of dusk. Peredyr slept there at the base of a spectacular tree, its roots sunk deep below the bed within his ultra-conscious mind, branches and leaves reaching up to a darkening star-dotted sky. He was the life of the tree, spiraling into the heavens, more alive than his youthful days of scaling the upper branches of the great elms and oaks of his homeland. For an instant of dream within dream, Peredyr held that innocence of spirit that the blessed king spoke about. He suddenly awoke, alone on the great bed.

The hall was empty. No servants had entered to clear the tables. He thought he might ask the servants about the night before. Did he dream all of this? Was he still asleep? He rose from the great bed, oddly hearing no activity beyond his own footsteps. He looked down a passageway, listening intently, but nothing could be heard. He stepped outside onto a terrace to see the citadel empty of all inhabitants – not a goat or a hen or a bird in flight. Peredyr hurriedly went down to the stables to find only one horse, recognizably his own, saddled, with a satchel tied behind.

"Hey there boy, did you just saddle yourself? Well done," he said to his complacent companion; then mounted the horse, slowly riding out through the open gate, perusing the landscape to see the river in the distance.

As the citadel gate closed behind him, Peredyr looked back shouting: "Is anyone in there?" Then quietly he asked himself, "where is everyone? What is this place? Where am I?"

Dumbfounded, he headed towards the main road, glancing back to see that the mysterious citadel had vanished completely from the stark barren hills. Peredyr journeyed on for what seemed several hours, until he saw a young woman kneeling by the side of the road, less than an ystaden ahead of him. As he approached, he saw that she was weeping over the body of a young man, bleeding into the dry earth of the roadside from a deep wound to his head.

She pulled his limp body towards her, sobbing and wailing: "My love, my love!" Startled, she noticed Peredyr approaching.

He slowly dismounted, walking his horse closer, asking: "What has happened? Has someone brutally struck down this fair lad?"

She did not answer for a span of time, holding her beloved's body close, rocking him in her arms, sobbing. Eventually she became more silent and still, just stroking her hand across his hair. Finally, she looked up at Peredyr with a strangely demented gaze to her eyes.

"I see your horse is fresh. You have not come far. My love is a stableman. He tends to all of the horses of the nobles. We are to be wed soon."

"I spent the night at Caer Grail," Peredyr responded.

"Ah, at the House of the Fisher King," she said.

"Oh, the Fisher King, hmm, well, the old lord of the manor was wounded, and carried out by his servants. I didn't know he was a king. I had seen him fishing earlier, before I entered the citadel and saw him in the great hall," Peredyr explained.

"He fishes because he was wounded, lanced through both thighs, unable to move forward, and cannot ride or rise to battle." The maiden told him. "Have you seen the white lance and the other wonders?"

"Oh, yes – amazing, I saw the white lance of light, the lads with the candelabras, the talking head on the silver platter, and the maiden with the golden chalice emitting brilliant blinding light. But I asked no questions about anything that I saw. Somehow I had fallen asleep on the great bed. Everyone was gone when I awoke. All had vanished. I doubt that I could even find Caer Grail again," Peredyr admitted.

"Gone? Pardon me, but you are lost. How could you fail to ask any questions about this spectacle? Don't you realize that if you had, the Fisher King would have been healed, and his legacy of wise rule would have returned to these lands of Prydain? Instead, much pain and suffering is repeated over and over from the failure to heal the wounded king. Those who inhabit his kingdom need to set him free, free from his endless wounding. My beloved would tell you, but he sleeps now. We all sleep now," she said calmly, staring into the distance, stroking her beloved's hair. Then turning slowly to Peredyr again, it dawned on her to ask, "I don't know your name, do I?"

"I am Peredyr of Ebrauc."

"Hmm, I believe I know your family. I think we are distant cousins. We are both of this line of the wounded king. Yes, I know of the death of your mother, and the death of your father, and the death of your older brothers. We carry the dead with us in the waking world. We will die too . . . or sleep, to wake again in another dream."

As she spoke, Peredyr saw vivid disturbing visions passing through his mind's eye – his first monstrous battle, the Battle of Arfderydd, the vicious mayhem of revenge, the rapes and murders beforehand of the maidens of the wells, their bodies bloodied and abused, their white gowns torn and stained red, and the vacant look of death upon the faces of the living and the dead. Then he saw a wounded dove with an arrow through her delicate wing, bleeding onto a crystalline white bed of fresh fallen snow. This immediately brought to mind his wife Blodgwyn, carrying their unborn child in her womb, her hand reaching out to him, blood dripping from her fingers – as Peredyr looked at the bloodied hand of the maiden by the road holding the fatally wounded lad.

"We can go on and on for years without asking the right questions, without seeing what we are becoming," the maiden continued, "without questioning what we believe we see, to step out of this realm of the dead and dying."

"Dear strange and distant cousin – who are you?"

"You may call me sorrow."

"How ever did I come to find you here?"

"I am another echo of the weeping maidens of the wells. Go on to restore the deep wells; so that everyone is served. Now you must awaken."

With the maiden's last words, Peredyr awoke, once again aware of his surroundings in the hills of Penllanw. It was just before dawn. His men were still asleep. He lay there contemplating the vibrant imagery of his dreams. "Will my unborn child live? What kind of world will this child know? What was all this blood and bleeding all about? What was the meaning of that lance of light? Can the wounded king be healed? Who is this king to me? What am I really searching for?"

Peredyr stepped outside of the cave to find that the rain had stopped and the wind had died down. He looked across the terrain to the east, wondering if the chalice or anything taken from the sacred wells could be found in these hills. Soon his men rose from sleep to get an early start searching to the northwest. Two men departed back to the nearest village they had passed, leaving four, including Peredyr to carry-on the quest. After traveling a few hours, exploring an abandoned mine and a rock-hewn cairn along the way, they heard riders approaching. It soon became clear that these were hostile marauders, possibly part of the few remaining allies of Gwenddoleu, running any treasure hunters off their native hills. Peredyr and his three men were suddenly under attack, arrows flying in advance of the riders' rapid approach. Two men fell quickly from the assault of arrows. Peredyr hurled a javelin to unhorse the lead attacker, before the young king and his last liegeman scrambled up toward the ridge on foot. There must have been over a dozen riders. Several were keen archers, much to Peredyr's dismay, fatally wounding his final companion, as he himself narrowly escaped into the backcountry. They failed to pursue the fleeing King of Ebrauc, not even knowing who he was, as he tenaciously ascended over the ridgeline, away from any trail suitable for horses. Without provisions, he managed to survive on berries and a rabbit he lanced with one of his few remaining javelins. Finally he came upon a trail descending into a forested region a couple of days walk into the northwest. A few leagues down that path he smelled the smoke of a campfire, quietly proceeding with caution. Nearing the campsite he spied-in from the woodlands, seeing an elderly man from behind, tending a humble fire. To Peredyr's surprise, the solitary elder spoke aloud.

"If you have come to rob me, I am an old man with no gold or coin, but you are welcome to share my fire."

Peredyr stepped into the clearing as the elder rose and turned to face him, peering into the darkness to see just who he had welcomed.

"Hello, I know you lad. You are Peredyr of Ebrauc!"

"Yes, Myrddin, how fortunate it is to come upon you here in the wild."

"How are you here lad, with no mount or provisions, no retinue of warriors? Have you entered the hermetic life like this old fool?"

"Not by choice, dear friend – no offence to you sir," answered Peredyr.

"None taken," Myrddin replied.

"I was on a quest, east of the ridge, with five able men, searching for the lost chalice and other treasures, believed to be hidden in a cave or an old mine. One of my men was injured by a fall, returning east with another to assist him; and then marauders attacked the rest of us. I am the only survivor of this ill-fated quest, aside from another patrol of six led by Gawain, headed southwest," Peredyr explained.

"You look rather trail-weary lad. Rest yourself and tell me of your new life as joint-ruler of Ebrauc with your brother, Gwrgi – isn't it? And, why was this quest so desired, at your near peril?"

"Yes, well, Ebrauc is still strong, although threats are mounting from Bryneich and the Angles to the south. And yes, Gwrgi is a fine brother and joint-king. We balance each other well: he as a statesman and me as battle lord – discounting this recent disaster in the hills. I'm expecting a child with my wife, Princess Blodgwyn of Powys. My sister Ceindrych Penasgell is there in Ebrauc with her now."

"Marvelous. It sounds like your life is quite full and content. Why are you on a daring search for this grail cup?" Myrddin questioned again.

"You must know, this curse upon the land since the assault of the maidens of the sacred wells requires the action of good men to restore what was taken and revenge this grievous attack," Peredyr declared.

"I know all too well of the horrendous attacks perpetrated by my own patron of verse. It is a shadow I will likely carry with me all of my days. As for revenge, Arfderydd should have satisfied that bloodlust. I do not believe any number of good men can restore what was taken; anymore than any atrocity is ever restored. It is an irretrievable loss. One cannot return a soul to complete a life cut short. One cannot expunge the pain etched in the hearts of others who survive. Maidenhood is not restored after an assault, neither is motherhood restored to virginity. What it means to carry a child, nurturing a new life into this world, is something a man can never know. The vessel is forever changed. How can the return of any cup or chalice restore these things of flesh and blood and the wounding of souls? Certainly one can conjure a disaster by either action or inaction; but once a disaster has occurred, it cannot be erased, anymore than time can be relived to bring about a different outcome," Myrddin expounded.

"I see that there is likely no other man alive better than you to understand the full scope of this disaster, wise Myrddin. Like so many, I became caught-up in this popular idea, or at least sought to allow it to be used to pacify the wounding of the land and people – which may never heal. There is clearly something sought by the masses and within every soul that desires to be filled from the emptiness of sorrow and loss. My brother had shared with me these tales of ancient times, where a golden fleece, a mighty sword, or the slaying of the gorgon – seeking one great deed or revered object to heal all ills. It seems that it is the unrequited desire of a suffering humanity to find the miraculous cure. I have seen this in my own dreams as well. Just days ago, obsessed with this adventure I dreamed of the grail, of a miraculous lance, a wounded king, and a sacrificial head of a blessed guide."

"Tell me about this dream that I might peer into your soul, and in turn it may help to heal my own," Myrddin requested.

Peredyr recounted the events of his visionary dream to Myrddin, recalling each detail, describing those powerful emissaries of spirit, and dynamic elemental forces that entered into his imaginal sphere.

"The force of water is a powerful element of nature." Myrddin began. "We all have felt its enormous strength and its immense calm. It reflects the undercurrent of the Otherworld: our dreams, our ancestral roots of spirit, and our origins of being. This common source of life and core of mind and emotion can only be described in symbol; and what better symbol than the elemental forces of nature that seem to have a life of their own, overwhelm us, and somehow course through us. There is a merging of inward and outward space that occurs in dream, shown within your enchanted night at Caer Grail, displaying the fluidity of soul. The wounded king, the beheaded king, the fact that you and your brother are kings, your long lost father was king, its affect on your mother, sister and lost brothers – all of this fluid nature of identity is at the core of the idea of yourself and your sense of emotional power. The fisherman is there, in stillness, in the midst of it all. He tells you where to rest. He is honored in the great hall, the hall of dreams, the hall of mind, of emotion, and of the soul. The fisherman – fishing, searching, and watching – is also the Fisher King, and the Priest King of a revered ancestral source. He is wounded. You sleep on his great bed of generations laid to rest. His servants carry him about; but does he move forward on his own? He is the center of it all: of the dream and the greater reality of the Otherworld. He is the rock. He is the island. He is the small boat of calm. He is the mystery. The current surrounds him. It is you who must enter the citadel. The Fisher King is already there. The fisherman was outside; but the Fisher King is inside. It is a spectacle before a great bed, within a great sleep, where the old lord watches the show.

"Then the young lad appears holding a ray of light from the past into the future and beyond. You lad, are the heir of the great javelin army. It has always been your weapon of choice. It reaches. It extends. It travels the great arc of forward movement. The tip, the leading edge – bleeds. Oh does it ever! We all know this wounding. We are at the edge: the leading edge of the blood and the light. We choose between the two, or realize them as one. The two lads with the candelabras are different versions of the same thing – the light refracted, the inverted, the mysterious, and the traditional. Yet both are blindfolded, proceeding by intuition. The maidens follow, serving their king and lord on a silver platter. They are untouched while carrying their lord, moving in pure innocence. He is a blessed lord. He is also a raven: as messenger, as harbinger, and as the call to awareness. He brings the song of his flock, descending and ascending, chirpping an ancient tune heard again and again. This is the blessed king of every time, beyond living and dying. We reside in Prydain, in the realm of time and forgetting. It is youth that carries the wonders. It is age that holds the wisdom. Your family lives in the light of your expanded soul. That impression forever resides in the light. Your memory is incomplete in the land of forgetting. But the light of your soul retains all. The last maiden is this last innocence revealed: the immeasurable light emanating from an indiscernible vessel – the cosmos, not to be captured in a cup. The old lord gets carried away. No one really follows him. He is wounded, wounded the moment he is identified, pierced and immobilized.

"You, however, sleep at the base of a spectacular tree, rooted in the heavens and your own innocence. There is no one else there. The outward spectacle is gone. This journey is yours alone. What is behind you will vanish, unless you carry part of it with you – your satchel tied tightly to the past. You vainly ask: 'Is anyone in there? Where am I?' You meet sorrow on the road, but also joy. The wounded lad is you. His caring lover is you. The dialog is your monolog to yourself. You are the stableman, tending to all of the noble horses, tamed or wild, broken or free. You heal the wounded king with the right questions, while living in the realm of time, the realm of sleep, the realm of dreams, and the realm of forgetting. Of course the sorrowful maiden is part of your family, as I am, another distant cousin. We speak to your soul. We are most familiar to you. We are the voices that echo from your depths. It is you that restores the deep well of your being. Other voices of guidance are available to help you find out where to look. Your search is to discover your own well, not recover an empty cup from the past."

"You have opened another world to me here, Master Myrddin," said Peredyr.

"That world is within you. Your dream held everything that I had to say about it," Myrddin continued. "When entering the dream, you become the dream. It is the fluidity of the grail, the drink of healing, and the awareness of infinite depth. As you enter the fluidity, you become the fluidity. We traverse the ever-flowing river of possibility, engaging a calm, centered eddy of being – Gwydd yn Ennyd – present in this moment. Your mother Erfiddyl and your father Eliffer are the expectant prayer of a flowing legacy realized in you and your brother and sister, continued in the womb of your wife and unborn child. Each and every soul is an heir to the divinity of being: an image of a wounded king, the wounded heart of a grieving bride to be, or a mother of sorrow – all children of one ancient family and source of origin. Their blood flowed for your life; and the wounded king and the severed head remind us of the shared wound, holding us to it, while also telling us to let it go, to be free. The bleeding and the healing continue, until each soul sees differently. The wounded one affects all; and the healing affects all. Whether a king or queen, father, mother, son or daughter is wounded – the healing is without gender, and so is love."

"Where do I go from here?"

"Home."

"I am turned around. Can you guide me back?"

"I can guide you forward to Ebrauc or to the road to Loidis."

"Thank you. I should be able to meet with Gawain and his men there. We can return to Ebrauc together."

Peredyr and Myrddin traveled down to Loidis from the hills, Peredyr staying there only one night before returning to Ebrauc, anxious to be with his wife for the arrival of their first child.

Gawain

Gawain and his five companions had traveled southwest, skirting the ridge toward the river Treante. The same storm that hit Peredyr and his men hit Gawain and his patrol too, yet much harder. They were hammered by the brunt of a deluge farther south, also taking shelter in a hidden labyrinth of caves. To their great surprise, these caves showed more traces of activity, inspiring deeper investigation. After hours of exploring, Gawain and his men discovered a narrow passage covered with stone fragments and rubble. Gawain tossed a stone into the descending passage to see how far it might go, when he heard the stone hit metal. They removed the rubble, working their way deeper, until they found the treasures that they had been seeking: a tremendous trove of gold and silver cups, jewels and finery. The men were elated, opening a goatskin bag of wine to celebrate their sudden fortune.

It was a crude bunch of men there with Gawain. Their stories soon degenerated into randy tales of ravaging women and the spoils of war. But here, the treasure required no battle. Gawain, the only sober member of the party, reminded them that the battle had happened at Arfderydd, these treasures were not for their profit, and the war ravaged spoils had been the maidens of the wells. This left the men quiet enough for a moment to hear the sound of rushing water increasing through the cavernous channels surrounding them beneath the earth. Gawain urged them all to quickly make their way out, lest the flooding of the caves overtake them. As they moved toward the entrance with treasure in tow, they heard a loud rumble. Soon they could see that a mudslide had sealed the entrance, a good hundred paces into the caves. Water was rising at their feet. Two men began to panic; another was far too drunk to move through the encroaching underground stream. Gawain and another man determined the most likely channel to find a possible exit point. Each carried a bit of treasure, Gawain holding what he believed to be that most sacred chalice of the wells. They worked themselves part way through a tight passage, until the heavier man couldn't crawl through the narrow channel any farther. They heard the others wailing in distress, but could barely save themselves. The second man wished Gawain good luck, and retreated back to search for another exit. Gawain, though tall, was lean enough to continue on. He became nearly stuck for a bit until increasing water and slime provided him with the needed slippery surface to finally slide through, dropping him into another tunneled stream, forcing him rapidly onward.

Banged about his limbs, fingers and head, Gawain was washed out into the open air, covered in mud, with his silent face gently breathing, unaware that he had survived. His hands were stiff, cold and battered from the travail, the chalice lost again in all the confusion. Within his mind he found still another channel to explore: as his soul continued to be open to the quest of the grail, and the search for his evolving sense of self. The sounds of rushing water and pouring rain filled his outer senses, as he lay partially covered beneath a blanket of mud, dreaming of the surf of the western shores, and of his past and future adventures there.

He stood on the rising cliffs across the distant sea from Afallon. It was winter. His cousin King Peredyr rode up and said: "thank you for your protection of my sister."

Gawain nodded in recognition, and Peredyr rode on. Looking down at the snow, Gawain saw a raven pecking away at a fallen dove. He was struck by the harsh contrast of the pitch-black raven, the white dove on white snow, and the rich red blood. A hawk called-out in the sky above, shifting Gawain's attention, when he noticed a rider approaching. A bold Christian warrior confronted him, demanding justice.

"You have killed my lord!" The Christian warrior claimed.

"I have not killed your lord. I do not even know your lord," replied Gawain.

"You must know of him. He is the greatest Christian lord of these lands," the warrior insisted.

"I do not know this lord. I am not a Christian, nor am I from these lands," Gawain affirmed.

"Then we must bring you to him by force," the warrior declared.

A patrol of twelve men bound and escorted Gawain to a nearby fortress where he was brought into the hall of the Christian king. Two spearmen pushed Gawain down on the floor to bow before the king.

"Who are you, lost warrior?" The king asked in a condescending tone.

"I am not lost. I am Gawain of the Orcades. Is this the manners and hospitality of the followers of the Prince of Peace?"

"Stand up then," said the king, waiving the guard away with his hand. "What are you doing here, so far from your homeland?"

"I am searching for the lost chalice of the sacred wells. Do you know where it might be found?" Gawain answered.

"Is it not the Holy Grail that you seek?" The king asked.

"Call it what you will. The last knowledge of this sacred chalice was in the hands of the maidens of the wells. I am a sworn protector of all maidens of these isles, be they of Afallon, Dalriada, Christian kingdoms, or even Pict Gwlad," Gawain asserted.

"And to whom have you sworn this pledge of protection? Are you a man of God?" The king queried further.

"I am a man of principle, a man of truth, and a man of spirit. My pledge is to honor, to justice, and to love," Gawain declared.

"Then you have no lord over you?"

"Spirit is my sovereign, and the innocent soul the only subject."

"You are a rare man, Gawain. My sister is in need of a new protector. Would you consider that appointment?" The king asked.

"Well, I don't know sire. I am currently engaged in another . . ."

Gawain's answer was interrupted by the arrival of the king's sister into the hall. Her eyes focused intently upon Gawain, he, transfixed by her gaze, unable to finish his words or complete his thought.

"Gawain – would you consider that appointment?" The king repeated.

"Uh, yes, uh, perhaps I would sire, if I could spend some time with the lady to see if we are well suited, and what she might require," Gawain answered, rather dazed.

"Alright then," said the king, directing his guards, "see that my sister and her ladies have some time with Gawain. Sister, if this man is suitable, let me know. Otherwise, he is free to leave, and will be escorted away."

Gawain and the king's sister were led out of the main hall with her ladies and attendants following behind. There was something sudden and extraordinary going on between these two: Gawain immediately drawn to the king's sister and she instantly intrigued with him, so powerfully, as if by an act of nature or divine will. Over the coming days, the two became inseparable, eventually eluding their chaperones, subverting all protocols, and finding ways to be with each other in intimate privacy. As time flew by, their head-spinning attachment created a scandal that aroused vehement public disapproval, he being seen as a pagan interloper of the kingdom's royal Christian dynasty.

The rebellious couple took refuge in a tower called the Magdala, just outside the citadel on a nearby hill. Crowds condemning them hurled spoiled food and insults from the surrounding landscape. Gawain responded in frustration by throwing game pieces from a Gwyddbwyll board down at the irate rabble. As the pieces fell, the darker ones turned into ravens and the lighter ones turned into doves, their claws drawing blood as they reached the angry mob. The king could not tolerate this continued unrest, agreeing to secure his sister and Gawain from the harassment, if Gawain agreed to embark on a quest for the grail cup, the grail lance, and the grail sword – the king believing that such a quest would be so consuming that Gawain would be unlikely to return for years. His sister might then forget this pagan lover of hers. Gawain agreed, confident in his immutable power to succeed, setting out to find the nearest location of one of the ancient wells. It wasn't long before he arrived at a venerated site, discovering a beautiful woman there, eagerly approaching her, inspired by his great quest.

"Oh dear lady, I am so glad to find you here alone at this secluded site. I believe you have what I desire. This meeting is truly ordained by all the powers of spirit," Gawain barreled-in with enthusiasm.

The lady, taken aback, believed Gawain's intentions were lustful advances towards her, fearing the rapid compromise of her virtue by this amorous zealot; she frantically announced: "Sir, I must caution you, my guardians are nearby. One shrill call of alarm will bring a world of trouble upon you. This is a sacred site, protected by forces of the goddess and her sisters of vengeance," those words ushering-in an apparition of a warrior goddess with flaming scarlet hair, appearing in a flash and then vanishing.

"I am sorry my lady. My zeal precedes me. I mean you no harm. My only desire is guidance, to find the sacred cup and other lost treasures of these sacred wells, serving the people of these lands," Gawain pleaded.

"If you desire to enter this quest, you must first retrieve a fine horse for me from the garden by the river Eden," the lady told him.

Gawain quickly departed. Heading along the Eden Valley, he heard voices from the woodlands warning him to be wary of what lay ahead. Ignoring these promptings, he went on to find the horse tethered to a tree in the garden by the river. As he prepared to release the fine horse from the tree, a dwarf attendant attacked Gawain, blindsided, lashing out from the shadows, taking the horse, leaving Gawain with nothing but a broken-down nag for his return. Gawain arrived back at the well site and the lady was shocked by his inept performance of the task.

"What manner of horse is this?" she asked with indignation.

"I was ambushed by a dwarf. He took the better horse. I believe he wore your colors; was he in your employ?" Gawain responded.

"What kind of man are you, that you can't retrieve a horse from a mere shadow of a man of your stature? This is an ill-fated quest, if this is your best effort," she chided him.

The lady eventually agreed to lead Gawain on to Caer Grail, where he might find what he desired. Nonetheless, she derided him all the way to the river. Upon arrival, Gawain was attacked again, this time by a full-size warrior, riding the robust steed taken by the dwarf. Stomping away in disgust, the woman abandoned Gawain, taking a shallow wooden raft across the river, piloted by a darkly-cloaked ferryman. Gawain handily defeated the warrior with a vigorous thrashing, redeeming his bruised self esteem and regaining the strong steed, as the mysterious ferryman returned. Gawain saw the lady beyond the distant shore, briskly walking-on.

"Can you ferry me across to where the lady has landed?" Gawain asked.

"There is a toll. Do you have coin, gold or silver?" the ferryman asked, looking suspiciously at Gawain.

"Well, no, I have no coin or valuables. But I can give you this nag."

The ferryman shook his head no, looking over at the other horse, saying with a larcenous grin – "I'll take the steed!"

"The steed – are you thinking about starting a stable on the side, expanding your predatory wealth? No . . . not the steed!"

Gawain stood firm, hand on his sword. The ferryman stepped back a few paces, folding his arms across his chest. As they glared at each other in a standoff, a few drops of rain came down to break the tension. The wind rose and the river got more turbulent beneath the darkening sky.

Finally the ferryman laughed and said, "Ha hah, the ferry is closed for the night, until the weather clears tomorrow."

"I can see that," said Gawain, reluctantly. "This journey just gets more troublesome with each turn."

Right then, the sky opened up with a tremendous downpour.

"Okay lad, stay the night in my cottage. I'll ferry you over in the morning," said the ferryman, as they both scrambled out of the rain towards his nearby cottage. The next morning he ferried Gawain and his two horses across the river, charging no toll.

"Thank you for your kindness," Gawain said to the ferryman.

"Take care lad, women will run you ragged," he responded with a cackle as he pushed off from the shore.

Gawain proceeded over the land until he reached a citadel on a hill. The gates were open, and a busy marketplace was thriving within the courtyard. After perusing the vendors and stabling the horses, Gawain entered the great hall at the far end of the courtyard. As he entered, three women began dancing around him, approaching him seductively, leading him over to an enchanted bed: its bedding slowly rising and undulating as if it was a living thing. The three women were quite enticing. One was much older, entrancing him with her eyes, gently touching his bare arms, sending a titillating surge over his skin. The second woman, somewhat younger, but still older than Gawain, looked at him with a longing that nearly brought him to tears. The third woman was younger than Gawain. She reached for him, pulling him into her upon the bed. As Gawain began to feel her flesh upon his, she whispered in his ear, "I am Cundri," as the much older woman whispered in his other ear, "I am Cundri." Gawain quickly withdrew from the young woman, jumping off the bed, seeing the face of the second woman as his own mother, instantly knowing the other two were his grandmother and his sister.

Gawain ran from the hall out of the citadel into an open field. The earth beneath his feet and the distant hills rose and fell with an undulating movement like the enchanted bed. He felt disoriented, his stomach rising with the unstable landscape surrounding him, causing him to bend over and throw up his last meal onto the unsteady ground. He wiped his chin with the back of his hand and then ran down to the stream, immersing himself in the waters again and again, as if to cleanse every layer of his troubled soul. As he looked up, finally feeling refreshed, he suddenly saw an apparition of the otherworldly scarlet-haired woman from the well. She appeared astride the handsome steed that he had fought so hard to recapture, the horse bareback, and she completely nude. Riding at a slow walk right up to Gawain, she began chanting in unrestrained revelatory expression an exhaustive list of names from the current generation into the ancient past – priestesses and priest kings, Sicambrians, Sarmatians, Arcadians, Greeks and Hebrews, including the names of the Fisher Kings, the Grail Kings, the Meira, the Maré, Saint Anne the mother of John the Baptist, Mary the mother of Jesus, her daughter Mary, and Mary Magdalene – finally pausing for a moment as Gawain stood in the shallows of the stream, drenched from head to foot, dumbfounded by her rambling oration.

In her pretentious naked glory, she pointed off towards a distant valley, saying: "Out there is your path to the grail. Follow this wise lineage walking before you. I am another sovereign woman of your extended clan. I am Marganna of the lineage of Afallach."

This outrageous apparition of the naked queen upon a steed vanished from Gawain's sight as he staggered to the shore. Astounded by these successive encounters, he tried to regain his bearings, deciding to follow the directive of the scarlet-haired queen, proceeding on towards the distant valley. Once he had entered the pleasant vale, he met another traveler.

"Good day, noble sir, I am Gawain of the Orcades. If I may ask: where are you from and by what name are you known?"

"I am called MacIlis, from the western isles beyond Gallwyddel."

"Near Arran or Islay then?" asked Gawain.

"Yes, my clan is from Islay. You know the west?"

"Yes, I do. I've spent many years on Ynys Manau, Iona and at Dun Airigh, fostered by Aedan mac Gabran."

"You have ventured far from the Orcades."

"Yes, but I prefer any of the isles to the inland kingdoms."

"I'm with you there mate."

As they traveled together for a time, the western warrior made some disparaging remarks about Gwenhwyfar, and the rumors of her infidelity. Gawain was about to silence the stranger, when as MacIlis spoke, he was shockingly slain by an arrow through the throat, coming suddenly out of sky. Quickly, Gawain took cover, pulling the wounded warrior close to the ground, and carefully peering up to catch site of the hidden archer's line of fire. Gravely wounded, MacIlis pleaded with Gawain to take his sword – a most unusual design with a leaf-shaped blade, so ancient in appearance it could have been crafted in Eden. Gawain removed the sword and its strange baldric made of braided hair from around the wounded warrior's shoulder. The dying man's final request was barely audible.

"Take my horse. Allow him to wander and guide you. His instinct is the way," the man coughed, nearly choking on his own blood to gasp with his last breath, "Lord, Lord, why have you forsaken me?"

Gawain buried MacIlis right there on a slight rise near the road. He never saw any sign of the deadly archer. Gawain mounted the horse, allowing him to act as his wandering guide, the horse leading him to a distant chapel at the edge of a Christian kingdom, as the weather turned threatening again. Gawain took shelter there, riding right through the partly unhinged open door. Inside a single candle wavering in the wind was soon snuffed-out by a sudden gust, accompanied by mournful groans and strange shadows sweeping through the chapel with an eerie foreboding. This wafting atmospheric pall spooked the horse and Gawain as well. When the windows and walls began to fracture, he quickly turned the horse to exit, deciding to brave the storm, rather than gamble on the uncertainty of this once holy structure. Returning to his storm-ridden journey, he clung close to his new mount, while the wind driven rain relentlessly pummeled them. Finally after several leagues of travel, the storm subsided.

By the time his cloak was almost dry again, Gawain had arrived at the Christian citadel. Alarmed sentries recognized the horse belonging to MacIlis. Gawain explained the tragic death of their comrade, his dying gift of the horse, and the location of his grave beyond the distant chapel. He was admitted into the gates of the citadel as they began to mourn the loss of the brave MacIlis. Entering the great hall, Gawain was amazed to see the body of that same warrior already laid upon a stone slab, partly covered by a gilded shroud, and holding a broken sword upon his chest – identical to the one given to him by MacIlis. Soon a procession entered the hall, their voices droning a reverent and mournful ritual chant as they moved slowly towards the dead warrior's body. They carried a vessel in the center of the procession, first appearing as a cauldron and then as a chalice, while they paused briefly to chant different verses in an ancient language of the east. A young priest held a long lance above the vessel, allowing drops of blood to drip into it from the tip of the lance. Each mourner from the procession drank form the vessel while it still appeared as a chalice, until the cup became a cauldron and then a platter, holding the severed head of a bearded saint, the crown of his head radiating a circular glow of celestial light. As the procession reached the dead warrior's body, an older priest-king stepped forward taking a fragment of the broken sword and handing it to Gawain.

"It is up to you to unite the broken pieces," the priest-king said to him.

Gawain bowed his head reverently, accepting the fragment; and to the amazement of the priest-king and the crowd, drew forth from his satchel the sword he had been given, identical to the broken sword, yet whole and complete.

Then Gawain asked the priest-king, "Sire, what is the significance of this ancient sword? What is the meaning of the ritual of the lance, the cup, and the cauldron? Who is this saint whose head is carried in reverence?"

The priest-king explained for all to hear, "This sword is the sword used in the beheading of Saint John the Baptist. It is his noble head that we carry. He was the cousin of our dear Lord Jesus Christ, heralding his arrival among us. This lance was used to pierce the sacred body of our Lord, for the proof of life, forever bleeding its essence. This cup was brought to us by Joseph of Arimathea, the Ram Theo, closest relation in the lineage of our Lord, carrying the cup containing the essence of the lifeblood of our Lord Jesus Christ."

As he spoke, Gawain recalled being told this story of the grail hallows as a lad by his mentor Colum Cille. The priest-king went on to explain the descendancy of the lineage of the Grail Kings, through the generations, citing many of the names that Gawain had heard from the apparition of Marganna at the river. During this long recitation of names by the priest-king, Gawain, so weary from his travels, gradually fell sound asleep.

Deeply fallen in dream within dream, bodily sensation stirred Gawain to open his eyes to find a young woman writhing on top of him, his leggings pulled down below his knees for her passionate mounting of his aroused largesse of manhood. Although her head was shaved completely bald, her face was quite pretty. Clearly distracted by her arousal of his pleasure and her lovely breasts joyfully dancing into his face, he suddenly recognized her to be his cousin Penasgell. With this startling awareness, he abruptly pushed her off to the side of his indiscriminately excited body.

She stood up, smiling, adjusting her disheveled garments, saying: "Beyond time we are free to love. I meet you there. You may embrace me as your otherworldly fortune."

As she turned away, her hair appeared fully grown again, braided in the back, exactly the same way as the braided hair of the baldric of the ancient sword. While Penasgell walked away from him, a peregrine falcon soared in a slow circular pattern in the sky above her, the high-pitched call of the majestic bird jarring Gawain awake from his stupor of near drowning.

He coughed-up some dirty water, rolling onto his side, dazed, and then quickly recalled his narrow escape from the cave. He frantically tried to find the point where he had slithered out of the cave passage; but layers of mud and debris had covered any trace. He knew that his companions must have perished, buried alive or drown, silenced by the massive power of the earth and the forces of nature. Gawain managed to reach a creek running closely below the trail, washing himself in the chilling waters. As he warmed-up in the morning sun, he pondered the fluidity of his dream reality, starkly contrasting the trapped and tragic deaths of the other men. He had hardly known them, struggling to even remember their names. Peredyr knew them. Peredyr would remember, he thought to himself. Gawain knew he must make his way to Loidis and meet-up with Peredyr and the others, share the grave news, and tell them that for a moment the grail was in their grasp, for a moment before near death, and for a moment before the death of all those who had ventured deep into the caverns of the earth.

Gawain was not out of danger yet. He needed to get back to Elmet, avoiding any marauders or the bastards that had put those treasures into the caves. Gawain heard riders on a couple of occasions; so he avoided them by altering his route to Loidis. By the time Gawain made it to a safe haven, Peredyr had left Elmet, returning to Ebrauc. Myrddin was still in Loidis when Gawain arrived. They greeted each other with a hearty embrace.

"Gawain lad, it has been far too long," said Myrddin warmly.

"Yes, how is it we two badgers of the north woods meet here?" Gawain responded.

"I ran into Peredyr, alone in the hills. He said you were planning to meet him here in Loidis," Myrddin told him.

"You ran into Peredyr alone? What happened to his men?"

"One broke his leg, returning early with another man. The remaining three were cut down by marauders' arrows. Peredyr escaped and made it here, but desired to return to his young wife with child. I told him I'd keep an eye out for you and your men. Where are they now, lad?"

"Tragically, also lost – we had found the treasure trove in some caverns to the south. A storm and sudden flood trapped us in the maze of tunnels. I am the only survivor," Gawain sullenly reported.

"Five men lost?"

"Yes."

"And the chalice lost too?"

"Yes, buried with those lost souls."

"Both you and Peredyr have had a rough return alone. How are you holding-up lad?"

"It was as startling as an ambush of battle; only the adversary was the elements: nature closing-in to strangle and suffocate the suddenly trapped and disoriented," Gawain sadly conveyed.

"Losing those men for this idea of a cup, or any sacred relic is a dreadful calamity. It brings to mind the fate of the maidens and loss of these relics the first time," Myrddin observed.

"Yes – and for what: lust, power, or a curiosity – I felt no power in that cup, only powerlessness beneath the immensity of the earth," said Gawain, shaking his head.

"Before his defeat and harrowing escape Peredyr had a visionary dream that he shared with me. He also faced the elemental powers within his dream vision, and saw the grail there."

"Extraordinary," said Gawain.

"He saw the Fisher King, his own ancestors, and his lost family," Myrddin continued. "It seems both of you were on a soul searching quest."

"After my escape from the caverns, I was knocked-out for some time, buried to the gills in mud and debris, yet carried-on in a dream vision. As you said, I was on that quest for my very soul, in that place where heart and mind rattle us about in the aether," Gawain confided.

"I am open to hear of your inner travels lad, if you wish to speak of them," Myrddin encouraged him.

"Most certainly, Master Myrddin, I am no stranger to this inquiry of the soul. As you well know my mother, Morcades, the great seer of the north raised me to reflect on these bedtime stories. The first thing that I recall was seeing Peredyr, thanking me for protecting his sister. And then, a strange scene of a wounded dove, pecked by a raven, the black feathers and red blood sharply contrasted by white snow upon the ground."

"That is quite astounding, because Peredyr had a similar vision of a bleeding dove, in which he held concern for his wife and unborn child," Myrddin interjected.

"Fascinating, it was clearly recognition of the importance of this dream vision to me, setting my intentions and awareness for what was to come. The raven and the dove suggest a shadow over love, with blood ties dramatically present. The scene quickly shifted to a sudden confrontation with a Christian warrior, challenging my intentions. This idea of Christian relics filled my mind, related to the quest for the chalice. While my life experience contrasts belief in these things, I find them intriguing," Gawain related.

"Yes lad, as I'm sure you know, the nature of these things touches the deeper nature of you. Christian symbols illustrate ancient elemental forces found in every culture, where dream visions occurred within aware souls all across the earth. You as the dreamer, your dreaming, and the dream itself are all one vision, common in its forces, yet held within your own unique perception. These visiting entities – Christian, pagan, familiar or foreign – are reflections upon your own sensibilities. You are the central identity within that visionary space. The dream vision is your threshold to the Otherworld, this curious place where the expansion of your soul continues," Myrddin elaborated.

"Yes, I understand that. This Christian warrior confronted me, accusing me of killing his lord."

"Ha, ha, ha – of course he would!"

"I denied it, stating that I did not even know his lord. This was surely my refuting the Christian belief in this imagined and isolated lord, residing in some other place; who as a non-believer of their doctrine, I must have killed or continue to kill or disregard, from the vengeful viewpoint of a Christian zealot," Gawain interpreted.

"The world of ideologies, like the world of dreams, is of course created in the mind, fed by the heart's passions, and defended by the emotions. Man created a world of temporal realties, imagining a greater creator – their lord – to give greater meaning to the unmanageable turmoil men create for themselves. This lord is found necessary to provide a higher purpose for the failings of humanity's many conflicting purposes and desires," Myrddin commented.

"Yes, the feudal lord who settles all feuds, or commands the forces of nature and the elements; when in fact, we are inseparable from the elements as manifestations of nature and spirit," Gawain added.

"So true, lad."

"The Christian king within the dream saw me as a lost warrior. I am not lost. I have been tutored in natural wisdom and the integrity of the soul. Once this king realized that I was a man of principle and a sworn protector of women, he offered me employment as protector of his sister. I feel this is another reference to Penasgell, who I dearly care for; and she represents that wise tradition of my own mother, and the natural realm of spirit. Of course I fall in love with the essence of this love, personified by the king's sister in the dream. The people of this kingdom, representing the outer world, were zealots who opposed my union with the king's sister. Even though it is a union of love and spirit. So we retreated to a tower called Magdala."

"Fantastic," said Myrddin.

"Yes, the lineage of the watchtower in spirit, self observing, as witness and closest love," Gawain expounded.

"Of course," Myrddin concurred.

"It's a game of mind and emotion when spirit becomes a debate of lesser 'truths'. So my love and I retaliate by throwing game pieces that turn into ravens and doves at the crowd. Awareness, intention, mysticism, shadowed emotions and love all descend, shedding blood and hopefully some light on the situation, prompting the king to send me off on an extensive quest. The outer authority separates the soul from its true love, distracting the soul with the desire to reach a seemingly impossible goal."

"I am amused and inspired," added Myrddin.

"So the quest resumed: truth must be victor, beyond conflict." Gawain continued retelling his inner saga. "I found myself at the site of a sacred well, where my intentions were challenged. Here I see a theme of my physical passions questioned in the face of my true spiritual path. A woman suspects me of lusting for her, and then sends me on an errand for a horse. I comply, but I am less than successful. The sovereignty of our matriarchal heritage is tied to spirit, the land, and the elemental powers of nature. Female entities within my dream, and therefore within my own mind, display this sparring of worldly and spiritual passions. The dream also connects to our heritage of origin: both elemental origins and mental origins, with Eden as the garden of this evolving tree of being; as I go to the Eden river valley to retrieve this illusive horse, for mastery of my own passions. A dwarf from the shadows thwarts my efforts – as they often do. My instinctual promptings, my passions, as the horse I ride or lose power over at times was continually reclaimed and redirected, yet sometimes let free to lead the way.

"The elements and terrain became active entities in my soul's journey as well. Water, rivers, floods, deluges of rain, served as the thresholds of fluidity. I either crossed over them, ride them, or wait them out. A ferryman toys with me, as my own inner battle with my time in this world. No man knows for certain his fate, or his point of departure from this life. The most disturbing scene of this rambling dream was where I encountered three enticing women who were revealed as my mother, my grandmother and my sister. This sensual confusion renders me, shall I say, impotent in evaluating this symbol," Gawain took pause.

"Yes, I can see that. I had similar dilemmas of my own with my sister, who I adored, yet emotionally seemed to hold me prisoner. In your dream vision, I believe they serve as symbols on many levels. I know your mother and have heard much about your grandmother. Your sister, as I understand, was not even known to you for many years. So we have the natural feminine wisdom as nearly forces of nature, as sensual power, in three phases: two relatively unknown and one actually birthing you into reality. The unknowns are past and future; the known is your point of inception, the center of known love, which set you free to discover yourself. The sister may also be an allusion to Penasgell, your younger cousin," Myrddin shared his insights.

"Did I say I had an attraction to Penasgell?"

"Ha, ha – you didn't need to say it lad. I heard it in your voice."

"Yes, well, no hiding it now. And you're also right about my sister: named after my grandmother Cundri, I didn't learn about her until years after she was born. This episode was followed by an apparition of Marganna reciting the lineages of the great dead masters and matrons of our heritage. She directed me to Caer Grail. On route, I witnessed the tragic death of a warrior called MacIlis. Fulfilling his dying request, I took his sword to the grail procession. I was told that this sword was the sword of Eden and the sword that slew John the Baptist – clearly the beginning and the end, or the beginning of the end. The sword is all at once the leaf of shame, the rib bone of Adam extended to Eve, the fractured judgment of humanity, and the death of the revered hero. I carried it all, braided over my shoulder, as I fulfill the mortal death wish. He, as the fallen hero of us all, died with his lord's final words on his own lips. At Caer Grail, the grail hallows were paraded before me. I witnessed the blood ritual and saw the severed head of Saint John. The priest king retelling the story and reciting the lineages rambled on, putting me to sleep within sleep, to dream within dream – until sensation, passion, desire, and shame stirred me to awaken again. I found myself mounted by Penasgell, her winged head of vision stripped bare and bald, enacting my uninhibited desires, telling me: 'beyond time we are free to love'. And beyond time is where I meet her. She is my soul exposed. As she turns her head, her braid of hair reappears, woven back into the origins of our heritage, as a spiraling double-helix, like the healing caduceus of the divine messenger, rising within me and every soul. I know that I am deeply connected to her in this life. And this is where I awoke."

"Magnificent lad, I must commend your mother and your teachers for giving you the understanding to interpret your own visions," said Myrddin. "This cave of the grail that you emerge from, as I see it, is an emergence from a womb of rebirth. Within its depths, you have faced or been exposed to the challenges of your soul, your desires and fears, your lust and illusions. The elemental world as portrayed by the goddess has birthed you into the waking world as a man of vision and passion. There is no lord over you, because you cut through illusion with the un-fragmented blade of realization."

"These are bizarre threads the soul uses to weave a complex tapestry, depicting the evolving story of our self to our self," Gawain reflected.

"Yes indeed, lad – we conjure a reality similar to the waking world, or what we assume the waking world to be, while still asleep. Experience exists in sensation, whether tactile, mental or emotional," added Myrddin.

"Certainly," Gawain continued the thought. "I have known warriors who have lost limbs, yet still feel them; just as broken hearts that have lost a loved one, still feel them. Pain, fear, loss, and suffering – all may occur in the dream world and the waking world. But can we awaken the troubled soul from both realms?"

"The soul can recognize this dilemma and become aware that both realities are fluid," Myrddin responded. "Our reality is not static or predetermined within dream or waking life. Our awareness changes our reality. This awareness is not limited to what we think we know. Dreams display things that we do not readily know about ourselves, but are aware of at a deeper level of being. There is an undercurrent of awareness exposed, within a background of reality available to us. You are on a grand journey lad. And you realize that your adventures have been created within your own imaginary world. It is the awakening of wisdom. Your wise mentors and partners in passion open and challenge your instinctual nature, and your intuition – streams that carry you or consume you. Each day presents its choices, as you navigate the turns of the stream. The mysterious ferryman as pilot or deterrent is also of your own imagining. You set the toll or waive it all together."

Myrddin journeyed on to the north, while Gawain acquired a new horse in Loidis, known for the able cavalrymen descending from King Maesgwid ap Gwrast, his own great-great uncle. When Gawain returned to Ebrauc, Penasgell greeted him at the gates, embracing him as soon as he dismounted from his horse, revealing her concern for his wellbeing; even though she knew he would return, secretly holding a vague visionary glimpse of that latent intimacy they shared within the Otherworld of dreams. He was almost shy during that welcoming embrace, cautiously sheltering his memory of the passionate dream encounter from being exposed.

"Where are the others?" asked Penasgell.

"Gone, all of them perished in the caves," said Gawain.

"That's terrible," Penasgell responded with a horrified look on her face. "I am so happy that you were able to return safely. It must be devastating, to have lost those men."

"Yes. It was sudden and overwhelming. I still can't quite believe it happened," Gawain confided.

"It is miraculous that both you and Peredyr returned, after losing all those lads," Penasgell said with loving eyes, affectionately holding on to his broad shoulders.

"It was so shockingly unexpected and tragic," Gawain responded. "I am lucky to be alive, and here, greeted by you, my dear cousin," he added in a stoic monotone, while his eyes revealed something much deeper, she recognizing immediately his great protected heart opening to her.

"I should have seen the peril of your comrades somehow beforehand. I was uneasy about this venture, but knew that you and Peredyr would return," Penasgell revealed.

"One of the strangest things emerging from this tragedy was meeting up with Myrddin in Loidis, after Peredyr had come upon him in the wilderness days before." Gawain told her.

"You cousin and my dear brother Peredyr are guided and protected. Our ancestry of wise souls does what they can to steer us along. Your mother's heritage aids you as well. And of course, Myrddin is our distant cousin, clearly guided by prophetic otherworldly mentors ever since his weird divergence into the wild. If only all of the Gwyr y Gogledd could hold true to the wiser strain of their heritage, our futures might be less precarious," Penasgell reflected.

"Now you speak of men, not saints. And even though women can be as fickle and ungodly as men, I believe our hope rests with the wise women of the north, not the beasts many of their sons have become," Gawain added.

Gawain and Penasgell joined their kindred and comrades in the great hall of Ebrauc, celebrating the safe return of Peredyr and Gawain, yet mourning the loss of the others on the ill fated quest for the chalice. Later that evening, Llen and Bercnaf arrived from the west, surprising all. They were part of a larger troop sizing-up the tense situation at the eastern borders. Prince Owain of Rheged led a smaller patrol into Bernicia, planning to join their brothers in arms in Ebrauc the following day. Concern arose when they didn't arrive.

Owain

Prince Owain's patrol had ventured deeper into enemy territory, trying to anticipate the next threat from the sons of Ida and their growing forces. During this spying mission, Owain's men were confronted by a Saesneg patrol, giving chase beyond Afon Tees. The Cymric party split-up to divide the pursuit, sending Owain and two of his best horsemen followed by six Saesneg riders. Both of Owain's comrades were picked-off by arrows and spears, while the Prince of Rheged raced to the woodlands for concealment. They were on him before he reached the wood, engaging in close combat with sword and shield. Even though outnumbered, Owain was able to take down two of his attackers before suffering a sharp blow to the head, rattling his helmet, sending his mind into a black-out, quickly consumed in vague delirium. At the moment Owain was struck, a dark warrior appeared from the dense woodlands, assailing the Saesneg with a fury. He was a formidable warrior – dressed in black robes, a black scarf around his dark-skinned face, wrapped and crowning his head, as is the custom in distant lands. The black steed he rode was both powerful and agile, even more intimidating than the fierce warrior; until an enemy lance skewered the majestic animal, forcing him to the ground. The dark swordsman sheathed his short sword, drawing an enormous blade from his back. Using two hands, he wielded the broad curved sword with such thrashing vigor, he dismembered two of his foes in passing, slicing into the horse of the third, dropping it to the ground, nearly cut in two. The final opponent died instantly as his head was sent flying into the field by one swift swing of the dark warrior's curved sword. He carefully surveyed the horizon before wiping clean his blade, sheathing it again, and looking to Owain. The prince had fallen from his mount, his eyes rolled back into his head. Carefully examining his head and neck, the dark warrior slowly lifted Owain to gently drape his limp body over his horse, and then chose another Saesneg mount for himself. Before he left the battle scene with Owain and horse in tow, he paused, bowing down to his own slain steed, reverently saying a few words in a strange and exotic foreign tongue. Then, turning abruptly, he spat upon the dead man who had slain his fine battle horse.

The dark warrior took Owain deep into the woodlands, making camp after dusk. He gently moved Owain to bed him down for the night, lit a fire, and began to perform a strange practice in the glow of the campfire light. The warrior removed his robe and unwound the scarf from his head. He stood very still for an extended length of time on one leg, first the right and then the left. His hands were held in front of his chest, as if in prayer, while he chanted unusual sounds, droning in his native tongue. Then he stood silent, with his eyes closed, the fire illuminating a painted spot between his eyes, appearing like a single open eye in the center of his forehead.

Owain remained still, yet breathing steadily, seemingly oblivious to the waking world; while his mind was reeling from the day's events with visions streaming through his attentive soul. Within that shadowy place of dream, thought and emotion led Owain into another adventure. He entered a vast clearing within an expansive forest. In the center upon a mound, a giant black-haired man stood on one foot, staring intently with his one eye in the middle of his forehead at Owain, as if to enter into his slumbering soul. The dark man held an enormous steel sword, heavy as an iron club. Two strong men could have barely lifted this powerful weapon. And yet, the dark man wielded if like a feather, sweeping from side to side, stirring the air to release all the forces of the living creatures inhabiting the surrounding forest. In a bellowing voice he called-out in his unusual native tongue, as the great blade hit the ground with an earth-shaking boom, Owain strangely able to understand the foreign words as: "Between me and God, all comes forth!"

With that, every imaginable creature began to appear from all directions. Ravens, hawks, and songbirds circled overhead, flickering the filtered light of the sun through the trees. Beasts of every size and form crawled out of the foliage, brush, and grounds surrounding the commanding dark warrior. Creatures swarmed the clearing to give homage to their mysterious dark master. Calls of the ravens and hawks mingled with the melodious songs of birds forming a crescendo of vibrant sound, only to suddenly cease and every critter to vanish with a wave of the dark master's sword. He looked directly at Owain, speaking to him within his mind, conveying instructions for his journey home.

"First, you must go down the road past the clearing, until you come to higher ground. Climb the hill, keep going, continuing to a river valley, following the call of your raven kindred. They call to you from above and beyond what you know. The ravens descend into a great tree, greener and more vibrant than any other tree you may see. At the foundation of the tree is a well. At the base of the well is a polished slab of stone. On the slab is a silver cauldron, fastened to a silver chain. It is always tethered to the stone, to the well, and also to the tree. Fill the cauldron with water from the well. Pour the water over the stone; be silent, and listen. You will know what to do – between me and God."

Owain followed the guidance of the dark master, continuing out of the forest and beyond the river valley. He saw the great tree, astounded by its radiant beauty, generating a profound sensation of vitality into every breath he drew into his chest. At the rooted foundation of the tree he saw the well, flowing with a satiating presence that quenched his thirst without even touching water to his lips. The stone slab at the base of the well held a sheen upon its polished surface that reflected his own image to him in a way he had never seen himself before. He paused for an instant, suddenly feeling complete within himself, momentarily held in repose from any idea of his station in life, of his chosen purpose or mission of discovery, of his identity, or of his relationship to any other person in his life. Then he recalled the dark master's directive to fill the cauldron. As the silver chain moved across the slab, he did not see himself reflected on the surface anymore – his attention had shifted to the links and their sound upon the stone. When he filled the cauldron with water and poured it slowly onto the slab, he watched the flow of ripples of water wash over the stone, revealing no image. Silently he waited, and listened

All of the sudden he heard a tumultuous noise thundering through the valley, unnerving him, quickly followed by the repeated heavy thumping of hail stones, stones the size of a man's fist, pounding the earth all around the great tree. Owain cowered in fear, huddling beneath the expansive tree, his body curled into a ball, holding his limbs tightly, feeling his back becoming covered with a blanket of fallen leaves, each added layer protecting him from the hammering hail. He waited. He listened. And then it all stopped. The leaves of the tree had completely covered him, falling off his back as he stood up. Every leaf from the great tree was gone, only the bare limbs and radiating twigs of branches remained. The sky began to clear as he walked around the tree, the well, the cauldron, and the stone – seeing that they all were miraculously unharmed. Out of the open sky an expansive flock of birds rushed into view, descending on the great tree to alight upon the bare branches, cluttering the vacant arboreal frame with feathered life, replenishing the towering form abundantly full with the layered plumage of hundreds of birds. Their songs filled the air, reverberating new life into existence, singing the most glorious sounds Owain had ever heard, standing there in rapture and awe. Stepping back, getting a wider view, he saw a line of ravens flying steadily to the west. He knew that they were guiding him to follow them, as the dark master had said. So he traveled on.

As Owain crossed the distant valley, he heard strange moaning sounds coming towards him from a dark figure on the horizon. It appeared to be one solitary rider rapidly approaching. Soon Owain was able to discern that it was that mysterious dark warrior, riding his black steed, carrying a lance with a black pennant whipping in the wind, its fluttering form turning into a flying raven, and then back into a pennant, over and over again, as the dark warrior came closer and closer. He rode right up to Owain, swinging his enormous sword, releasing a shuddering flock of ravens from its sharpened edge, the whoosh of their wings knocking Owain to the ground.

Owain bounced back on his feet shouting – "What do you want of me?"

The dark warrior just rode off, back in the direction he came from; and Owain wandered-on following the direction of the ravens. After a while, Owain heard a strange moaning again, this time sounding more like a wounded animal. He followed the sound, exploring beyond some crags and boulders on the hillside rising up from the valley. As he rounded the rocks, he saw a young lion deliriously gnawing at his paw, moaning in pain. Owain surmised that the cat had become ill from a wound. The lion soon appeared to fall asleep. Owain was able to get close enough to the wounded cat to see that his paw was swollen. Using a belt to cinch the lion's three other paws together; Owain secured the animal, and carefully removed a nasty thorn from the cat's paw with a quick gouge and twist of his short sword. The lion immediately woke up, fiercely irritated, swinging his one free paw at Owain, only to roll over tangled in the belt. Owain waited around for the lion to fall asleep again, gently releasing the belt and quietly moving on.

Farther down the road, Owain sensed someone behind him. At first he saw no one, then turning again to see out of the corner of his eye the young lion following along. At nightfall Owain made camp, built a fire, and prepared a rabbit he had caught for his supper. While the prince enjoyed a roasted chop, the lion strolled into his camp, crouching by the fire.

"You must be feeling better to follow me all the way here, young cat. I see . . . you're not much for conversation, are you," jested Owain, as the cat continued to watch him eat the roasted rabbit. "Are you hungry? Silly question – you're probably always hungry," Owain continued, tearing-off the other chop and tossing it to the lion, the lion quickly snatching it in his jaws and slinking away into the dark.

The next morning Owain traveled on, noticing the lion following closer, as the prince carried-on his one-sided conversation. Rounding a hill, Owain saw a fine looking dark brown palfrey with a reddish mane, just standing there, fully saddled, and casually grazing along the roadside. He slowly approached the horse, walking right up to take the reins.

"Well hello – who left you out here all alone?" Owain inquired, looking around for any sign of human life. "You're about as talkative as a young lion. Do you know that? I am Owain, Prince of Rheged. I'll be your new master. And if you see a young lion, don't worry – he prefers roast rabbit."

Owain slowly mounted the horse and rode on, following the call of a soaring raven. Around midday he came upon the dark warrior again, waiting at a crossroads to confront the wandering prince. As they met in combat, contending with blow after blow, Owain eventually was able to strike the dark warrior severely over the head, surely cracking his skull – the prince eerily feeling the wounding within his own challenged brain, down through the core of his body, and out through his battling limbs. Suddenly the young lion leapt from a large stone at the side of the road, landing on the dark warrior's horse, causing it to rear-up, the cat then jumping down, and the dark warrior's horse carrying his master at a gallop on up the road. Owain followed in fast pursuit, as the lion ran along on a parallel path through the open fields. The dark warrior reached a walled citadel, entering the gatehouse with Owain close behind. As the dark warrior passed through the gatehouse into the citadel, the gate closed abruptly after him; with the portcullis crashing down upon Owain's horse, nearly severing it in two, trapping the prince inside the gatehouse. Owain could see the dark warrior within the citadel, his black scarf and robes turning into the black feathers of a raven, as he laughed, cackled and crowed, his face becoming a raven's head, then his own dark visage again, and then a vague resemblance of Owain's great uncle, Master Myrlyn. A maiden quickly approached the gatehouse, horrified by the calamity, attempting to offer assistance. She handed Owain a ring and a small stone through the portcullis.

"Wear this ring, now, before the guards arrest you; and hold this stone with the same hand. Hold it tight within your fist; and between God and me, you will not be seen. Remain hidden in this way, and follow me closely. Touch me on the shoulder; and I will know that you are there; even though no one will be able to see you."

When the guards arrived, Owain was nowhere to be seen. The maiden bewailed the fatally injured horse, as the guards fumbled around, looking for the missing rider. Owain followed the maiden into the citadel and up a long flight of stairs to a bedchamber and secluded rooms at the end of an upper floor hallway. He touched the maiden on her shoulder, handing her the stone, and appearing again in plain sight.

"You must wash yourself. You are completely spattered with blood. I'll find some fresh clothing. Quickly, go in here," the maiden directed Owain to a side room, bringing him a silver bowl of water and a fine linen cloth to wash himself, leaving a clean tunic, hauberk and leggings to wear.

As Owain dressed he heard the maiden in the main bedchamber with another man. Quietly, he stepped closer and peeked inside the door to see the maiden in bed with a man who resembled his half-brother Deifyr. And the maiden, clearly no maiden now, resembled Owain's wife, Princess Penarwen. This was quite startling just for the infidelity, but also because he had not seen this maiden appearing to be his wife before. Slipping silently back into the other room, he felt a throbbing in his head as he tried to understand what was going on. When the maiden returned, he looked at her strangely, trying to see how he thought she resembled his wife.

"Are you alright? You look a bit ill, or stunned. Stay quiet, I'll get some food. That should set you right," she said as she gently closed the door.

Owain just sat there puzzled, wondering what would happen next. The maiden returned with a large tray of abundant food and drink. After dining, Owain fell fast asleep, dreaming within his dream of his half-brother and his wife running away from him through the halls of the citadel, laughing and toying with each other to taunt him. Searching other rooms, he found his half-sister Morfudd beckoning him to come to her bed, with a raven perched on the bedpost, turning his neck side to side, observing the odd affairs of these humans. Owain quickly closed the door and ran down the hall, hearing moaning sounds echoing through the passageways. He could not discern whether they were sounds of pleasure or pain. Then he awoke from this dream within dream, still hearing the obscure moaning. The maiden entered the room and he asked her what the doleful sound was that he kept hearing.

"Oh dear lad, you do not know. The king of this land has died. You hear the sounds of sorrow and mourning. A great funeral procession is underway for the beloved king."

Owain went to the window and could see that the streets were filled with crowds honoring the sudden passing of the king. His body was carried into the great hall, the bier draped with white linens. Beside the bier a veiled lady wearing a dark gown was weeping. As monks chanted, wafting incense over the fallen king's bier, the lady's gown and veil changed from dark to light and back again. When her gown appeared light in color, almost pure white, wounds beneath the sheer garment began to bleed through. Then the gown shifted to black again, as she continued to weep and moan over the king. A procession of twenty-four maidens walked around the bier, each of them holding a chalice, each of them bleeding from their hands, and each of them crying tears that turned to blood as their tears welled-up and rolled down their veiled faces. One by one as the maidens passed by the widowed queen they disappeared, leaving only their veils upon the floor beside the bier. Later on that day, Owain was brought before the Queen.

"Now **you** shall be guardian of the wells," the widowed queen told him.

"Your Majesty," Owain said, bowing, "the wells are dry and the maidens are long lost."

"You have been satiated by the presence of the well of the great tree, pouring waters from the silver cauldron. You have suffered the severe hail storm, faced the relentless dark warrior, and heard the glorious song of the returning birds. You have proven you have the heart of a lion. It should be clear to you, you cannot deny this appointment," the queen responded.

Reluctantly, Owain traveled back toward the place of the fantastic well, still mulling over in his mind all he had seen and experienced. He soon became lost, deep in a visionary forest, filled with fallen trees enmeshed in overgrown vines. A distorted sense of time and rapid aging began to envelope him, the vines alive as veins flowing within his imaginal body. He took-on the battered visage of the dark man, and then becoming the bizarre semblance of Myrddin Wyllt, as he was described gone mad in the wood. Owain's hair and beard had grown long and matted, with wounds and scrapes covering his arms and legs, as if he had been lost in the wild for months or years. As coal-black feathers sprouted from his arms, head, and his grossly feral body – he imagined that he might even fly. His voice became coarse from growling at wild wolves, badgers and lions. At one point he saw the young lion he had helped on the road, and followed the cat into an open valley. The sky was expansive, brilliantly blue, with countless fragrant flowers filling the air with the potent scent of springtime. Soon Owain saw a young woman amidst the field of color gathering a bouquet of flowers. As he moved closer, he recognized her as the maiden who had rescued him at the citadel. He quietly came up behind her and touched her shoulder, as he had before. Startled at first, then shocked by his wild appearance, she quickly saw in his eyes who he was.

"Between me and God, I believe I know you, gentle sir," she said with a loving lilt in her voice.

She took him back to a cottage outside of the citadel, cut his hair, bathed and shaved him, treating his wounds with ointment. After he was well fed and rested, she showed him a strong battle-horse in the stable, with a fine hauberk, helmet, sword and shield hanging there on the wall.

"These things are of no use to me. I want you to have them. Take them on your journey. The well awaits you." She said to Owain, with kindness in her eyes.

"Thank you my lady. I do not know where I was, or for how long I have been lost. All sense of time has escaped from my addled mind. But now, I know that I can continue. Thank you for your kindness, and for seeing me when I could scarcely see myself. When I was at the well before, I was able to see a reflection of myself that I must find again," Owain confided.

Owain embraced her; and she kissed him on his brow, sending him on his way. He was not certain of his direction, but followed his intuition, aware of the distant call of the ravens. After traveling a good number of leagues, he saw the dark warrior down the road ahead of him. Once again, he prepared to defend himself. The dark warrior slowly rode closer; but something was different.

As he approached, the dark man dropped his black scarf from his face and said, "Between me and God, I believe I know you."

Owain was stunned, immediately asking, "Are you the warrior that I fatally struck, splitting your skull?"

"You cannot split what remains whole." The dark warrior responded.

"I don't know what that means. Either you are dead or alive, a man or a ghost," Owain declared in frustration.

"I am spirit. God is one. This soul is undivided," the dark warrior answered, as he clanged his short sword against the metal boss of his shield.

The sharp ringing sound of a metal bowl hitting a hard stone suddenly awakened Owain.

"Pardon me, I have disturbed your sleep," the dark man said to him.

Owain sat up, touching his head, "Ah, ah."

"You had best move slowly for a while. Your skull may be cracked," said the dark man as he handed Owain a chilled damp cloth from the nearby stream.

"What happened?"

"You were attacked."

"Who attacked me?"

"I think they were Angles from Bryneich, at least six of them. Do you recall any of this?"

"Hmm . . . oh, yes, six Angle bastards, they took out two of my men. I think I took two of them down; and then everything went black."

"That's when I arrived and slew the other four; although I didn't take the time to find out their parentage," the dark warrior said with a smirk.

"Where did you come from?"

"The East."

"Who are your people?"

"My people? You wouldn't know them."

"What are they called?"

"Hanif."

"Why did you help me?"

"The fight seemed unjust. You appeared to be a man of nobility, and they – mercenaries and cutthroats."

"You risked your life at those odds?"

"Odds . . . what does this mean: odds?"

"There were four of them, and only one of you."

"There were two of us, until the blow to your head. And, it seemed unjust. I could not pass by and do nothing. I would carry that choice with me. So I risked my life, for your life, to unburden my journey," he explained.

"Thank you, for risking your life for mine."

"I believe you would have done the same."

"I hope that you are right. How far have you traveled?"

"Very far."

"What is your homeland like?"

"It is very dry and hot. It is quite wet and cold here. But, I am drawn to the difference. The world is much bigger than I thought."

"Yes, well, this island is smaller than you might think, especially with more invaders arriving."

"My people would not likely invade you."

"And why is that? You're here."

"It is too far, too wet, and too cold."

"Then we can send the Angles to your homeland."

"They will soon follow the Romans. I am sure of it."

"You have saved my life, and I don't even know your name."

"I have taken the name Bylal; but I do not know my parentage. I was a student of Waraqah ibn Nawfal. He found me and raised me as his own. This foster father is all the family I have known – between me and God."

"I have heard this phrase over and over: 'between me and God'. What does it mean?" Owain questioned.

"Everything we imagine is between us and God; and yet, God is in everything," answered Bylal.

"How is God in everything, and everything we imagine between us and God? It makes no sense." Owain challenged him.

"It is a paradox. We imagine realities and place God outside of them; when God is reality. God is one, whatever name we use: God, Allah, Abba, Brahma, Elohiym, or Jehovah. Everything imagined exists from the source of imagining. Once we have named it and claimed it as ours, it becomes something between us and God – an idea, not reality."

"You are a puzzling man Bylal."

"Yes . . . between me and God," he responded, rousing their laughter. "What are you called, my puzzled friend?"

"I am Owain ap Urien, Prince of Rheged."

"Of course, a man of nobility . . . how are you feeling now?"

"My head and neck are still quite sore," said Owain, lightly touching the crown of his head. "Every limb feels as if it had been pulled from my body."

"You were stretched over your horse for a while," Bylal reasoned. "I shall travel with you, to see you to your homeland."

"Rheged is many leagues to the west. I have family nearby in Ebrauc. That is where I wish to go."

"Then I shall travel with you to Ebrauc," said Bylal. "I have heard of this kingdom of Rheged. You are descended from the Fisher Kings, are you not?"

"Yes, that is what I have been told," Owain answered.

"I have not been told of my lineage. I am what you call a bastard. But more rightly, in spirit, I am descended from my teacher and his lineage of teachers – between me and God."

"Ha, ha, ha," they laughed together again, traveling on to Ebrauc, continuing their conversation.

"You said that your teacher came from a lineage of teachers – what was that teaching?" asked Owain.

"It is a teaching of the one God," Bylal answered.

"Is that what 'Hanif' means?"

"No, 'Hanif' means . . . to lean away, that is, to find one's own way, like the prophet Ibrahim, leaning away from the many gods and idol worship, to find the one God within all. I have traveled to many distant lands, discovering different paths and teachings that guided me to find the one God, found within the heart and soul. I have sat with very many teachers, speaking diverse tongues; and yet they have found one voice as their own."

"What is this voice?"

"It is a voice that has no language, no doctrine, no deity, no image, and no church or temple. This voice speaks in a breath like the wind, but is not the wind. It is in the rhythm of the ocean waves, but it is not the waves. It is in the warmth of the fiery sun, but it is not the sun. It is in the stillness of the mountains of the earth, but it is not the mountains. It is the voice that speaks to the soul in an unspoken language of the unspoken name of God."

"I believe that I know this voice too," said Owain. "There is a practice that was handed down from a lineage of teachers through Master Myrlyn of the Cymri. It is known as the power of the mountains and streams, empowering us with an elemental spirit that is the essence of all things."

"Ah, I have heard of this," said Bylal. "It began in a place called the Llydaw, near a mountain in the west."

"Yes, that's right. My Master Taliesin trained there. He has taught this to my brothers-in-arms. You will meet some of them in Ebrauc."

"Very good, I am looking forward to it."

Owain and Bylal arrived safely in Ebrauc, much to the relief their comrades, as they were assembling a search party for the Prince of Rheged.

"Owain!" Llen exclaimed, at first sight of his lifelong friend. "We thought we might have lost you."

"I nearly lost myself, if it wasn't for this brave soul who pulled me from death's door. Lads, this is Bylal, a wise and powerful warrior from the east."

Llen was the first to greet Bylal with a firm Roman handshake. "We are all indebted to you for bringing Prince Owain back to us. I am Llenlleawg of Afallon, and here is Gawain, Bercnaf, over there King Peredyr and King

Gwrgi our hosts, and their sister Penasgell – you will meet all of the others in due time."

"Thank you for your warm greeting. I knew instantly that Prince Owain was a noble soul. I was compelled to do whatever I could to ensure his safety," Bylal responded.

"He took-on four Angle bastards, cutting them to pieces; while I had fallen off my horse, out cold, from a hard blow to the head," Owain related.

"Well, at least you weren't hit anywhere important," Llen jested.

"Like the royal family jewels," Bercnaf added.

"Yes, you could probably sire progeny without a brain," Gawain chimed-in. "It has been done countless times before."

"And evidenced in mindless royal heirs we have come to know and love," said Peredyr, as he placed his hand on Gawain's shoulder.

"I must apologize, Bylal, for subjecting you to the abusive banter of my demented cousin – all of them great warriors, yet sad examples of tragic inbreeding," Owain bantered back. "Except of course, Penasgell, who seems to have escaped this rampant hereditary illness."

"It is my pleasure to meet you, your highness," said Bylal as he bowed before Princess Penasgell. "It is clear that you carry the gift of wisdom. I see great light surrounding you, my lady."

"And I see that clarity in you as well, Bylal. I am intrigued to hear of your people and your long journey, most certainly filled with light and insight," said Penasgell.

"Nothing would give me greater pleasure, my lady," said Bylal, as they all began walking towards the main hall.

Ebrauc was one of the old Roman citadels, standing for hundreds of years, rebuilt and repaired by generations of the Gwyr y Gogledd. King Peredyr and his cousins were the proud descendants of Coel hen, the last Dux Britanniarum of the north. In those ancient days, the northern Picts were their main foes. By this time, Saesneg territories nearly surrounded Ebrauc, and neighboring Bryneich was more duplicitous than ever. Recent reconnaissance made it clear that a mounting effort was underway to attack the Cymri.

"As soon as your heir is born," Owain told Peredyr, "I recommend that you send your wife and child to Caer Lliwelydd, while all the Cymric kingdoms begin to marshal troops to come to your aid."

"War is that evident to you?" asked Gwrgi.

"Yes cousin, Ida's sons have amassed a large army, and may have Deira with them," Owain urged him.

"He's right," Llen added. "We believe the Saesneg will make a move against Ebrauc and Ynys Medcaut soon. If they lay siege here, you will want your wife and heir in a safe haven. We can take them west, and return with troops from Rheged."

"Blodgwyn's time is near. The midwife is with her now. As soon as my wife and child are fit for travel, I will send them with you," King Peredyr replied. "Gwrgi, we should prepare for a siege, stock the storehouses, and secure the battlements."

The child was born that night, a fine wee lad who they named Gwrgant. Blodgwyn recovered quickly. Within a few days, Owain was to lead his small troop and the royal entourage first to the west and then northwest into Rheged. Before leaving, Owain and Bylal had time to describe their fortuitous meeting in Bernicia to Penasgell. She was particularly fascinated by Owain's dream, envisioning Bylal's exotic appearance.

"You must have been seeing and hearing Bylal, even though you were nearly dead to the waking world," Penasgell observed.

"Yes, in my dream vision Bylal was an Otherworldly being, appearing to balance on one leg and having only one eye, peering directly into my soul," Owain confirmed.

"I was applying my spiritual practice, right there by the campfire. I did not know if you would ever wake up. My intention was to join the healing of your mind, body and spirit, believing that healing was well underway," Bylal explained.

"Somehow that healing power encompassed every creature and element of the surrounding wilds, as he uttered for the first time: 'Between me and God'. This of course led to a later discussion of the meaning of that phrase," Owain recounted.

"In essence," Bylal interjected, "all these imaginings are between us and the deeper presence of God, as source and center of all natural elements."

"The image, however, taking on more significance than the essence that it conveys," Penasgell added.

"Exactly," Bylal replied. "The dreamer is completely engrossed in the dream, unaware of where it comes from, or where it can take him."

"I was continually being guided by ravens: advised to follow the call of my raven kindred, my own ancestry of Emrys Myrlyn, the Raven of Awen," Owain described, "being told that they call from above and beyond what I know."

"Yes, of course, as that revered lineage, touching the elemental source of all things, represented as images reflecting a presence of God," Penasgell interpreted.

"Then the appearance of the great tree with the sacred well at its foundation, linked to a silver chain and cauldron, enlists me early-on as a guardian of that satiating presence," Owain revealed.

"The tree here is our ancestry again, but also the source of creation, renewal, and the mystic path of the tree of life, growing and resilient through shifting seasonal storms. We are tethered to it by a direct line, a silver cord of innate understanding, connected link by link, exposing a refined self," Penasgell elaborated.

"When that torrential hail storm hit me, with hailstones the size of my own fists, I did not know if I would live through it. All that I could do was to wait and listen, believing I would indeed survive. And it did become clear again: the expansive sky releasing countless songbirds, filling that great barren tree."

"Clearly the brilliant return of your very own inspiration and higher aspirations," Bylal observed.

"But then again, the dark warrior returned to confront me. It seems that this image is both my guide and my shadow: a facet of myself, releasing ravens with the movement of his blade, and throwing me off-balance."

"You were confronting and challenging yourself," said Penasgell.

"Frustrated, I shouted – 'What do you want of me?' As if I could release myself from my own self-challenge. My roar or whimper illustrated farther down the road, I removed a thorn from a young lion's paw, befriending him for the rest of my journey."

"Your courage, healed from wounding, no doubt, while befriending that emotional strength to stay with you," Bylal surmised.

"During the next confrontation with the dark warrior, I struck his head and felt it within my own. The young lion came to my aid, sending the dark warrior galloping away. I followed him into the gatehouse of a citadel, where my horse was cut in two by the descending portcullis – as you had cut down the Saesneg horse with your broadsword, Bylal. I can scarcely make sense of this episode," Owain admitted.

"Again, it is self-confrontation: a violent racking of your own mind, finding courage, trapped in the gatehouse between worlds, your entry into another world blocked for the moment – your future, your inheritance, your passion and stability split in two," Penasgell discerned.

"I see . . . I am in a repeated battle with myself in these visions," Owain reflected. "I can't get that image of your grand sword out of my mind, Bylal. Does it have some significance or even a name?"

"Yes. It is called 'saif al-haqq' – sword of truth."

"Alright, that's significant. This entire journey, my inner story, is a search for truth, isn't it?" Owain realized.

"Between you and God," said Penasgell.

"The truth became even more elusive once I entered the citadel. A maiden helped me to escape from the gatehouse by handing me a ring to wear and a stone to hold, rendering me unseen – between me and God again. Within the citadel, I saw her in bed with my half-brother Deifyr; and she suddenly looked like my wife Penarwen, leaving me dizzily confused. I soon fell asleep after a hearty meal, only to dream within dream of chasing my wife and half-brother through the halls of the citadel."

"Dear cousin, the stone and the ring were most certainly the Oathing Stone and wedding ring of your marriage to Penarwen. And I dare suggest that there is trouble in your future with her, if not your past. You might feel trapped in the gatehouse, with half your mount lost to your half-brother; while you have become invisible to them." Penasgell untangled the mess.

"I see, the husband is the last to know," Owain responded. "In another room of this illicit citadel, Morfudd, my half-sister, beckoned me to bed with her as a raven watched from the bedpost. I ran from that invitation, and woke from the inner dream within dream. Hearing the funeral procession for this strange land's dead king, I went to the main hall of the citadel. The ceremony surrounded his body with a weeping queen and weeping maidens: their gowns and veils concealing their wounds; while their wounds bleeding through, bleeding tears and bloodied hands revealed their pain."

"Your future as King of Rheged will begin with the death of your father, King Urien, who sired Morfudd your half-sister, emotionally wounding your mother the queen. Your father betrayed the marriage and perhaps Penarwen betrays your own marriage. Your half-sister was born on the same hour and day that you were: on the winter solstice, the turning point of the year between darkness and light. She is your twin in spirit, in shadow, and in illicit conception. A raven feather was found in your crib at your birth, and was kept by your bed throughout your infancy and childhood. The raven kindred watch over you. Did the queen in your dream speak to you?" Penasgell asked.

"Yes, I met with her later and she told me that I am now the guardian of the wells."

"Of course, because the legacy of the tragedy of the maidens of the sacred wells is handed down to you as the future King of Rheged, and perhaps one day as the Pendragon," said Penasgell. "The maidens with bleeding hands were handing this to you. Their bleeding eyes have witnessed betrayal. Your half-sister is part of another legacy of betrayal looming over the Cymric kingdoms. Her daughters are the duplicitous queens of Lothian and Bryneich, our northern neighbors. Was there anymore to your dream vision?"

"Yes, I was sent by the queen back to the well and the great tree; but I became lost, returning to the wild, like Myrddin Wyllt, only to be saved by the young lion and the maiden again," Owain continued. "After that, I encountered the dark warrior once more. He did not fight me this time. And when I questioned whether he was man or spirit, and how he survived the fatal blow to his head, he said: 'You cannot split apart what remains whole.' Then I awoke at Bylal's campfire."

"Myrddin Wyllt held himself responsible for the tragedy of the maidens and went mad, for a time." Penasgell recalled. "You, in this dream, feel the weight of great responsibility, and might run mad into the wood, if you let yourself go. But courage and innocence came to your aid, once again. You cannot split apart what remains whole. That refers to you and the cosmos – between you and God. When you become aware that you are dreaming, you will either affect the nature of the dream, or wake up. If you remain attached to the dream and its outcome, you will continue dreaming. If it no longer fulfills you, the only resolution is to awaken. That is your responsibility as the guardian of the well. Fists of hailstones or glorious songs filling the tree of life await you, dear cousin."

"There are certainly some stone fists preparing to hammer at us from Bernicia. I am grateful to you both for your insights. But now, I suppose it is time for us to escort the future royal family of Ebrauc to secure lands in the northwest," said Owain.

"I am grateful as well for your welcoming kindness to me here; and I will travel with you to the west," said Bylal, "but my journey continues farther south, to explore the expanse of the Llydaw.

"You are following the heart of wisdom," said Penasgell.

"Truly, that is the way I must always go," Bylal responded.

The well equipped entourage left Ebrauc the next morning, including Queen Blodgwyn, the newborn prince, Owain, Llen, Bercnaf, their troop from Rheged, Gawain, Penasgell, and the eastern warrior Bylal. After reaching the northern crossroads to the west, Bylal departed for the southwest, bestowing his unusual foreign blessing upon his new friends and the entire troop. The northern journey to Caer Lliwelydd took several days, with an advance courier riding ahead, while the full entourage traveled south of the Wall of Tyne safely into Rheged. Owain met with his father, King Urien, and they assembled an army to move against the Saesneg straight away. The young Queen of Ebrauc and her infant son were cared for by Queen Orwen and the ladies of the court. Llen, Bercnaf and Gawain hastily departed for the north to Alt Clud and Lothian, alerting the northern kingdoms about the stirring of war in the east. Llen and Gawain hadn't found time to talk to each other about their encounters in the Otherworld, since Llen's injury and recovery and Gawain's failed and near fatal quest for the sacred chalice.

"Before we left Caer Lliwelydd, Penasgell told me that I would likely recall my dream vision played-out in the waking world after arriving at Arthsedd," Llen told Gawain.

"She has a way of doing that, much like my mother Morcades, and I would assume your mother, Lady Vivianne," said Gawain.

"We are both guided by very prescient woman, my friend," Llen continued. "When I was left for dead and recovering for months, thanks to the clever tracking and rescue by Bercnaf . . ."

"He was a mess, even more than usual, that is . . ." Bercnaf added.

"Coming from a master of hounds that is a very low evaluation," Gawain quipped.

"Rightly justified, I do confess. I was in the worst state of being, my body and outward senses shut down like nothing I've known before," Llen went on. "Regardless, I traveled in the Otherworld; and I know you have taken that trip as well, where visions of people we think we know meet us in strange encounters."

"Yes, most definitely," Gawain agreed.

"This Marganna," said Llen, "sister of Loth's wife Anna Morgause –"

"Yes, she is an aunt to me, of sorts," said Gawain, "and a cousin, as daughter of Morfudd, Owain's half-sister. Truly, she is more like a scorpion queen or a dangerous black widow with a living spouse."

"Dangerously ready to strike-out for her lust . . ." Llen added.

"Or her lust for power – both sisters capable of covertly striking with a deadly sting," Gawain concurred.

"Marganna had, in fact, staged the abduction of Gwenhwyfar at her father Morcant's direction, taking me captive as well. In the Otherworld she held me prisoner again, allowing my release under the promise that I would arrange an interlude with you, Gawain: her interest aroused by the inflated reputation of 'your manhood' – as she put it."

"Ha, ha, ha – I'm flattered that my prowess has aroused the interest of rogue queens in the Otherworld," Gawain responded.

"You should be. You're not only a man of the world, but a man in demand in the Otherworld," Llen remarked. "But at the root of this lustful farce, there is treachery being abetted in Bryneich, fed by this manipulating Marganna; and I fear her sister, Anna Morgause, may be in league with her."

"Thank you for the caution," Gawain began to assess the threat. "Anna Morgause is unstable, yet more likely the victim than the perpetrator. Your continental cousin Llamorhad paid the price for her careless sensual entrapment of his lusting death wish. I agree that this is a dangerous female lineage, going back to Gwallwen, the mother of Rhun Hir, or even earlier."

"I assume Vivianne told you of my heritage," said Llen.

"Vivianne and my mother often confer about their visions. Morcades told me of the revelation of your noble birth – no surprise to your comrades who have fought beside you, witnessing your courage and character first hand. Since the age of Clovis, however, there has been an import of dynastic treachery from Francia. You are one of those redeeming veins of Frankish nobility that still flows with regal blood," Gawain acknowledged.

"Thank you, my friend. If I had known earlier, I may have gained the hand of Gwenhwyfar."

"Perhaps, but noble lineage and fate do not always align in the most pleasant ways for the descendants. Pricks in bedchambers and assassins' daggers will continue to complicate the lives of royal heirs," Gawain mused. "You should know Marganna entered my dream vision too: in the nude, riding bareback. Does this woman possess a master's power to enter our dreams and cavort about in the Otherworld?"

"She does descend from the lineage of Afallach, known to be powerful masters of the mystic arts," Llen reminded him.

"Yes, and ever more strangely, she recited the mystic lineages just as a master druid would – except without the hooded robe in utter nakedness."

"That would tend to capture your attention. If Marganna decides to visit her sister at Arthsedd, we may be in for another bizarre encounter," Llen predicted.

Exile of the Fisher Kings

When Gawain, Llen and Bercnaf arrived at Arthsedd, the guards had been doubled on the walls, the gate, and the long road approaching the fortress. They soon discovered a noble party had arrived from Francia, narrowly escaping capture by their dynastic cousins. Upon entering the main hall, Gawain and Llen were introduced by King Loth to his guests.

"Your highness, King Pelles, and Princess Elaine, may I introduce my son Gawain and Llenlleawg of Afallon."

The young warriors bowed to Pelles and his daughter. Llen was transfixed: seeing King Pelles seated on a throne alongside Loth, he and his daughter identical to the king and princess who appeared in Llen's dream vision. He knew they were his future father-in-law and future bride. It was clear by her expressive smile that Llen caught Elaine's eye; although she soon turned her face away with a look of shy innocence.

"King Pelles of the Corbenic has come to us for sanctuary, after a forced exile from his homeland in Francia," King Loth explained. "Dynastic wars and treachery have divided the Frankish kingdoms, endangering the lives of royal heirs."

"It is our pleasure to be here under the protection of Lothian, and to meet the kings and princes of the Cymric kingdoms," said Pelles. "Since the passing of Chlothar, and before, the dividing of lands and the vying for dominance of our native kingdoms has created turmoil between Chlothar's heirs. Sigebert and Chilperic were fierce rivals until Sigebert was murdered, his wife and young son barely escaping with their lives. The lad was actually lowered in a bag from a tower window by his mother. Other lines of the Merovingian dynasties are in even greater peril. Our lineage, descended from Zambor of Burgundy, has been exiled and hunted for decades."

"It is an honor to have you and the princess here with us, Sire," said Llen. "I have only recently become aware and confirmed my own lineage, after being fostered in Afallon by the nobility of Rheged. I am a descendant of Galains, and the only surviving heir of Ban of the Benoni. I believe we are fourth generation cousins, Sire."

"Astonishing! How is it that you are here now?" asked Pelles.

"We have come to alert King Loth of Saesneg advances near Ebrauc, and the urgency of a Cymric response," Llen answered.

"The Angles have fought and wed their way into Frankish dynasties as well. Our lineage of the ancient priest kings is in grave jeopardy. You must know of the Fisher Kings, descended from the ancient tribes of Palestine, Sarmatia, and Arcadia," said King Pelles.

"Yes Sire, I have been learning more and more about our heritage in recent months, now knowing that I am part of this legacy," Llen replied.

"Your father was a courageous man. I knew that he and his young bride had fled to Britannia, here in the north. The sad news of his death came to us more than two decades ago. We did not know that he had a final heir," Pelles recalled.

"Luckily, my father's assassins did not know of his heir either. Thanks to the wise vision of Lady Vivianne of Afallon, that heir stands here today," said Llen.

"This is a grand day of reunion, and calls for a celebration," King Loth announced.

While the hall was being prepared, King Loth, Llen, and Gawain met in a side chamber to discuss the situation in Ebrauc.

"They have amassed an army of thousands, father. And it was clear from our reconnaissance that they are preparing for war," said Gawain.

"Ebrauc is the nearest target. We expect them to advance there first. If Bryneich allies with the sons of Ida, Lothian will likely be a future site of attack," Llen explained.

"Coledauc and my wife's sister Marganna have been eager to claim this keep as long as or longer than they've been wed. Don't be surprised when that conniving she-devil shows up tomorrow to size up the furnishings. Is Rheged up to date with this latest news?" asked Loth.

"Yes father, Owain was in Ebrauc with us just days ago. They are preparing a force from the west," said Gawain.

"Alright then, we must do the same. Try not to let your Aunt Marganna know what were up to. She is in the very least sleeping with the enemy," Loth asserted.

"Gawain should be able to distract her with other sleep habits," said Llen, slapping his comrade on the back.

"Don't get caught in that viper's trap, lad. She has no conscience; and has bedded men just to see one of her Bryneich bastards slay them right where they lay," Loth cautioned.

A grand feast was held that night, giving Llen the chance to spend time with Princess Elaine; although the attention of the court soon shifted with the sudden arrival of Queen Marganna of Bryneich. Queen Anna Morgause announced her flamboyant sister, who entered flanked by two dashing greyhounds as if she was on an evening hunt. And when her eyes landed on Gawain, she was.

"I love to come to Lothian, just to marvel at the strong warriors and handsome bastards my sister's husband has assembled," Marganna said as she walked right up to the table were Gawain and Llen were seated.

"Hello Auntie, I see that you've been running your dogs again," Gawain greeted her.

"Oh yes, I have to let them loose, or they might forget why they were bred," Marganna responded.

"And why is that?" asked Elaine, catching Marganna's attention for the first time.

"The chase of course, my dear," Marganna answered. "I don't believe I know your new little friend, Llenlleawg. You must introduce her to me."

"Queen Marganna of Bryneich may I introduce Princess Elaine of Burgundy," Llen replied.

"Ah, a continental princess, a wise distraction from the local queens, lad," Marganna mockingly responded, abruptly turning to Gawain again, pausing just long enough to say with a wink, "I'm not your Auntie by blood, so anything we do will be okay."

It would have been difficult for anyone to upstage Marganna, except possibly her sister, especially if she had drunk too deeply into her cups again. But that unusual night, one or maybe two gentle visitors took center stage, for at least a few moments. Amidst the clucking of the court and the waves of boisterous laughter, an instant of silence descended upon the great hall as a pure white dove suddenly flew-in from one of the upper windows. It seemed to be drawn to a small silver incense burner, catching the light of the fire as it gently swung from its chain. The dove glided down, taking the chain in its beak, carrying it around the hall as guests dodged the dove's erratic smudging of the court with incense – until one startling move by an annoyed courtier caused the dove to drop the flying incense burner onto the floor. While the bird flitted about in a panic, beyond the commotion, Princess Elaine had carried a precious chalice over by the fire. Polished and gleaming, the chalice caught the attention of the dove. So the pure white bird alighted on the delicate rim of the chalice as Elaine held it out before her, walking slowly to an open doorway. The court silently watched her move with rhythmic grace out of the door, holding the chalice high, releasing the dove into the crisp night air, fully illuminated by the rising moon. Elaine viewed the dove's triumphant ascension and flight out into the clear sky, standing alone on the terrace. And then, returning to the court, she was received by an uproarious round of cheers and applause. She bowed slightly, humbly making her way back to her place at the table near Llen and Gawain.

As she came closer, Llen leaned over to Gawain and whispered: "She is my future wife and mother of my son, to be named Galahad."

Gawain embraced his dear friend in that private moment, while everyone in the great hall resumed their joyous evening festivities. Marganna continually tried in vain to lure Gawain to her bed that night; but he resisted the repeated verbal and physical harassment. She simply wouldn't stop until she held him at least for and extended moment, pressing herself upon the virile lad, he finally plying her off with an uncomfortable laugh. The next day Marganna departed with her hounds, liegemen and all, quite possibly suspicious of the increased troop activity around the fortress. That same day, Llen, Bercnaf, Gawain and a sizable force of Lothian warriors departed for Ebrauc. Llen was able to meet with Pelles just before he left.

"Sire, it was a momentous occasion to meet you and your daughter last evening. I do not know what will come of our days ahead in Ebrauc; but I believe fate has reunited us as surviving heirs of the Fisher Kings for far more than one night. So if destiny holds true to my belief, I will return to pledge my future to you and your family, and that extraordinary daughter of yours. I must leave you today, but will return as soon as my earnest sincerity can bring me back safely," Llen told the king.

"You are an impressive young man, Llenlleawg. I must confess, our thoughts seem as allied as our heritage. I know my daughter well; and I believe her heart will be overjoyed by your earnest pledge," King Pelles responded.

"Thank you, Sire."

"May the light of spirit surround you, lad."

A short time after that conversation, Llen and the army departed to the south. They had yet to receive any courier messages from Rheged, but assumed a meeting would occur near the crossroads below the Roman wall. During those recent days of the amassing of forces from Rheged and Lothian, Ebrauc had already come under siege from the Angles. Peredyr and Gwrgi held the citadel as long as they could, until it became clear that the overwhelming forces of the Saesneg were decimating their numbers by the hour. The citadel was certain to fall. They knew that this enemy would give no quarter. Kings Peredyr and Gwrgi recognized that there was a slight chance of retreating to Caer Gwyr, an outpost to the north established by the Gwyr y Gogledd, if they could take their dwindling troops out silently in the night, hopefully joining reinforcements arriving from the north. It was a daring gamble: slipping out in the darkness through the hidden passages of the ancient Roman tunnel system. By the time the sun had risen the following day, the Saesneg had stormed the vacant fortress. Once the Angles saw that their foes had fled, they sent half of their forces after the Cymri, while the other half remained to hold Ebrauc.

The Cymri sent a courier north to alert their Cymbrogi reinforcements of the rapidly shifting situation. Another factor soon left Peredyr, Gwrgi and their men in peril – the arrival of warriors from Bryneich in league with the Saesneg, attacking their own countrymen at Caer Gwyr. The courier could see the two advancing enemy forces as he reached a ridgeline to the west. Peredyr and Gwrgi were two of the last men to hold on to the embattled timber hillfort. In those final hours, they talked of their father, their mother, and their five brothers that they never knew.

"She tried to keep us protected from all of this grand gore and glory," said Peredyr.

"Yes, even her 'man of letters', as she would say – is here in this fateful trap. It appears inevitable that all the men of our clan are just meant to die in the jaws of this beast of war," added Gwrgi.

"I thought we had it by the tail for a moment at dawn; but now, it has become a two-headed treacherous monster that is certain to consume us," Peredyr replied.

"Well, we were able to get Penasgell, Blodgwyn and your son to safety," said Gwrgi.

"They'll have to carry-on without us . . . one last charge, brother?" Peredyr said to Gwrgi after a short firm embrace.

With those last words, Peredyr and Gwrgi ran out from their final barricade toward the enemy, hurling their last javelins at the advancing invaders, rushing to their deaths, swords and shields in hand, cut down by the Saesneg and the traitors of Bryneich.

As the reinforcements were reaching the Tyne, the courier arrived from the south. He rode immediately up to Llen, Gawain and the other leaders of the army. The look on the messenger's face revealed the solemn news before he spoke.

"Grave news Sires, Ebrauc has fallen. Kings Peredyr and Gwrgi retreated with the last of us to Caer Gwyr, making a final stand. They were surrounded and outnumbered, both royal souls and all the men have surely perished," relayed the courier.

Llen, Gawain, and the others hung their heads in silence, until Llen spoke: "What was the size and make-up of the enemy forces?"

"Thousands, Sire, mostly Angles; but I saw the advancing troops of Bryneich meet the Saesneg from Ebrauc, from a ridge west of Caer Gwyr."

They quickly sent another courier to alert Owain and his advancing troops from Rheged, expected to arrive soon. The tragic news was shared among the men, reflected in the hundreds of sullen faces. The leaders met in council to plan their next move, after Owain had arrived. It was agreed to stage their battle west of Ebrauc, rather than enter the newly captured Saesneg territory. Llen proposed an additional assault by sea, holding Ynys Medcaut and invading Bryneich. He and Gawain would raise forces from Dalriada and Alt Clud, while Owain would bring in more forces from Elmet.

Gawain and Llen first returned to Caer Lliwelydd to break the news to Penasgell and Blodgwyn of the devastating loss. Peredyr and Gwrgi's prophetic sister knew in her soul, before her cousin Gawain arrived. She met him outside the citadel, running into his arms on the road. He held her tightly as they cried together. Vivianne arrived from Afallon within hours of Llen and Gawain's return to Caer Lliwelydd. She consoled the grieving sister, her dear protégé Penasgell, and the new mother of Peredyr's only son. Vivianne held the babe in her arms, still innocent, safe from harm, leagues and leagues away from that family's tragedies. The young grieving widow Blodgwyn was in shock and disbelief.

"How could he be just gone: a vibrant man, a loving man, a man of skill and honor? This, this death . . . is such an odd and terrible thing. What has become of this man that I love and bled for, and known as much a part of me as my own flesh and blood and bone and tender life – now just gone? What becomes of that one so dear?" Blodgwyn cried out.

"There is no answer that can satisfy a heart and soul suddenly severed from that love held dear," Vivianne began. "It is an abomination to the love we shared and still carry. We are the ones entombed within the cairn of time; while our loved ones have stepped out of time. For them, time has collapsed into love. They are that love, more clearly, entered into the Otherworld. Departing this world, time and identity are collapsing into love. This is of little comfort to us within the waking world. We are still here, in this identity, in loss of that other, who was just with us. Our fallen brothers and the line of ancestors is a line of identities, each identity representing an arc of love and awareness from their own place in the waking world and beyond. To know them, to observe them, to love them, is to know, to observe, and to witness the arc and heritage of awareness. Any appearance or idea of these identities may enter our minds, our hearts, or our dreams and visions. Each one is representing a witnessing of the deeper reality that we are all part of, in life or beyond life. Each identity becomes one with us as a witness, as we expand in awareness, an awareness expanding within this field of infinite being. Our identity, their identity, all identity becomes merged as a limitless sense of awareness. This awareness, this undying love is the grail – where we may drink of the indescribable draught of boundless being – and be immersed in the well of love."

Chapter Eight ~ **The Ash and the Elm**

The well of love flows through the most ancient verses that have been conveyed from mouth to ear and quill to page. Aware souls attuned to those profoundly common echoes of origin set the standard for generations of descendant bards who would follow. Within the origins of every culture, that resonant voice speaks of the seeds cast from the prima materia – a tree, a vine, a spark of life reverberating into the essences of form. Conjured of ruddy clay, fashioned by divine imagination as spoken rib from hub of sacred center, revolving out into manifested space and time, a branch of that primordial tree is remembered: as the first fruits, as man and woman, as Adam and Eve, as Ash and Elm, as Llen and Gwen, as sacrifice and vision, as will and intuition, and as vital breath made flesh in speech and motion. This is the source of heart and form birthing our joys and sorrows.

Within the mythic understanding, everyman is the first man; and every woman is the first woman – each entity finding their persona, as that point on the page of the human story, where they see the world and their own soul as a flowering of awareness. Is each one aware enough to perceive a reflected self, as a transient image creating its own shadows? All recognition becomes a duel of self and other, engaged in conflict, or embraced as love. The tangible is felt and the intangible imagined both as interpretations of the unmanifested made manifest and lived in choices held by our own repeated assumptions. All we know is assumed by what we have lived day to day, year to year, in an endless history of lifetimes. We are wooed or entrapped by what has come before, carried-on again and again after we depart.

The Romans had treaded over the ancient dales where ash and elm held roots as sentinels of the Afon Swale. Centuries have passed and now these arboreal beams shield our native peoples from new invaders. The black faced sheep still roam about these hills and dales, generations after past slaughter. They meander between the dense groves, wary of predators masked by the shadows of primal ash and elm, grazing on ancient fields of battle, only paces or leagues away from the deeply rooted forests where the Cymri had made a stand against the Saesneg, avenging the loss of their brothers of Ebrauc. One clear morning of a slowly warming dawn, a brave few faced the Bernician flame-bearer, known for his trail of ashen destruction upon the land, like the brutal Roman scars burned against the Pict Gwlad. King Fflamddwyn sent a call for ready hostages from the Cymri. Prince Owain refused, challenging the sea dogs to hunt the whelps of Coel Hen, the Gwyr y Gogledd and their kin of Rheged, and ready themselves to leave this world, if they dare chase the Cymric wolves and ravens into the wood. The enemy was drawn into the shaded forest-lined road of Argoed Llwyfain, where ranks of the raven armies of Rheged waited in that wild un-harvested timber fortress, with spears and staves to snare the unsuspecting invaders. It is baffling how the flame-bearer could fall for such a trap, when his own ancestors had used such tactics against the Romans in continental battles. And yet, his own arrogance bred undue confidence, believing the small band of Rheged and Ebraucan warriors to be the last surviving remnants of his fateful conquest of the eastern citadel. Fflamddwyn led his four columns into a single cue, blustering after the taunting Cymric horsemen. Once the Saesneg troops were well within the wooded corridor winding through the shadows of Argoed Llwyfain, Cymbrogi emerged from ash and elm, from thickets and crude palisades, to assail a great decisive victory upon the invaders. Any who retreated to the open fields beyond the wood were soon run down by the formidable horsemen of Elmet, rounding-out the Cymric forces. Forest and field were strewn with many dead, "reddening ravens and wolves from the warring of men", as Taliesin's verse had said. Among them, the corpse of the flame-bearer, snuffed-out in the evening light, "run down as a wolf-pack would pursue sheep", the proud leader beheaded by Prince Owain's swift blade.

While Owain and the sons of Gwallog waged their successful inland battle, Llenlleawg and the ships of Dalriada landed on Ynys Medcaut, securing that eastern island and preparing an offensive against Bryneich. Medcaut was the holy isle of the east, standing in its own natural moat of the northern sea. For centuries, the medicinal herbs of the island had been sought by the druids of the northern tribes. Many ailing souls had journeyed to this isle seeking healing, braving the shifting tides to reach its benevolent shores. With the support of Aedan of Dalriada, his sons, and their fleet of ships, Llen became the protector of Ynys Medcaut, a guardian of peace over its newly established fortress that he rightly named Joyous Guard.

Joyous Guard

Llen's joy had been illusive, after his challenged love affair with Gwenhwyfar due to his uncertain heritage. But now, he knew at last that he was the descendant of a great lineage from Francia and ancient priest kings. His future bride had been revealed to him in dream visions, presenting him with a son, fulfilling generations of destiny. Ynys Medcaut and Joyous Guard furthered that fulfillment as a holy citadel and plot of land to hand down to his heirs, if he and the Cymri could hold on to this small island realm. Llen's return to Lothian after the Cymric victories was his moment to renew his commitment to Princess Elaine. Her father King Pelles was eager to re-establish their lineage of the Fisher Kings, seeing Llen as the ideal son-in-law: raised in Afallon and acknowledged as successive champion of Aenach Garman. Llen arrived at Arthsedd with Bercnaf and a small patrol, after weeks of battle campaigns, to find Princess Elâine and King Pelles patiently awaiting his return. Llen entered the main hall, greeted by King Loth, Queen Anna Morgause and their guests.

"Welcome Llenlleawg of Afallon, or is it Llenlleawg, King of Medcaut?" King Loth inquired.

"Greetings Sire, Queen Anna Morgause, King Pelles, Princess Elaine, I am not as yet crowned king of our eastern isle, but rather Protector of the Isle and Lord of the fortress Joyous Guard," Llen responded.

"Joyous Guard – a fine name for a beacon of vision upon our eastern coast – what has inspired this grand name?" asked King Loth.

"I was guided to this recent victory and these steps toward my destiny by my vivid dream visions. And I return here today to complete that joyous fulfillment, by seeking the hand of the future lady of my Joyous Guard to join me there," Llen adroitly stated, without hesitation, kneeling before Princess Elaine and King Pelles. "King Pelles, we spoke before my departure of my intentions; and I assume that we are still in agreement. The destiny of your daughter's future life with me is clear. But I would not propose our union without her desire and consent. Princess Elaine, I realize that we hardly know each other, and yet our future together is so certain to me. I am drawn to you as if I had been guided to you and this sacred moment all of my life. I hope that you feel that same irrepressible bond already forming between us. If you do, I request your pledge of love in return for my love and devotion. Will you consent to be wed to me, to bear our children, and share our lives together as husband and wife?"

"Yes I will, with all my heart," Princess Elaine answered, rising to her feet, embracing Llen for the very first time, as he stood-up to hold her.

Queen Anna Morgause promptly said to King Pelles, "I'd say you have a match!"

"This match was formed beyond this little world; and I accepted it the moment that I met this fine lad," Pelles responded.

Princess Elaine and her father were greatly relieved by Llen's safe return and his immediate honoring of his pledge. They lost no time in preparing for the wedding, with the help of Queen Anna Morgause and King Loth who had become their family of nobility in these Cymric lands. The ceremony took place at Arthsedd, presided over by Bishop Cyndeyrn and attended by the kings and queens of Alt Clud, Rheged, Dalriada, and Elmet, as well as Lady Vivianne and Taliesin of Afallon – the only parents Llen ever knew. Prince Artúr of Dalriada and his wife Princess Gwenhwyfar did not make the short journey from Caer Ystrellyn at the west end of the Firth of Forth. Gwen suddenly felt ill, upon learning of the event, although Artúr believed this wedding had quelled the rumors of Llen's scandalous attraction to Princess Gwenhwyfar. Of course Queen Marganna and King Coledauc of Bryneich also did not make an appearance at the impromptu wedding – having set themselves as enemies of the Cymric Cylch by their deadly betrayal of Ebrauc.

The royal wedding was a pleasant respite from the increasing turmoil across the land, with Bryneich and the Angles to the southeast, and the Picts of Bruide to the northwest. Tensions were subdued between the diverse spiritual beliefs among the Cymri and Scotti, even as Christianity was spreading into the north. Danger of the invading pagan Saesneg posed a common threat for both druids and Christians. While tolerance of each other served them for the moment, eventually Christian zeal began grating against the ancient ways of the land and its people. Prince Artúr had become an ardent Christian, influenced by his uncle Eoganan and Bishop Cyndeyrn. Afallon held a balance between divisive beliefs: with Vivianne's own heritage of the Fisher Kings, spiritually descended from ancient priest kings and the Gnostic mystery schools, while also firmly rooted in the traditions of the elemental world, and the wisdom of the Meira and the Maré. Taliesin was a voice supporting the elemental spirit of the people connected to the land, and the noble heritage of the kingdoms evolved from tribal roots, even though tempered by Roman influence, but never spiritually conquered by Roman Legions or the priests of the Roman Catholic Church. Having been raised in Afallon myself – just as Llen, Bercnaf, Gawain to some degree, and others – I saw Vivianne and Taliesin as guardians of the Cymri: each of them influencing generations of priestesses, bards, warriors, druids, princes and kings. The soul of these lands and our people had been a hybrid culture for centuries. However, since the encroaching influence of the Christian Church and the battling continental invaders landing on our shores, the old ways were eroding under new factions of dominance, resentment, and division. This was the world that Llen and Elaine's son would be born into.

Galahad

During the last full moon before Beltaine, nine months after the wedding of Llenlleawg and Princess Elaine, Galahad was born on the holy isle of Medcaut at the fortress of Joyous Guard. The babe appeared perfect in every aspect, growing into a beautiful fair-haired child. Vivianne had foreseen that the lad possessed a second sight – confirmed as his infant crystal blue eyes saw the presence of the Sidhe surrounding his crib. The High Priestess of Afallon told his parents to nurture this gifted wee lad.

"You have given birth to a wise soul, destined to fulfill the fruition of a sacred lineage of spirit. He will stand apart from the other lads; because he will be led by divine currents most of us can scarcely imagine. Train him well, as you were Llen, my dear son. And Elaine, never let him forget that he is not only born of love, but he is the love of the sacred heart manifested into life. He will know his path more readily than any of his peers; so listen to him; because he hears a deeper calling. He is surrounded by an angelic presence that has planted the seed of the cosmos within his heart, and divine vision within his mind. Whatever time and turmoil may bring into your own later years, remember that your union brought forth this child, opening a window into timeless peace."

Llen and Elaine were stunned by Vivianne's words, both of them embracing her with tears of joy, Elaine saying: "Thank you Lady Vivianne, for your blessing and shared vision."

"The blessing is born from you to us all, dear child," said Vivianne, wiping a tear from Elaine's eye.

"Thank you Mother," said Llen. "You have been that guiding light, with you, Father," reaching his hand to Taliesin, "all of my life, carrying me from the threshold of death as an infant, and raising me into a vibrant life of fulfillment."

"You were, and are, a delight to us, born to us as if from our own seed, and flourishing as the finest of men," Taliesin responded.

Vivianne and Taliesin stayed-on at Joyous Guard for several months, showering the babe Galahad with love. Before the wee lad could walk, Llen and Elaine brought him to Afallon, where they retreated to the western isle for a time, as new threats along the eastern shores were mounting. Galahad began to walk his first steps and utter his first words months before most children his age. Taliesin and Llen marveled at the wee lad's ability to even mimic the movements of the power of the mountains and streams as they practiced in front of the babe. They both wondered if the wee lad actually felt the current of power flowing through his tiny limbs, or was he just following their movements.

"Are you wondering what I'm wondering?" asked Taliesin.

"Yes," answered Llen, "but I don't see how, so young, he couldn't possibly . . ."

"And yet," Taliesin interjected, "he smiles so with each movement; and he appears to feel that surge and flow."

"I don't suppose we will know for certain unless he becomes the first infant to wield Caladbolg," Llen quipped.

They both laughed, and Taliesin said, "That would be a sight to see. Can you imagine the faces of the Cymric kings and princes who could not even hold the sword, seeing a toddler carrying the sacred blade around like a wooden toy?"

"Ha, ha, ha," Llen laughed. "This jesting fantasy could hardly be true; but we will see how he fares as a lad with an ash axe-handle and a buckler."

Just then a raven landed on the nearby wall, arching his neck, cawing three times, and then flying away. The babe Galahad laughed with glee, while Llen and Taliesin just looked at each other with brows raised, momentarily speechless.

"I know the presence of Master Myrlyn," Taliesin confirmed. "His eternal spirit is giving us a nod lad."

"Mother had spoken of her father Myrlyn and Master Blaise seeing your own arrival into Dinas Emrys Ysgol in their dream visions," said Llen. "It is so marvelous that you are part of Galahad's young life, as you were for me, carrying-on this lineage of light."

"It is an inspiration to me to see this heritage continue," Taliesin responded, "with the Raven of Awen calling to us from the threshold of the garden wall."

"It seems there are so few of us that have caught and carried this light in these times of turmoil," Llen reflected. "The sons of Aedan are being drawn into the Christian fold. Peredyr's son doesn't seem to shine with any glimmer of his father. The bards and druids you have mentored live as observers on the edge of life, mainly as voices to echo into the future."

"I'm afraid this has always been the case," said Taliesin. "In every age there are but a few aware souls to carry the light into future generations – many are ignored or forgotten. While others have held that light quietly, as dormant seeds awaiting a new spring. The light never dies. It only appears to be overshadowed by the events of history. We keep the light living, as we cultivate that divine seed, as a continuous pulse of truth within this body of illusion. I am grateful for you my son, and your new lad. That is the light that I see right here, right now."

Galahad was a surprising little lad. I first met him at Afallon when we were both quite young. He was about seven years younger than me; but even then he had a presence, as if he already was a druid or a priest. This seemed a bit odd to the other children, who didn't quite know how to relate to this unique lad. I befriended him straight away, feeling like an elder brother of the odd birds. Soon I found out he knew the movements of the power of the mountains and streams; so we practiced together. I understood his solitary nature; and he looked up to me – something I had never felt before.

Trial by Fire

I traveled about the north with Aneirin in those early years; and we frequently visited Afallon, Caer Lliwelydd, and Alt Clud, establishing Aneirin's reputation as a bard of the Gwyr y Gogledd. Being taught at a young age to observe human behavior, I could see the strained relationship between Prince Artúr and his wife Gwenhwyfar. She struggled to accept the marriage. It was her duty. However, she resented Artúr, appearing more irritable ever since Llen had found his bride and sired his son Galahad. Gwen remained childless, while Artúr blamed her for her unchaste past and her inability to accept Jesus Christ, as he did.

"The Lord will grant us the miracle of a child if you would simply open your heart to Christ Jesus," Artúr told her repeatedly.

"What would you know of my heart?" Gwen challenged him.

"I married you and pledged to honor our love and your heart. And yet, I confess, I don't know what that is," Artúr rebutted.

"Our marriage was never a union of the heart. It was an arrangement between kingdoms, each of us acting as dutiful heirs of our kings. I never have been able to embrace any lord with my heart: perhaps because I was a wounded child and never healed after my mother's death. A distant god and his son are no more than another king and a prince who demand something from me that I cannot give. The goddess of the earth and her sovereignty are the only stable comfort I have found. This is neither otherworldly nor religious, and certainly not patriarchal. It is rooted here and now as a nurturing presence. Even your Jesus abandoned this world; and he still hasn't returned," Gwenhwyfar declared.

"You are a blasphemous woman. It is your pagan ways that leave both your body and soul barren. You are a captive of Satan and his consorts!"

"I certainly have been abducted more than my fair share," Gwen responded. "I don't recall meeting Satan; although some men seemed like the prince of darkness in their dominance over me. Queen Marganna was the one female exception; surely a woman who you would describe as the devil's consort."

"Don't you understand that if you refuse to repent, your heresy and blasphemy will be extricated from you by the court of this kingdom and the authority of our Holy Church?"

"What possibly can be extricated from me that men have not already taken? Is there no god of love? Is my only choice to submit to be dominated by patriarchal power? Haven't I been doing that all of my life? . . . and whatever for? You do not bring relief or comfort, only threats – to suffer in this world or the next. I will rest in the bosom of the goddess of the earth, when my abused body is dead and buried, free of pain," Gwen stated with stark finality.

"You will be tried then, by a council of clergy to determine the nature of your corrupted soul," said Artúr.

A council of clergy was assembled at Caer Ystrellyn, chaired by Bishop Cyndeyrn and including six other orthodox clergymen. Gwenhwyfar was held under guard prior to her trial. Word of her arrest spread across the kingdoms, arriving at Dun Airigh to King Aedan from Prince Eoganan and his brother's fellow Christians.

"Artúr has actually imprisoned his wife . . . and will try her for what – the heresy of passion or the crime of barrenness!" Aedan exclaimed.

"Yes, and most likely consorting with the devil, and being under Satan's demonic possession," Eoganan explained.

"I can't believe this is my own son, persecuting his own wife. We must go to Caer Ystrellyn and also urge King Rhydderch as Pendragon to intervene," Domelch pleaded.

"The poor woman is unstable, but this Christian demon-hunting is beyond reason. We must send a courier to Afallon and depart for Caer Ystrellyn straight away," Aedan advised. "Rhydderch is unlikely to go against the Church. We must seek aid from Gawain, Llen, Loth and Urien. Send couriers to other Wledig of the Cymric Cylch who will be sympathetic to Princess Gwenhwyfar's plight."

"And what of Laigin sire?" asked his liegeman.

"No, not yet," Aedan cautioned, "We don't want to start a war ensnaring us with Alt Clud and the kingdoms of Eirenn."

Llen and Gawain soon received news of Gwen's arrest. Llen and Bercnaf put a plan in motion; while Gawain petitioned his father King Loth for his support. In the meantime, the trial for Gwenhwyfar's soul had already begun. Gwen was first interrogated and threatened with torture, urging her to confess, which she resisted. Prince Artúr would not have her visibly abused; although the use of painful restraints soon brought out her inner protector – Gwenhwyfach. This sudden shift in her persona shocked her captors, who brought her before the clergy.

One robust clergyman called out: "Gwenhwyfar, Princess of Laigin and Dalriada, you are accused of consorting with demons in league with Satan. Do you confess to these crimes against Christ and our Lord God?"

"I only confess to being a woman among impotent men, who use their religious power to inflict pain on those that they can dominate!" Gwen lashed back.

"You respond to these charges with the anger and fervor of a soul enflamed by demonic possession," Cyndeyrn confronted her. "Do you have anything to say in your defense?"

"My anger and fervor is my only defense against womanly costumed men who hide behind the trappings of a vengeful god. Whatever I say, you will twist to meet your own desired ends. You fear me because you are weak inside. Malicious outer force is all that you have. This is what you will use to silence me," Gwen combatively answered him.

"Again, you speak as if you are possessed by an evil entity, giving you this false inner strength. Unless you repent, we will have no choice but to execute you, and free you from these demons," Cyndeyrn warned her.

"Repent? I hold no commitment to your god with his unjust laws and biased beliefs. I am unable to repent for something I do not believe I have done in error. In fact, I stand here as a voice of truth in the face of your continued attempts to deceive, corrupt, manipulate and exploit with false authority. You men of the Church, kings, Wledig, and princes – you are in need of confession, repentance, or whatever pious lies you need to tell the world to satisfy your loveless souls," Gwen railed against the council.

"Gwenhwyfar, you are clearly a heretic and a blasphemer, speaking the voice of your master, Satan himself. We will convene and convey sentence upon you directly. May God have mercy on your soul," Cyndeyrn concluded.

"Bishop Cyndeyrn, If I may speak," Prince Artúr requested, Cyndeyrn nodding and motioning him forward.

"Thank you, your holiness – Gwenhwyfar, I beg you to reconsider, to repent, and accept the Lord Jesus Christ into your heart. Let his love save you," Artúr pleaded with her.

Gwenhwyfar, or Gwenhwyfach, just stood there, glaring at him, silent, until he turned away and left the hall. The council deliberated briefly and returned their verdict. Six members sat quietly while the robust fellow stood forward and stated their findings.

"Gwenhwyfar, Princess of Laigin and Dalriada, you have been found guilty of heresy, and blasphemy, and are determined to be possessed by demons of Satan, unable to recover your immortal soul. You are therefore sentenced to be taken from this hall and executed, by being burned alive at the stake, to free your soul, if you can repent before your death. If you are unable or unwilling to repent, your soul is condemned to the fires of hell for all eternity, in the name of our Lord Jesus Christ."

Gwenhwyfar was led away; while a tall, heavy, hewn-oak stake was erected on a mound not far from a hangman's elm in the open field beyond the fortress walls, where any and all who gathered could see the swift justice of righteous retribution by king and clergy.

Llen, Gawain and Bercnaf had rallied forces from Lothian, bringing ships deep into the Firth of Forth from Arthsedd. A sizable crowd had gathered around the execution pyre, while Llen and company landed and made their way closer to Caer Ystrellyn. Gwen was bound with ropes to the stake, her gown soiled and torn from rough handling by her captors. As heaps of dry branches and straw were piled up at her feet, Cyndeyrn questioned the princess once more.

"Gwenhwyfar of Laigin, do you repent your sins and beg for forgiveness from our Lord Jesus Christ?"

Gwenhwyfar just stared into the sober face of Bishop Cyndeyrn, without uttering a word, as if she looked through him to see beyond the confines of his harsh judgmental mind. That leap was more distant than the parapets of the fortress, where Artúr watched the spectacle. After a distant nod from the Prince, Cyndeyrn signaled for the fire to be lit. Two men with torches ignited the base of the pyre and stood back. Within moments, a rapidly running fox dashed through the crowd and around the pyre, pursued by a pack of hunting hounds, creating instant chaos all over the surrounding area. Men on horseback soon followed, led by Llen and Bercnaf, Bercnaf whistling commands to the hounds, Llen riding to the center of the scene, leaping from his horse onto the pyre to cut Gwen free. Just as he pulled her safely onto his horse, the pyre burst into flames. The rescuers quickly rode away, toward the shore of the firth. Bercnaf herded his hounds out from the crowd, making a rapid dash after Llen, Gwen and the other horsemen. The wily fox found his way to the nearest wood, most likely unaware of his heroic role in the rescue. Gawain and the warriors of Lothian slowly approached on the field beyond the crowd in a massive column, standing shoulder to shoulder, pounding their shields, creating a barrier of men, thwarting any attempt to follow Llen, Gwen and the others. Artúr was not about to engage in battle with Lothian. He was secretly relieved that Gwen had escaped, but remained conflicted about her and their tumultuous life, unable to reconcile his faith in his Lord with the troubled nature he saw within his wife. Gwen appeared to be in Llen's possession now. His daring rescue of Gwenhwyfar made it clear to Artúr that rumors about the two lovers were true. Llen was his comrade, his elder brother in arms – but now seemingly the enemy of his marriage, his faith, and his domain.

Llen had left Elaine and young Galahad in Afallon to lead the rescue of Gwenhwyfar. It was an uneasy departure, Elaine well aware of Llen's past romance with the Princess of Laigin. She had thought it ended with Gwen's marriage to Artúr, now fearing Llen's old flame would be rekindled – when the affair had been smoldering beneath the surface all these years. What had suddenly come about sent Llen sailing away from his new marriage with the lover of his past. It was a quiet voyage along the northern shores. Llen held Gwen close to him, comforted by a heavy cloak, as they renewed their forbidden bond of souls, formed so many years ago. The ships heading out from the Firth of Forth landed at Ynys Medcaut, taking Llen and Gwen to Joyous Guard, the precarious fortress of Llen's new life.

The ill-fated couple was alone, together again, free to abandon all caution and immerse themselves in their passion for each other. Tensions of the past hours, days, and even years were rapturously released as they merged in their complete nakedness of unhampered desire. They awoke to the soft morning light, hearing the crashing waves beneath the cliffs outside the windows of the keep. Time announced itself with the rhythm of the surf, reminding the adulterous pair of the paths they had departed from, and the circular nature of events that would crash against them once again.

Back at Caer Ystrellyn, Artúr paced across the field beyond the walls of his citadel; between the hangman's elm and the smoldering ash that was hours before the execution pyre of his rebellious bride. Gawain and the warriors of Lothian had long since departed. In dawn's silence, Artúr was faced with the decision whether to attack Ynys Medcaut and retrieve his wife, or suffer the humiliation and dishonor of a jilted prince, losing his princess to the most revered and honored warrior of the Cymri, who now lay with his wife.

"He will bring his forces here to fight you. Artúr is too proud to just let me go," Gwen told Llen as they lay together that morning at Joyous Guard.

"His religious zeal gives him the righteous justification, even beyond his obvious marital rights. We are in the wrong, despite the love of life we restore in our true embrace," said Llen.

"I was sorely wounded again by you, ever since you married Elaine and she gave you a son. I have been barren with Artúr. He is certain it is because I reject the Christian faith, to which he so fervently adheres. I would assume to him, you must be my demon lover," Gwen confided.

"I can't say that I feel very demonic; but I don't feel very saintly either, by betraying my wife. She is a dear and earnest woman, and a fine mother to my beautiful son. I thought our marriage would heal all discord within my soul and restore my identity in this life. But alas, I realize all too clearly this morning that my sincere love for her pales against our fiery passion. I am a man split in two," Llen admitted.

"I understand, my love. I have been a woman torn in two ever since I was a child, never knowing true love until we met. And yet it feels as if we are only healed in our mutual wounding, bound by a tattered bandage of passion that sooths our souls, but betrays the outward body of our lives," Gwen reflected.

"I do not know how we can continue either side of our lives as they are," Llen said in frustration.

"There must be another way," she responded.

"I cannot let a battle between Cymric kingdoms over infidelity destroy what has been built here at Ynys Medcaut. We must find a place of exile and sanctuary for you, where Artúr will not pursue you or battle me," Llen contemplated.

"He would not find me in the north, in Pict Gwlad or the Orcades," suggested Gwen.

"And I could still come to you there, living this divided life, if it were not too distant," Llen considered.

"I believe that I would feel free, alone, away from Artúr, and resolved to waiting for our time together. At least half of my distress might be removed," Gwen conceded.

"We must act quickly, before Artúr mounts an assault against this island. Once you are gone, he may see that he has little to fight for," Llen reasoned.

Llenlleawg and Gwenhwyfar departed that same day, sailing north with a small patrol to the Firth of Tay, along the north coast. Gawain's mother Morcades had spoken of a community of Attacotti priestesses who lived near the village of Migdele. The surrounding territory was in the tribal lands of the Miathi. Gwen was graciously welcomed by the women of the secluded community. Just the mention of Morcades, Vivianne and the sisters of Afallon reassured them of what they could clearly see within Gwenhwyfar – an emerging soul set free. Llen embraced her for a few heartfelt moments and then departed for Ynys Medcaut.

Days after Llen's return to Joyous Guard, Artúr had arrived with a fleet of ships to confront Llenlleawg and retrieve his wayward wife. To Artúr's surprise, the fleet was welcomed, as any allied kingdom's ships would be. Llen presented no resistance, admitting Artúr to search the fortress and the entire island, all the while insisting that Gwen had departed for the continent.

"She said that she needed to find a new world to live in," Llen told Artúr. "The lands she knew held too much memory and pain. She thought the foreign shores and distant breezes might help to cleanse her soul and heal her wounds."

"I do not trust either of you: but it is clear that she is gone. We are still Cymbrogi, whether I despise you or not. If that woman does not come between us anymore, then perhaps we can fight shoulder to shoulder again, instead of face to face," said Artúr.

"The Cymric Cylch is our bond. You are wise to see that, Sire," Llen acknowledged.

Artúr sailed his ships back up into the Firth of Forth, returning to Caer Ystrellyn – the threat of civil war quelled for the time being.

Cyndeyrn

Cyndeyrn had been a strong influence upon the earnest religious faith birthed in Prince Artúr. The bishop's severe condemnation of Gwenhwyfar did not sit well with King Rhydderch the Pendragon. And, at the urging of King Aedan and other Cymric allies, Rhydderch pressured Cyndeyrn to redirect his zeal farther south, to the kingdom of Powys, before his brother Morcant Mwynfawr or neighboring King Loth and his brother King Urien devised some plot to send the bishop directly to his final resting place among the Christian martyrs. During his exiled travels south, Cyndeyrn established a church in Rheged nearly twenty leagues south of Caer Lliwelydd. He erected a cross there that stood for generations, giving name to the place of Croesaidd. Farther south, Cyndeyrn gained the favor of young Prince Cadwallon and King Cadfan, who secured lands for the exiled northern bishop along the Afon Elwy. This period of Cyndeyrn's life gave the Church a strong foothold in the Cymric kingdoms. After years away from the north, Cyndeyrn left his able protégé Father Asaph to oversee his southern churches and monasteries, returning to Alt Clud. Many of the northern kings had not embraced Christianity in the way that Prince Artúr had. Rhydderch Pendragon was Cyndeyrn's strongest ally of faith among the Cymric kings.

Cyndeyrn's spiritual battle against the old religious practices of the Cymri and the Picts, and his harsh condemnation of lustful and adulterous behavior began early in his life. He had learned of his own unsavory origins from the monks of eastern Lothian who had traveled along the northern shores during Cyndeyrn's early years. They were quite familiar with the lustful appetites of King Loth and his many illegitimate children dotting the villages and farmlands of the north. Loth had sired a daughter with a woman from eastern Lothian, who had two daughters by different fathers. One she named Ddenyw and the other Beren. Ddenyw caught the attention of young Prince Owain who quickly seduced and bedded the lass, never seeing her again. Loth found out that his bastard daughter was carrying the child of his nephew and consulted his druids about this potential offspring from these first cousins. The spurious druids advised Loth of their cloudy vision of his grandchild leading to the downfall of his domain. Loth arranged to have the pregnant lass Ddenyw killed, attempting to avert an inbred heir from toppling his kingdom. The inept henchmen assigned to the task could not bring themselves to murder a young lass carrying a child; so they abducted her in a cart, uncertain as to what to do to fulfill their contract.

"We took the lord's coin. We have to get rid of her somehow; or he'll just send someone to kill us," said the taller of the two halfwits.

"Then why didn't he send them to kill her in the first place?" asked the shorter of the two.

"Likely because we're cheap and expendable," answered the tall one.

"What's exbendable?" asked the short one.

"No, expendable – that's you, no one would miss you," he answered.

"Me Mum would miss me, wouldn't she?"

"No one important would miss us."

"Me Mum's important to me."

"That's very nice, but we have to do something with this lassie so she won't be seen again," the tall henchman continued.

"You mean like magic?"

"No, I mean like dead, without killing her and her babe, maybe take her to the shore and . . . holy shite – didn't you secure that cart!"

Both men sprang after the rolling cart, the wheels picking up speed as it careened toward the edge of the steep bluff of Dun Pelydr. Frantically they stumbled to retrieve it as it got away from them, reaching the sheer cliff edge, plummeting down the precipice. All that they could see below was battered to pieces, reduced to scattered rumble, with no sign of the lass. The two hapless henchmen scrambled the long way around to hunt for the remains below the cliff, unable to find the poor lass at all, as nightfall obscured their search.

Some fishermen returning from their days outing heard the inept assassins ranting in a panic over the need to be certain the lass was dead. The fishermen had already discovered the lass – quite young, but very much a mother-to-be. Realizing this attempted murder must have been a plot to dispose of an unwanted child, the fishermen courageously carried the young lass to the shore of Aberlessic. Desiring to spirit the lass away from her pursuers, they set her adrift in a coracle, following ancient tradition, allowing the gods to decide the fate of the lass and the bloody show of the birthing. After kneeling for a prayer to the sea, to the sky, and to great mother earth, the fishermen returned to Dun Pelydr, passing by the bumbling would-be murders, who awkwardly pretended to be repairing demolished fragments of the escaped cart.

The young lass Ddenyw was gently rocked across the Firth of Forth, delivering her newborn lad as the coracle touched the shores of the Pictish lands of Fib. Some shepherds retrieving a lamb from the marshes heard the cry of the newborn babe, discovering Ddenyw and her son. They took them to a local monk known as Father Serfan, who cared for the lass and child with the help of two sisters of the Church. The lass lost a lot of blood, barely staying awake as the sisters vainly attempted to revive her. She waned further during their all-night prayer vigil, passing away before dawn. Her body was burned on a pyre of elm branches, slowly reduced to ash, tragically vanishing from the world in that secluded refuge, removing all evidence of the lamentable lass cast to see. Father Serfan named the surviving babe Mungo, meaning dear pet, raising him at the orphanage he had established there for abandoned children. The lad Mungo had trouble getting along with the other lads, constantly being bullied and harassed because he was favored by Father Serfan. He saw something in the lad. Mungo took well to learning scriptures, showing the first inkling of his future vocation as a priest. The cook at the orphanage took to the lad as well, seeing he didn't quite fit in, teaching him a bit of his craft in the kitchen. When Mungo was about ten years of age, the cook suddenly died; and the lad was forced into the position of cook for a time, until someone else could be found. He had a knack for cooking, although he despised it intensely, secretly desiring to poison the bullies; while at the same time terribly guilt-ridden for his evil thoughts. Finally escaping his new duties, he crept-out one night, pirating a coracle at the shore, setting-off into the firth and his expanding future, paddling all the way up to Ystrellyn. The lad traveled across the northern terrain and along the Afon Forth to the west. At a crossroads upon his uncertain adventure, he crossed paths with the entourage of Morcant Mwynfawr heading east, at the same time in a chance meeting with a patrol led by Prince Owain, arriving from the northern direction.

Morcant questioned the lad, with a craven undertone to his voice, "What is a handsome lad like you doing out here all alone? Would you like to ride with us and have a fine supper?"

Mungo was surprised by the generous offer, but sensed that this noble was a bit two-faced, like some of the lads that bullied him back in Fib. Owain and his armed company stepped up, the prince knowing of rumors of Morcant's depraved buggery of lads. Seeing the licentious expression on the predator's face, he addressed the lad directly.

"You look like a wise lad, and appear to be traveling south. We are making camp down the road a few more leagues. We'd be glad to share some roast venison with you – and a safe camp for the night."

Mungo looked at the two men, one he was already leery of, and the other somehow familiar and trustworthy; bowing to Morcant he said: "Thank you Sire, I'm not going your way. These men have kindly offered a meal; so I will make camp later on the southern road."

Morcant gave Owain and the lad a disgruntled and distasteful look as he motioned to his entourage to continue on. As they rode away, Owain said to Mungo – "Smart choice lad! He's a buggery old lord with a dastardly reputation. I am Owain, Prince of Rheged. What are you called, lad?"

"I am called Mungo."

"Ha, ha, well Mungo, you just escaped becoming that nasty old bugger's dear pet. Maybe we can direct you to a better destiny."

"He wasn't about to touch me! I'm a survivor! That's what Father Serfan told me. I'll be bishop of this land one day," Mungo declared.

Owain responded with a hearty laugh: "Ha, ha – I believe you lad. "You are a stubborn one. Maybe you should take on a new name and claim your desired destiny."

"I think I just might, Prince Owain."

Mungo shared a much needed meal with Owain and his men, quickly drifting off to sleep by the campfire, becoming peacefully rested for his continuing journey. Owain stirred the lad the next morning.

"Well lad, we're on our way back to Caer Lliwelydd. What's your plan?"

"I don't have a plan."

"You're just a wandering pup then, are you?" Owain prodded.

"No, I'll be a bishop, you'll see. Is there a monastery with an ysgol at Caer Lliwelydd?" The lad asked.

"Rheged has a few, you tenacious pup. And maybe, as the Prince of Rheged, I could put in a good word for you," Owain offered.

"Thank you. That could be quite helpful, although nothing will stop me – no matter how long it takes."

"You are such a stubborn pup . . . that's what we should call you – Cyndeyrn – the stubborn lord of the hounds," Owain decided.

"Cyndeyrn – I like it," said Mungo.

Owain took the lad with him to Caer Lliwelydd. His wife Penarwen embraced Mungo immediately.

"He looks like a younger you, Owain," she said.

"Huh, maybe . . . there is something about the lad. He is determined," said Owain.

"You mean he's stubborn, like you," said Penarwen.

"Yes, determined, like me," said Owain.

"Ha, ha, yes, determined and stubborn, like you," Penarwen laughingly answered him.

Owain and Penarwen became Mungo, or Cyndeyrn's foster parents, supporting his education until he was ready to go on his own to Eirenn or the continent to study to become a priest. His ambition was stubborn and determined, rising him rapidly to become Bishop of Alt Clud. It was Vivianne who first suggested to Owain that Cyndeyrn really was his son. The monks from eastern Lothian confirmed the stories of the lass Ddenyw being cast adrift and Father Serfan raising the lad. When Cyndeyrn became aware of his origins, he was at first ashamed; but later turned that shame into a vengeance against Loth his grandfather, his own father Owain, and any lustful sinners who failed to repent. Gwenhwyfar had narrowly escaped the fires of redemption once. If Cyndeyrn ever found her, he would most certainly be determined to raise her upon a pyre again.

Caer Morwynion

Owain's youthful siring of Cyndeyrn was years before his marriage to Penarwen. He had been loyal to her, resisting temptations to stray as his father Urien had with Eliwri daughter of Gwyddno, and Modron daughter of Gwallwen of Gallwyddel, and likely many others. Urien and Modron's daughter Morfudd had been a shadow sister to Owain, born on the same day and hour as he was on the winter solstice. They were celestial twins of different mothers, continuing parallel divergent clans among the northern Cymric kingdoms. Morfudd had married Morcant Mwynfawr, devious brother of King Rhydderch of Alt Clud. All that could be said good of Rhydderch was starkly contrasted by all that could be said bad of Morcant Mwynfawr. As we know, Morcant sired the two daughters of Morfudd: Anna Morgause who married King Loth, and Marganna who married King Coledauc of Bryneich. These sisters being the namesakes of their maternal ancestors from the fifth century, the daughters of Gwyrls of Dumnonia and Ygerna, coincidentally the spiteful half-sisters of that eras Owain ap Einion. Marganna's husband Coledauc – like Loth, Urien and his son Owain – was a descendant of Coel Hen. Although rightly members of the Gwyr y Gogledd, Coledauc and his branch of the northern dynasty never held the luster of the sons of Meirchion Gul and Maesgwid Gloff, claiming Merovingian heritage as well as holding the kingdoms of Rheged, Ebrauc, Elmet, and Lothian. Coledauc married into the heritage of Dyfnwal Hen, Meirchion Gul and Afallach of Gallwyddel through his queen Marganna. Those sisters of Gallwyddel, however, had not received the traditional northern matriarchal inheritance of land and sovereignty. Coledauc, Morcant Mwynfawr and his daughter Marganna were lusting for the lands of Lothian, Alt Clud, Ebrauc, and even Rheged if they could claim the bedding of their heiresses as the hand-fasting of the deed, or engage foreign interlopers to open other nefarious means of succession. Rhydderch Pendragon and his fostered Prince of Dalriada, Artúr, were the dominant Christian defenders against this destabilizing scheme; while Loth and Urien were the remaining crown heads standing in the way of a dynastic coup from the east to the west. When the unpredictable Bruide of the northern Picts saw the divides in the Cymric Cylch, he set his sights on the siege of Arthsedd.

Aedan of Dalriada had been battling his brother-in-law for more than a decade, interrupted by Baetan's invasion of Ynys Manau and Aedan's eldest son Artúr's attempt to incinerate his bride. Alt Clud, Lothian and Ystrellyn held the narrow girdle of the island that Bruide desired to claim for his own, to virtually capture the entire north as his domain. This was the overreach that was his undoing, when he laid siege on Arthsedd. Marganna had been planting seeds of conquest in the north, courting Pictish warlords who might serve Bryneich's aims in the future. She was even rumored to have seduced young Artúr of Dalriada on his first campaign in the north, disillusioned with his recent marriage to Gwenhwyfar, unaware of who was enticing his wounded libido, and likely driving him guilt-ridden headlong into devout Christianity. Marganna could have that chilling effect upon her conquests. Her father Morcant Mwynfawr used her as his covert siren, luring kings and princes into the rocky shoreline of changing alliances.

These decade long disturbances to the resonant unity of the Cymric Cylch gestated alarming visions in the aware souls of Afallon. Penasgell found herself guiding her cousin Owain and a young Galahad through the dreamscape of the Otherworld, on the eve of Bruide's invasion of Lothian. Penasgell described to Prince Owain her nocturnal journey involving him, the seasoned warrior, alongside the innocent child Galahad, traveling together within this illusory world of portentous imagery.

"We were wandering across the northern terrain beyond the elevated crags in western Lothian," she began. "It felt like a pilgrimage of sorts, with discarded relics discovered along a road leading to a secluded religious site on the plain – an ancient chapel, abandoned and in ruins. There was nothing inside, the ceiling open to the sky, emitting a voice within my own open awareness telling me: 'These are warriors of the soul. Lead them to the citadel of the sovereignty of your mothers and grandmothers of the matriarchal lineage, connected to the land and the heavens. Go to Caer Morwynion. Defend the coastal keep from the painted king, from the boastful king, and from the perverse king.' Then we rode across the land to the great inlet of the northern sea, until we saw the citadel crowning that immense mound of earth and stone, seemingly alive, like a giant crouching bear. An aging hermit met us at the base of the mountainous landmark, pointing upward and saying: 'The people do not know their true queen, sovereign, and goddess. There is a harshness of the heart that has captured them. Shame has fallen upon the lady of the keep, her husband, and her kindred. They block the entry of their earnest defender, until you state your intention. If you enter, they will try to sap your rightful power from you. Beware; you enter at your own peril.' Un-dissuaded, we moved forward, as an army of support appeared behind us. Soon a battle began. Our warriors fought with seven brothers from one king and four brothers from another. The battle became confusing: as to who was friend or foe – until we did not know how to defend ourselves from our own brothers and cousins. The old hermit appeared again and told us, 'the key is in your own history: to know who your mothers are.' Then a young woman came up to us and handed a great ram's horn to Galahad, saying that 'he must call the dead to rise.' Gawain and his brothers were on top of the wall looking down from the parapets. The wee lad blew the horn, and we could see the images of the queens of the ancients hovering in the sky over the citadel – Ingenach Hen, her mother, her grandmother and great grandmother, Ingenach's daughter Nyfain, and her daughter, my mother Erfiddyl. And to my amazement, I saw myself, suspended in the air, as I stood on that imaginal ground, watching these fantastically elevated images overhead. I recognized the elder queens as if I knew them all, but cannot recall all of their names. They were finely dressed and adorned, fittingly for their times: one wearing a purple Roman mantle, another tattooed like a Pictish Priestess, another with the breastplate of a warrior queen. Their intent, conveyed to me without voices, was to reveal the presence of the matriarchal power. Each of them had come to their thrones as maidens, as their husbands and kings wed both the maiden and the sovereignty of the land. This lineage had changed when my mother Erfiddyl handed that right to her brother Loth, with the blessing of her other brother Urien. As these grand images of the matriarchs had ascended into the air, ships arrived from Pict Gwlad at the shore. We could see Bruide's banner waving above the main mast of the lead ship. It lashed against the air like a flame, threatening turmoil and destruction. I pulled Galahad close me, thinking he might be afraid; but he bravely blew the ram's horn again – and I awoke in Afallon."

After hearing Penasgell's visionary dream, Owain immediately gathered a force of warriors, heading north to Arthsedd. He was the eldest of the seven sons of Urien, joining the four sons of Loth to defend Lothian from the Picts. Gawain and his brothers were battling against Bruide's assault when Owain and the forces of Rheged arrived. Bruide couldn't contend with the cavalry of Rheged striking at his troops while they laid siege on Arthsedd, so they retreated to the northern shores of the firth to regroup. Their Pictish rivals the Miathi were waiting for the fatigued and diminished army of Bruide to land, attacking them by surprise. Bruide was slain and his forces defeated.

This turn of events left the Cruithni Picts of the north without a leader. King Aedan's Queen Domelch was Bruide's sister, and the matrilineal heiress of their mother Dwysedd, daughter of King Grom of the Cruithni, affording Aedan and his sons a dominant position to gain greater control of the north, if they could forge an alliance with the Miathi. Queen Domelch had a younger half-brother, Gartnait, a Pictish prince who was an amiable ally, looking up to Domelch as the mothering older sister of his youth, and seeing Aedan as a mentor or foster father. Gartnait readily stepped up to lead the Cruithni. The Cruithni held the north, from east to west, and the western islands north of Dalriada: the Scitis, the Hebrides, at times even the Orcades. Aedan held all the islands north of Gallwyddel and west of Alt Clud, and the lands from Loch Lomond to the Firth of Forth. His son Artúr held Caer Ystrellyn, where the Teith meets the Forth. Aedan set the foundation of the Scotti in the north when he wed his beloved Domelch, Princess of the Cruithni. Not even Rhydderch Pendragon, his corrupt and perverse brother Morcant with his subversively beguiling daughters could now rattle the Scotti above the Wall of Forth.

Coming of Age

The insidious plans of Morcant Mwynfawr, his daughter Marganna and son-in-law Coledauc were thwarted for the moment; although, these predators of power continued to plot their way into position for another assault. Marganna's son, named after her father Morcant, was being weaned on deception and treachery within the viperous nest of Bryneich. Many believed he was not even Coledauc's son, with Marganna's notorious reputation of sexual aggression making it nearly impossible to follow the web of patrilineal threads spun by her appetites.

Marganna was far from the only duplicitous child of the Cymric dynasties. Within the house of Rheged, Penarwen, Prince Owain's wife and Deifyr his brother had been involved in a lustful affair for a couple of years before Owain learned of their betrayal. He and his brother drew swords against each other during the Battle of Arthsedd, before their cousin Gawain stepped-in to stop the impending fratricide. It was all a few brave souls could do to hold the Cymric Cylch together. Artúr held back his troops at Caer Ystrellyn, failing to assist Lothian after they had protected his faithless wife Gwenhwyfar's escape from certain death. These grudges and personal wounds among the kings, queens and nobles of the Cymri were festering ill-will across the land while Saesneg invaders lay-in-wait to topple any crumbling kingdoms.

When young Morcant of Bryneich had come of age, his mother Marganna sent him out into the dynastic courts to find their most vulnerable veins of assault. Urien of Rheged and his brother Loth of Lothian were aging leaders of the north; both waning in strength as their sons vied for control of their inherited kingdoms. Loth, though resilient, was slowly recovering from wounds suffered at the Battle of Arthsedd. Agrefain was the assumed heir, but Gawain had achieved significant recognition among the nobles and Wledig of the north. In Rheged, Owain's wife and brother had all but publically admitted their affair, without remorse. Bishop Cyndeyrn, the adopted bastard son of Owain's youthful sexual exploits, had personally and spiritually rejected his immediate and extended clan, finding kinship with Christian King Rhydderch and Prince Artúr.

Prince Morcant weaved his way into the outer circles of rebels seeking to undermine the dynastic pillars of Rheged and Lothian. He was able to hire assassins within Rheged's own troops, attempting the murder of Prince Owain, and succeeding in the murder of King Urien. The court of Rheged was in a panic, with no one sure who might be the next targeted victim. Princess Penarwen and Prince Deifyr appeared to be as shocked as anyone, even though suspicion surrounded them. Kings of the Cymric Cylch were reeling from the tragic news. Llywarch Hen, first cousin of the king, composed tribute to the much revered Urien of Rheged, describing the events surrounding his death and the retrieval of the crowned remains from the northern shores beyond Lothian, where Bryneich forces drew attention away from the assassins concealed within the king's own ranks. Urien had been in a secure encampment, surrounded by his own men, in the midst of planning a defense against the forces of Bryneich and their Saesneg allies. Feeling safe within his own camp, Urien had stepped out of the command meeting briefly, when a treacherous blade struck-off his regal head, the king releasing his last utterance at death, announcing the brutal assault. Another complicit assassin stabbed Llofan Llaf, the beheading assailant, attempting to cover his own covert role in the murder. With the king dead, and his first heir in danger, soon to be crowned king, a hasty retreat was called; and the men of Rheged returned home, retrieving the head housing the soul of Urien, their beloved and fallen king. Llywarch's words carry a sorrowful echo of that fateful day that will resound throughout the centuries.

Urien's Head

The head that I carry at my side,
from an attacker amid war bands,
was the proud son of Cynfarch's head.

This head that I carry at my side,
the head of generous Urien Rheged,
was still wont to guide all the host,
but now on his breast are black crows.

Oh the head that I carry on my left,
better ye live than go to your death,
you were the wise elders' strong fortress.

That head I have carried on my arm,
made a load for the funeral biers,
out of Bryneich after battle cries.

And this head that I carry in my arm's hand,
the powerful chieftain who led these lands,
is Prydain's chief pillar – taken away.

A head I carry from the darkened hill,
on its mouth spattered with foam and spittle,
blood and sorrow – woe be to Rheged today.

Morcant, son of Marganna and Coledauc, did not swing the blade that killed Urien, but blood was on his hands nonetheless. His conspiracy was revealed, confessed by the assassins. The grandson of Urien Rheged himself would forever be known as the red-handed murderer – Morcant Llofrudd. Morcant was as much older than me, as I was older than Galahad. I was born in between two of the most extremely divergent souls of a generation – one so near saintly, the other nearly a diabolical beast. Entities of both goodness and evil seem to be born into this world, while most of us stumble along through this life somewhere in the balance between. It is often the best we can do to lean towards the good; because in this warring world, we all have a bit of blood on our hands. Galahad faired far less bloodied than others, as did I, as a bard, and only a reluctant warrior, if I need be at all.

Young Galahad received the same training as most noble lads, with sword and shield, mace and axe, lance and bow. Even as a young lad, he was quite adept at basic skills, making his father Llen very proud. Early training in the power of the mountains and streams surely enhanced his natural ability. I spent a lot of time with the lad when he was near ten years of age. We both were in Afallon for a number of months, his mother residing there for a season or two, and his father defending Ynys Medcaut, off on strategic battle campaigns, or stealing away to visit his mistress Gwenhwyfar.

Artúr had not given up his periodic search for his fugitive wife. Finding little evidence that she had departed for the continent or her native land of Eirenn, he sought her out along the edges of the northern kingdoms. This brought Artúr to Afallon, where he intended to question Vivianne for her prophetic knowledge and any rumored reports of Gwen. He arrived with an armed entourage, eager to interrogate the High Priestess. Old Galehaut, still living, still standing, supported by sheer cantankerous will, stopped Artúr and his liegemen as they arrived.

"No weapons are allowed within the halls of Afallon," Galehaut announced, baring the door.

"Stand aside old man. I must speak with Lady Vivianne – urgently," said Artúr.

"Then urgently remove your weapons. It is quite simple, lad: assume you are entering a sacred place, like the churches that you frequent," replied Galehaut.

"All of our weapons? I carry the sword Caladbolg. It is sacred as well," Artúr responded.

"I see that. I have seen the blade myself, as you might have remembered; if you weren't so busy pissing yourself. Now, leave all of your weapons here – swords, axes, darts, whips, chains, knives, cleavers – unless you're the new cook or a scullery maid."

Artúr stood there glaring at him.

"No, I didn't think so," Galehaut concluded, holding out his hand to accept the sword Caladbolg.

"Men have died for this sword," said Artúr, as he handed over his prized possession.

"I know. I killed a few of them," answered Galehaut.

Most of Artúr's men remained outside, fully armed, while Artúr and a couple of his liegemen entered the building unarmed, leaving their weapons on a stone slab outside the entrance. They were greeted by a novitiate who led them in to see Lady Vivianne.

"Prince Artúr, to what do I owe the pleasure of this unexpected visit?"

"Unexpected? You are too modest, Lady Vivianne," Artúr sarcastically replied.

"Alright, you are here looking for your wife, who escaped a fiery death at the hands of Bishop Cyndeyrn. She is not here. And if she lives, I could not tell you where to look for her," Vivianne responded succinctly.

"You could not or would not tell me where to look?"

"It amounts to the same thing. I have no information for you, lad. Let the woman live her life in peace."

"I intend to search the island."

"Would you search the private chambers of the bishops of Rome and Constantinople?"

"This is hardly the center of the Holy Christian Church, my lady."

"No, it is older and even more sacred to us, and to our people, as our spiritual center, located in the physical center of these isles, housing the devoted women of Afallon, whose privacy you will not violate. Your father and mother would not approve of this intrusion. Please give us the same respect that you would give to a sanctuary you do respect," Vivianne said with finality.

"Gwenhwyfar has betrayed our sacred marriage. She does not respect me as her lord and master. She is disturbed by demons and must be cleansed to save her soul."

"This religious fervor is very unbecoming. You were such a promising lad, at one time. It dismays me to see who you have become. Gwenhwyfar is a beautiful, but tragically wounded soul, who was on her way to healing, before she was tormented back into her wounded self. Every child deserves a chance to reclaim their innocence. Please allow her that chance. There must be plenty of young Christian princesses who would love to have you for their lord and master, obeying your every command. Take one of them home to your keep. Let them give you sons who will carry your bloody banners of Christ. And please, leave this island undisturbed. It is a sanctuary of peace," Vivianne concluded her remarks, turning away from the young prince.

Artúr left, without another word, his liegemen trailing behind him. While he was meeting with Vivianne, I had wandered over with young Galahad to see what these warriors were doing in Afallon. Galahad was curious to see the sword Caladbolg close-up. As he reached to touch it, one of Artúr's men stopped him.

"Not for you laddie: it's Prince Artúr's sword."

"Ah, let the lad have a look. He might just fall over dizzy from the power of the blade," Galehaut said with a smile and a nudge.

Artúr's man looked around, then grinned and said, "Alright lad, but ye can't say we didn't warn ye. Grown men get weak in the knees just touching this mighty blade."

Galahad looked at Galehaut. He winked and nodded to the lad. So Galahad reached over, first merely lifting the pommel above the stone slab a bit, looking up for approval. Artúr's man raised his brows, expecting the lad to pass out at any second. Instead, Galahad pulled the sword smoothly out of the scabbard, lifting it with both hands above his head. Artúr's man looked around in a panic, stepping towards Galahad as Prince Artúr stepped out of the building to see Galahad wielding Caladbolg. Taking a wide stance that he had learned in his training, Galahad swung the long blade in a spiral motion in the air, as if he knew the blade, and it was accustomed to his young hands. Soon the divinely tempered steel began to hum, singing an ancient song with its resonant tonal voice. Galehaut and Artúr's men just stood there, dumbfounded, as I was too, watching the lad, hardly taller than the sword itself, dancing with its vibratory rhythmic power. Then he stopped, allowing the blade to rest on one open palm as he slid it back into the scabbard.

"That was fun!" Galahad exclaimed.

Artúr scowled at his liegemen standing by the weapons, who simply shrugged his shoulders, saying, "Forgive me Sire; the lad surprised us all."

"Shut up you fool," said Artúr, grabbing his weapons, and securing Caladbolg to his belt. "Good day, Galehaut – watch that lad!" He added, as he pointed at Galahad, turned, and departed with his men.

"Yes, it is a good day, isn't it," said Galehaut, with his hand on Galahad's shoulder, "a very good day indeed."

Vivianne soon came outside to be sure that Artúr and his men had actually departed.

"Did Prince Artúr finally leave for the shore or inland?" Vivianne asked Galehaut.

"It appears he went back to the shore, my lady. I sent a man to be certain." Galehaut answered, smiling. "You missed young Galahad's stellar performance."

"Oh, what kind of performance?" she asked with anticipation.

"The lad picked up Caladbolg and gave us a demonstration of its power and song," Galehaut relayed with delight.

"And did Artúr see this?"

"Oh yes, my lady, and was none too pleased. The lad must be five or more years younger than the prince was when he first held the blade at Maen Gwregys," said Galehaut.

"Yes, you're right, five years younger," Vivianne confirmed, turning to young Galahad. ""What made you believe that you could wield the sword, lad?" she asked him.

"Galehaut gave me a nod," the lad explained; "but I also had a dream vision last night, with the sword, a chariot, and strange kings, queens, priestesses and odd things happening, as they do in dreams."

"Tell us about this dream vision, laddie," said Vivianne.

"I was driving an ancient chariot, which seemed to be like a backwards throne," Galahad began. "It was being pulled by four horses, taking me through kingdoms and worlds that were alive in a strange way – everything moved as if it was a living thing – towers, walls, rocks, mountains, lakes, and streams. Everything was as alive as a stream or an animal. Along the road I passed by kings, queens, warriors, priests and priestesses. The road was leading to a giant tree in the distance. I felt the tree, maybe its roots, inside me or under the road. I thought the roads going everywhere were the branches of the great tree.

"Everyone I met on the road was a branch or path of that same tree. There was a young woman, crowned like a queen, seated on a throne. She was very smart, and talked to me with her mind. She said that she was the daughter of great and mighty beings. She told me that she waited at the gates for the mighty ones, and for all those who sleep. Her world was a world of action and of waiting – waiting for everyone to wakeup. She could tell who was ready to wake up. She looked at me, and then waved me on; and I soon came to a young man who tended to a great big machine. It had gears and pulleys like a gatehouse to a fort; but it looked like it connected to the sky and the earth, which were as alive as any living creature. The man was completely naked; and he moved perfectly along with the machine, as if they were one living thing. He was there by himself; but he was somehow everything else too. Whatever he was doing appeared to be creating worlds, and kingdoms inside those worlds.

"I rode on and found another man – at least I thought he was a man – but at times he also looked like a woman. It was very confusing. All of these people in the dream were very smart, like mentors who knew a lot of things. I knew this because they all could see inside my head and know what I was thinking, and teach me other things that I can't even remember, but know I know it somehow. It sounds crazy, but makes sense to me inside my head, in my thoughts and feelings. This man-woman person was teaching me to be honest with myself. I don't quite know what he-she meant; but it made sense to feel the truth.

"The next person was some kind of a priestess. I was sure she was a woman; because she was bare-naked and very beautiful. She smiled because she could tell I was trying not to stare at her breasts; but I couldn't hide anything from her. She knew everything I was thinking and feeling. She knew things that are strange and mysterious, like you, Mam-gu, like how planets and stars are also gods, and were in the sky a certain way when I was born, and that told how I would be in my life, or might be when I grow up. She was also very sexy. I guess because she was naked. It made me feel all tingly inside. She was also very kind and loving, like a teacher or priestess who gives a lot to others all the time. She waved to me, smiling as the horses pulled the chariot; because she knew I wanted to stay longer.

"Then I traveled up a hill, a moving hill that kept turning around when the chariot stopped. At the top was a priest king, a very handsome man who looked at me and really understood me, as a young lad, soon to be a man. Even though the woman before was beautiful, this man was somehow beauty itself – in his heart. He touched something in me that I can only say is love, like my Ta, or Tad-cu Taliesin, or mother, or you Mam-gu. He held it and gave it to me as if it was the balance of everything. I felt very safe. He told me that I would do great things; because I would live the truth.

"After I left the priest king, another warrior was riding along beside me in another chariot. He looked like me, only older. I think I was seeing myself in the future. This gave me courage. We both rode by another king on a throne that looked like Tad-cu Pelles, holding a shepherd's crook. And a woman was there too, holding a fish. She looked like you, Mam-gu. The fish was glowing with light. This priestess understood who I was, and who I would be. Tad-cu Taliesin was there too; at least he looked like him. He was very wise, and funny. His robe was magical. When he opened it, it glowed. He pointed to a standing stone on the horizon; and when I looked, a sword floated over it. Tad-cu said, 'It is yours for the taking.' Then I woke up."

"Well, laddie, that is quite a dream," said Vivianne.

"What does it all mean, Mam-gu?" asked Galahad.

"It certainly explains how you knew you could take hold of Caladbolg, and says a lot about you, confirming much that I have always known about you, dear lad."

"Like the chariot – will I drive a chariot?"

"Ha, ha, maybe so – but I see the chariot as a symbol of something much greater. This dream reminds me of a dream that your father had, many years ago."

"I had the same dream as Ta?"

"Well, no, not exactly – there is a greater meaning to both dreams; and that, you have in common with your Ta. The ancient chariot is really about your shared heritage with your Ta, with Tad-cu Pelles and with me. The priest kings and priestesses belong to your ancestral and spiritual heritage. The chariot is about your inner journey, taking you for a ride through a greater and greater understanding."

"Understanding of what, exactly?"

"Your dream answers your own question. It is the understanding of how to 'live in truth', as the priest king said in your dream. At your young age, you are in touch with the greater understanding of your own higher intelligence. That's what all of those smart beings were telling you. You're still a lad, so they appear as others who show up along the 'living road', as you called it. They are all part of you, the deepest part of you. This deeper part of you is like a tree, a tree of life connecting every soul to the greater truth of being. Your journey is an adventure into the understanding of the deeper qualities of your soul. The tree of life has been a spiritual tool since ancient times used to explore these qualities. The dream illustrates these deeper qualities and virtues of understanding.

"All of this is within you. You will realize it more readily as you grow up. The queen at the gate is your discernment. The naked and powerful man turning the wheels between earth and sky is your independence. The man who was also a woman is truth and honesty revealed. We are all male and female in our essence. That is birthed and expressed in love. The sexy priestess is the generosity of that love; followed by the priest king who saw right into your depth, as the balance and fulfillment of the beauty of that love, encouraging you to do great things. You found your own courage reflected in the mature vision of yourself as the other chariot driver. Your

Tad-cu is of the lineage of the Fisher Kings: the priest kings of ancient times. You honor that heritage with this dream, and your future of living that truth. I am here and Taliesin is her to help you with that wisdom and understanding. Your father's dream did not go as far as yours has, even now at your youthful age. It is the relative age of your soul – your timeless ageless soul – that matters here. As Tad-cu said, 'It is yours for the taking'. Take the inner journey lad, and there is no limit to how far you will go."

"I felt that in the dream, Mam-gu, like something deep inside was set free, free to be anything," said Galahad.

"It is your time of maturing from lad to young man to warrior, prince or priest," Vivianne responded.

"I cannot say I would be a priest, not of the Christian Church, anyway; but there was something holy happening there in the dream. I could feel it. Everything was holy – the land, the road, and all the people I met – and the great tree was in everything too."

We were transfixed by the majesty within his dream imagery. Just a lad myself, barely a novice bard, I stood there in awe of the lad's inner vision. I had seen the gifted presence of this lad bubbling up to the surface in plain sight before; but after this dream and the raising of Caladbolg, I knew that he was a beacon to follow. He had looked up to me, this stumbling bard, trailing behind Aneirin for poetic guidance. Now I looked to Galahad, whose soul I was privileged to glimpse into that day he shared the dream. It wasn't long after that, I noticed his mother showed distress and longing for her absent husband Llenlleawg. The lad missed his father too; but other mentors appeared in his young life, like Galehaut, who mentored his father, Taliesin, Gawain, and even me. I encouraged the lad's spiritual gift, desiring to align myself more and more to that refined resonance. Galahad brought more of that out of me in my own youth. I saw the resilience of the young Galahad come to light when a great shift occurred in that new family of Joyous Guard.

Cyndeyrn had returned to the orphanage in Fib to see his old mentor Father Serfan, before the aging priest died. While Cyndeyrn was there, he heard about a group of pagan priestesses to the north, practicing what the Christians called the "dark arts". Whatever they feared was a dark art, because it wasn't sanctioned by the Church. When Cyndeyrn went to investigate this heretical community of women, he saw Llenlleawg arriving at the Firth of Tay. Cyndeyrn sent one of his monks to follow Llen, leading him to the village of Migdele. Llen was seen from a distance in a romantic embrace with a woman who resembled Princess Gwenhwyfar. They departed on horseback, the monk unable to follow. He asked a local villager and his wife who the passionate couple was.

"There's a romance this village must be talking about," said the monk.

"Oh yes," the woman responded, "every few weeks they meet-up here and scurry off."

"I see . . . they're not a local man and woman?" the monk asked.

"We don't know them. And I'm not one to get into someone else's affairs," said the man, as he gave a sideways glance to his wife.

"Then you don't know the woman? She doesn't look familiar?" The monk pursued his questioning.

"Vanora," the woman said, as her husband looked at her with dismay. "She's one of those women of the old ways, The Attacotti."

"The Attacotti – then there is a sect of that ancient belief around here?"

"I think we've said enough. We don't need to stir-up something with the Church," the villager said, his arm around his wife, pulling her away. "They're just a pair of young lovers, that's plain to see; and that's all we need to know. Good day, father."

The monk hurriedly returned with his report to Bishop Cyndeyrn, who asked: "What did you discover?"

"Your Holiness, I followed Llenlleawg to the village of Migdele, and saw him embrace a woman in plain view, whom I do believe was Princess Gwenhwyfar," the monk reported.

"Are you sure it was her? Did anyone else in the village see them?" asked Cyndeyrn.

"I inquired, your Holiness; and a local woman said her name was Vanora, not Gwenhwyfar, and a member of a sect of Attacotti who lived near the village," answered the monk.

"Yes, but of course she could have changed her name. She wouldn't announce herself as Princess Gwenhwyfar," Cyndeyrn reasoned.

"Quite true, your Holiness," the monk affirmed.

"These lands and its people are much steeped in the tribal culture, with few Christians, although that is changing. What better place for the princess to hide than among the Attacotti. I didn't really believe any of them still existed. Prince Artúr will be eager to hear this news," said Cyndeyrn, with a smile of satisfaction.

Days later when Llen and Gwen returned to the village, the woman who spoke to the monk approached her, asking: "Vanora?"

"Yes," Gwen answered, a bit startled.

"I am Alys. I live here in the village, sorry to startle you. I've seen you and your beau before. And, just the other day, A Christian monk saw you here too. He was asking a lot of questions, and seemed to recognize you. My husband pulled me away. He didn't want to start something with the Church coming in and all. I did tell the monk that your name was Vanora, and that you were one of the Attacotti women. I thought you should know. This monk was insistent. And, well, it felt odd to me – like he was snooping about. I had to tell you."

"Thank you, I will let my sisters know that a man of the Church has been asking questions in the village," said Gwen.

"Yes, thank you, dear lady," said Llen. "The Church can become quite zealous in their intrusion into other beliefs. You and your husband are wise to be wary."

"Love should never be something to fear," the woman said, gently touching Gwen's arm. "Take care you two."

"Thank you," answered Gwen, as the woman simply smiled, turned, and walked away.

"It isn't safe for you here anymore," said Llen.

"I'm afraid you're right. If the monk has any connection to Cyndeyrn or Artúr, it wouldn't be long before they find me," Gwen agreed.

"Where will you go – north to the Orcades, Francia?" Llen asked.

"I only have affection for one of the Franks, and he's a Cymbrogi, my 'Man of Eirenn'!"

"I'll never forget that first night at the falls, in Laigin. Well, come now; let's get you away from here to the Orcades. I have heard of a place from Gawain and Morcades where you will be safe," said Llen.

"We should alert the sisters, and collect a few things before we go north. I'm sorry to put you through all of this," Gwen said with love in her eyes.

"It's not your doing: it's Artúr and the Church, and this insane world we live in. It will give us that much more time together, for now," Llen added.

"But when you leave, we'll be farther apart," she said.

"Not in my conscious heart, my dear," Llen answered.

After their journey north, securing a place for Gwen in the Orcades, Llen returned to Joyous Guard to find a Cymric fleet anchored at the shores of Ynys Medcaut. He was greeted by Owain and to his surprise, Princess Elaine, young Galahad and King Pelles. Llen warmly embraced his wife, hugged his son, and gave Pelles a strong Roman handshake, as Owain explained their sudden arrival.

"After the death of my father, a show of force in the east was necessary to dissuade these Bryneich traitors and their assassins. Elaine and the lad insisted that they come see you. I felt with the extra troops here, she and the lad would be safe," said Owain.

"Thank you, my Cymbrogi, for protecting my family and fortress," Llen responded.

"You'll always be my brother-in-arms, so your family is mine as well. I'll let you have some time with them before we talk strategy," said Owain.

"Thank you, we'll talk soon," said Llen.

"It's a fine fortress, son. Ban would be impressed," said Pelles as they walked on, Elaine staying behind, retiring to her chamber.

Llen spent some time with King Pelles and young Galahad touring the battlements, seeing and hearing what the lad had learned: his skills with arms, his dream visions, and the mature young man he was becoming.

"I am so very proud of you son. I wish that I could have been there to see you tackling these fine skills. I'm sorry that I have been away so much. It appears that your mother, Vivianne, Taliesin, Galehaut and Tad-cu Pelles have done a marvelous job teaching you all of these things that I can see within you now," Llen told him.

"Thank you father, I know that there is much for you to do away from home, as there will be for me someday. You never even knew your father, and yet had wise mentors. I have you in my life and also have many of the same mentors that you did. We are together now; but with battles, invaders, and assassins about, no one really knows how much time we ever have, do we?" Galahad graciously acknowledged.

"Sharp lad!" said Pelles.

"Yes indeed, you are such an incredibly wise lad. I could not be more proud," Llen answered, embracing his son. "And you are right, my wise lad. There is a fragility of life, even for the strong. That is why it is so important that you and your mother were kept safe in Rheged or Afallon. One day I hope to secure these eastern shores for us and all the Cymri."

When Llen and Elaine finally had some time alone together, it was clear that she was far more ill-at-ease than their son.

"I was so surprised to see you, Galahad and Pelles here with the fleet," said Llen, after kissing Elaine gently on the lips, immediately feeling her resistance.

"I was surprised that you weren't here, and that no one seemed to know where you were. Where have you been? No one has been able to tell me where you have been for weeks," Elaine questioned him.

"For weeks . . . ? I would have thought my liegemen would have given you at least some information about our reconnaissance in the north," Llen answered.

"In the north, where in the north?" she asked.

"North of the Tay, with the Picts; since the death of Bruide, the Miathi have become more of a factor at play in holding the east from the Saesneg."

"Why is it I don't believe you?" Elaine challenged him. "It seems there is something you aren't telling me: just like when you went back to save Gwen. She is gone now – isn't she?"

"Yes, of course."

"Where, where did she go?"

"No one knows."

"No one – you raise armies to save her and then no one knows where she went?"

"It is best that way. Artúr still searches for her. Cyndeyrn still desires to cleanse her soul with fire. It is best that no one knows. That is her only chance for freedom."

"What about you?"

"What about me?"

"Do you know where she is?"

"I told you, no one knows?"

"You said it was best that no one knows. But, do you know? How can you or anyone continue to protect her if no one knows?"

"It would be best if few people knew."

"Then you know where she is."

"I've told you all there is to tell."

"Would you tell me where she is if you knew?"

"No."

"Why not?"

"Because it would endanger her."

"You don't trust me?"

"When it comes to her, no, I don't."

"Then why should I trust you?"

"Because you love me."

"Do you love me?"

"Yes, of course I love you."

"Do you love me as much as you love her?"

"I married you. You are the mother of my son. There is no way to compare that love with any other."

"Make love to me," she said in a hushed voice, as she threw her arms around him.

Llen began kissing her and undressing her; and she undressed him until they were both naked within each other's arms on the bed. Then she abruptly stopped, pushing him away.

"You have been with her. I know it. I just know it."

Llen rolled over on his back, letting out a deep sigh, with his arms over his face.

"Why can't you admit it? You have been with her."

"I have been with her in the past. You know that. I may never be with her in the future. I don't even know how long I might live, or whether for certain, she is alive or dead. Life is uncertain. All that is certain is that one day each of us will die; and for me, I am certain that I love our son, and I love you – even when it pains me to do so," Llen said as he dressed himself, leaving the room.

Elaine sat on the edge of the bed and wept, believing she had driven Llen further away from her heart, believing he still loved Gwenhwyfar.

Aside from delivering Llen's family to Joyous Guard, Owain had amassed a sizable force of the Cymri to attack Bryneich. He spoke with Llen about his plans.

"Has there been any movement in the north, or are the Miathi stable for the moment?" Owain asked Llen.

"I don't believe the Miathi have any interest in attacking Lothian," answered Llen.

"At least that's one bit of good news," said Owain. "You must be glad to see your wife and son again."

"Yes, Sire, the lad is growing up so fast. I'm proud to see the young man he is becoming. I was stricken to the heart when Urien was slain. It must be a heavy burden upon you, to mourn him and take on your sudden kingship of Rheged," said Llen.

"Indeed it is. This rally to battle meets both things that I face at once. Thank you for seeing that."

"Certainly Sire."

"Have you settled your affairs in the north, if I dare ask?"

"They are held at bay Sire, at a very distant bay. I will leave it at that."

"Of course. Good luck my friend. I knew you would have insight for this campaign against Bryneich, so that we might act swiftly, but not rashly."

"Yes Sire, the fleet at the shores of Bernicia has no doubt alerted the Angles and Bryneich."

"Yes, I realize the surprise factor has been lost," Owain admitted.

"Perhaps not entirely, Sire. Part of Bryneich's longevity depends on the alliance with the Angles and their holding of the shore," Llen explained.

"Yes, of course, so we must reduce the Angles hold on the shore, or push them to distrust Bryneich, so they will invade them – which will eventually happen anyway," Owain surmised.

"Right now, Bryneich is useful to the Angles, because they have taken down your father, and potentially other kings," Llen added.

"The traitorous bastards! That is why we are here in force, to show that Rheged is as strong as ever."

"I understand Sire, but you are exposed as the new king to that same treachery from Bryneich. It was a tough choice to show your military and naval power and courage. The other part of Bryneich's longevity is the mountains to the west, limiting attacks from the Cymric Cylch. That, I believe is our best option. While they are near certain of an advance from the northeast, with our fleet sitting here at the northern shore of Bernicia, we might find the mountain routes to be their weakness," Llen proposed.

"Do you have a plan?" asked Owain.

"I have spent time in those mountains. There are routes older than the Roman roads, known by local tribesmen. We could get Nudd Hael of Selgow, who has no love for Bryneich, to provide scouts and additional troops. If our troops from the fleet land from the Tweed Water at the north of Bryneich, we might slip past the Angles of Bernicia. We will need Lothian behind us, and possibly Alt Clud. I can talk to them when I take Elaine, Pelles and Galahad back to Lothian, where they will be safe if all goes against us here at the shore."

"I will hold tight until I receive word from you," said King Owain.

"I will send a courier by sea, Sire," said Llen.

With the plan in place, Llen took Galahad, Elaine and King Pelles with him to Lothian, where he conferred with Loth about the attack of Bryneich. Loth was still recovering from the last battle siege of his own kingdom. He agreed to give support to Llen and Owain; but his wife Anna Morgause was distressed that things had led to the inevitable attack of her sister's kingdom. Llen sent a courier to Owain, and began marshalling troops to march through Selgow with Nudd Hael and his men. Before they departed, King Loth suddenly died. This sent the royal court of Lothian into chaos, the eldest heir, Agrefain, now becoming king. Queen Anna Morgause persuaded her son to hold back the invasion of Bryneich. Llen now found himself at odds with the new young King of Lothian and his brothers. He sent another courier to Owain; but news had already been leaked to Bryneich. Prince Morcant Llofrudd was able to intercept the second courier, sending assassins to slit his throat and sink the courier's boat, leaving Owain to believe that the invasion would proceed as planned. Bernicia's ships were prompted by Prince Morcant to attack Owain's fleet waiting offshore; informing them that neither Lothian nor Ynys Medcaut would be rallying to their aid. A sea battle ensued, sinking several of Rheged's ships and killing the newly crowned King Owain; still mourning his own father's passing. As the surviving ships retreated, they raised their ash-hewn oars in homage to their lost king and Cymbrogi, while ravens circled the returning fleet. When Llen met with Nudd Hael to discuss a future assault of Bryneich, he was shockingly informed of Owain's death and defeat. These events all took place in a matter of hours, leaving the lands between the Tweed and the Tyne in turmoil, as Bernicia gained a stronger hand. With the death of Loth and Owain, the courts of Lothian and Rheged were at best in flux. Llen, realizing that even Joyous Guard may no longer be his, took Elaine, Pelles and Galahad west to Afallon.

I was at Caer Ystrellyn at that time, with Aneirin at the court of Artúr. We had been traveling from Dun Airigh and Dun Barton. Aneirin had a circuit of bards in the north he would join at Gorsedd. Artúr was less inclined to accept the bards who weren't Christian, but was still a gracious host, even without his lady by his side. News had reached him through Bishop Cyndeyrn that Gwenhwyfar was seen in Pict Gwlad in the lands of the Miathi, near the village of Migdele. Cyndeyrn was eager to ferret out the priestesses of the "dark arts", spurring Artúr to send a patrol of righteous men, who would know how to deal with them.

"It is likely the type of nest that your bride was corrupted by years ago," Cyndeyrn advised Artúr. "The right men sent into this den of heresy would clear it out for good."

"Do you believe Gwen is still there?" asked Artúr.

"It is likely, sire, unless she was alerted by my monk's inquiries."

"Well, either way, these heretical nests, as you say, need to be cleared out. Send your monk and select some volunteers among my men who are willing to punish these women most severely," Artúr ordered.

Aneirin and I overheard this plot and saw the patrol being formed with some of the most unsavory Christian warriors we had ever seen. It was clear that they were chosen to do the darkest deeds of the so-called righteous men. Aneirin decided to leave Caer Ystrellyn straight away to possibly warn Gwen and these Attacotti Priestesses of the impending danger. We arrived before dawn the following day, discovering their community with little trouble.

"Lad, they are doves for the slaughter," Aneirin said, as we walked right into the center of their sacred space.

We quickly found the High Priestess, who wasn't the least bit concerned by our warning, inviting us to join them in their evening celebration. We politely accepted, all the while believing that we could convince them to seek refuge from an imminent attack. The entire community was un-phased, even after Gwenhwyfar's sudden departure. They were intently focused on the event at hand, and were most pleased that we had arrived – as guests of honor and reverence, we soon discovered. They were especially attentive to me, determining that I had never been with a woman, and still in my teenage years, of chaste and eligible bridegroom material, as it would seem. I had also never had strong drink before, becoming quite evident as they insisted that I enjoy the generously flowing refreshments. Aneirin tried to caution me, in his particularly tutorial way, yet was imbibing pretty well himself.

"Take care lad, the northern people worship the mead of song," he told me, "consuming a strong beverage made of honey and the blood and spittle of the gods, believing that it arouses wisdom and the poetic imagination."

This was little to caution my overconsumption, which seemed to approach and overtake me quite rapidly. Rather than any arousal of poetic wisdom, I found myself aroused more by the erotic dance of the women, one lovely maiden near my age in particular, taken-in as I was with her poetry of motion. She and the other women drew me to my unsteady feet, supporting me in their ritual dance. At some point I was aware that both the young maiden and I were utterly naked. I was wearing nothing but my boots and a headdress of the antlers of a ten-point buck. My body was being fondled and aroused by the swirling hostesses of merriment, until I was lying on a soft bed of furs, mounted by the young maiden, whose beautiful naked body consumed me with her tender exposed maidenhood, as if I was the erected monument of her salvation. The only thing I recall of this first physical experience was the tremendous surge of elemental power I felt rushing through my every follicle and fiber of flesh; and, that it was over so very quickly. As soon as my part was complete, the maiden was lifted away, immediately covered in a white gown, bowed to and praised as if she was the expectant mother of a future god. From there, I vaguely recall my body was gently washed. I awoke the following day, wrapped in furs beside a smoldering fire. Aneirin was oddly amused by my encounter, congratulating me for coming of age in the most glorious way he could have ever envisioned.

"Thank you or I suppose I should thank her, whoever she was. Where are all of the priestesses? Did they vanish in the night?" I asked Aneirin.

"I believe they are engaged in a group prayer or silent ritual in that round structure over there," he said, pointing to a large dwelling, less than an ystaden away.

"Do you think they expected us last night?" I asked.

"Oh, I'm sure of it – especially you. They didn't seem overly interested in me. Not that they weren't gracious and generous; but you had arrived expressly for that maiden," Aneirin explained.

"Do you think I'll ever see her again?"

"Oh dear lad, it isn't a courtship. You are the catalyst for her consummation as a priestess – the seed of the tree of life."

"I had the seed of the tree of life?"

"It is the essence of life, which appears in many forms," Aneirin tried to explain to me.

I was so momentarily exhilarated on that night, and yet still so terribly naïve, that I just tried to absorb all that he said and all that I experienced. My clothes were neatly folded beside my fur bedding; so I dressed and waited to see if any of the women would make an appearance. Aneirin and I walked down to a nearby creek, when we suddenly heard horsemen approaching. As we came back towards the site of the gathering, we saw through the brush that the riders from Caer Ystrellyn had pulled the women out of the round dwelling and herded them together. I started to step forward, but Aneirin stopped me.

"Stay here, keep still and quiet lad, or you'll likely be dead before your next step."

A monk among the warriors shouted, "Where is the woman called Vanora?"

Several women, one after another, shouted back: "I'm Vanora, I'm Vanora!"

"None of you are Vanora!" The monk yelled at them. "Vanora is not even Vanora. She is the Princess Gwenhwyfar."

Then the High Priestess stepped forward and said, "I am Vanora, what do you want with us?"

"If you can't tell us where this Vanora or Gwenhwyfar is, I will let these men have their way with you, and then burn you all to death for heresy – for your salvation!" The monk declared with malicious rage.

Then the High Priestess raised her hands high, spreading her arms wide. The women suddenly shifted from their momentary terror to a calm, peaceful, attentive focus on the High Priestess. She chanted words in an ancient tongue, strange and haunting, yet similar to the unusual dialect of the Miathi Picts.

Rousing the women, she then said: "Join me in calling the kindred hounds of the Venicones!"

The next thing we knew, they all began to howl and chant and utter such bizarre and unnerving sounds, beyond anything we had ever heard. Within moments, vicious hounds appeared from the wood, approaching the monk and his men. Several attacked the monk, tearing him to pieces before our eyes, as the other men scrambled to mount their horses to escape. Some were able to ride away; others were pulled down and devoured – until the High Priestess raised her hands again and the hounds quickly departed. The women slowly moved the bodies of the monk and his men to a fire pit, piling branches on top of them and lighting the fire.

I looked to Aneirin asking him, "Is it safe for us to go out there?"

"If they were going to kill us lad, we'd be dead already. But be careful, they might just love you to death," he said with a smirk, as he stepped out of the brush. "Fine day for a burn, ladies, I hope you all slept well. I see there was no need for our warning. You seem to be more than able to protect yourselves from unwanted intruders. We thank you for your hospitality; but we will be on our way shortly."

"Thank you for your concern Aneirin," said the High Priestess Vanora. "Take care of yourself, wise bard, and that fine lad. He will have stories to tell after we're all gone. And . . . you be wary of axe wielding men of battle, as you compose your great songs of flowing verse. Your kindness will be honored by the goddess."

"Thank you, my lady," Aneirin responded, bowing, while contemplating her every word.

The lass that had made wild love to me smiled intently, as I mounted my horse. She was wearing a different gown, the color of peach or saffron. As we rode towards the river we saw an ancient standing stone, draped with the white gown that the beautiful maiden had worn the night before. People from the village later told us that a gown would appear on the stone certain seasons. It was called the Maen Gwyngwn – stone of the blessed gown.

Aneirin and I started back toward Arthsedd; but soon heard of the death of Owain and Loth, and the Angles on the rise; so we stayed out of Lothian, even bypassing Caer Ystrellyn, likely just getting news of the hound ravaged monk and his henchmen. We returned to Rheged. Owain's brothers were posturing over who would rule, now that both their father and elder brother were dead. Their elder cousin, Llywarch Hen, was presiding over the debate of rival siblings. He was King of South Rheged, and well respected as a wise bard rather than a military leader. Even so, many of his compositions were questioned, as well as the conception of his multitude of children and grandchildren. He is ascribed to more than would seem humanly possible. But then, he is of the bloodline of Urien and Loth.

Llen, Elaine, young Galahad and King Pelles, along with many other nobles were in Rheged, both mourning the loss of King Urien and King Owain – and with concern for the future of Rheged. The Cymric Cylch had convened with King Rhydderch now the wise elder Pendragon, while many were resistant to his Christian faith. Aedan of Dalriada was there to balance his son Artúr, Aedan being wise enough to embrace the both old ways and the increasing number of Christian kings. Little was accomplished at that gathering, with the royal family squabbles needing time to sort out, when time was encroaching from the east with the emboldened Saesneg.

As the kings and nobles retreated from their diverse family councils, returning to their own kingdoms, Llen departed again for the east, or north, or wherever he could convince Elaine he was going. He was in fact, going to be with Gwenhwyfar. Elaine knew it – even if Llen would never admit it. She was becoming increasingly difficult to be around, for Llen and even young Galahad. He loved his mother and knew about his father and Princess Gwenhwyfar, but was beginning to understand the complexities of the human heart. He discussed some of these things with his Mam-gu Vivianne and Tad-cu Taliesin, who were continually impressed by the lad's maturity. He was by this time entering his teen years, when in the ancient traditions a lad became a man.

"I do not like the fact that father loves, and possibly has always loved another woman besides my mother. He is a good man. It is clear to me his heart is torn. I love my mother very much; but I must admit she is not an easy person to be with. I do not know if it is because my father abandons her, or if there is something more that torments her." Galahad confided in Vivianne.

"You are so wise to see this, dear lad. I know your father better than anyone alive; and I have seen his inner struggle and his love for you and your mother. He is not the first noble prince to have a mistress. This is not a fact most wives would choose; but it is the way of this world. Your mother is wounded: wounded by the battles of the heart, wounded from her family's life of exile, and wounded in ways she has wound around her own heart. I am seriously concerned for her – that she may not be able to weather this storm inside of her soul. We need to hold her gently within our own hearts, and help her to find that joy she once had," Vivianne explained to the lad.

"I am worried too. She is so sad so often lately. I can feel her slipping away from me, from everyone."

"Keep an eye on her lad. Let me know if she becomes worse. We should get her back to Afallon soon. Perhaps the sisterhood can give her comfort."

Their concern for Princess Elaine was sadly too late. As soon as she found a space in time to get away unnoticed, she exited the gates descending down to the gardens along the River Eden, mourning her lost sense of self: suspended between gates of life and gates of death. She had been the faithful virgin, descendant daughter of the wise and mighty ones, and bride of an honored and beautiful man; but the inertia of her broken heart was too great. After taking strong herbs to rapidly induce a deep sleep, she lay her body down into the waters of the Eden, submerging the manifested beauty that she was into the unmanifested reality that she was becoming. Her cold pale body was later found by fishermen, where the empty form had settled, mired in roots and branches along the shaded shoreline. Galahad saw his mother's body when she was brought back to Caer Lliwelydd. She lay in a casket made from red elm, draped in a purple mantle. Pelles had his hands on the shoulders of the lad to comfort him, while the lad was more of a comfort to Pelles, having now lost his wife, daughter, and most of his family. Galahad shed a tear and kissed her icy lips, knowing she was not really there. He was able to talk to his Mam-gu Vivianne alone about what he was feeling.

"It hurts my heart that she is gone, even more so that she felt so sad that death was her only way out. That is what hurts: that she could not find her way to live," the lad told her.

"I know dear. I don't believe there was anything we could do. Even if your father had come back and stayed with her, I don't know if it would have been enough. Would she ever let go of her pain from the past? That is a question we cannot answer," Vivianne reasoned.

"It is a strange thing when someone dies." Galahad contemplated. "I have seen dead bodies before, from war, disease or old age; but she was young and beautiful and alive. I did not see that life in her, when I saw her body. She did not look real. There was no life there. She was not there."

"It is strange, laddie." Vivianne considered. "In all that I know and have seen, this thing of death, of leaving the body, is a fading shadow before the light – a light that lives. Her soul is free now, free from worldly concern."

Galahad was surprisingly calm and reflective about the loss of his mother. He wouldn't see his father again for weeks. It would be nearly that long before Llen even knew of his wife's passing. Galahad slept restlessly that first night and dreamed about his parents. He told Vivianne about his vivid inner journey of the soul, the day after his mother died.

"I dreamed that I drove a chariot again, pulled by four horses. I can remember their names: Dechrau, Dychmy, Emosi, and Amly. Each horse came from its own world, but ran together within the same kingdom. Even though I drove the chariot, it carried me of its own intent and movement. I felt as if I was on that same road from my other dream: the living road that moved with the power of the roots and branches of the great tree, which seemed to be the center of the tree as well. I could feel all of its roots and branches moving through me – thousands and thousands of vibrating fingers of life and imagination moved with the power of water or wind or sheer will of their own.

"Beneath the great tree, a wedding ceremony was taking place. I recognized the bride and groom, not by their faces, but by their way of being. I could see who they were, or who they were becoming. The bride was a young woman, very much of the earth – simple in her honest emotions. She had been living in a place where she lost her balance, emotionally, like my mother; until she could no longer see the virtues of living. She had stepped into the gate of death, from the gate of Eden. But then she met her bridegroom, who rescued her heart. He had done this before with another wounded heart, a lover from his past who also struggled with demons of the mind. I could see and feel within both the bride and groom, as if they were within me and part of me. The groom was the messenger or mentor of the bride's soul, and she was also in some way that for him, each as a being of love – although, they were one love inside of me. It was a radiance that the bridegroom brought out of the bride, as she reflected that radiance back to him. They became a merging of worlds. The grand tree presided over the ceremony, as the presence surrounding all of us, and the formation of all worlds and kingdoms. The tree held an unknowable and unspeakable wisdom. Even though it guided the ceremony, it did not show itself as a person or a thing. It was somehow fully present, and yet hidden as the concealed of the concealed – allowing each of us to open to it within a core of love.

"The ceremony brought together all that was lost or wounded between the bride and the groom. That healing of souls was happening within me, as I watched it happening within them. They were me. They were the heart of my parents. They were the beginning of me. I knew that my mother was gone from this world; but her love was still part of me and part of my father. Their union was born as me. It had a beginning before me, and then was birthed as I am. That great presence of love, that was guiding the ceremony, was wedding or crowning these two as one, as me – not as king and queen or prince or saint – but as a crowning of creation itself. No ornament was placed on our heads; and no jeweled ring was placed upon our hands; and no face or voice spoke any words of command or desire. There was no vision of a great being with arms or a head: like a fallen king whose crown is handed down from the head that is not, from the king who once was, to the heir that now is. All of this was going on inside of me, as I watched it take place; until the chariot carried me away across the living road again. I could feel the endless future stretching out in front of me, and the fading past dissolving behind me. What was once seen and felt was an unseen memory. What was yet to come was my unseen imagination. I could feel a current that was my journey from the unseen to the seen and back into the unseen again. Then I woke up, still feeling that love, which was my creation and my birth."

"Oh my dear lad," Vivianne began. "You surely must see all that is here. I scarcely need to interpret what you have so clearly revealed. I am so very proud of who you are. You are so young, but your wise soul is so open and dear to my heart. This is a divine outpouring of your soul's insight: the horses – the origin, the imagination, the emotion, and the revelation – driving you on and on. This vision exposes our divine roots and branches: the tree of life as our living road of elemental source and being. Birthed of a sacred marriage, we are born into a world of wounding and healing, all of us messengers and mentors to each other. In timelessness, without past or future, we are crowned and wed as love within the majesty of creation."

He was indeed a wise soul, evident even as a lad. I was there to see him at that young age. Unlike his father, Galahad knew his heritage at birth, connected to a lineage of priest kings of a sacred bloodline. He had only lived a few years more than a decade, and like his father, sheltered by the idyllic world of Afallon. Until the loss of his mother, there was no memory of pain or suffering. He was born into innocence and learned to move into radiance. Joyous Guard was his place of birth; but he held few memories of it, nor held any responsibility for it. It appeared neither he nor his father would rule an earthly kingdom or would ever wear a worldly crown. Galahad's own image, although commonly handsome, was to him comprised of the vast countenance of the cosmos; and yet, not at all – as the mythic head which is not, as the king who once was or could be, as a descendant priest king, that he may never be. He was born of a branch, of a root, and of a seed of the prima-materia, his soul honed into an acutely guided and released arrow, sent to hit its true mark, defined by the path of the arrow. He would move with mildness through a world of severity and mercy. His new devotional companions were inner radiance, the natural elemental realm, and the maturing awareness of mysticism. He found himself unbound by ideas of man and woman, young and old, life and death – nothing drew him to partake of the conflicted tree of the knowledge of good and evil. He was rooted in Eden's eternal tree of living will and intuition, beyond his own birth and death, beyond the harvested ash limbs for oars and axe handles, beyond the elms cut down for barrel staves and caskets – he had opened to the essence of being.

Chapter Nine ~ **Blood and Light of Song**

What is the essence of being? To the bard, it is the creation of song, rising up within the creative spirit as art, as the love of words, and as the voice of all living hearts. To the saint, it is the light of the soul, as faith and communion on a path of light, and as the love of God as source and origin of all life and love. To the warrior, the king or the queen, it is the blood and bloodline that defines their place in the world, as the surviving sovereignty of their domain, as the pulse and passion of their lives, and as their love of family, tribe and kingdom. Each soul wields a sword, a voice, or a loving hand to take their place in the waking world. Hearts and kingdoms are captured by the song or the sword; while light surrounds and permeates all that lives and loves, in one inseparable current of radiance. It is the claim of pride and power to divide that conquers a people or a soul. So we conjure a hero, a savior, or a god to guide us back to the essence of love.

The bard paints a picture of the hero with words, describing the many faces – both human and divine – that express hope for every mortal to transcend human frailty. A perfect hero becomes a saint, if the human qualities are purified, at least by reputation, and the miraculous appears to radiate from the loving action of the saintly hero. Legend and myth merge to convey the story of such a person, who behaves more godlike than human. Soon the deeds of one include the deeds of many, and all human flaws are forgotten, rendering the immaculate conception of a perfect entity. And yet, wouldn't any flaws give hope to the rest of us mere mortals struggling within our own reality? Or, does this messianic figure need to be unsullied by matter, descending from and ascending to the heavens? In the guise of the infallible ideal, the king of kings or the bear king can leave a trail of stars from Pleiades to Draco to Ursa for us to follow and cast our wishes upon the infinite sky. For the Cymri, the bear king or "the Arthwyr" was this hero of a northern people, who would once, and in the future, rescue us from our conflicted selves and our violent neighbors.

It appears we never fully rise above our tribal past. Any dynastic prince, would-be king, Pendragon or chieftain named Arthwys, Arthen, Arthmael, Artorius or Artúr may see himself as "the Arthwyr", as that heroic immortal bear king following the northern star of destiny. Artúr mac Aedan also had his Christian faith and righteous enablers cheering him on to conquest and control of the north. The enemies, of course, were the pagan peoples and their kings. Conquest or conversion became the credo of the battle-arm of the Church. Artúr saw himself as at least that bloody arm, and likely as the chosen "Arthwyr", even before his own foot grew to fit the imprint on the stone of kings at Dun Airigh. Now he held Caladbolg and a bishop guiding and sanctifying his moves across the borders of the north. Artúr meant well. He was overzealous, not evil. Right was on his side: within his belief and mission to right the wrongs he perceived, regardless of the wrongs he committed in the process. In his mind, he fought for the greater good. One can debate what, exactly, that greater good may be.

Peace is the greater good. But in hindsight, we may see the diminishment of a people, divided and decimated by a difference in ideals. The only ideal outcome of war is peace, which arrives by conquest or is achieved and sustained by compromise. One faction can often force another faction to submit to domination, only to instill resentment. Peace requires the discovery of grace within the divergent factions who desire the end of conflict more than domination. Clearly, it is not the enlightened and peaceful minded who instigate war and conflict – it is the malevolent and self-righteous who strike for first blood, leaving peace to be rediscovered later, beneath the ashes, the graves, and the wounded souls.

Miathi Tribes

Artúr's pride was wounded; and Cyndeyrn perceived the pagan priestesses of the north and their protective hounds of nature as demonic minions of Satan; while the Miathi provided the fertile land for these abominations to continue. Prince Artúr and Bishop Cyndeyrn saw it as their duty to cleanse the land of this evil. Their mission began with a march into the tribal lands of the Miathi, the descendants of the Maeatae, ancient people of Alt Clud and Manau Gododdin, flourishing tribes pushed farther north, first by the Romans, and then by the Cymri. Two great walls in the north had been built by Roman Legions to combat and contain these fierce woad and tattoo painted warriors. Now Artúr and his zealous bishop believed they could conquer them like the Christian Emperor Constantine, fully justified by superior faith. The bishop and his prince had their biased interpretations of the lessons of the ancient biblical tribes who warred and lost, tribes who began as brothers but suffered as slaves to Pharaohs and kings, tribes who wandered in exile, eventually kneeling to Rome, or engaging in a final suicidal battle from a hillfort. History embellished by parable and metaphor often buries the truth from the eyes of the faithful, determined to claim land and people for themselves and their silent gods. Artúr saw himself and the Church as the overlords; while the Miathi were part of the land. Lords will come and go – it is the land that will survive. Artúr's own great great grandfather founded Dalriada, migrating from Eirenn, bringing the Stone of Destiny, believed to be the sacred pillow of the biblical patriarch Jacob, who became Israel and whose twelve sons founded the twelve tribes of Israel. Tribal peoples of the east have divided and scattered to distant lands in the west and north for millennia. Battles, warfare, and marital unions created the paths toward peace, endowing tribal cultures with a rich inheritance of blood and light. All people carry the same fears, passions and aspirations as members of the human family. Their conflicts begin within themselves, soon directed against those closest to them; until a family, a tribe or a kingdom can agree on a common enemy to inflict with instruments of cruelty.

Prince Artúr of Dalriada fought more than a dozen battles in the north. He desired stability, and yet his rigidity led to instability. His self-will forged resentment among his neighbors who revered the land and the elemental world as the life-blood of their goddess, rather than the dominion of a god and his kingdom. The common enemy was not the tribal people of the land. It was the foreign yet inherent states that have always invaded the common peace, covering the landscape of experience like an invasive tree of greater good and lesser evil: until the roots are enmeshed throughout this earth, miring the sprouting seeds of our awareness. Youth, in their zeal, are often unaware, and as unstable as water. Artúr's assault on the Miathi was not condoned by his father Aedan. Reality is rarely as simple as a battle of good versus evil. These northern lands belonged to the Miathi centuries before the Scotti landed on the western shores and founded Dalriada. Legend tells of the ancient kings of the southern Picts, the kings of Scone, the Brude, known as the conquerors of their enemies and the nurturers of their people, honoring the matriarchy of their mothers and grandmothers, and holding back the Romans across the northern lands from the Tyne and the Eden into the highlands, generations before the Romans built their coast to coast walls and milecastles. The ruling descendant of these Miathi kings was Nechtan Mawr, a tribal crowned head not about to let a young Christian prince and his bishop go beyond the Roman ruins with their mission of greater good. Artúr and his troops headed northeast from Ystrellyn toward the village of Migdele. Vanora and her priestesses were aware of this force of arms approaching, quickly abandoning their sacred settlement, alerting Nechtan Mawr of Artúr's advance. The Miathi hillfort was only a few leagues beyond the village. Nechtan sent a small troop to meet Artúr, turning in retreat once they were seen by Artúr's forces. This maneuver enticed Artúr to pursue them, leading him into a trap set below the hillfort of Dun Nechtan. A narrow roadway traversed the marshlands surrounding the hill. As soon as Artúr's troops were spread along the ystryd, Miathi cavalry from the fort, with archers and spearmen from the marsh, inflicted serious harm to Artúr's men. Trapped by the mire of the marsh on two sides, and barred access to Dun Nechtan, Artúr had only two ways out – retreat or death. His army returned to Ystrellyn defeated. This was only the beginning of his troublesome battles.

King Aedan of Dalriada went to his son Artúr's fortress in Ystrellyn soon after he heard of the failed assault on Dun Nechtan. Artúr was still assessing his losses, while planning another attack. Aedan interrupted Artúr's meeting with his chiefs and liegemen.

"It appears you are planning another assault on the Miathi," Aedan addressed his son directly.

"I need some time alone with King Aedan," Artúr dismissed his men.

Cyndeyrn was the last to leave the hall, telling Aedan: "The warriors of our Lord will always prevail."

"After how many martyrs die, led by ignorant lads and overzealous priests?" Aedan challenged the bishop.

"Your eminence, please, allow me some time alone with my father," said Artúr, Cyndeyrn bowing graciously, leaving the hall.

"How was your trip father?"

"Hurried," he answered curtly.

Aedan glared at his son and then continued, "Your attack of Dun Nechtan should have been reviewed by at least Rhydderch and me if not the entire Cymric Cylch. There may have been other agreements with the Miathi underway that may now be impossible."

"I believed there was an urgency; and thought the element of surprise would catch Nechtan off-guard," Artúr explained.

"The surprise element for you was your defeat – no surprise to Nechtan! He's been fighting the Cymri, the Cruithni and the Scotti for decades. No pup with a mythic sword is going to catch him off-guard. You clearly cannot see what is at risk here: we need the Miathi as allies, with Lothian and Rheged nearly headless, and their courts of bed-hopping queens a tumble away from being buggered by Bryneich and the Angles. Now with the Miathi on edge, we are nearly surrounded by enemies!"

"Rhydderch would surely recognize the threat to Christian kingdoms by these pagans. My own wife was corrupted by their abhorrent priestesses."

"Rhydderch recognizes more than anyone the value of alliances. He is the reason you and I and the Scotti of Dalriada are part of the Cymric Cylch, ever since that meeting at Maen Gwregys, when they handed you your sword, instead of your head. They now question the wisdom of that choice; but you are my son; and you cannot let this Christian god and your damned bishop ruin you and the kingdoms of the north with foolish strategies. Let me remind you that your mother is also a pagan – which is a foolish term! Anyone born outside of a citadel, raised on the land with reverence for the elemental world is a pagan. Adam and Eve in Eden before their fall from grace must have been pagan. How does this religion reconcile the exile of divine children and the sacrifice of the only son of their god to the Romans, to their pagan overlords? Should I do the same with you, my eldest heir? Or should I simply wait for you to destroy yourself and your allies in the name of your jealous god?"

"I forgive you father, for your blasphemy against God. Can you forgive me for my attack of our enemies who killed a monk and a patrol of my men, while they were seeking my adulterous wife?"

"Your wife has done no more than many husbands have done. Not to say her disloyalty should not be reprimanded; but to burn a wife to death for failing to love you is hardly a loving act of forgiveness. Let her go to her lover. Disown her, and disavow your love for her. Find another young bride who will be loyal. These things are not valid grounds for war; although they have been far too many times. Wounded pride is the death of men and kingdoms: where perhaps you think you will find your place in heaven, more likely create a hell that will be your legacy. Furthermore, in this rash charge towards heaven's gate, you are clearly unaware that Colum Cille has been meeting with Nechtan Mawr, and believes he may even become a Christian convert, at some point in the future – if you and your bishop haven't closed that door to an alliance with Rhydderch and other reasonable Christians."

"I had not even considered the possibility that King Nechtan might become a Christian. I will not stage another attack on the Miathi without consulting you or King Rhydderch, father," Artúr conceded.

"Now it is likely that the Miathi will be the next to strike at us, lad. Nechtan Mawr will see your assault as an invitation to regain the ancient lands of the Miathi, while we are clearly in disarray," Aedan forewarned.

King Aedan didn't stay long in Ystrellyn, returning to Dun Airigh to meet with King Rhydderch about the increased Miathi threat. When Aedan arrived home, Rhydderch and Colum Cille were there to greet him.

"At last, some wiser Christians to discuss the mounting threat of 'pagan invasion'," Aedan said as he embraced each of them.

"Perhaps it is the sword Caladbolg that gives your son the heavy hand to his good intention?" Colum Cille replied.

"That, and the angry zeal of your fellow bishop, Cyndeyrn, still battling his bastard origins, beyond their graves," Aedan retorted.

"But as you have said: wiser heads of church and crown are here now to repair past aggressions, or prepare for what may come," Rhydderch added.

"Yes, thank you both for meeting with me here. I believe you Rhydderch, are at the greatest risk, with the Miathi just to the north of Dun Barton. And Colum Cille, I don't know how to approach this Christian zeal; while you so earnestly build bridges, others are burning them down. You have lived through this kind of conflict in Eirenn, exiling you here in Dalriada years ago," Aedan stated.

"And it was a godsend. You and my other cousins were so generous in embracing me, all too aware I am sure, that a time like this might arise," said Colum Cille.

"We were aware indeed; and yet I never imagined that one of my own sons would be an aggressive arm of the Church," replied Aedan.

"Clans are divided by the different ways they carry the cross. I was at odds with my own bishop, back in Eirenn, God rest his soul. The Celtic Church of Eirenn is not the Catholic Church of Rome. Even among the so-called pagan priestesses of Afallon, there is a strong vein of Gnosticism and reverence for Mary Magdalene. These divisions among Christians are making their attacks upon those that they deem pagan even more severe. I believe it is to instill fear among their own not to waiver," explained Colum Cille. "And still, I hope to bring Nechtan Mawr across that welcoming bridge that is at the heart of Christianity. With this attack, we have surely lost some ground. There are many of the Miathi who need little provocation to attack Christians, when overzealous Christians have harassed and burned Miathi priestesses alive."

"Nechtan Mawr is a fierce adversary. We must prepare for his likely advance south," said Rhydderch. "I hope that you, Father Colum, can find a way to dampen the fervor of our flame bearing Christian brothers, while Aedan and I deal with the military threat."

"If you could speak to my son, as a Christian, father, perhaps you can give him wiser spiritual guidance than he has been receiving. His views have become so narrow as to allow little light to break through. I believe he will listen to you and Rhydderch," Aedan pleaded.

"I believe that I can find a way to his Christian heart. Your son is full of youthful zeal. He must see Nechtan as a potential Christian brother. But here, I have his two fathers before me: one of blood and one of spirit, fostering his soul in this life. I must confide with you, Aedan, what I have seen in my visions of your Prince Artúr," Colum Cille aroused his attention.

"Will he indeed succeed me?" Aedan asked.

"I do not see that as his future," Colum Cille revealed.

"Then it must be Domangart or Eochaid Find, surely one of them?" Aedan asked further, as his wife Queen Domelch and his three youngest sons entered the hall.

"The one who runs to me, Aedan – he will be your successor," said Colum Cille as he turned to face the wee lads, Eochaid Buide running straight up to the holy man, embracing the robes of his godfather with glee. "There is your answer Aedan. Raise him wisely. Your legacy will be secure in his hands."

It was only a few weeks after that meeting that the Miathi descended around Loch Lomond. As much as Aedan, Rhydderch and Colum Cille desired to reign-in the Christian zeal, they did not foresee the march of over a hundred Christian novitiates, devoted students of Cyndeyrn, approaching the Miathi with prayers and choral chants; only to be mowed down by the relentless tribal warriors, gathered at Loch Lomond for battle – not to be converted to a new faith. Cyndeyrn and Artúr were furious. While Rhydderch and Aedan were shocked and saddened by the senseless massacre of scores of the naively ignorant, parading like bleating lambs before lions. Over a period of months, five battles ensued between the Miathi and Artúr of Dalriada, with the support of Rhydderch and Aedan's additional forces. The Miathi used the terrain well to their advantage: staging attacks in mossy or marshy lands where the cavalry of the Cymri and Scotti were less effective. Losses multiplied on both sides, as autumn leaves changed color from green to blood red, falling quickly to earth, with flurries of icy lace dropping from the darkening skies, allowing the perpetual change of seasons to create a needed hiatus from the bloodshed.

Artúr and his troops were weary after this onslaught of Miathi tribal attacks. The Miathi realm of the vast northern lands of Prydain was a diverse territorial region where tribes and clans had banded together against a common threat ever since the Roman occupation. Artúr announced himself as a new common threat to their ancient way of life and to the sacredness of their native spiritual beliefs. Many tribal peoples of Prydain would have been quite content to live in their secluded havens by the sea, in the quiet solitude of the mountains, or hunting within their rich dense forests. Aggressive kingdoms disturbed this peace with willful force, imposing their agendas to re-conceive the known world as a power structure of foreign kings, requiring the conquered to conform to the belief systems of distant gods. To the native tribes, their gods were within the land and the elements, and within the Otherworld of their dreams – realms of the souls of their ancestors. This land embodied their place of peace as the landscape of their spirit. Ironically, battles began again in the spring at Dun a Bhais, "the hills of peace", each side falling back into conflict, justified in their own motives and judgmental bias.

Celyddon Dreams

The greater blows to the north came later, with battles beginning in Coed Celyddon, the forests at the center of Cymric held lands between the Roman Walls. Bryneich's alliance with the Angles was a writhing serpent in the way of unity for the north. Anna Morgause, widow of King Loth was now even more influenced by her father Morcant Mwynfawr, and her sister, Queen Marganna of Bryneich. Within this viperous clan of in-laws, Marganna was the venomous adder on the path, seducing Wledig when she could, creating discord, biting at the heels of the Cymric horsemen, perilously engaged on two battle fronts. The wise observers of Afallon or the druids of the wood found little recourse to the paths of destruction cut through their fields and forests of tranquility. Myrddin Wyllt made his way through the Celyddon Wood to meet with the Christian Prince Artúr who instigated or was lured into this conflict at the edges of the sacred forests. Artúr had found a secluded spot within the dense wood to practice his movements with the sword Caladbolg before dawn. Myrddin appeared suddenly out of the shadows.

"Who goes there?" Artúr called out, poised in battle-stance.

"A forest ghost from your past, lad," said Myrddin, as he quickly became more visible in the dawning light.

"Oh, Myrddin, I thought you were the enemy," Artúr responded, relieved.

"Am I the enemy?" Myrddin challenged him.

"Well, of course not, dear old friend, I meant that I thought you might be a spy from Bryneich or Bernicia. How are you old man? And, what on earth are you doing here in this embattled wood?"

"I step out of time here, out of the realm of Prydain, into an expansive nemeton. This wood is my sanctuary. Your battles, dear prince, intrude upon this sacred space," Myrddin answered.

"You might want to tell Marganna and her bastard son and the Angles of the east your grievances. If not for them, I would not be here thrashing about with an army of weary men."

"Thrashing about is it?" Myrddin confronted the prince. "I watched your practice of the power of the mountains and streams for a while before you realized that I was here. How do you reconcile your practice of these ancient movements and all that they entail with your newfound Christian faith? Are you here to be one with the natural world or to conquer it?"

"I see no need for any reconciliation. My practice of these movements has no relation to my faith," said Artúr, defiantly.

"Ah, then it appears your old mentor has failed you, since you fail to see that the movement in harmony with the natural world is the essence of what you call 'pagan'. The failure is in your self-deception: because the natural world and the divine reality are inseparable. Life, with its movement and vitality, is an aspect of God, demonstrating features of the divine whole. This wood is not a pagan temple, it is the embodiment of divine life," Myrddin declared.

"I respect you, my dear old friend; but your words are blasphemous to me," Artúr responded.

"And your actions are hypocrisy to me. You cannot separate yourself from nature. You are a natural being as well as a spiritual being. The power of the mountains and streams flows through you. Your blood is fed by the earth, by the creatures of nature, and by the light that is the essence of life. I too have battled with the darkness of the mind – but the light prevailed. Ideas that divide, separate and subjugate are shadows we create, concealing the light, love, and essence of our souls. Your savior did not battle and draw blood. He brought light. He would not even allow the ear of his enemy to be severed. He wanted to be heard, for love to be heard, for divinity to be heard, not just from him, but heard in the wood, in the stone, in the air, and in the earth as in heaven."

"These pagans have killed men of God!" Artúr shouted.

"Christians have killed countless men and women whose spirits were pure and loving, darkening the name of their vengeful god. Didn't your savior say, 'whatsoever you do to the least of these, you do to the one spirit'? Isn't that the message he wanted you to hear?"

"You are not a Christian, dear old friend. I rely on Bishop Cyndeyrn for his understanding of the words of our Savior. The Church is founded on the Word of God and His apostles, for centuries now. That is where I place my faith."

"It appears that the Church has lost the truth to the structure built on a failed foundation. Hidden voices of the apostles have been silenced. The 'word' and love of divinity has been divided, with a separated message for those who follow the Church. My church is everywhere and within everything and everyone. It is in the air we breathe, the water we drink, in the warmth of the sun, and on every path of the earth. That is the voice of divinity heard directly. I hear it through the day and night and within my dreams – beyond the encroaching din of battle. I hope that you listen for that divine voice, deep within yourself, instead of biased priests; and even possibly listen with the ear of your enemy. You may think that you battle for a greater cause; but it is not the cause that bleeds. Men battle and die in their own person. Take what I say to heart. That is where the soul hears divinity," said Myrddin, before embracing Prince Artúr and vanishing back into the woodlands.

Artúr and his men, along with a legion of warriors from Alt Clud and Dalriada had been battling Angles and mercenaries from Bryneich in and around the forests of Celyddon for weeks. The Cymri had made some ground, pushing the enemy northeast toward Bryneich, Artúr finally taking a stand at the old Roman fort, Caer Guinion, most of the Roman buildings still standing, stark-white against the rich green terrain and shadowy edge of the woodlands. The fort was near the eastern line of defense held by Nudd Hael and his men of Selgow. Artúr's army had the strength of the fortification, out from the forests and protected from the sporadic attacks within wood and thicket. The Angles were similar to the Miathi in their reliance on battle by attrition, wearing down the garrisoned armies with sudden strikes and raids.

At Caer Guinion, Artúr had time to ponder Myrddin's rebuke. He had carried the image of the mother of Christ on his shield, yet somehow forgetting to listen for her gentle guiding voice within his heart, and failing to feel her loving touch on his shoulder, if he could possibly open his awareness to the level of depth suggested by the mystic Myrddin Wyllt. Artúr had lapsed from his early mentoring by Myrddin, Gawain, Owain and the lads of Afallon. He also failed to fulfill the opportunity of having been placed in the unique position to forge a bond between northern kingdoms, and between the Scotti, the Cymri and the Picts. He held the heritage of all three. The power of the mountains and streams were imbedded into his development as a warrior; and he was exposed to both native and Christian beliefs. He chose one ideology over all others, believing his Christian Lord God did ultimately rule over all others. There was much to be reconciled between Artúr's faith and practice, as Myrddin had pointed out. The warring world of Prydain would not readily conform to his beliefs.

Artúr's first night at Caer Guinion he dreamed that he was in the forests of Celyddon again. Myrddin was ranting obscure verses, standing atop a large stone within a small clearing. Artúr attempted to clearly hear and fully grasp each word; while ethereal pagan priestesses scantily clad in silken gowns, laughed and whispered, disappearing between the aisles of ascending timbers of the darkened wood. They seemed to hear his puzzled thoughts, mocking his straining reach for an understanding of the enigmatic import of Myrddin's verse. Cyndeyrn appeared, rattling a crosier at the druid bard, as Myrddin continued his supernatural oratory unabated.

"And now the foreign church, void of birch or elder vision, upholds its shepherd's crutch, to rail against the stone, beheld by raven, crane and lynx, standing over bone – of Adam's rib – so pulled that ash and elm begat the world; and sleeping man was lulled, into his fallen stupor, and sword of flame concealed the gates, for murdering our brothers, clan, and distant kin – the raven, buck and peregrine – and claim this life a sin."

At this point, Cyndeyrn held up with his other hand an ornate cup filled with blood, splashing it upon the towering standing stone, the maen expanding in its size and significance. Artúr then noticed at the base of the prominent stone a footprint filled with blood. As he stepped forward, an ancient man arose from sleep, disturbed by Artúr's sudden appearance. Artúr mouthed these words that the ancient one spoke in unison with an oddly echoing voice: "from Dan even to Beersheba." Then the ancient one walked off into the trees, seemingly climbing a stairway into the darkness; when there was no stairway to be seen. High within the treetops, the ancient one wrestled with another being of light, illuminating the crowns and foliage of the great trees. As the struggle continued, Artúr could scarcely see the figure of the ancient one, but could feel the wrestling within himself.

Artúr called out: "Who am I? Why am I here in this confounding grove? What is this struggle all about?"

Myrddin answered by resuming his ecstatic verse once more. "You struggle for your soul, immersed within a well; a thirsting image you had thought could shelter you from hell. In heaven, you are not to play an earthly role; but something you might be, as true as ever spoke, and would not be a tree: willow, hazel – even oak. If all display in verse, upon immortal yew, were seen in stark reverse – a tree, a leaf, a sprout, a seed – as all the pages torn of leaves to hide and live and feed, from books of self reborn."

Artúr reeled in vision, as if wise Myrddin's bardic words had etched upon his mind the reprimand he had delivered days before. The forest of Artúr's dream was alive with a myriad of beasts and fowl. He heard the call of creatures, of every shape and form. His senses were immersed in a world of fluid imagery, in-touch with the elemental realm, a realm he seldom thought of during his waking hours. The dream world seemed to be taking Artúr into places he would not choose to go. Perhaps Myrddin had opened a window into other aspects of Prince Artúr's conflicted soul. After Myrddin's delivery of verse, Cyndeyrn ranted away, as if to counter Myrddin's verse with scriptural refrains.

"Many false prophets shall arise and deceive many. Take heed that no man deceive you. You shall hear of wars and rumors of wars. All these things must come to pass; but the end is not yet. For kingdom shall rise against kingdom, and there shall be famines, and pestilences, and earthquakes in diverse place. All these are the beginnings of sorrows."

Myrddin quickly responded: "Because iniquity shall abound, and the love of many shall wax cold. You call on your sacred book; and I answer in kind. Your fires of redemption have left this lad's heart cold. Now he finds himself in the midst of battles he must endure. And you offer him nothing but the beginnings of sorrows? You are an echo of a book of another time; and the shadow of a hatred that continues. Though you speak with the tongue of men and angels, and have not love, charity, and compassion – you are the harsh sound of rash symbols. Men have made themselves slaves to myths by making gods of brass, clanging then about, battling truth with beliefs, draining the well of life beyond completion. This is the world of our creating, revealing moment by moment, in dream or awake, what we create and conceal, what we sustain, and what we may eliminate and illuminate. It is each one of us who must awaken."

With those words, Artúr woke up, not quite sure where he was. He saw the Roman masonry of Caer Guinion lit by the dawning sun, recalling his surroundings, astonished by how much the teaching of Myrddin Wyllt had lingered in the recesses of his mind all of these years. That brief encounter in Celyddon Wood must have triggered all that he had once known and believed. Now he questioned the integrity of his attacks on the Miathi, while still battling his pagan rivals in Bryneich.

It was a quiet morning. The enemy had retreated to the eastern hills; but soon a courier brought word of an assault being mounted by the Angles in the west at Caer Lliwelydd; while these recent battles had diverted substantial Cymric forces to the east. Artúr rallied the troops, sending couriers to Rhydderch and Aedan, all heading to Rheged for a joined battle. As he secured his armored hauberk, he suddenly recalled these lines of scripture: "A troop shall overcome him; but he shall overcome at the last. Hold to the wilderness, with men of might and men of war fit for battle, that can handle shield and buckler, whose faces are of lions, and are as swift as the roes upon the mountains."

Prince Artúr, like most of his peers, had romanticized battle, believing their persistence would bring victory and glory – the makings of myth and legend. Bold confidence would face failure or success, mustering will, or at least trust in each man who fought beside him. There had always been a grotesque indulgence of some kings who waged wars while never entering the fray. Artúr led the field, believing his God would ride before him, as he wielded Caladbolg – confident that the sword was God's divine gift to him.

Anglican armies had been attacking Caer Lliwelydd for days before Artúr and the troops of Dalriada and Alt Clud had arrived. The Angles also assailed Artúr's men en-route, but Artúr prevailed, heading on to Rheged. The fortress withheld the siege, even after relentless night raids by the Angles. Once reinforcements had arrived, the Cymri, the Scotti and Prince Artúr defeated the invaders, sending them retreating into the wilderness, no match for the cavalry and archers of the Cymri. Finally there seemed to be a lull in the waves of battle after battle. Artúr and his troops returned to Ystrellyn. Rhydderch and Aedan left part of their armies in Rheged, bolstering the forces of Llywarch Hen and the sons of Urien. Caer Lliwelydd was a strategic point near the west end of the Wall of Tyne. Kings and Wledig of the Cymric Cylch knew the Angles, Saxons or even the Miathi might attempt another strike there in the future.

It was only the morning after Artúr's return to Caer Ystrellyn that the Miathi staged another attack at his fortress. They were likely hoping to hit their nemesis when he was weakened and recovering from his battles in Celyddon and Rheged, surprising his weary troops on their home ground. But Artúr's cavalry were able to hold the Miathi at the Ford of Frew before they reached Caer Ystrellyn. Nechtan's men backed-off, but had seized an ancient hillfort to the west called "og nyth" meaning the nest of harrows, mentioned in tales told by the local elders about the abandoned Miathi stronghold used against the Roman legions. Nechtan Mawr was breathing new life into this ancestral fortress on Myot Hill. These battle sites near the tributaries of the Firth of Forth were strike points for the Miathi to inflict blow after blow upon Prince Artúr's troops, while the Angles continually encroached on Cymric lands to the east.

The night after battle, Artúr dreamed again of the Celyddon forests. He was riding away from a battlefield toward Caer Ystrellyn with his full retinue behind him, suddenly to find himself riding all alone into Celyddon Wood. Myrddin appeared on the road in front of him, surrounded by birds and beasts of the woodlands, moving towards the baffled prince, Myrddin reaching his arms forward, with every creature coming at Artúr like eager pups – only to quickly vanish within a stone's throw of his approach. Artúr pulled the reigns of his horse to a dead stop, looking about, astonished, his heart pounding fast, wondering if what he saw was even real. He stepped down from his mount, looking into the shaded wood for any signs of life. When he faced back toward the road, Cyndeyrn was standing there right beside him.

"You are the first born, your foot perfectly fit to the Stone of Kings," Cyndeyrn kept reinforcing Prince Artúr's role as the eldest son of King Aedan, chosen heir of Dalriada, and chosen by Rhydderch Pendragon as battle lord of Caer Ystrellyn. "Aedan could have chosen one of your younger brothers, and Rhydderch could have chosen his own son to command Ystrellyn. Our Lord God has smiled upon you, Artúr of Dalriada."

At that point, Myrddin re-appeared with a bear cub on one arm, and a raven on the other. The raven took flight. Myrddin gave the bear cub a quick hug, gently letting him down to the ground to scurry off into the forest. Then Myrddin turned to Bishop Cyndeyrn saying, "Your ingratiating is relentless, Cyndeyrn: for you know full well that your holy book is filled with instances of the second or youngest heir being chosen by some act of divine providence over his elder brothers. The patriarch of the Stone of Destiny, Jacob was chosen over Esau, and Jacob's eleventh son Joseph was favored over all of his brothers. Who is to say what destiny awaits Prince Artúr? You flatter this Christian prince to further your own ambitions. Joseph ben Jacob was a visionary, and an interpreter of dreams, clearly displaying divine favor, his treacherous elder brothers jealously selling him into slavery, only to unwittingly further Joseph's destiny to become governor of Egypt."

"Our Lord Jesus Christ is the only true heir of God, not any of these ancient patriarchs," Cyndeyrn rebutted.

"Ah, well, let me add to them. Your book begins with Cain and Abel, as first and second sons, one exiled for the murder of the other. And let us not forget the prodigal son; or is that just a parable? But then, aren't they all parables – for these our brothers who are dead and are alive again, who were lost and are found? We find them within ourselves, not in our mythic stories," Myrddin audaciously illuminated scripture for the bishop.

"You speak in riddles, blasphemer!" The bishop barked.

"Myths are riddles, or clues, clues to the greater experience of being; while we repeatedly riddle ourselves with incoherent religions," Myrddin responded.

"You are a heretic and a demon of the beasts that you embrace. God is our creator. We owe praise to Him," Cyndeyrn proclaimed.

"I don't owe allegiance to an imaginary apparition, believed to be separate from the being that I am. I am that essence of being. The beasts of nature appear to me. I observe them. Creation appears around me; but I am the center that observes it or fears it or loves it."

"You are born in sin, only redeemed by God's grace!" Cyndeyrn shouted.

"I experience and observe my own birth and death. I meet my fate within myself. But the vision, the point of observation – does not die. Everything imaginable is conjured in the mind: beasts or benevolence, demons or angels, gods or devils. Artúr finds us in his mind, in his dreams, and observes us in his sleep. We live or die; we are found or lost, as he sleeps or wakes."

Artúr awoke in his own bed at Caer Ystrellyn, his mind divided between his two mentors. He prayed to Lord Jesus to guide him through this turmoil.

The Gododdin

Within months, the call to battle rose again, near the border of Bryneich at the southern slopes of the Eildons. Nudd Hael and his clans of Selgow called the place Bowdon. This was the first battle in years where Artúr, Llenlleawg and Gawain were all three together on the same side of the conflict. It was hoped that they could stop the Angles and Bryneich with a strong victory for the Cymric Cylch. The region held reverence for Christian and pagan, with legends of saints and the Sidhe having long standing there. Llen and Gawain had been defending lands in the Lothians since the passing of King Loth. Predictably, Queen Anna Morgause and her sons were now overshadowed by her father Morcant "Mynyddog" Mwynfawr. He was as ravin as a wolf in his seizure of power, during the mourning period of his son-in-law's demise, well before his grandsons could claim and divide their inheritance of the Lothians. Gawain held no claim, and had no desire to rule his father's kingdom, or incite a war with his half-brothers. There was no matriarchal descendant, other than possibly Ceindrych Penasgell as daughter of Loth's sister, daughter of Nyfain and Cynfarch, and matrilineal descendant of Ingenach Hen. Penasgell had no desire to rule, even if Loth's in-laws would consider the renewal of matriarchal sovereignty – which they would not. The great divide there rested in the alliance of Morcant Mwynfawr with his other daughter Marganna, Queen of Bryneich, Coledauc her king and husband, and Morcant's grandson and namesake Morcant Llofrudd. Lothian was now in effect allied with Bryneich and the Angles. The Battle of Bowdon was an effort to weaken that dark alliance – and it did. The duplicitous King Coledauc, influenced by the mountainous pressure of his father-in-law Morcant Mwynfawr, now the de facto ruler of Lothian, withdrew his army of Bryneich just prior to the battle, enabling the Cymri to gain a greater victory over the Angles. This was all part of Mynyddog Mwynfawr's plan to regain the graces of the Cymric Cylch, secure his hold on Lothian, and to protect Lothian from a future advance of the Angles to the north.

Morcant Mynyddog Mwynfawr played it up in grand style: hosting warriors and nobles at Arthsedd for an entire year, punctuating battle training with feasting and a seemingly endless fount of mead and wine. Lads came from the farthest Cymric kingdoms to the south, and most distant Cymric outposts of the north. Bards from all over arrived to present their verses of song at this crossroads of their prodigal journeys. Aneirin and I were there part of the year to see the spectacle and ply our craft. The aging Taliesin was also there with us, recognized by most every bard as the elder master of the art. Gawain and Llenlleawg guided part of the training, both in their forties at that time; committed to their private lives to the west and north, neither would take part in the much anticipated battle. Prince Artúr utterly detested Morcant Mwynfawr, the vile brother of his fostering mentor Rhydderch Pendragon. So, Artúr would not take part in Morcant's battle plan. The most incredible moment of the yearlong event for me was the discovery of a lad from beyond Bannog and Maen Gwyngwn named Llif.

Aneirin and I both noticed the lad at the same instant, in the midst of training with Llenlleawg. Vivianne was there, seeing the look on my face she voiced what I knew in my heart.

"Yes, Cian, he is you son, born near Migdele nearly two decades ago," Vivianne whispered in my ear as the chill of realization swept across my flesh.

When the men had paused from their training, Llen and the lad were talking together; and I approached.

"The lads look good," I said to Llen.

"Yes, there are some sharp lads, like Llif here, trained in the north with the power of the mountains and streams," Llen replied.

"I can see that," I said, reaching out to take the lad's hand. "I am Cian, bard of Rheged and Afallon. Llif is a fine name for a lad trained in the power of the streams, the current, and the flow."

"Ha, ha," Llen and Llif laughed. "Yes, only those trained in the art get that, Master Cian," said Llif, acknowledging that I knew his name actually meant current or flow.

"I am hardly a master, just Cian is fine . . . so, you were born in Migdele Vivianne tells me?"

"Yes, Llen mentored me over the years, when he traveled through the region. His lady has known my mother for quite some time," said Llif.

"And your father, did he practice the art as well?" I asked.

"I never knew my father. I lived with the Miathi for a time. My mother is a priestess of the Attacotti," Llif explained.

"Ah, well, the power is strong with you lad. It shows your heritage, and at such a young age. I hope we can speak again," I said, holding back the truth simmering inside of me, ready to overflow.

"Thank you," he said with a warm smile. "I look forward to hearing your verse tonight."

"Certainly lad," I answered, resisting the urge to throw my arms around him and tell him who I was.

I could hardly sleep that night, realizing that I had a son, a fine lad, mentored by Llenlleawg. I could not have imagined how powerful this connection would be to me – as if the source of creation had suddenly flooded my life with a vibrant new stream. It was strange to think that he had existed all of these years and I did not have any idea of it. I thought of that night, years ago, dancing around the fire with those priestesses, my mind reeling, during my body's ecstatic release. That instant was the inception of my son, my son – even those words felt strangely beyond belief. Somehow I knew the moment I saw him: not in my mind, but much deeper, from seed to offspring within my core of being. I pondered those thoughts throughout the night, rising the next day to watch my son from a distance, training for battle, a battle he may not return from. What is this life, where some live long and others leave much too soon? There are no easy answers. It is the bard who brings voice to what we all question deep inside. That following night, gathered around a fire, many of the lads, my son among them, sat to hear the songs of the bards, after a long day of training. It was my turn to sing verse from my heart; and so I sang these words, birthed from my hours of contemplation, but never voiced before.

> "The wind may cast a seed,
> from the tree of life;
> and from it we may bleed,
> and carry on in strife,
> to find our purpose here,
> in art, in love, in battle fray,
> to conquer hidden fear,
> and let our hearts display,
> a window to the sky;
> where we may travel on,
> in earth, or when we die,
> upon the air beyond;
> because we hold a fire,
> that simmers in our water,
> to feed endless desire,
> in every son and daughter:
> that from a single tree,
> countless seeds belong,
> to grow, expand, and be,
> blood and light of song."

I received a round of applause and cheers as I gently wept. Aneirin took my hand and raised it high, shouting: "Cheers one and all to Cian – the wheat of song – feeding us divine bread once again!"

I finally had a chance to speak with Llif alone after the last bard sang. Llif stood tall and sure of himself: as a stronger reflection of myself in my youth, but favoring his mother, as much as I could even recall her countenance.

"Master Cian . . . surely I can call you Master after that verse – so bold and true," the lad said to me.

"Thank you, lad, there is something I am compelled to tell you, that Lady Vivianne has told me. I had been to Migdele only once, nearly two decades ago. What Vivianne told me, I feel it in my bones; lad, she says I am your father. And, I know you go off to battle soon. This may be our only chance to know each other. Forgive me for not seeking you out. I did not know until yesterday that I even had a son."

The lad's eyes began to tear-up as he embraced me with two decades of love all at once. We cried together for a moment, and then quickly regained composure to talk well into the night. He spoke about being raised among the tribe of priestesses, with male mentors entering and leaving his early life, Llen being the most consistent and stalwart. I told him of my strikingly similar youth, raised in Afallon, mentored by Morfyn, Taliesin and Aneirin. It was an incredible exchange, both of us seeing our parallel fates, aligned yet separate: one as a bard and one as a warrior. We finally retired to rest nearing dawn. He had a vigorous day of training ahead. Taliesin and Vivianne left for Afallon that morning. The Master had sung a number of splendid compositions honoring Urien Rheged, and other epics of bold warriors traversing worlds. Taliesin appeared old and frail, until he sang out his verses with a surge of power coursing through him, illuminating us all.

The lads trained hard during the weeks that followed. Young Galahad trained with then, but Llen kept him out of this impending battle. Vivianne and other seers did not carry positive visions of the coming conflict. There were plenty of other regions to defend in those days. Battle strategies were formed during that year in Lothian at Arthsedd. Techniques of shield walls and spear defenses were mastered by scores of lads: learning to fight as one mind in unified action. The lads would lead others, adding to their numbers before the final conflict. Over three-hundred comprised an elite force, backed by several thousand on the battlefield.

Two days before their departure south, we received news from Afallon telling us that Taliesin had passed away quietly in the night. I had one brief moment to say goodbye to Llif, my rediscovered son, before leaving with Aneirin, Llen, Galahad and Gawain for Afallon to mourn the loss of our great mentor and Pen Bard. His towering verse eclipsed us all, from his time as protégé of Master Myrlyn, to carrying on his own legacy as a unique guiding voice of vision. A memorial was held at Afallon, but the Master's body was interred at Llyn Geirionydd, celebrated by a Gorsedd, attended by bards from across the land.

After the memorial, Aneirin and I went back into eastern Rheged to find the troops from Arthsedd assembled for battle against the Angles. The site was near the borders of Bernicia and Deira's acquired territories of the former Cymric Kingdom of Ebrauc, between Afon Tees and Afon Swale, on the plains of the Swale Valley, in the region called Catraeth. Although we still mourned the loss of Taliesin, we honored him as bards of the Cymri, as witnesses to tell of the battle that was meant to define the future of the Cymri in the north. The Angles of Bernicia and Deira had amassed an enormous force of thousands of warriors. Even with few horsemen in the Saesneg ranks, the sheer numbers presented a staggering opposition for the Cymri. Aneirin and I were bards, not fighting men. Traditionally, bards were not even armed, and never attacked during conflicts among the Cymri, Scotti and even the Picts. There was no such guarantee with the Saesneg. They were from the foreign cultures of the northern continent, never conquered by the Romans. We knew this and felt it with unsettling waves of fear through our bodies, untempered by battle.

The battle began with both armies moving as vast entities of thousands of men. We observed from a hillside the mechanized attacks of giant forms of shielded warriors: the Angles as a wedge, and the Cymri as a wall or solid citadel of men and arms; except for the Cymric cavalry who would strike at the flanks of the enemy formations, and then retreat to strike again and again. The battle raged from dawn until dusk, day after day, with the Cymri inflicting losses against the Saesneg far beyond what their numbers would have suggested. It was a stark task against overwhelming odds. I could not help but think of my son, so young and strong, spending his last drops of blood upon a field of grass and carnage – to what end? These devils from across the sea will not stop invading our lands. The massive forms of battling men pushed each other against the edges of the plain, trampling saplings along with the spent and fatally bloodied youths. Although they no longer looked so youthful, appearing like old battered and weathered men, their faces painted dark blood red like hardened wood, their beaten legs reddened to the thighs. This carnage carried on for seven days. The Saesneg emerged victorious, losing half of their force, it seemed; while we two bards and a few Cymri were the only souls on our side still wandering around stunned within our bodies.

We were captured, and chained to a small tree near the edge of the riverbank. I thought our fates were sealed. Aneirin chanted verse, line after line; and he bid me to remember. I echoed him, as to retain each word he crafted from his soul, until we were one song sounding against the silent heart hollowing echoes of war. We sang of all the fallen lads, some well known, and others only memorable strangers to us; mostly lads of the Gododdin, the lands south of the Firth of Forth, the lands of the Votadini, of Cunedda and Coel Hen. We were no threat to our Saesneg captors. At first they were amused by our endless chanting of verse, laughing at us, throwing stones at us, believing perhaps that we were singing a ritual prayer. Finally they grew impatient with our chatter and shouted at us to halt our recitation. Aneirin and I spoke enough of their tongue to surmise what was said, while their tone left no doubt. One of them, called Eddan the Elder, ordered Aneirin to stand up, the bard's old knees pained by the weight of the chains.

"Du bist ein bard, ya?" asked Eddan.

"Ya, ich bin ein bard," Aneirin answered.

"Besingst du uber Odin?" asked the Angle.

"Ya, ich können," said Aneirin.

"Do you know songs of his people?" Surprised, I asked Aneirin.

"I recall a few. My use of his language is a bit shaky. I'll give it a go, and hope for the best," he answered.

Although he sang the first seven lines in an Anglican tongue, they were simple enough for me to understand and retain. I translate them here, and remembered them for the rest of my life.

From prophesy it is held:
The sun was not,
Where she was held.
The moon was not,
What he beheld.
The stars knew not,
What light compelled.

At that moment, without warning, that Angle bastard Eddan the Elder swung an axe into the skull of my dear mentor, severing his head in two, right before my horrified eyes. Aneirin slumped and fell to the ground, collapsing on his knees, leaning slowly over to the left. I trembled in abject terror as his murderer laughed with his comrades, saying something about a song to Odin. He approached me with the bloody axe, taunting me as if I would be his next victim. But he turned away; and as he walked away from me, he muttered something about "morgen nacht"; that I discerned he meant tomorrow night. I feared that I had only one more day to live. That night the Saesneg drank themselves into silence, as their array of campfires waned in the distant darkness. Later, I heard a rustling nearby, believing it was an animal scavenging the dead. But to my amazement, it was young Galahad, his face painted over with river mud, still revealing his angelic countenance to me.

"Dear lad, how ever did you find me?

"I've been watching for a while, hoping these Angle devils would spare our bards, shocked to witness Aneirin's murder," the lad explained.

"It was utterly devastating. I fear that I am tomorrow night's merciless entertainment," I responded.

"Not while I live, dear friend," said the lad.

"I met my son just weeks ago, and now he and my father of song, Aneirin – both gone, gone from this dark world."

"Let's get out of here before these devils wake from their stupor and add to the tragedy," said Galahad, as he found a way to free my chains from the tree to which I was bound.

I lugged the chains along, careful not to make any sound of metal against metal, we crawled our way through the ravine cut by the river, until we reached the place where he had two horses waiting, making our escape to the west. Shortly after dawn, a pair of riders approached us from the east. Galahad sent me riding on, as he turned to face them.

"They'll catch up to us with your iron chains rattling off this horse. Take to the hills and head west!" He shouted as he charged full tilt at the enemy.

I viewed the encounter from the hillside. The lad was masterful, felling both Angle warriors like saplings. It was so quick; I could hardly believe my eyes. He searched their bodies, bringing their horses up to me on the hill.

"That was quick work," I said.

"No time to dally, they may send others, perhaps a troop. These horses will help us outrun any other trailing devils. I found keys to your shackles. That should speed our retreat as well," Galahad commandingly stated.

"Thank you dear friend," I said, as he removed the chains from my hands and feet. "You're a miraculous lad."

"Well, let's keep this miracle running to the west," he said with a smile.

About halfway to Caer Lliwelydd we were relieved to see a patrol of Cymric warriors riding towards us, led by Gawain.

"Your father warned me that you might break your curfew," Gawain scolded the lad. "I fear the Battle of Catraeth was a complete loss, just as the seers had foretold."

"Not a complete loss – I retrieved one bard. Others may have wandered away. As predicted, it was senseless carnage. The Saesneg forces far outnumbered the Cymri. These Angle hordes are here to stay. We had best prepare Caer Lliwelydd, or set sail for the distant islands," said Galahad.

"The islands sound better and better each season," said Gawain. "Cian, how are you holding up? You must surely be shaken by what you have seen and survived."

"Yes sire," I said. "Aneirin was murdered before my eyes. My newly found son is gone forever, along with the sons and fathers of thousands."

Unable to speak further, I wept as we rode on into the west toward Caer Lliwelydd. Warriors become numb to the slaughter somehow. These scenes of darkness are not for the temperament of most bards. A bard is trained to open his heart and soul to sing of greater light. Young lads crave the honor and prestige of victorious battles, proving themselves stronger that their foes, protecting land and clan, earning a golden torc to adorn their thick necks. We bards follow the lead of the Great Crane Taliesin, the Raven of Awen Master Myrlyn, and Aneirin of the Flowing Verse – great birds of a feather, soaring high in song, dipping quills like oars into the nectar of the gods, to glide within each song we sing, blessed by words and tones to heal the wounded soul.

If Aneirin had not sung the song of Gododdin to me, many of those lads would never have been known to the world and the distant future. For seven days these warriors waded in blood, only one or a few to survive. Each lad's life cut so short, never to sire a child of their own. My own son Llif ap Cian, called "the fierce" by his Cymbrogi; Buddfan ap Bleiddfan "the brave"; Tudfwlch Hir ap Cilydd "the heart of his tribe"; Eithinyn ap Boddw Adaf "the wild bull and battle wall"; the maiden warrior Bradwen, worth any three men; and Aneirin's own brother, Cynwal ap Dynod, and countless more; and one who catches notice for Aneirin's oft-mentioned phrase: because "he was no Arthwyr." None of them were that mythic bear-king; none of them were ferried off to Afallon. All of that mead and blood was poured out into light, upon their darkest day. And when the dark earth covered Aneirin, poetry departed from Gododdin. The verses are long, though much remembered. I was there beside Aneirin to retain all that will be carried on. Here are but a few of those verses, to taste a bit of the mead and blood held in their final breath, that it may shed light on the fallen dead.

Y Gododdin

Men went to Catraeth with the dawn
> gwyr a aeth Gatraeth gan wawr
disheartened by the price of their lives
> dygymyrrus eu hoet eu hanyanawr
their yellow sweet ensnaring mead
> med evynt melyn melys maglawr
in a quick yearlong stupor with scores of troubadours.
> blwydyn bu llewyn llawer kerdwr.

Red neither swordsmen nor ankles
                              coch eu cleddyfawr na phurawr
their swath spearheaded four-part whitewashed
                              eu llain gwynglach a phedryollt bennawr
by means of installation of Mountainous Mwynfawr.
                              rac gorsgord Mynyddog Mwynfawr.

Lads with instincts of men	gredyf gwr oed gws
'round valorous cry	gwrhyt am dias
fleet thick-maned horses	meirch mwth myngvras
under their honorary riders	a dan forddwyd mygrwras
light broad shields	ysgwyt ysgauyn lledan
upon swift lean flanks	ar bedrein mein vuan
swordsmen pale and pure	cleddfwr glas glun
their arms golden.	ethwy eur arfan.

We, who he, for whom	ny bief a vi
gives to these enemies	cas e rof a thi
what better make do	gwell gwneif a thi
upon their strike at unity	ar wawt dy uoli
sooner the wait to the grave	cynt y waet elawr
than to the marriage feast	nogyt y neithyawr
sooner a food for ravens	cynt y vwyt y vrein
than to the bereavement.	nog y argyurein.

Men went to Catraeth with the dawn
                              gwyr a aeth Gatraeth gan wawr
faces unified like a shielded citadel
                              wyneb udyn ysgorva ysgwydawr
rock-solid in plot of a riot
                              crei kyrchynt kynnullynt reiawr
in time the ground roared with their thunder
                              en gynnan mal taran twryf aessawr
men laid down men, pounding men to the ground
                              gwr gorvynt gwr etvynt gwr llawr
oddly high and wide killing blades
                              od uch lled lladei a llavnawr
in swaths of iron and steel mastery.
                              en gystud heyrn dur arbennawr.

I am not whatsoever grievous	nyt wyf vynawc blin
I avenge my imprisonment	ny dialaf vy ordin
I scoff at the laughter	ny chwardaf y chwerthin
– a grain under foot –	a dan droet ronin
my knee stubborn	ystynnawc vy nglin
for allegiance	et ty deyern
to iron chains	cadwyn heyernyn

to cart about both knees
from mead of the drinking horn
of the peasantry of Catraeth
I, not myself, Aneirin
as one knows Taliesin
ovate word-master
to sing Gododdin
before dawn of day follows.

am ben vyn duelin
o ved o vuelin
o Gatraeth werin
mi na vi Aneirin
ys gwyr Taliesin
oveg kywrenhin
neu cheint Gododdin
kynn gwawr dydd dilin.

Men went to Catraeth, for swift fame
    gwyr a aeth Gatraeth, buant enwawc
drank wine and mead from their gold cups
    gwin a med o eur vu eu gwirawt
for a year in preparation, in honorary custom
    blwydyn en erbyn urdyn deuawt
three-hundred and sixty gold-torqued men.
    trywyr a thri ugaint a thyrchant eudorchawc.
Skillful spearmen assembled
    kywyrein ketwyr hyuaruuant
they were there as one assault
    y gyt en un vryt yt gyrchassant
short their lives, long their life's grief
    byrr eu hoedyl hir eu hoet ar eu carant
seven times their number of Saesneg were slain
    seith gymeint o Saesneg a ladassant
out of anger, wives become widows wailed
    o gyvryssed gwraged gwyth a wnaethant
many mothers were wrought tearful eyes.
    llawer mam ae deigyr ar y hamrant.
From the wine and mead feast they went
    o winveith a medveith yd aethant
into genesis – mail-clad – in damp clumsy gown
    e genhyn llurugogyon nys gwn lleith llekynt
before their wide place to dawn
    cyn llwyded eu lleas dydaruu
by means of Catraeth in time to ready their host
    rac Gatraeth oed fraeth eu llu
avoiding mountainous dawn's door
    o osgord vynydawc wawr dru
out of three-hundred, but only one man came back.
    o thrychant namen un gwr ny dyvu.
From the wine and mead feast they made haste
    o winveith a medveith yt gryssyassant
men in need of their soul's fate
    gwyr en reit moleit eneit dichwant
in a bright manner, 'round the wine cup, feasting together
    gloew dull y am drull yt gytvaethant

– wine and mead, a blight and feeble
>
>> gwin a med a mall a amucsant

avoidance – from mountainous but devout ruination
>
>> o osgord vynydawc am dwyf atveillyawc

an oar who dips from my truth of the crane
>
>> a rwyf a golleis om gwir garant

out of three-hundred, some of them made haste
>
>> o thrycant, riallu yt gryssyassant

to Catraeth, sadly, but not one man returned.
>
>> Gatraeth, tru, namen vn gwr nyt atcorsant.

In testimony sung to grasp fellow
>
>> ardyledlawc canu kyman caffat

fighters scattered in shock about Catraeth
>
>> keywyr am Gatraeth a wneath brithret

tread and trampled, scattering of blood
>
>> brithwy a wyar, sathar sanget

made trampling of trees
>
>> sengid wit gwnedd

what mead bears vengeance for
>
>> bual am dal med

and carnage mediates.
>
>> a chalaned kyuurynged.

In testimony sung to fellow prodigals
>
>> ardyledlawc canu kyman ovri

tumult of fire and thunder and tempest
>
>> twrf tan a tharan a ryeurthi

among excellent valorous horsemen
>
>> gwrhyt arderchawc varchawc mysgi

who desire ruddy war
>
>> ruduedel ryuel a eiduni

men made to deprive and dissect
>
>> gwr gwned divudyawc dimyngyei

the gate of measure of land in their earshot.
>
>> y gat or meint gwalt yd y klywi.

On Tuesday they donned their dark armor
>
>> diw mawrth gwisgyssant eu gwrym dudet

On Wednesday they scraped clear their limed shields
>
>> diw merchyr peri deint eu calch doet

Thursday they counted the dead
>
>> divyeu bu diheu eu diuoet

On Friday carnage about was endured
>
>> diw gwener calaned amdygnet

On Saturday they judged their joint effort
>
>> diw sadwrn bu divwrn en kytweithret

On Sunday their blades had endured red
>
>> diw sul eu llavneu rud amdygnet

On Monday they all appeared old and bloodied to their thighs.

                      diw llun hyt benn clun gwaetlun gwelet.

Three-hundred gold-torqued men made haste

                      thrychant eurdorchawc a gryssyant

in the face of turbulence, quickly appearing

                      ym am wyn breithell, bu edrywant

together they liberate, and they slaughter

                      kyt ryladded wy, wy lladdasant

they, who are faithfully admired, until the end of the world

                      a hyt orffen byd edmyg fyddant

and of those who were grieved together with the crane

                      ac or sawl a aetham o gyd garant

sadly, but not one man reappeared.

                      tru, namyn vn gwr nyt enghysant.

He struck while three-hundred were unseated

                      ef gwant tra thrychant echasaf

he who was utmost numb to the slaughter

                      ef lladdai a pherfedd ae eithaf

this time worthy to appease the host stone

                      oedd gwiw ym maen llu llariaf

blazing, he drove horses in winter

                      goddolai o haid meirch y gaeaf

wary of black ravens on fortress walls

                      gochorai vrein du fur caer

though he was no Arthwyr.

                      cyn ni mai ef Arthwyr.

Three-hundred gold-torqued	thrychant eurdorchawc
combatants bloodied	gweddgar gwaenawc
Three-hundred arrogant	thrychant trahaog
united, assembled	cyfun, cyfafog
Three-hundred horses reddened	thrychant meirch godrudd
that even of powerful tendency	a grysiws ganthudd
Of three-hundred cut down	trychwn a thrychant
Sadly, none returned.	tru, nid atcorsant.

I thought that I was the only survivor, but two wounded and bloodied lads were found in the wilds surviving on herbs and berries. The images of Aneirin's head split in two, just steps away, haunted me for the rest of my years. He had such a fine mind. I am shocked to my soul by the brutality of this waking world, still deeply asleep within the grotesque nightmares of violence. Never having known my father, likely a violent man, siring me in violence – Aneirin was my true father figure, mentor, and dear friend. He brought the love of verse out of me, and taught me the elevated love of language, awakening this voice of the human spirit. I learned from him and Taliesin that it is the bard's duty to be that voice of hope and reason in the face of brutal tragedy. We are observers of this waking world and comprise the background of vision that permeates reality, bringing forth glimpses of humanity caught in our own time, creatively spiriting them off to future generations. As long as our voices echo forward into the infinity of time, there will be some trace of these souls who lived, loved and died here.

Battles waged on in the north, with the Miathi continuing their attacks against Artúr and his troops of Caer Ystrellyn, west of the firth, near Afon Carron, north of the Wall of Forth, where Artúr and his brothers battled year after year against Nechtan's raids. The king of the Miathi Picts was wearing them down, until a massive confrontation near the Wall of Tyne, outside the old Roman fort of Camboglanna proved to be the decisive victory for the Miathi. Artúr and two of his brothers were killed. Cyndeyrn managed to wander off the battlefield with Artúr's sword, after delivering a distraught prayer over the prince's body. The bishop trudged into the wetlands, muttering away in Latin, submerging himself in the reedy mire again and again, seemingly trying to purge clean from his mind what he had witnessed that day, his vision of a Christian kingdom dissolved in battle trauma and death. Myrddin Wyllt was the first to find the departed bishop huddled in the marsh, clutching the sheathed Caladbolg as if it were a treasured crucifix. Found hours after the bishop had drowned; Myrddin pried the mythic sword from the holy man's cold, brittle fingers and carried it away. Few knew what happened to the sword. Some believe Myrddin brought it to Rhydderch the Pendragon, his brother-in-law. Some say Llenlleawg and Gwenhwyfar hid Caladbolg away in the north. Others have said Aedan took it to Dun Airigh with his sons for burial. Aedan was able to eventually bring the northern tribes together with his Cruithni in-laws, finding common ground with the Miathi, and keeping the Saesneg below the Wall of Forth. Llen had seemed to disappear. Rumors of him living in the Orcades with Gwenhwyfar continued for decades. Gawain frequently traveled to the Hebrides, maintaining contact with his mother Morcades, Aedan of Dalriada, and Colum Cille. The aging priest of Iona had died before the Battle of Catraeth, leaving a legacy of peace within the western isles. For many, Colum Cille was their Christian Father of the North.

Aneirin was my holy father, baptizing me in the flowing verse and the dynamic spirit of Awen. He and the priestesses of Afallon were not biased against the Christian faith. They were aware of other paths apart from Christianity, and yet knew the teachings of secret and sacred Gnostic texts conveying the hidden voices of Mary Magdalene and the twelve disciples of Jesus. Aneirin had committed many of those texts to memory, as well as epic Greek compositions and the scripture of foreign lands. I did not know the entire pagan song that Master Aneirin drew from in those final minutes of his brilliant life; but I knew that it was a song of creation: a song etched within my mind that seemed to carry Aneirin from Eden to Gododdin and to his return to the Otherworld. I wrote down those last lines he spoke, and continued the song with my own words.

From Prophesy it is held:
the sun was not, where she was held;
the moon was not, what he beheld;
the stars knew not, what light compelled.

And thus it was, when all was laid,
and how it was, that earth displayed,
the world made round, with oceans found;
and giants roamed, the distant sound,
as titans laying fertile land,
conceived upholding mythic vows,
how from their brows, a burg began,
home for reason, to guard and stand,
that from these minds cast into air,
were formed as clouds of angel hair,
so braided and entwined in seasons,
they spread their vines most anywhere.

The flesh of earth and sweat of seas,
were clothing for the bones of dead,
and heirs of trees combed to the skies,
of vaulted skulls, beyond the heads
of dragon hulls, of mortal ties,
consumed in folly and melancholy,
besotted ills, from dual trees,
below, above, where man and mate
begat their fate ~ the life and spirit
of soul and love, and power of motion,

and choice to fear it, with pride of wills,
and senses found, and senses lost,
and every notion of ill or good,
in wounded cost, where one once stood,
at crossroads of this place,
to feel the innocence and grace,
seeing clear, beyond the fog,
carving from that ancient log,
a vessel formed of heart of wood,
that every soul is understood,
to be that life of holy spark,
in covenant with sacred arc,
and in calamity of time,
to resonate with mortal rhyme,
eternal metre held sublime,
that sun and moon and stars reflect,
our light beyond the intellect,
our roots beyond the fallen tree,
our birth within infinity,
as dreams of human destiny.

Chapter Ten ~ **Beyond the Grave**

We may ask ourselves: how and when will it all end? Our lives are patterned with dreams, some as aspirations, and others as haunting visions. If we live long enough, most everyone that we have loved departs this waking world, to step from limited experience into infinite expanse. So we remain, attempting to open to that inevitable bliss that we were born from and return to; while our bodies and minds revert to the clumsiness of infancy. Our awareness can find comfort in the inherent innocence, if we can only release all that we have accumulated to crowd our minds and emotions. Some find religion as their final comfort. I know too much of myth and dreams to swallow metaphor as doctrine without feeling that I have ingested something terribly ill-conceived. There is truth there; but the trappings kill the prayer. The prayer, of course, is that union with the infinite, beyond any self-serving petition for assistance from a colossal arbiter of fate. Lately, I feel the intensity and directness of my mentors, the way they rapped on my noggin of understanding with the sharpness of truth, all those years ago, reminding me that prayer is the intention of an innate strength, guidance and understanding that leads us beyond our limited sense of self. Within that awareness, visions may come as dreams or direct revelation. The priestesses of Afallon devoted their lives to this endeavor, as did the purest of Christian monks and nuns, many becoming recognized as saints.

The priestesses of Afallon remained largely unrecognized, their prophetic gifts ignored, and their guidance unheeded. Afallon's most loyal sons: Llenlleawg, Gawain and Galahad, who were raised with the wisdom of Afallon, eventually walked away from conflict, unless it was forced upon them. During the early decades of the new century, northern Cymric kingdoms began to fall, one after the other. The Anglo-Saxon invasion of Caer Lliwelydd was a major defeat for Rhydderch as Pendragon, handing his mantle over to Aedan of Dalriada to stand with Scotti and Picts against the Saesneg invaders. Llywarch Hen was exiled into the south, losing most of his extended clan in the Anglo-Saxon conquest of Rheged. Ynys Mon and Ynys Manau were struck from the sea, sending the priestesses of Afallon and the druids of Mon to scatter among the western isles of Dalriada in the north. Descendants from two centuries past had held Ynys Manau together for generations, but could not secure the safety of the priestesses of Afallon against invading pagans or Christian zealots any longer. More and more pagans were converting to Christianity, making the double threat increasingly insidious. The Isles of Scitis and the Hebrides became the new refuge for wise souls of the north, protected by the Scotti of Dalriada and the Cruithni Picts. Aedan lived only five years after the passing of his three eldest sons. His youngest, Eochaid Buide, held the north with his Scotti cousins and the Cruithni clans. Rhydderch died quietly at Dun Barton in his sleep. Rule of his kingdom was succeeded by Neithen, Rhydderch's distant cousin, and his sons, also descendants of Dyfnwal Hen. Morcant Mwynfawr died of drunken debauchery and disease, handing Arthsedd and Lothian over to his grandson Morcant, who died defending Arthsedd against Edwin of Northumbria, his newly acquired citadel renamed Eidyn's burg, known to the Cymri as Dun Eidyn. After the Saesneg conquest of Deva in the west, the Cymric kingdoms were severed in two: Alt Clud allied with Dalriada and the Picts of the north, and the south was ruled by descendants of Cunedda, Cadwallon ap Cadfan and later Cadwalladr Fendigad, "the blessed" – becoming the last Pendragon. Pendragons had been the protectors of the Cymric kingdoms since the time of Christ, starting with Cymbeline in the year 10, the first Pendragon. A new era of Anglo-Saxon domination had arrived, along with the spread of Christian kingdoms. The last vestiges of the old ways barely held to the western edges in the south, the northern isles, and the northern lands above the Roman walls. Songs of the bards echoed through these quiet corners to keep the spirit of Afallon and the Cymric Cylch alive, if only in the memory of their descendants.

Gawain and Penasgell

Descendants of the Cymri, Gawain and his cousin Ceindrych Penasgell had embodied the dynastic lineages of the north as heirs of patriarchal and matriarchal succession – choosing not to pursue them with any sense of inevitable destiny or fate, but instead, carry-on their heritage of ancient mystical legacies. Both of them chose independent paths for their early lives, although they were soon drawn together by family tragedy. There was always an unspoken affection between them, until they could no longer suppress the dynamic otherworldly attraction to each other. During one of their travels across the northern kingdoms, all imagined barriers to their embrace came tumbling down. One night the weather took a sudden turn, with chilling winds forcing them to take shelter in the ruins along the Wall of Tyne. They huddled close together, unable to resist the welling passion that had been building for years. The next morning they awoke to a calming peace opened up all around them.

"Do you have any regrets?" Gawain asked as he held her close, gently caressing her head.

"Absolutely not – I can't imagine why I resisted for so long to entirely surrender to this love," answered Penasgell.

"Yes, yes – I have been so self-controlled around you, I felt as if I might explode," Gawain responded.

"Well, now you have, several times," she said with a smile.

"Was I too forceful?"

"Oh no, I was pleasantly overwhelmed."

"Then you really feel we are not wrong in this, as cousins. I am your protector, after all."

"Please, never protect me from yourself again. The kingdoms and courts of the world are full of wedded cousins. This union is meant to be, and long overdue," Penasgell declared.

"I feel relieved, fulfilled and joyous – you are everything that I ever desired in a woman. We are spirits truly bonded," Gawain lovingly confided.

"I feel the same way. And now, this inevitable bond is complete, in the flesh as well as spirit. Our lives have suddenly begun again. I love you, and it seems that I always have," Penasgell openly expressed.

It wasn't long before Gawain and Penasgell did wed, in a quiet ceremony performed by Lady Vivianne and attended by Taliesin, Morcades, King Aedan and Queen Domelch, just a few years before the Battle of Catraeth. The newlyweds eventually settled on Ynys Ulva near Mull, raising a son and daughter in idyllic seclusion. Penasgell continued to care for the sick and afflicted, after her children had grown. Gawain was a trusted advisor to King Eochaid Buide of Dalriada, but Gawain avoided committing himself to battle. Penasgell's visionary gift provided Gawain with the perfect confidant, as challenges of conflict appeared on the eastern horizon of their western isle. Morcades and Vivianne were still Penasgell's active mentors, although they felt as equals as time went on. Penasgell was quite in tune with her ancestral heritage of wise women and the elder sisters of her lineage of light. Penasgell told us of one of her visionary dreams during my travels with Galahad through the western isles.

In her dream, she said, "I was sailing on a boat in the Hebrides and steered into a corridor of caves within one of the isles. The light of the sun shined through an opening to the sky, illuminating the sail, brilliantly reflecting a glow all over the striated stone walls. The boat glided to a bank within the cave where I disembarked, miraculously carried by the light, requiring little if any movement of my legs as I hovered just above the surface of the sea-eroded stone floor. In front of me was an enormous corridor of light between the cavern walls. A giant slab of rock had rolled away to the side, allowing me to continue into the light. As I moved on, the light shining between my arms and my body formed rays extending behind and around me, feeling like four wings had in a flash sprouted from my bare shoulder blades into the air – two ascending up and two descending down. And as I imagined the idea of flight, I rose-up into the encompassing luminous rays, leaving the cave and my little boat behind, to ascend higher and higher into the open sky. I soon felt the presence of other entities all around me. I knew that they were the Maré: our ancient and eternal sisters of spirit. I was engulfed by a love and light more glorious than I can possibly describe. The hearts of these entities were merged with my own, permitting me to enter a sense of self that was infinite and eternal, inclusive of every loving pulse of life sustaining the cosmos, beyond beginning and ending, immediate and expansive, as the constancy of love. When I awoke, my emotions ran from tears of joy to uncontrollable laughter, in waves of inner sensation. I was not entirely certain whether I had lost my mind."

"I wasn't sure about her either," said Gawain. "But I had seen my mother enter this state before, and like my mother, Penasgell settled-down after a few days."

"What do you believe that is?" I asked her.

"I believe that I became so completely free of everything, I was ecstatic with that potential, as the reality of us all, the reality of any soul," she said.

"Gawain, did you ever have an experience like that?" I asked him.

"No, I would dream of her, until we embraced in the flesh." He said.

"And now?" she asked pointedly.

"I still dream of you," he answered, reassuringly.

We all laughed. It was clear to see that those two held a deep bond of love for each other. They had found that island sanctuary away from the embattled world, a serene place to raise their children. Before we left that western isle, Galahad discovered a tarnished silver cup in his satchel. It was a bit worn and bent at the lip. He brushed the dark filigree to expose the name Ambrosius inscribed within the detail.

"Did you put this in my satchel?" He asked me as he handed over the old cup.

I looked at it closely saying, "No, but this is a fascinating find. Gawain, did you put this cup in Galahad's satchel?"

"No, but it is amazing, especially if it once belonged to Ambrosius Aurelius." Gawain responded, as he examined the cup. "It reminds me of some of the treasure that I discovered in the hills of Penllanw, years ago – lost again in the torrential rains and flooding that nearly took my life, and did drown five men of Ebrauc that were there with me. When we discovered the treasure trove it was quite exhilarating – a fascination cut short. I held there to my breast in the depths of that abandoned mine, treasure that could be the foundation of a new kingdom, or a kingdom revived in any grand features imaginable. There were cups and challises of silver and gold, and bracelets and torques and ornaments – and gems of every aspect – diamonds, sapphires, agates, chrysolite, carbuncles, emeralds, sardius, topaz, onyx, beryl, jasper and amethyst: the dream stone. I was out cold for a while, traveled in my dreams, and dreamed of Penasgell, years before we were wed. I held a cup in my hand for as long as I could; but that too was lost from my grasp as I fought for my life."

"And we are so grateful he survived," added Penasgell, wrapping her arms around him, "to be the loving husband and father he is today."

They embraced and Gawain kissed her gently on her brow, while handing the cup to her, saying "It's quite a find. What do see in this cup my dear?"

Penasgell held the cup in her hands, closing her eyes for a moment, then handing it back to Galahad, telling him, "I believe it holds your legacy: as a cup of an ancient Pendragon; and you as a son of a sacred lineage. Ambrosius was that unifying voice of leadership that brought the Cymric Cylch together, generations ago, honoring the ancestors and guiding their descendants. It is a legacy of light. You are the youngest here, besides our children, who all carry that light."

We thanked Penasgell for her vision, leaving Galahad plenty to ponder. They were gracious hosts and like family to us. There is a mystic bond among the sons and daughters of Afallon that clearly continues into the Otherworld. Gawain and Penasgell lived on Ynys Ulva for the rest of their lives. Their son Guari and his sons kept the island in their family for generations. Legend says that the regal ern or sea eagle returns each April or May to mate and nest on Ulva in honor of Gwalchmai – the hawk of May.

Llenlleawg

Galahad and I traveled on through Gallwyddel, the lands where the old mentor and guardian of Afallon Galehaut hailed from, and where each generation handed down their knowledge of the land and the skills of hunting and tracking. For years, we heard stories form Galehaut about the lands of his youth, about Myrddin's mystical journey across the land, about Llen and his mastery of the bow, and about Bercnaf and his hounds. Old Galehaut was long gone now. Years after our journey across the west, Galahad told me about his last hunting trip with Bercnaf and Llen. Bercnaf had been living in Gallwyddel with his young wife, raising children and hunting-hounds.

Llen, Bercnaf and Galahad were hunting very near that place in eastern Gallwyddel where Llen and Bercnaf had hunted years ago as lads. They had been following a large ten point buck for a number of leagues, until they reached the crest of a ridge. Llen had a clear shot of the buck in the distance. His bow was set. He drew back the bowstring . . . but then didn't release the arrow. Instead, he lowered the bow, suddenly clutching his chest, dropping to his knees. Llen looked up at his son, about to speak, half smiled, until the life of spirit leapt out of him in an instant. Llen collapsed in his son's arms, still holding that half smile, his eyes lifelessly gazing up into the treetops.

"Look there," Bercnaf said, pointing to the ten point buck, standing still, staring intently at the three men on the ridge. Bercnaf nodded his chin upward slightly as he and Llen had done to each other thousands of times, acknowledging a signal, a moment, a call to shift action in time. Straight away the great buck nodded back in the same manner, turned, and bounded off into the distance. Galahad looked down at the limp form of his father's body as the buck disappeared, shed a tear, and looked up to Bercnaf, saying:

"He is free to the wild now. We saw it. His spirit gallops into the Otherworld."

Bercnaf wiped his eyes and said, "Certain we are, that buck was his spirit's farewell. I know him true enough, after all our life together. He was so very proud of you lad."

Galahad and Bercnaf brought Llen's body down to the sea. Vivianne had known the instant he had passed. They immediately sent for Gwenhwyfar. Llen's body was later buried in a cairn near the shore, with a view of Ynys Manau and Ynys Eirenn in the distance. He was remembered as Llenlleawg Gwyddel, Man of Eirenn, three time champion of Aenach Garman, son of Ban of the Benoni of the Fisher Kings.

Vivianne spoke with Galahad after the burial, telling him, "Your father was a fine man. I know that he was not always there for you; but I know he truly loved you. My heart ached at your mother's passing. I am the only mother that your father knew; and he was, all but in birth, a dear son to me; just as you are, and always will be my dear grandson. And you also know, you carry his birth name – Galahad. Forgive me, as an old woman, that I repeat things that you well know. Your name is very ancient, derived from Galaad or Gilead – which means the enduring witness, from a rock of witness, originally a mound of stones as a watchtower of prayer, established by the patriarch Jacob and his father-in-law Laban as a stone monument – a cairn for the fallen. You see why I remind you lad: because you are of this line of Benoni, descended from the line of Benjamin, Jacob's most cherished and youngest son. The ancient tribes have a bloodied history, but also portray an emergence into light."

"I will do my best to live up to that heritage of light, Mam gu," he said, kissing her softly on her brow.

Vivianne gently touched the top of his head, saying, "I am sure that you will, lad. We all have a rich heritage of spirit; and we are blessed if we can touch those ancient souls in our heart or in our dreams."

Vivianne

Beginning thirty leagues beyond Ynys Manau, scattering into the colder northern regions above Ynys Eirenn are countless islands, many with standing stones of the ancients, or housing cliffs and caverns carved by the sea, washing tides against the earth for millennia. These were the rarely charted regions of travelers from long departed civilizations, and the outer reaches of seafaring pilots from Greece and Rome. Legends connect biblical tribes, wise lineages, and spoken paths of distant languages settling here, in the western most isles of Prydain. Vivianne and her sisters, the priestesses of Afallon, and druids of the north found refuge from the long arm of the Roman Catholic Church, extending its religious mantle far beyond where the Roman Legions had marched.

We spent several days in the western isles with Lady Vivianne. She told us of a dream vision she had, soon after receiving word of the declaration of the new Pope, Gregory the First, defaming Mary Magdalene from his highest pulpit of the ecclesiastical power of the Church, spoken nearly seven years before the Battle of Catraeth. Vivianne had seen a scribed quotation of the Pope's words stating: "She whom Luke calls the sinful woman, whom John calls Mary, we believe to be the Mary from whom seven devils were ejected, according to Mark. And what are the seven devils to signify, if not the vices? She washed the feet of Jesus with tears, wiped them with the hair of her head, kissed his feet, and anointed them with an ointment. It is clear brothers, that the woman previously used the unguent to perfume her flesh in forbidden acts."

"The utter gall of this man is abhorrent," Vivianne expressed her outrage. "It is important," she continued, "that men, women, lads and every maiden know of Mary Magdalene as a master of her own merit, not as a penitent prostitute, as the Pope would portray her and have us all believe his distorted speculation and lies. I spoke to Mary Magdalene in a dream vision about this slanderous assault on her character. I was walking in the cool of the evening through a garden within my dream, and a woman was approaching me. I knew immediately in my soul that she was Mary Magdalene, the Maré, and confidant of Master Jesus. I said to her, 'Dear sister, I am blessed to have this moment with you. I am very disturbed by the defamation committed against you by the new Pope of the Roman Catholic Church. How can he say these lies? What are these claims in scripture, referring to seven devils? Are they also lies?'

"She smiled, emitting an outpouring of love that I felt directly and so profoundly, and then she said: 'Thank you for your tireless work in continuing the legacy of our sisters in spirit – the Maré, in Afallon and these northern islands. I have been characterized by religious patriarchs as defiled and unsavory in contrast to the virginal and pure portrayal of the Master's mother, also a Maré, our dear sister in the great work. This notion of devils is an attempt to give cause to something inexplicable to common understanding. Language is meant to convey ideas, impressions, and images which can be interpreted in many ways, depending on the intention. As Maré, we choose to be aware of what we carry within our minds, hearts, and souls that keep us from clarity – the clarity to receive divine grace. The Master helped me to release any barriers that I might have retained, to be free and open to grace. To characterize that as casting out seven devils is a colorful use of language, easily misconstrued, and an issue to be addressed by the ancient bards and scribes. But if the patriarchs are looking for devils, demons, or deadly sins, they need look no further than themselves; and would be wise to seek the Master's assistance to set themselves free.'

"'You are so very dear, Maré Magdalene. This overwhelming problem besieging humanity seems to be the dual nature of the mind, creating a severance between masculine and feminine and between innocence and experience. The idea that virginity defines innocence and purity is a sanctimonious judgment against the natural world by hypocritical priests. Every newborn soul is innocent and pure in their nature, as is any young mother. But when men decide which woman or child is innocent or pure, and when dominance becomes a force applied in defense of an idea or to institute violent control and punishment, any innocence is soon lost through corrupted intention. Men can dominate women, and women can manipulate men, and vice versa. We women are less prone to use violence to dominate and control; and we tend to be more nurturing, by our very nature as potential mothers.'

"Mary smiled lovingly at me again, and I felt a calming come over my mind. Then she responded, 'The Master said that we are to make the two one . . . to make the male and female one and the same. In other words, our true nature is not solely masculine or feminine, but rather a merging of our dual nature into wholeness. Unfortunately, the differences between masculine and feminine natures are more often exploited than appreciated.'

"I looked at her and felt my mind reeling around her every word, responding: 'Yes, religious zealots continue to condemn the flesh, because they are irreversibly attached to the flesh; believing if they could sever themselves from the flesh, that the soul would return to the grace of innocence. Separating men and women, suppressing and numbing sensation, even by violent means, has become a drastic yet vain effort to control temptation; when temptation is only the natural response of sensual awareness. For these zealots, the senses are the enemy; the body is the enemy; and women are the enemy. For them, passion and desire become directed toward God and only God; who is portrayed as male, dominant, and a force to be feared. And if he is not frightening enough, his other apparently misbegotten son, Satan, will serve as the patriarch of utmost cruelty and retribution.'

"'It is the strange belief of dualism,' Mary agreed, 'to have a force of evil somehow created by a force of good. When, according to this belief, the worst one can be within the waking world is to be in league with Satan, his devils, and his demons. However, he seems to provide a most desired service for the Church in the reclamation of souls: within this calamitous bond, this specter of evil serves good by fulfilling the dark extremes of duality, forcing the fearful to cower under the mantle of the Church. This belief in love out of fear is a dangerous course for the human heart to navigate.'

"'It is difficult to understand how fearsome entities are the answer to human fears,' I said to her. 'I find that even the ancient belief in the Goddess as our acknowledgement of unity with nature, brings in the elemental forces as part of one encompassing realm of wholeness.'

"'This is a noble intention,' Mary responded, 'as long as this belief does not become another form of dualism, with the deity on one side of reality and humanity on the other. It is within manifestation that unity is expressed through duality, with every conceivable part completing the whole. Understanding this perspective, we sisters know that there is a current of grace within wholeness that can be followed. We need not call it the grace of the Goddess or God's grace or even nature's way. It is the essence of being aligned in love, resolved in the courage of surrender to that wholeness, away from fear, hate, and conflict. Until the balance of the human spirit shifts into this greater awareness, there will be battles within each soul over their own true nature, reflected into the waking world. This struggle has continued since the beginning of time, through those days when the Master and I walked the earth, and likely far into the future. This is the nature of time and duality in manifestation. The tribes of Judah, the children of Dan, the descendants of Benjamin, the Ephraim and the Fisher Kings, along with Tamar, Cambra, and the Maré have all wandered these isles of Prydain, to once again enter the drama of time and space in the waking world, becoming lucid within dream. It is the density of physical life that many have become attached to: as a thickening of blood, rather than a translucency of light. You have been a beacon of that light for many souls.'

"'Thank you, my dearest sister and gracious Master of Love and Light,' I responded; as I reached my hand out to her – when she suddenly vanished, gone from my vision, then I awoke. The age of matriarchal succession has also vanished; and the age of Afallon and our priestesses are soon to follow. Do not let the feminine power be lost, dear lads. It is the balance within the waking world that must remain, or the elemental forces will right themselves to the stability of the cosmos despite humanity."

That was the last time I saw Vivianne. She was a bright shining light in a time of encroaching darkness. She too stepped into the Otherworld to join her sisters, the Maré of ages past.

Galahad's Vision

Galahad truly took Vivianne's words to heart. He was a man who carried that balance of masculine and feminine within him. He was most accomplished in combat of arms, and yet most sensitive to the hearts of others. He was decisive and keen of mind, and yet patient and intuitive in his spirit. We had often practiced together the movements of the power of the mountains and streams since we were lads; but Galahad had learned the ways of prayer and contemplation from druid mentors, priestesses of Afallon, and wise priests of the Christian faith. He told me of one amazing spiritual vision that he experienced, immersed in a deep state of awareness.

"I had entered my daily practice of silent contemplation and prayer," Galahad related, "when in that place of focused being, opening my heart to the spirit of that immensity of love we have called God, I seemed to have drifted within that silent space into another sphere of relative awareness: neither asleep, nor awake, nor in a dream, but rather in an awareness of another realm, observing this waking world. I could see myself in quiet contemplation, as if I had stepped out of my body. There was a great light of spirit surrounding this image of myself, seen as I viewed myself, sitting apart from this observing and highly aware sense of being. I could clearly see the front, back, top and all sides of myself at once. Within my back, there was a light of extraordinary intensity, pulsing at the center of my still, and seated body. I stepped towards this radiant image and immediately understood that I could actually step inside this body of light; and as I did, I entered an infinite corridor of all-encompassing light. As I descended, or ascended, into this timeless, formless space, I began to see a figure before me, within this profound saturation of light. He appeared as a man, unlike anyone that I had ever seen; although he was strangely familiar, with long auburn hair, and a very handsome bearded face. His eyes were the most loving and penetrating pools of pure awareness I have ever known. I knew in that instant that he could see all aspects of my mind and soul. He knew all that I had ever felt or dreamed, imagined or desired. He heard me and spoke to me as if we were of one mind and voice. I conveyed to him that I knew who he was: Yehoshua ben Yusef, the one known as Jesus the Christ.

"He conveyed to me: 'I know you as Galahad, descendant of the line of Benoni, of the ancient tribe of Benjamin, and the lineage of priest kings, of the Order of Melchizedek, a sacred order of Zadok, Archangel Michael, and Emmanuel.'

"I was so stunned by the profound nature of the experience; I could scarcely absorb what was happening. I asked him: 'How can you be so much a part of me, and a part of this brotherhood of priest kings, and this presence of light, and yet appear as an image standing here before me? I have not known anything in my journey of life that has been as powerful as this moment, here, now, with you.'

"'I have come to you before, in your dreams.' He said. 'You may not have recognized me there, because I had merged with your mind. Life in neither the dream world nor the waking world is what you think it is. It is a journey of innocence and experience, and of awareness – awareness of love and action from love.'

"'Isn't this life also a journey to discover and know God?' I asked.

"'Whether you discover the beast or God in nature and humanity, the journey is determined by your intention within reality. There are many ideas about God, but very few clarify the truth of God.' He answered.

"'What is the truth of God?' I asked.

"'Truth, God, and the essence of being are one inseparable reality,' he began to explain. 'The individual mind is by its nature active with the perception of separateness. How can one possibly discover and know the source and essence of being from a point of view declaring separateness from the source?'

"'What did you mean when you said: 'I and my Father are one,' I questioned.

"'What I said,' he clarified, 'was closer to: I am one, as source – meaning the source and essence of being. The word that I spoke, Ab, means father, but it also means source, origin, and one – just as Elohiym means the one as the many, and the many as the one. Things that I said were not always taken as I had intended. Those present and aware could feel what I conveyed, but may not catch the full meaning of what was said. The words are only of the mind. Each mind or point of view may not perceive what was intended.'

"This prompted me to ask, 'Why aren't you here in the world clarifying what was said about you, and about life, truth and the nature of reality?'

"'I am here now,' he said. 'I am always one with reality. Each soul, each identity, has free will to be aware of love and the nature of reality. Each identity can perceive itself as a limited body, and therefore see me as a limited body: a separate body that was there, but is not here. The reality that I know is always here, now, as the essence and the body of the cosmos.'

"This brought me to ponder all of the other apparent masters, living lives in bodies that existed three-score or more and vanished, so I asked: 'What of the other prophets or the beliefs of their religions – are they one with their gods? Is there one true path?'

"He smiled as he conveyed love that embraced my soul and calmed my mind, answering: 'Yes, there is only one true path; but it has nothing to do with gods, prophets or religion. The one true path is love, wisdom, compassion, awareness, innocence, equity – none is better than another, because that implies division, separateness and disunity. I am one as source, as love, as truth, as reality. You will find me there, and also any other who conveys that reality.'

"I tried to grasp all that he conveyed, to feel the expanse of that reality. My mind continued to question all of the different beliefs about saints and holy prophets and the artifacts that they had used or touched, asking: 'Do relics or artifacts, the bones of saints, the grail cup, that men seek to possess – do they carry or convey that greater reality in their essence?'

"'How could they,' he answered, smiling compassionately. 'However, belief is very powerful in conjuring illusion. Everything seen in the world is an interpretation of the greater reality through illusion. A cup holds love and healing, if love and healing are fulfilled when one holds a cup. Love and healing are eternally present. The cup is lost or found. The bones of a saint hold only as much love as the beholder. Many have been healed holding the bones of a hen. Was the hen as holy as a saint? Maybe so, if the belief and love is invoked strong enough to provide relief.'

"Will there ever be enough relief for all of the suffering in this world? I pondered. 'Why is there so much division, brutality, war and hatred in a world meant for love and unity?'

"'This is the nature of free will,' he conveyed with a measure of sadness. 'The multiplicity of experience illustrates the completion of experience. Each solitary point of view has the capacity to open and to see as one: to observe with all-inclusive wholeness. Completion is fulfilled by its diversity: with many parts comprising the whole. One intention affects the whole, for ill or good. We may see this as unjust, because the consequences often strike the innocent. The perceived separateness creates the imbalance. Brutality and war are born in the hearts, minds and souls intent on justifying separateness. Peace, love and harmony are innate qualities of wholeness, born within every soul, at one with the essence and source of spirit and divine life. This wholeness is fulfilled in awareness and immersion into that essential source stream of love.'

"'What is this source stream of love?' I asked. 'Is it God? Is it the Holy Spirit? Is it the soul?'

"He looked at me, as one with that source, within that love, imparting: 'All is one, as source, as stream, as awareness, as the constancy of love. The awareness is the power and truth of constancy. Elemental constancy prevails in the midst of apparent change. Healing occurs when the underlying constancy is revealed and embraced by the innocence of the soul.'

"This led me to ask, 'Then are the elemental qualities of reality, love, nature, innocence, and life one, as an underlying constancy of experience? And if we are innocent and whole within our souls, are we judged in a final judgment for our love?'

"'The final judgment,' he said, "is the ending of the judgmental mind, which is difficult to imagine. And yet, that is what is imagined within divine understanding. To love without biased judgment is the nature of divinity. Humanity has separated their behavior from their divine nature and the essential reality, as children from the source of love. In the waking world, nature has become an allegory of reality. The ancient allegory of the tree of the knowledge of good and evil bears the fruit of the judgmental mind, leading to division, dualism, and conflict. The innocent heart is the gateway to wholeness. Love is the essence of being. It is up to each soul to discern whether their love is self-serving, or the life-blood of a light illuminating the world.'

"After he spoke those words, I suddenly realized that I was seated in contemplation again, aware of my physical body; and yet enriched with a light of such radiance that I felt no separation from my sensation of self, and the love surrounding me. I was love. I am love. And although I do not feel it now as utterly and supremely intense as I did when it was coursing through me on that day, I carry this love, and the love of my eternal brother Yehoshua ben Yusef with me at all times. I am forever changed. I cannot engage in battle, but to save a life. I cannot live in anger, but must expose injustice. I cannot live in lust, but can only act in love. This is my quest: to embody that immense love now opened wide within me."

Galahad was truly an awakened soul. When I was his age, I was still searching, wandering through the Cymric kingdoms with Aneirin, singing our songs of adventure and wonder. Before Taliesin passed away into the Otherworld, he told me where I might find direction in my search; so I went to seek it out.

Dinas Emrys

The aging Taliesin had sent me to The Glaslyn Valley, in the south. He told me that there was someone there that I needed to meet. I had heard all of the heroic legends of the south, of Myrlyn and the sword Caladbolg, of Dinas Emrys, the property deeded to Master Myrlyn by Ambrosius, becoming the esteemed ysgol of the first five lads taught by the Raven of Awen. So I journeyed south, south of Yr Wyddfa. I could see the craggy hill from the valley floor, when crossing the Glaslyn before entering the wood. Much of the path was overgrown. The trace of any track was vague, few treading this way anymore. Taliesin had given precise directions noting landmark sightings. Even so, I nearly lost my way. The narrow path toward the top was partially blocked by a fallen boulder, covered with vines and a thorny bush at its base. I hacked my way around to find the steep track up, farther ahead. Then I saw it. The gateway was weathered, broken on one side, barricaded with an old cart, stood on end. I knocked at the active side of the gate, as Taliesin had instructed, feeling a bit foolish, as if I was summoning a ghost from a long abandoned fortress.

After the third knock, a voice shouted: "Go away! Plague and pestilence lurks beyond this gate!"

"I was sent by Taliesin for the philosopher's stone!" I shouted back, as instructed, hearing a muffled laugh from within the battered estate.

"Swords and stones will build no thrones!" The voice responded.

"But words will be remembered!" I volleyed back the correct response.

The gate opened and a curious fellow pointed the way for me towards the main hall across the courtyard, the entrance stacked with crates and barrels, some covered with tarps, others pried open and empty.

Once inside, the disheveled little gatekeeper said, "Wait here."

The large room was dark, trace lighting spilling-in from a few high windows. As my eyes adjusted, I could see worn patterns of footwork on the stone floor, sending a sudden chill rushing across my flesh. I felt the movement of spirit through my soul in recognition of the practices that had gone on here, beginning more than a century ago. Soon a small figure of a man emerged from the shadows. He moved slowly, holding a torch in his left hand, its flame seeming to rise as he gazed intently at me.

So Taliesin sent you off with some riddles; are you a bard?" The nearly ancient druid questioned me.

"Yes, I've studied with Taliesin and Aneirin in Rheged and Afallon, and elsewhere in the north."

"Ah, Afallon, the isle of apples, first fruits of our lineage, held in trust – what do you seek, young bard?"

"Well, I was told that I would meet someone here with answers."

"Answers to what?" he asked, looking at me with a wry smile.

"Answers to the meaning of all this that we endure and experience – and to the mystery of the grail."

"The grail . . . ? Ha! You are the grail, fool! The center of the cosmos is right here, right where you stand. Drink it up, or keep moving on your quest. You'll find yourself eventually, or die. That's all there is."

"That's all there is – quest or death?"

He looked at me like a lad that didn't know a bloody thing, but then responded with a slight tone of sympathy in his voice, explaining: "it has been this way with mankind for thousands of years, and will be for thousands more. Human nature remains the same. You stumble about in the dark or wake up to the light that you are. The grail quest is a search for a mythic cup hidden in a satchel that you've been lugging around within your own bloody bag of bones. Stop it. And be still. Listen . . . and sing from your core. The mountains and stream are bounding and flowing through you."

I stood speechless, his cloak falling down to his elbow as he spoke, his hand reaching expressively into the air, seemingly releasing an invisible javelin out into the cosmos. That's when I noticed his right hand, turned and withered, yet extending from a powerful vein-patterned forearm. Stunned, I thought, it can't be.

Then I asked, "Are you Bedwyr?"

"I have been called that, yes."

"How can you still be alive?"

"Huh ha! I ask myself that same question from time to time. But then, time is not what it seems to be."

"You trained here, with the Myrlyn – my God, you are one of the first five!"

"Yes, but you can leave God out of this. There's the most misinterpreted moniker ever conjured by human speech. Come this way, into the library by the fire."

Looking at the shelves filled with scrolls and dust covered bound books and stacks of loose pages, I said: "I hardly know where to begin, to ask you what you know, and what you have learned.'

"I know nothing." He said definitively. "I have only un-learned what I did not need to know."

"You must know something of God; but you seem to take issue with the name of God."

He paced in front of the fire, poking at it a bit before responding.

"People everywhere are reaching for God in name only, without realizing it. Names identify and separate without really clarifying anything.

So much evil has occurred in the name of God that 'his' reputation has become almost entirely fictitious."

"Are you suggesting that God doesn't exist?"

"No. I'm saying that God is all that does exist; but in naming this primary essence and source of existence, and characterizing that life essence as a fickle, moody, and biased entity of vengeance, humanity unleashes more mayhem and havoc upon generations of souls struggling for answers than is godly."

"So, God is not the answer?" I queried.

"No, God is the question – because the word has been abused as a term referring to that which is indefinable," he said forcefully.

"Is God, then, an idea, like the grail cup?"

"All words are ideas. What they represent can be distorted or corrupted into mythic illusions."

"Then of what value are the myths?" I asked.

"As a bard you must know that myths are the artful use of language to convey concepts that are nearly indescribable. A myth taken literally, believed as a reality, loses most of its deeper significance and takes on a false identity of its own."

"What is the significance of the grail? Is the quest for the grail just a myth that has lost its deeper meaning?"

Bedwyr paused for a moment, staring into the fire, and then continued, "The soul is on a quest for experience that illuminates spiritual essence, existent within all being. By the nature of exploration it appears to transpire as a gradual process. 'Graal' or grail is a term of the same root as gradalis, gradual or graduated. It represents the step by step endeavor to the realization of wholeness. Wholeness, however, is complete, not incremental. Therefore, the steps are as much away from the goal as towards the goal."

"Does that mean the pursuit of the Holy Grail is a futile endeavor?"

"No quest is futile that ultimately dispels ignorance. It simply may not be necessary. If one discovers a cache of gold in his own garden, he would not need to dig a mine in the distant hills to find gold."

"Are you saying that our own garden, our holy grail, our Garden of Eden – is right here where we stand?"

"Yes – if we are aware," he said with a grin, as I pondered his claim.

"What is the significance of the Garden of Eden myth? Was there a fall of man and a banishment of humanity from the divine garden?"

"Man is falling all of the time. We fell into time: living time asleep to the awareness of timelessness."

"What of the Otherworld? Isn't the Otherworld timeless? Can't we enter the Otherworld through our dreams?" I questioned further.

"The Otherworld and our dreams are realms of human awareness. Most human beings are unaware of the depth of these realms, confused by them, or create myths about them."

"Are these realms real?"

"They are as real as any image in our mind's awareness; because what these energies and events portray within these realms is real to the soul's journey – a journey that ultimately leads one back to center, to wholeness, to the essence of creation."

"Are we creating these realms?"

"Yes. We are creating, concealing, revealing, eliminating and sustaining the garden, the treasure, the dream, and the myriad of forms from the essence of all conceivable realities."

"Then is everything imagined as a story told to ourselves . . . and to what purpose?"

"Purpose, hmm," he stood silent for a moment, and then continued, "Once the essence releases into all potential, all that can be conceived or believed is eventually imagined: as a story, as a life, or as an identity. We identify with an idea, a feeling, or a sensation as purpose."

"Is purpose just a feeling or desire as a potential? I have been searching for my purpose, as a bard, and to find my place in the world. You must have had a dream of a future, a purpose to your life. You were a prince. Your father was the King of Meirionydd; your elder brother Cadwaladr was his heir. When or how did you realize your purpose, your dream?"

He gazed out of the library window at the glow on the distant horizon and said, "I dreamed of throwing a spear or a javelin as a lad. I knew that I held more within myself than any sense of limitation. Eventually, I reached for the unlimited, the infinite that exists within us all. Much like throwing the javelin, it is a reach and release all at once – within the same infinite instant. My father did not understand this infinite inner life. Instead, he held strongly to the conviction of his own ignorance: he hid his shame behind pride; he concealed his guilt with blame; he covered his fear with anger. His outer kingdom was a fortification to protect an embattled soul from its own diminished awareness. My mother was the opposite of my father – open, loving, and optimistic. She named me Bleiddud as the call of the wolf sang out at my birth. Like a wounded whelp, I lost the use of my right hand, due to my father's carelessness and cruelty; while my mother taught me the intuition stemming from the left. I lost the respect of my father, because he saw me as a weakened extension of himself. My mother saw an inner strength in me, and took me to the Myrlyn. Master Myrlyn began calling me Brydiwr and then Bedwyr, encouraging my inner opening, and teaching me the power of the other side, the power of the Otherworld, and the insight of a prince of spirit. The Master and Nimue were my otherworldly father and mother. I saw a new depth of love; and I felt a new strength of life and limb – limbs of my earthly body and limbs branching out of the tree of eternal life. I found the love of my wife and children. I found all that I thought was lost as a child – yet retained the joy and wonder of a child. I became a piercer of the veil, a shifter between worlds – a mabinogi."

"I have tried to imagine the impact of learning from Master Myrlyn, and I wondered about the life of young Emrys Myrlyn, the life that shaped him. Did the Master ever speak of his youthful experience of nearly dying?"

"Yes. He spent much of his life endeavoring to understand and cultivate the awareness he attained in the Otherworld. He said that he came to realize that his near death sparked a unified and complete experience of his soul;

although upon his return to the waking world, he was ill-equipped to describe this fulfillment in the dualistic terms of our common reality. He said, 'One embodies wholeness, then returns to separateness, only able to express the boundless love and expansion through the heart, indescribably perplexing to the mind.' It was a great gift for my mother to bring me to the Myrlyn and Nimue. Once I had these masters as surrogate parents, my intention and awareness was forever changed."

"I never knew my birth parents. I too found otherworldly parents and mentors: Taliesin, Aneirin, and Lady Vivianne, Myrlyn and Nimue's daughter. I suppose that gives us some kind of kinship in spirit. Maybe the reason Taliesin sent me to you. Even after all of those years of loving guidance, I still search for my place in this waking world."

"What inspires you?" Bedwyr asked. "What do you feel conveys the essence of being through you? What do you draw from the stream of being?"

"Language," was the first world that entered my mind. "I was embraced and raised by bards. They saw this in me. Although I am most inspired by the bold souls who have discovered what you have discovered – souls who love from that essence of being, souls of the Fisher Kings."

"So be that," he encouraged me, "convey that in your presence and your gift of language, live that as your purpose in the world. There is nothing to stop you but yourself."

"Yes, I see that now. I will tell this story, this story of princes, kings, saints and prophets," I said, brimming with new inspiration.

"Everyone seems to want a story," said Bedwyr. "Some want answers to questions and others just want to escape, to drift off into the mystery of it all. You cannot help but convey all that is imagined. There is a part that you can choose to play in the drama, in the history, in the dream. This is your dream. You can wake now, in this infinite instant, or dream on."

I reflected on his words for a moment, and asked again, in another way, about the depth of his extraordinary life. "Within your very long life, after all of those years of mentoring by Master Myrlyn, in your deepest understanding, what do you experience?"

"Do you see all of these ancient scrolls, books, and notes and verses on random loose pages," Bedwyr said as he waved his left hand towards the shelves of Master Myrlyn's extensive library, "they contain knowledge from wise sages and mystics across the world, spanning centuries, revered by their students and followers. If I were to write on one long parchment scroll everything that I know, everything that I understand, everything I perceive – and then poke a tiny pinhole in that parchment, holding that lengthy unraveled parchment up in the air to allow a beam of light to come streaming through that pinpoint – all that is written upon the parchment would be in shadow, illegible, indiscernible, and inconsequential. That beam of light, connected to an infinite stream of light, at one with all light and ever-expanding space surrounding this room, the world, and our intimate sense of being – that is what I experience. I allow that pinpoint of light to open me to the infinite and the eternal light. What is written or believed, or believed to be understood is inconsequential. There is only the light of being, the light of love, a light encompassing every soul – unfathomable to the mind, but simple to the heart."

"I tried to take-in all that he was saying and apply it to my renewed sense of purpose, asking him, "Can a story possibly convey all of this?"

"It is there," he said, "but we complicate it all. We create, we conceal and reveal. We sustain and eliminate lives and our reality within our minds as a dream. We cannot separate our minds and emotions from ourselves. When we stop looking for purpose within the dream of our own making, perhaps we may wake up from the dream, and realize the simple truth of the infinite and eternal love and light that we are, beyond dreams, and beyond the dreams of the Fisher Kings."

Cian's Dream

That night at Dinas Emrys I dreamed the most prophetic dream of my life. It is surprising that I even slept with the intense charge of spirit that rushed through me from the moment I stepped into that hallowed hall. The vision was so vivid and lucid that I question to this day as to whether I was transported directly into the Otherworld, taking my earthly body with me. I sat up in my bed to see a figure entering my room, a room once occupied by the brilliant young charges of Emrys Myrlyn. And to my astonishment, the Master himself entered with a torch following him at his side, hovering in the air as if held by unseen hands.

"Master Myrlyn," I said with awe. "It is an honor to meet you."

"I have been with you all along, lad. What took you so long to get here?" The Master responded.

"I, I don't know. I suppose I just failed to imagine being here," I fumbled with an answer.

"Confidence is all that you needed," said the Master. "It is like flight: until you catch the air surrounding you, you do not realize that flying is so accessible."

With those words, the windows of the bedchamber sprang open and he carried me into the night air, soaring like a bird into the moonlight, realizing I had in fact become a bird: a jay, flying there beside Myrlyn, who was also a jay. As we flew towards the full moon, we both became ravens, first black and luminous, our coal-dark feathers shimmering with lunar light, then as white ravens, merged with a mystical light, not reflected from the moon, but rising within us as light fills a room, quite suddenly and completely. At this peak of radiant brilliance, we were once again transformed, no longer ravens but doves, quickly flashing again into the essence and appearance of our human forms, moving in the phases of the power of the mountains and streams, standing in those well-know postures by the shore of a flowing brook. I felt Myrlyn's presence moving with me, as strongly as if he was the atmosphere surrounding me and coursing through my veins and sinews. We moved in unison for what must have been hours, yet seemed immeasurable. After we stood in silence for an equally undetermined space of timelessness, he finally spoke to me again.

"This ysgol is open to you. You are the surviving heir of its legacy within the waking world. As bard and druid, as a fatherless son of shifting worlds, you were born to continue this work, if you accept it as your purpose. Your verse and other writings are already the fluid conveyance of this purpose; but you must choose to teach those with ears to hear and hearts to embrace what you impart. Bedwyr has held this place for you; but he has chosen to move on to the Otherworld and continue his work from there. Taliesin and Aneirin are of the Otherworld as well, and will surely guide you from time to time as you carry on. The vision that you impart will be received by many. However, as with much of this form of conveyance, it will tend to be distorted into mystery, magic, and wonder, held in the storied mind of human fascination. Do not be discouraged. Follow your inspiration. The voice of Awen sings through your wheat of song."

I awoke at Dinas Emrys, weeping, overwhelmed with joy and gratitude for this overflowing embrace of my being. When I saw Bedwyr that morning, he saw deep into me, without my telling him anything.

"I see that the Master has conveyed the gift of his property to you, if you accept its stewardship," said Bedwyr, so matter of fact.

"Yes, of course," I said haltingly. "I am humbled and joyous, to be welcomed into this grand lineage. As a man of words, they seem to escape me now – insufficient to express this encompassing fulfillment. You must know, having been the recipient and steward for all of these years."

"Yes, it is an astounding experience. It is not being thrust upon you. You will know when it is time for you to step-in, as I did," said Bedwyr, as he reached out and embraced me with a love that bridged worlds.

I didn't spend much time in the north after that day. I had journeyed to see Gawain and Penasgell with Galahad in the western isles. I kept the Gorsedd at Llyn Geirionydd active over the years. And as I grew older, I spent more time in Dyfed and Carmarthen nearer to the shore, mentoring young bards in that corner of the Cymric lands, less overrun by the Saesneg. I have feared they might weed out our embattled tongue over time, leaving it to the bards to carry both the song and natural voice of our people.

As long as a language survives, so does the identity of a people, born of one voice to echo their song throughout time, reminding each longing heart how to return to the innocence and joy of the timeless sense of being. All that bards can give us are words: sounds and silences forming images in our own minds, touching cords that stimulate memory and passion. We bards are the voices of a people and their living language, beyond the words and phrases, portraying characters of the collective spirit in ancient tales, resonating with the mythic images found within every soul and their infinite dreams. We open doors and windows of awareness for new ways of seeing; and with that vision, every wounded soul ascends, to re-imagine each ash and elm within the waking world, and fulfill the dream of each Adam and Eve, and every leaping brother, son or father, and every drowning sister, daughter, mother, and every burned or buried love, and each scorned Magdalene, and every scarred Fisher King, born into blood and light within this realm of passing time, to wake, to sleep, and dream again.

GLOSSARY AND PRONUCIATION GUIDE

Glossary & Pronunciation Guide

Here are some general notes for pronunciation of Welsh words for readers unfamiliar with the Welsh language: a, e, i, and o have short vowel sounds, as in cat, met, pin, and not; u sounds like a short u or short i; w usually sounds like the vowels oo as in nook, though it can sound like a consonant before a vowel; y acts as a vowel and usually sounds like a short i or a short u; c always sounds hard like k; and ch always sounds hard as in Bach; f sounds like v; only ff or ph sound like an f; g is always hard as in girl; s sounds soft, never like z; dd sounds like th as in then; th sounds like th as in thistle; ll sounds like hl, softened by the tongue against the roof of the mouth; ae and ei sound like the ai in main; eu, and ey sound like the long i in tiger; oe sounds like the oi in oil; words in languages other than Welsh are marked with an asterisk* and pronounced according to their language of origin.

Achnabreac* [Ak-na-brāk] – forest of Dalriada

Aedan mac Gabran* [Ā-dan mak Ga-bran] – late 6th century King of Dalriada (Argyle, Scotland)

Aenach Garman* [Ā-nak Gar-man] competitive games held in Laigin (Leinster, Ireland)

Afallon [Av-**ahl**-on] – mystic school on Ynys Manau

Afallach [Av-**ahl**-ak] – King of Gallwyddel (Galloway, Scotland)

Agrefain [Ag-**re**-vain] – 6th century Prince of Lothian

Alban [All-ban] ancient name for northern kingdoms (Scotland)

Alt Clud [Alt Klut] – northern kingdom (southern Scotland)

Ambrosius Aurelius* [Am-**bros**-ē-us Aw-**rē**-lē-us] late 5th century Pendragon, son of Cystennin Gorneu

Aneirin [An-**ai**-rin] 'Gwodryd' [Goo-**od**-rid] late 6th century Cymric bard – "of the flowing verse"

Anna Morgause II [An-na Mor-goz] Queen of Lothian, wife of King Loth, daughter of Morcant Mwynfawr

Annwn [**An**-noon] – deeper realm of conscious being

Arfderydd [Arv-**der**-ith] late 6th century battle near the Solway "weapon of the oak"

Argoed Llwyfain [**Ar**-goid Hloo-**i**-vain] elm forest (Yorkshire)

Argotta* [Ar-gotta] – ancestral Sicambrian Queen

Armorica[Ar-**mor**-ika] – mainland kingdom (Brittany, France)

Arthsedd [**Arth**-seth] – northern fortress (Edinburgh)

Arthwyr [**Arth**-ooir] – name meaning: descendant of the bear

Arthwys [**Arth**-oois] – name of several 5th & 6th century princes

Artúr mac Aedan* [**Arth**-ur] – 6th century prince of Dalriada, son of Aedan mac Gabran

Attacotti [At-ta-**cot**-ti] "toward thy coat of thyself"
– mysterious tribe & mystic sect of the northern Cymri

Awen [**Ah**-wen] mystic core of the soul – inspiration

Baeddan or **Baedd** [**Bāth**-an] exiled Frankish prince

Baetan mac Cairill* [**Bā**-than mak **Cā**-rul] 6th century High
King of Eirenn, King of Ulaid (Ulster, Ireland)

Balchder O'Rhywun [**Balk**-der Ō **Hri**-wun] (pride of anyone)

Bedwyr [**Bed**-ooir] – aka Bleiddud [**Blī**-thud] son of Meirion

Beltaine* [Bel-**ta**-ne] – mid-spring festival (May 1st)

Benoni* [Ben-on-i] – descendants of the tribe of Benjamin

Bercnaf [**Berk**-nav] – lifelong friend of Llenlleawg

Bernicia* [Ber-**nē**-sē-a] – 6th century Anglican kingdom
(Eastern Northumberland and Durham)

Blaise* [**Blāz**] – master druid, son of St. Digain

Blodgwyn [**Blod**-gwin] – wife of Peredyr

Bruide ap Maelgwyn [**Brī**-de ap **Mail**-gwin] 6th century
King of the Cruithni Picts, son of Maelgwyn Hir

Brychan [**Bruk**-an] – 5th century King of Brycheiniog

Brychan II – Peibo, son of Brychan, late 5th early 6th century
King of Manau Gododdin (the Lothians, Scotland)

Brycheiniog [Bruk-**ain**-ē-og] – southern kingdom of the Cymri
(Breconshire, Wales & parts of Herefordshire, England)

Bryneich [**Brun**-aik] – northeastern kingdom of the Cymri,
allied with the Angles (Northumberland)

Bylal* [Bi-**lal**] – middle-eastern traveler

Cadel Ddyrnllwg [**Ka**-del **Thurn**-hloog] – "gleaming hilt"
mid 5th century king of Powys, grandson of Vortigern

Cadwalladr 'Fendigaid' [Kad-**wahl**-adr 'Ven-**di**-gaid']
'the blessed' 7th century King of Gwynedd, The Last Pendragon

Caer [**kai**-er] – fortress

Caer Leon [**Kai**-er **Le**-on] – southern citadel (Caerleon, Wales)

Caer Lliwelydd [**Kai**-er Hli-**wel**-uth] citadel of north Rheged
(Carlisle, Cumberland)

Caer Guinion [**Kai**-er Gwi-**ni**-on] roman fort, south of Lothian

Caer Morwynion [**Kai**-er Mor-wi-**ni**-on] aka Arthsedd
"Castle of the Maidens" (Edinburgh, Scotland)

Caer Ystrellyn [**Kai**-er U-**stre**-hlin] Prince Artúr's fortress
(Stirling, Scotland)

Cairn [**kāirn**] – subterranean tomb or temple

Caladbolg* [Kal-**ad**-bolg] – "hard lightning" – legendary sword

Camboglanna [Kam-bo-**glan**-na] roman fort at Hadrian's Wall

Catraeth [**Kat**-raith] – late 6th century pivotal battle
(Catterick, North Yorkshire)

Catwg [**Kat**-oog] – 6th century Cymric saint (aka Cadoc, Cadfael or Cathmail)

Ceindrych 'Penasgell' [**Kain**-drik 'Pen-**as**-gehl'] daughter of King Eliffer, sister of Peredyr, of Ebrauc – "winged-head"

Cenfigen [Ken-**vi**-gen] tutor on Ynys Manau

Ceretig [Ker-**e**-tig] – son of Dyfnwal Hen, 5th century Patriarch

Chlod* [Klod] – son of Chlothar, Prince of Soissons, Francia

Chlothar* [Klo-thar] – early 6th century King of Francia

Cian 'Gwenith Gwawd' [**Ki**-an **Gwen**-ith **Gwa**-ood] late 6th century Cymric bard – "wheat of song"

Clovis [**Clō**-vis] – late 5th early 6th century King of Francia

Coed Celyddon [Koid Kel-**u**-thon] – northern forest, south of Lothian (southern Scotland)

Coel Hen [Koel Hen] – 4th century Pendragon, Patriarch of the Gogledd (Old King Coel)

Coledauc [Kol-**e**-dawk] – late 6th century King of Bryneich

Colum Cille* [Kol-um Keel] – 6th century saint of Iona (Saint Columba of Ireland and Scotland)

Conall mac Comgall* [Kon-al mak Kon-gal] – mid 6th century King of Dalriada (Argyle, Scotland)

Constantinus* [Kon-stan-tin-us] 5th century prince of Dalriada

Cruithni* [Kru-**ith**-ni] ancient people of Northern Highlands & Strathclyde, Northern Picts

Cunedda [Koo-**neth**-a] – 5th century Pendragon, Patriarch of the Kings of Gwynedd

Cwm [koom] glacial valley; (esoteric: energetic abdominal core)

Cymbeline [**Kum**-be-līne] – The First Pendragon, 10 AD

Cymbrogi [Kum-**bro**-gi] – fellow countrymen

Cymri [**Kum**-ri] – "the allied" – the Welsh & early Britons

Cynan Meiriadoc [**Kun**-an Mai-ri-**a**-dok] – Cymric Patriarch, First King of Armorica (Brittany, France)

Cyndeyrn [Kun-**day**-ern] 6th century Bishop of Alt Clud aka Saint Mungo, bastard son of Owain, Prince of Rheged

Cynfarch [**Kun**-vark] – early 6th century King of Rheged

Dalriada* [Dal-**ri**-a-da] – Scotti kingdom (Argyle, Scotland)

Ddenyw [Then-**i**-oo] – mother of Cyndeyrn

Deifyr [**Dai**-vir] – half-brother of Prince Owain of Rheged

Deira [**Dai**-ra] – 6th century Anglican kingdom (Eastern Yorkshire)

Dewi [**De**-wē] – 6th century Cymric saint (aka David or Dewidd)

Digain [**Di**-gān] – son of Cystennin Gorneu, father of Blaise

Dolmen [**Dol**-men] – ancient megalith, or standing stone

Domangart* [Dom-an-gart] 6th century Prince of Dalriada

Domelch [**Dom**-elk] wife of Aedan mac Gabran, daughter of Maelgwyn, sister of Bruide of the Cruithni Picts

Dumnonia [Dum-**non**-i-a] – southwestern Cymric kingdom (Cornwall, Devonshire, & Dorset, England)

Dun Airigh* [Dun Ā-rē] – 'fort of kings' citadel of Dalriada (Dunadd, Argyle, Scotland)

Dun Barton* [Dun Bar-ton] – fortress of Alt Clud

Dun Nechtan* [Dun Nek-tan] – fortress of the Miathi Picts (Dunnichen, Angus, Scotland)

Dun Pelydr [Dun Pel-**i**-dr] – fortress of East Lothian

Dwysedd [Doo-**i**-seth] – daughter of Girom of the Picts, 4th wife of Maelgwyn of Gwynedd, mother of Bruide & Domelch

Dyfed [**Duv**-ed] – southwestern Cymric kingdom (Carmarthen & Pembroke, Wales)

Dyfrig [**Duv**-rig] – late 5th early 6th century Cymric saint

Dyfnwal Hen [**Divn**-wall 'Hen'] 'the old' – early 5th century Patriarch of the northern Cymric kingdoms

Dyfrwyr [Duvr-**oo**-ir] – "watermen": disciples of Dyfrig

Ebradil [E-**bra**-dil] – mother of Dyfrig and Emrys

Ebrauc [**Eb**-rawk] – northern citadel & kingdom (York)

Einion Yrth [Ai-**ni**-on urth] – late 5th century Pendragon

Eirenn [**Ai**-renn] – western ancestral island (Ireland)

Elaine* [**Ē**-lain] – exiled princess of Francia, daughter of Pelles

Elffin [**Elf**-in] – bastard son of King Urien of Rheged

Eliffer 'Gosgorddfawr' [El-**i**-fer 'Gos-gorth-**va**-oor'] "of the great army" – early 6th century King of Ebrauc

Elidyr 'Mwynfawr' [El-**id**-ur 'Moo-in-**va**-oor'] 'the wealthy' – cousin of King Rhydderch of Alt Clud

Elmet [**El**-met] – northern Cymric kingdom (West Riding)

Emrys [**Em**-ris] – childhood given name of Master Myrlyn

Eochaid Buide* [Uw-kaid Būd] youngest son of King Aedan

Eochaid Find* [Uw-kaid Find] middle son of King Aedan

Eoganan mac Gabran* [Uw-gan-an] King Aedan's brother

Fergus Mor* [Fur-gus More] – 5th century King of Dalriada

'Fflamddwyn' [Flam-**thoo**-in] – 6th century King of Bernicia "flame-bearer" (agnomen for one of the sons of King Ida)

Galains* [Ga-lains] – ancestral Patriarch of the Fisher Kings

Galahad* [Gal-a-had] – son of Llenlleawg of Afallon

Galehaut* [Gal-e-hot] – battle lord and guardian of Afallon

Gallwyddel [Gahl-**with**-el] – northern Cymric kingdom (Dumfries & Galloway, southern Scotland)

Gawain* **'Gwalchmai' ap 'Loth'** [Ga-wain '**Gwalk**-mai'] "Hawk of May" – bastard son of 'Loth' Llewddan ap Cynfarch

Gawain Gwinau [Ga-wain Gwin-aw] early mentor of Gawain

Glywyssing [Glow-**us**-sing] – southern Cymric kingdom (Glamorgan & Monmouthshire, Wales)

Gododdin [God-**o**-thin] – northern region and its people (West, Mid, & East Lothian, Scotland)

Gorsedd [Gor-seth] – a gathering of the bards

Grechion [**grech**-i-on] – greyhounds

Gwallog 'Marchog Trin' [**Gwaw**-hlog '**Mark**-og Trin'] son of Llaennog, 6th century King of Elmet 'battle horseman'

Gwallwen [**Gwahl**-wen] – wife of Maelgwyn Hir

Gwawl [**Gwa**-ool] – daughter of Coel Hen, wife of Cunedda

Gwawr [**Gwa**-oor] – wife of Elidyr ap Meirchion of Rheged, daughter of Brychan II

Gweheris [Gwe-**hair**-is] – 6th century Prince of Lothian

Gweirydd [**Gwair**-ith] – 6th century Prince of Lothian

Gwenddoleu [Gwen-**tho**-lī] – mid 6th century King of Solway

Gwendydd [**Gwen**-dith] – twin sister of Myrddin Wyllt, and wife of King Rhydderch of Alt Clud

Gwenhwyfar [Gwen-hoo-**i**-var] – Princess of Laigin, and wife of Prince Artúr of Dalriada

Gwenhwyfach [Gwen-hoo-**i**-vak] Gwenhwyfar's dark alter-ego

Gwrast 'Lledlwm' [**Goo**-rast '**Hled**-loom'] 'the ragged' – early 5th century King of Rheged, son of Ceneu

Gwrgant [**Goor**-gant] – son of King Peredyr of Ebrauc

Gwrgi [**Goor**-gi] – late 6th century joint-King of Ebrauc

Gwyddbwyll [Gwith-**boo**-uhl] – ancient board game like chess

Gwyddel [**Gwith**-el] people of Eirenn (Irish & Gaelic dialect)

Gwyddno [**Gwith**-no] maternal grandfather of Elffin ap Urien

Gwyl Awst [**Goo**-ul Owst] – Cymric late summer festival (1st full moon of August, Welsh Lughnasadh)

Gwynedd [**Gwin**-eth] – northwest Cymric region (including all or parts of Anglesey, Caernarvon, Denbighshire, Merionethshire & Montgomery, Wales)

Gwyrls [**Goo**-urls] – 5th century 'duke' or ruler of Tintagel

Gwyr y Gogledd [**Gwē**r i **Gog**-leth] "men of the north"

Hanif* [Han-ēf] – pre-Islamic monotheistic religious sect

Hibernia* [Hī-bern-i-a] – ancient name for Eirenn (Ireland)

Ingenach Hen [Ing-e-nak Hen] – 5th century Queen of Manau Gododdin and ancestral Matriarch of the northern kingdoms

Laigin* [Lai-gin] eastern kingdom of Eirenn (Leinster, Ireland)

Lailoken* [Lai-lo-ken] – Myrddin Wyllt's alter-ego

Lamech* [La-**mek**] – archdruid of Armorica & Narbonne

Llaennog [**Hlain**-nog] – son of Maesgwid, King of Elmet

Llalwc [**Hla**-look] – archdruid of Ynys Mon

Llamorhad [Hla-**mo**-hrad] – older cousin of Llenlleawg

Llenlleawg 'Gwyddel' or **Llen** [Hlen-**lai**-ook] – exiled prince of Francia, "Man of Eirenn' – champion of Aenach Garman

Llewyrch or **'Llew'** [**Hloo**-erk] – exiled prince of Francia

Llif [Hliv] – bastard son of Cian of Maen Gwyngwn

Lluan [**Hlū**-an] – mother of Aedan mac Gabran, granddaughter of Brychan II, and grandmother of Artúr mac Aedan

Llydaw [**Hlud**-ow] – mountainous region in Gwynedd (Snowdonia Park, Wales); also, an alternate name for Armorica

Llyn [Lin] – lake or pool

Llyn Geirionydd [Lin Gair-ē-**on**-ith] – a lake in Gwynedd, 6th century site of the Gorsedd

Llyr Marini [hleer Mar-**i**-ni] – son of Meirchion Gul

Llywarch Hen [**Hli**-wark Hen] – 6th century Cymric bard, mid 6th century King of South Rheged

Loairn mac Erc* [Lo-airn mak Erk] – brother of Fergus Mor, 5th century King of northern Dalriada

Loidis [**Loy**-dis] – citadel and seat of Elmet (Leeds, England)

Loth or **Lleuddan** [Lōth **Hlī**-than] 6th century King of Lothian

Lughnasadh* [**Lū-nā**-sā] – late summer festival (Irish origin)

Lymer [**Li**-mer] – leashed hunting hound

Maelgwyn Hir [**Mail**-gwin Heer] 6th century Gwynedd King

Mael Umai* [Mile U-mai] – 6th century Prince of Ulaid, son of Baetan mac Cairill

Maesgwid 'Gloff' [**Mais**-gwid] [Gloff] 'the lame' – son of Gwrast Lledlwm, late 5th century King of Elmet

Maen [**Mā**-en] – ancient standing stone

Maen Gwregys [**Mā**-en **Goor**-eg-is] – ancient stone circle, (Girdle Stanes, Dumfries, Scotland)

Maen Gwyngwn [**Mā**-en **Gwin**-goon] – "white gown stone"

Magnus Maxen* [Mag-nus Max-en] – 4th century Pendragon, Romano-Iberian Cymric Patriarch

Mam-gu [Mam-gu] – Grandma

Manau [**Man**-aw] – western island kingdom (Isle of Man)

Maré* [**Ma**-ray] – female spiritual masters of ancient eras

Marganna II [Mar-**gan**-na] – Queen of Bryneich, daughter of Morcant Mwynfawr, wife of King Coledauc of Bryneich

Miathi* [Mi-a-thi] – southern Pictish tribes

Migdele [Mig-**del**-e] northern village (Meigle, Angus, Scotland)

Meirchion 'Gul' [**Mair**-ki-on] [Gul] 'the lean' – son of Gwrast, late 5th century King of Rheged

Meirion [**Mai**-ri-on] 5th century King of Meirionydd

Meirionydd [**Mai**-ri-**on**-ith] – kingdom of southern Gwynedd (Merionethshire, Wales)

Merovech* [**Mer**-o-vek] – 5th century Frankish King

Merovingian Kings* [Mer-o-**ving**-i-an] Sicambrian Frankish dynasty, descendants of Merovech & ancient Priest Kings

Modron [**Mo**-dron] – mistress of King Urien of Rheged, Princess of Gallwyddel, and daughter of Gwallwen

Mon [Mon] – northern Cymric island (Anglesey, Wales)

Morcades* [Mor-**ca**-des] mother of Gawain, mistress of Loth

Morcant 'Llofrudd' [**Mor**-kant '**Hlo**-vruth'] 'murderer' 6th century Prince of Bryneich

Morcant 'Mwynfawr' [**Mor**-kant 'Moo-in-**va**-oor'] 'wealthy' aka 'Mynyddog' [Mi-**ni**-thog] 'mountaious' 6th century King of East Lothian, brother of King Rhydderch of Alt Clud

Morfudd [**Mor**-vuth] – bastard daughter of Urien and Modron, wife of Morcant Mwynfawr, and cosmological twin of Owain

Morfyn [**Mor**-vin] – early mentor of Cian

Myr 'Heliwr' [Mur 'Hel-**i**-oor'] – 'the huntsman'

Myrddin 'Wyllt' [**Mur**-thin 'Wilt'] – 6th century Cymric bard, druid and seer – 'the wild'

Myrlyn [**Mur**-lin] late 5th early 6th century Cymric seer & bard (agnomen meaning: pool of myrrh, or higher lucid qualities)

Nascien* [Na-sē-en] – ancestral Patriarch of the Fisher Kings

Nechtan 'Mawr' [**Nek**-tan '**Ma**-oor'] – 'the great' 6th century King of the Miathi Picts

Niall 'Noigiallach'* [Nī-al 'Nu-ē-gē-ul-ak'] – legendary ancient Patriarch of Eirenn (Niall 'of the Nine Hostages' of Ireland)

Nimue* [**Nim**-u-e] wife of Master Myrlyn, Princess of Rheged

Nudd 'Hael' [Nuth 'Hail'] – 'the generous' – 6th century King of Selgow (Selkirk, Scotland)

Nyfain [**Nuv**-ain] – daughter of Brychan II, wife of Cynfarch

Orcades [**Or**-kades] – northern island kingdom (Orkney Islands, Scotland)

Owain ap Urien [**O**-wain] – 6th century Prince of Rheged

Owain 'Ddantgwyn' [**O**-wain '**Thant**-gwin'] – 'white tooth' youngest son of Einion Yrth, 5th century King of Rhos

Pelles* [Pel-les] – exiled king, descendant of the Fisher Kings

Penarwen [Pen-**ar**-wen] wife of Prince Owain of Rheged

Pendragon [Pen-drag-on] highest battle leader of the Cymri & Britons, "Protector of the Isle"

Penllanw [Pen-**hlan**-oo] – mountainous Cymric kingdom (the Pennines & Peak districts, Derbyshire, England)

Peredyr [**Pe**-re-dur] – late 6th century King of Ebrauc

Powys [**Pow**-is] – central Cymric kingdom (including all or parts of Montgomery & Radnor, Wales; Shropshire, England)

Prydain [**Prid**-ain] – ancient name for Britain, meaning: realm of time and form, from the Cymric root word 'pryd'

Rheged [**Hreg**-ed] – northern Cymric kingdom (Cumberland, Westmorland, Lancashire, & Cheshire, England)

Rheu [Hrai] – Galehaut's lead huntsman

Rhun 'Hir' [Hrun 'Heer'] – son of Maelgwyn 'Hir', 'the tall' and late 6th century King of Gwynedd

Rhydderch 'Hael' [**Hrith**-erk 'Hail'] – 'the generous' 6th century King of Alt Clud, and Pendragon of the Cymri

Saesneg [Sais-neg] "outsiders" or "outlanders" (Germanic or Scandinavian invaders)

Scotti* [**Skot**-ti] the people of Eirenn, the kingdom of Dalriada & the northwestern islands (Irish)

Selgow [**Sel**-gow] northern Cymric kingdom (Selkirk, Scotland)

Serfan [**Ser**-van] – a priest of Fib [Vib] (Fife, Scotland)

Sicambrian Franks* [Si-**cam**-bri-an] descendants of Cambra, 4th century BC Queen & ancient dynasties of the western Steppe

Sidhe* [Shē] – entities from spiritual realms or the afterlife

Soissons* [Soo-son] – a kingdom of Francia

Suibne Buile Geilt* [Shuv-i-ne Bul-e Gelt] (legendary madman of the woods)

Taliesin [Tal-i-**e**-sin] – 6th century Cymric bard

Talhaearn [**Tal**-hairn] – early 6th century Cymric bard

Tewdr 'Mawr' [Te-**oo**-dr Ma-oor] 'the great' – 6th century King of Armorica (Brittany, France)

Tuatha de Dannan* [Tou-tha de Dan-nan] "people of Dan" mythic ancestors of the isles, of the Otherworld, of the goddess Danu, or descendants of the Tribe of Dan

Tudwal [**Tud**-wal] – 5th century Patriarch and King of Alt Clud

Tywysog [Ti-**wis**-og] – "prince"

Tywyswr [Ti-**wis**-oor] – "leader"

Ui Nell* [U Nel] – dominant clan of northern Eirenn (Ireland)

Urien [**Ur**-i-en] – 6th century King of Rheged

Vanora [Va-**nor**-a] – legendary priestess of Angus, Scotland

Vivianne* [**Viv**-i-an] – High Priestess of Afallon

Vortigern [**Vor**-ti-gern] – 5th century King of Powys, High King, or "Gwrtheyrn" of the Britons

Wall of Forth [Forth] – Antonine Wall (from the Firth of Forth west to Dumbarton, Scotland)

Wall of Tyne [Tīne] – Hadrian's Wall (from the Tyne River mouth west to the Solway Firth, northern England)

Wledig [**oo**-le-dig] – regional leader, prince, or king

Yehoshua ben Yusef* [Ye-hōsh-wa ben Yoo-sev] – Hebrew name for Jesus: Joshua son of Joseph, aka Iesous (Greek)

Ygerna [Ig-**er**-na] – daughter of Amlawdd, wife of Gwyrls, 2nd wife of Einion Yrth

Ynys [**Un**-us] – island

Ynys Medcaut [**Un**-us **Med**-cawt] 'The Holy Isle' (Lindisfarne)

Ynys Padrig [**Un**-us **Pad**-rig] (Saint Patrick's Isle, Isle of Man)

Yr Wyddfa [Ur **Wuth**-va] – "the prominence" (Mt. Snowdon)

Ysgol [**Us**-gol] – school

Ystaden [us-**stad**-en] – furlong (200 m., 220 yd. or 1/8 ml.)

Ystrad [us-**trad**] – river valley

Ystrellyn [U-**stre**-hlin] – northern citadel (Sterling, Scotland)

Ystryd [us-**trud**] – street

Ywrhica [U-oo-**hrik**-a] – wife of Gwrast, daughter of Merovech

CHARTS OF THE DESCENDANTS

OF CYMRIC, SCOTTI, AND

FISHER KING DYNASTIES

DESCENDANTS OF CENEU, SON OF COEL HEN

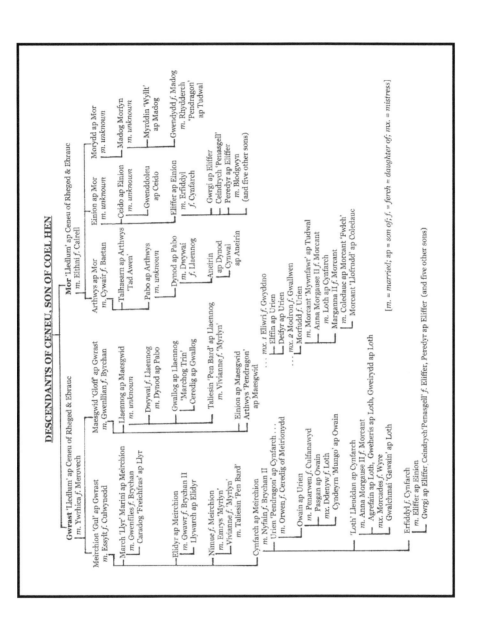

[*m.* = married; ap = son of; *f.* = ferch = daughter of; *mx.* = mistress]

DESCENDANTS OF FERGUS MOR & MAELGWYN HIR

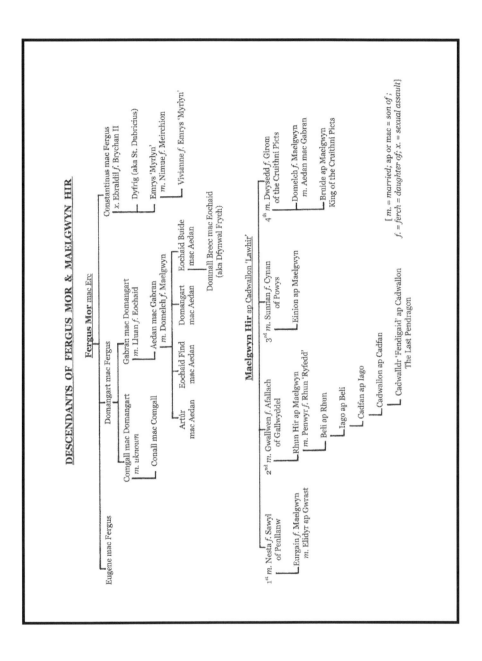

Fergus Mor mac Erc

Eugene mac Fergus

Domangart mac Fergus

Comgall mac Domangart
m. uknown

Conall mac Comgall

Gabran mac Domangart
m. Lluan *f.* Eochaid

Aedan mac Gabran
m. Domelch *f.* Maelgwyn

Arthir
mac Aedan

Eochaid Find
mac Aedan

Domangart
mac Aedan

Eochaid Buide
mac Aedan

Domnall Breec mac Eochaid
(aka Dyfnwal Fryeh)

Constantinus mac Fergus
x. Ebraldil *f.* Brychan II

Dyfrig (aka St. Dubricius)

Emrys 'Myrlyn'
m. Nimue *f.* Meirchion

Vivianne *f.* Emrys 'Myrlyn'

Maelgwyn Hir ap Cadwallon 'Lawhir'

1st *m.* Nesta *f.* Sawyl
of Penllanw

Eurgain *f.* Maelgwyn
m. Elidyr ap Gwrast

2nd *m.* Gwallwen *f.* Afallach
of Gallwyddel

Rhun Hir ap Maelgwyn
m. Penwyr *f.* Rhun 'Ryfedd'

Beli ap Rhun

Iago ap Beli

Cadfan ap Iago

Cadwallon ap Cadfan

Cadwalldr 'Fendigaid' ap Cadwallon
The Last Pendragon

3rd *m.* Sunfan *f.* Cynan
of Powys

Einion ap Maelgwyn

4th *m.* Dwysedd *f.* Girom
of the Cruithni Picts

Domelch *f.* Maelgwyn
m. Aedan mac Gabran

Bruide ap Maelgwyn
King of the Cruithni Picts

[*m.* = *married*; ap or mac = *son of* ;
f. = *ferch* = *daughter of*; *x.* = *sexual assault*]

DESCENDANTS OF DYFNWAL HEN

Dyfnwal Hen ap Ednyfed ap Anwn Dynod

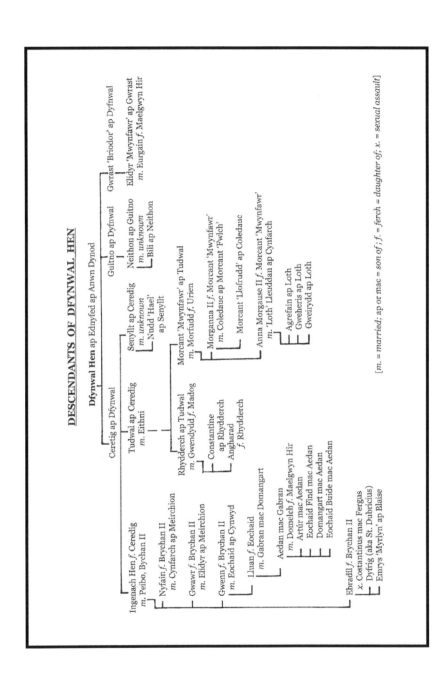

[*m.* = *married*; ap or mac = *son of*; *f.* = *ferch* = *daughter of*; *x.* = *sexual assault*]

DESCENDANTS OF THE FISHER KINGS & THE SICAMBRIAN FRANKS

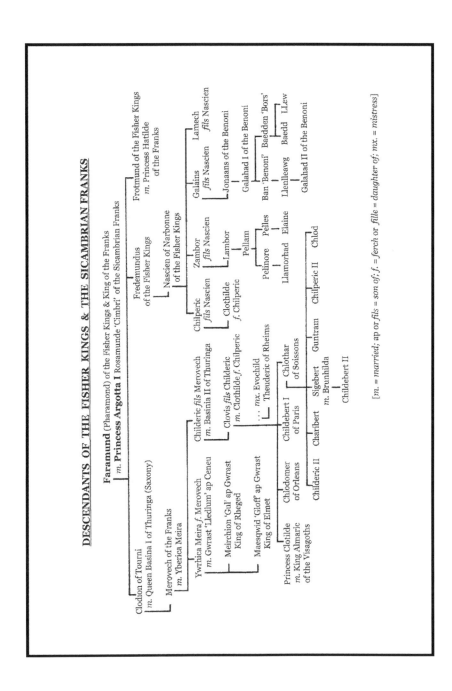

Faramund (Pharamond) of the Fisher Kings & King of the Franks
m. **Princess Argotta I** Rosamunde 'Cimbri' of the Sicambrian Franks

[*m.* = *married;* ap or fils = *son of;* f. = ferch or fille = *daughter of;* mx. = *mistress*]

Made in the USA
Columbia, SC
24 November 2024

46951886R00205